The Guardian Angel

Kay Seeley

To Nathan

And all children who struggle to make sense of the world around them.

Also by Kay Seeley

Novels

The Water Gypsy

The Watercress Girls

The Guardian Angel

The Hope Series

A Girl Called Hope

A gGirl Called Violet

(All Kay's novels are available in Large Print)

Box Set (ebook only)

The Victorian Novels Box Set

Short Stories

The Cappuccino Collection

The Summer Stories

The Christmas Stories

Chapter One

1890

The first time Nell saw the child her heart crumbled. It was the day she left the workhouse. The carrier dropped her off in the lane and she'd walked the length of the tree-lined drive carrying her small bundle of belongings.

She pulled her shawl closer around her against the March wind. As she turned a bend in the path Inglebrook Manor came into view, its ivy covered walls and tall windows glinting in the early spring sun. Nell's eyes widened, her jaw dropped. Set amidst stately trees and beautiful manicured lawns, the majestic building took her breath away. A chill went through her. She'd never seen anything so magnificent and yet so forbidding. A lump rose in her throat. She swallowed and walked on.

She'd been told to go to the tradesman's entrance and ask for the governess, Miss Bannister. Her breath caught in her throat. She couldn't believe this was to be her future home. Her hands trembled as she went up to the side door and knocked.

A young girl with a red face and harassed expression opened the door. "What do you want?" she said. "We don't buy at the door."

Taken aback Nell said, "I'm not selling anything. I'm Nell Draper. I was told to see Miss Bannister and that there was a job for me here. The Board of Guardians sent me."

The girl's features lightened. "Ah. You're the workhouse girl. Well, you'd better come in."

Nell stepped into the kitchen, her face reddening in the sudden warmth. A fire burned in the huge range, its glow reflected on copper pans lining the walls. Pots bubbled on the stove and a mouth-watering smell filled her nostrils. A heavy set woman with rolled up sleeves stood at a large oak table rolling out pastry. She glanced up as Nell walked in.

"It's the workhouse girl come for Miss Bannister," the girl said.

"Well, best take her through then," she said, glaring at the girl.

Nell followed the maid through the kitchen and along to a small parlour off the servants' hall.

"The workhouse girl's here," she said, pushing Nell into the room. Nell glanced around. Her eyes were drawn to the woman sitting behind a solid desk. Thin faced and harried looking, she wore a severe black gown with a pinned-tucked bodice. Her dark hair was drawn into a bun and her angular features could have cut glass with their sharpness. She looked Nell up and down and sniffed. "She's to see Miss Bannister in the Nursery," she said. "You'd better take her up."

The girl nodded and Nell followed her up a flight of stairs. "It's on the top floor," the girl said.

"Oh," Nell said. "Who was that?"

The girl grimaced. "That was Mrs Grindley, the housekeeper. If you've any sense you'll keep well clear of her. Miss Bannister's all right though."

Nell smiled. "Thanks for the advice." She took an immediate liking to the girl. "What do you do here?" she asked.

"Me? I'm Jenny, the in-between maid. That means I help out upstairs and downstairs, it's all the same to me. A sort of maid of all work I am."

By the time they got to the third floor Nell was quite out of breath.

"You can leave your things in here," Jenny said softly, opening the door to the bedroom. "Then I'll take you to meet Miss Bannister."

They crept into the room. Heavy curtains drawn across the tall window made the room appear dark but Nell could make out two beds arranged at right-angles to each other. A large chest of drawers stood against the wall. A fire burned in the grate, protected by a colourful fire screen. Nell saw a small child asleep in the bed nearest the window. That surprised her. She understood the child she was to nursemaid was five years old. Where she'd come from boys of five were worked to exhaustion and beaten if they stopped work or answered back. They'd be expected to do a full day's physical work as well as having lessons. They couldn't sleep in the afternoon. She realised working here would be very different.

"Best not to wake him," Jenny said. "Miss Bannister will be cross if her afternoon is disturbed before she's finished her tea."

Nell didn't have much to leave, all she possessed were the clothes she stood up in; the dress, undergarments, stockings, boots and shawl provided when she left Salvation Hall House; a bar of soap, a comb and a book she'd been allowed to take. She put them in the chest of drawers and laid her shawl on the bed.

A cheval mirror stood in front of the wardrobe and several chairs were grouped around a low table. She glanced in the mirror, bit her lips to bring a little colour, removed her bonnet and smoothed her chestnut hair. The wind had brought a glow to her cheeks and she hoped she looked presentable enough to please the governess. She paused for breath, squared her shoulders and followed Jenny to meet the woman who would be in charge of her future.

The nursery playroom, next to the bedroom, was light and airy. A dappled rocking horse stood in front of the window where a sliver of sunlight penetrated the lacy curtains. Various toys were spread over the rug, as though a sudden interruption had called their owner away. Nell couldn't help but compare the luxury afforded to the child here to the deprivation of the workhouse children. A rock hardened in her stomach as it always did whenever she thought about those children.

Miss Bannister sat at a small round, white clothed table, set out with the finest china. Nell guessed her to be about thirty. Blonde waves framed her face. Several strands of hair had escaped the tight bun at the nape of her neck to fall onto the cream collar of her blue day dress. Her face lit up at the sight of Nell. "Ah, the workhouse girl," she said, her gaze washing over Nell. Every fibre of her being hoped she would meet with this woman's approval. If not she'd be sent back until another job came along.

Miss Bannister smiled. "Please come and join me; I was just about to have tea." Nell eased herself into the chair opposite the governess, horribly aware that if she was to be working under her it would be as well to make as good an impression as she could.

"Now, you must tell me all about yourself. Do you have a name? What do they call you and how old are you?"

In the workhouse she'd been 'girl number 27' but she could still remember when she was called Nell and she lived with her mother many years ago, in happier times. It was something she'd vowed never to forget.

"Nell," she said. "My name is Nell Draper and I'm sixteen."

Miss Bannister poured the tea and said, "My brother is on the Board of Guardians. They speak very highly of you."

Really, Nell thought. That was another surprise. She was always getting into trouble for cheeking Matron or speaking up for those too sick to work.

"I believe they have given you a reference."

Nell pulled the letter she'd been given from her pocket and handed it to the governess, who read it while Nell sipped her tea, her heart pumping.

Miss Bannister nodded. "Excellent," she said. "They say you have a way with children, are not afraid of hard work and excel at obeying orders. Is that correct?"

"Yes, Miss." So that's what the Master had told them. She hoped the shock she'd felt at hearing the words hadn't registered on her face. Blind obedience had never been her nature but she guessed they had to say that to secure her place.

"I understand you have experience of working with the sick, both mental and physical. In the infirmary?"

"Yes, Miss," she said, unsure what else to reply. She didn't know where this conversation was leading but she'd have said anything. The fear of not being good enough loomed large. She swallowed the dread rising up inside her.

"You'll be on a month's trial as nursemaid to Lord Eversham's son, Robert. A shilling a week, all found. I understand you have no family so you'll not be needing any time off, which is just as well."

Nell swallowed again. "Thank you, Miss," she said.

"Good. Now let me tell you about the family you will be working for. Lord Eversham is in Government and well respected in the county. He has two daughters, Ellen who is nine and Martha who is seven. They are a delight, very bright and willing to learn. They are my charges. You will see them occasionally about the house and gardens, although most of the time they are out riding, at music lessons or in the schoolroom. They sleep in the west wing of the house as do I."

She took a sip of her tea. "You will sleep in the nursery with Robert. The schoolroom is on the floor below, but I see no reason for you to bring your charge there."

Nell nodded.

Miss Bannister picked up a piece of paper from the table in front of her and handed it to Nell. "I have made a list of your duties, his daily routine, which you are to follow to the letter. You will report any difficulties to me personally. I hope that is clear."

Nell glanced at the list. It didn't look too daunting. "Yes, Miss," she said.

"Good." Miss Bannister smiled. "Robert, although just five, is proving to be a bit of a handful. The last girl left after only two days." She looked Nell over again. "I do hope you are made of sterner stuff."

"Yes, Miss," Nell said. She felt sure that her past experience would stand her in good stead. "I'm sure I'll love it here. I can't wait to meet young Robert and get to know him."

The governess laughed. "You haven't met him yet."

Nell wondered what could be so terrible about the child. In Hall House she'd cared for all sorts of people, from the very young to the elderly and infirm. She was sure she'd be able to cope with anything that a five-year-old could throw at her.

Miss Bannister checked the fob watch she wore pinned above the breast of her smart blue dress. "He should be awake now," she said. "I think it's time you met your charge."

Nell followed the governess as she walked towards the bedroom. She heard an ear-shattering crash. Miss Bannister hastened her step. The nursery chair lay on its side, fragments of the cheval mirror scattered around it. In the middle of the room a small boy stomped up and down pushing the other chairs over, toppling them against the wardrobe with loud bangs.

"Robert, stop that at once," Miss Bannister said. The authority in her voice had immediate effect. Robert stopped, a bewildered look on his face.

"He's had one of his tantrums," she said. "He doesn't have them often, but when he does they're impressive." She moved to the bell pull and rang for Jenny to come to clear away the glass and have the mirror replaced.

Nell stared at the child and her heart lurched. He was the most striking child she had ever seen.

Curls of blonde hair accentuated his fine-boned, delicate features set in a face as pale as an angel's wing, but the look in his piercing blue eyes appeared defiant. It reminded Nell of the gaze in the eyes of recently orphaned infants when they first entered the workhouse; brimming with bravado but unsure of what might lie ahead of them. She'd seen so many pale-faced, vulnerable children she didn't think her heart could be moved by another but this small boy with his questioning gaze stole it completely.

The governess strode over to the window and drew back the curtain. Light flooded the room revealing sky blue patterned wallpaper. "Robert, meet your new nurse," she said.

"This is Robert," Miss Bannister said. "You'll be responsible for his care."

Robert was dressed in grey knee-length breeches with a grey waistcoat, a high necked white frilled shirt, dark socks and black shoes. He appeared smartly dressed and yet heartbreakingly fragile. Then his lips spread into a ridiculously radiant smile that lit up his face like a sparkling shaft of sunlight. Nell found herself held captive in his gaze and falling totally under his spell.

She crouched down. "Hello, Robert," she said. "I'm Nell, your new nursemaid. I'm very glad to meet you."

"He doesn't speak," the governess said. "In fact he does very little, but you'll find that out."

Nell stretched her hand towards him. He stepped forward, took her hand and sank his teeth into it. Nell didn't flinch. She'd had worse. She merely removed her hand from his mouth and said, "We don't bite people." He raised his hand to hit her. She caught his fist. "And we don't hit either," she said.

Then, before he could recover, she jumped up and said, "Come on, let's find some toys." She walked away into the playroom. The boy followed, his face creased with interest.

In the playroom she took some bricks from the shelf and put them on the rug. "Show me what you can build with these," she said.

Robert started to play with the bricks, picking them up and throwing them into a wooden box already out. He rarely missed. "Well done," Nell said, clapping her hands. She went to the box and tipped the bricks out so he could start all over again.

All the while Miss Bannister watched them. "If he gets out of hand and needs to be punished please don't hesitate to let me know," she said.

Nell got the impression that punishment was not an uncommon fate for the child. "Oh, it's just high spirits. He'll soon settle and we'll get on famously."

The governess grimaced. "If you say so, but don't forget I'm here to help you. He can't learn much but he does need to learn how to behave. Good manners are the least we expect from him and it's your job to see he has them."

"I'm sure I'll do my best to see he behaves in the future," she said. But she wanted to know more. "You say he can't learn much and can't talk. Is there some reason for that?" She was used to children in the workhouse being so traumatised by the brutality they experienced they no longer spoke but couldn't believe that to be the case in this instance.

Miss Bannister sighed. "I suppose I'll have to tell you about him." She walked over to the table, felt the teapot and poured herself another cup of tea. "It was a difficult birth," she said. "His mother died having him." She paused. "The birth of a son and heir to a noble family like the Master's should be a cause for joy and celebration, but his birth is something we've all come to regret." She sighed again. "Robert's been seen by the best doctors in London, but the prognosis is poor. They say his brain was addled at birth. He'll always be backward and probably feeble-minded."

Feeble-minded! The expression shocked Nell. That description didn't fit the boy she'd just met. Unruly and young for his age maybe, but that could be down to his lack of speech. She'd come across feeble-minded before. It was a world away from what she'd just seen.

Miss Bannister shook her head. "It's such a shame. He'll never amount to anything, well, nothing of which his father can be proud. We just have to look after him until a decision is made about his future."

A cold chill rang through Nell's veins. What did she mean – a decision about his future?

"He's to have his meals with you in the nursery. The Mistress doesn't want him mixing with his siblings. Doesn't want them getting attached," she said. She placed her cup and saucer back on the table. "Well, I think you have everything you need. Jenny will bring tea and supper for you and Robert. You will stay in the nursery until he goes to bed. Once he's asleep you may use the servants' hall downstairs." She indicated a bell rope by the fireplace. "If you need anything else just ring and Jenny will see to it. Now, I'll leave you to get acquainted with your charge. If you need me I'll be in the schoolroom on the next floor down." She turned to leave but stopped and, glancing at Nell she said, "I hope you will be happy here. You seem like the sort of person who may do Robert some good. Heaven knows he needs all the help he can get."

With that she swept out of the room. Nell didn't know what to make of her or Robert, but she was new and perhaps there were things about the boy she didn't yet understand.

Chapter Two

Nell walked around the nursery. A large wooden doll's house with a white painted front and red roof, stood along one wall next to a collection of miniature prams and a push-along dog which she presumed had once belonged to Robert's older siblings. A tall bookcase contained an assortment of books and small toys. A closed cupboard stood alongside the bookcase.

She went to the cupboard. As she opened the door a worn rag doll with an embroidered face somersaulted out. She picked it up and replaced it on the shelf next to a row of exquisitely dressed china headed dolls. Stuffed toys and a box of tiddlywinks sat on shelves unused. The musty smell of neglect reached her nostrils. She saw a box of toy soldiers complete with barracks, Noah's Ark with all its animals and a toy drum with its drumsticks all neatly packed away. She picked up a clockwork toy and wound it up. The smiling faced monkey clapped his brass cymbals and jumped around on the shelf, toppling off as it turned around. Nell laughed with delight.

It seemed that no expense had been spared in providing things for the boy, but any sign of affection from the family was definitely lacking. It felt as though he'd been put away, out of sight, like a toy for which they had no further use.

She picked out a jigsaw puzzle and took it to a small table near where Robert was playing with a spinning top, intently watching it circling around. "Come on, Robert, come and help me with this puzzle," she said, tipping the pieces onto the table.

Robert shot her a glance, picked up his top and moved to the corner of the room away from Nell. He spun his top again. Nell sighed.

"All right then, what about a game of soldiers? Boys like to play with soldiers." She put the puzzle back in its box and went to fetch the soldiers. She called to him again to join her in a game, but he just kept on spinning his top. He seemed to be in a world of his own. All her attempts to interest him in anything other than spinning his top ended in failure.

Just as she was losing hope, he moved towards her, drawn to her side to watch the clockwork monkey clashing his cymbals. He clapped along with the toy, giggling at its antics. I'm getting somewhere at last, she thought, although she had to wind it up again and again.

All of a sudden she wanted to get to know this strange, solitary little boy Miss Bannister said had been damaged at birth: to get to know his likes and dislikes, what he enjoyed and what he stubbornly refused do. It would take time, but she was in no hurry.

The clapping of the tin toy, the clicking of the clockwork winder and Robert's giggle were the only sounds in the room. She glanced around, amazed at the light and space. So much space for just the two of them. She never thought she'd miss the remorseless noise, crowding and unrelenting work of the workhouse, but suddenly she did. The isolation felt unreal and strange. A shiver ran down her spine. Had she made a mistake coming here? Would she have been better off staying where she was, where at least everything was familiar? She shuddered at the thought.

It was getting dark when Jenny arrived with tea for Robert and a hot cottage pie for her. She placed the tray on the table. "If there's anything else you need just ring," she said.

"If you could stay a while and talk I'd appreciate it," Nell said.

"Talk?"

"Yes please. I'm feeling a bit lost here in this big house on my own. I was hoping you could stay and keep me company for a while. Tell me a little about the other staff, the family and... Robert?"

"I don't know," Jenny said, pushing a stray curl of dark hair back under her cap. Then she smiled. "I suppose it'll be all right. I could say I was helping you with Robert, you being new an' all."

Once Jenny was satisfied that she wouldn't get into trouble by staying, Nell was able to persuade her to join her for a cup of tea. She even managed to produce some biscuits from a tin she found in the small kitchen next to the playroom. She called Robert to come and have his tea.

"It's your favourite," Jenny said as he opened and inspected each sandwich. "Eat up." So he did. "Cheese sandwiches," Jenny said. "He likes cheese sandwiches and you have to crumble the scone. He'll like that."

Nell picked up the scone and crumbled it. "Miss Bannister said to keep Robert up in the nursery. Does he ever go downstairs?"

Jenny shrugged but Nell guessed she knew plenty she wasn't telling.

His earlier tantrum had been quickly forgotten once it was over so Nell said, "I'm confused. He doesn't seem to be any more trouble than most boys his age. I can't understand why he's not in the schoolroom with the other children. Surely he should be having lessons or at least playing with other children."

"He never has," Jenny said. "Perhaps Miss Bannister thinks he's too young." Nell could see from the look on her face there was more to it than she was saying.

"Does anyone else come up to the nursery?" Nell asked. "Does he have anyone to play with?"

Jenny shook her head. "As far as I know he's to stay up here. Never seen him downstairs, not since..." She pouted. "Alice, the chambermaid comes up in the mornings to do the beds, tidy and clean, old George the handyman sees to the wood for the fires. Other than that, no one."

She put her empty tea cup on its saucer on the table. "I really must be going. Cook'll have my guts for garters if I don't get back and help with dinner. Just ring the bell when you've finished and I'll come and clear the plates."

Nell ate her dinner in silence, her head filled with questions about this absurdly adorable boy. Once she'd put Robert to bed she'd go downstairs and find the answers.

She looked again at the schedule Miss Bannister had set out for her. It showed the times Robert was to rise, wash, eat and play. There was no mention of him doing anything else.

After they finished eating their tea Nell sat in the nursery chair. "Would you like a bedtime story?" she asked Robert, showing him the book she'd picked from the impressive collection on the bookshelf.

He gave a dazzling smile and climbed onto her lap. She sighed with relief. At least this was something he was used to. Perhaps all was not lost.

He nestled against her and turned the pages while she read. For the first time that day a feeling of warmth and happiness flowed through her. This was where she belonged, looking after this small, helpless boy who couldn't speak up for himself. The joy on his face and his tiny body pressed against hers as she read made her want to protect him. She wasn't sure what she'd need to protect him from but knew in her heart that she'd die rather than let anyone hurt him. After the story she helped him get ready for bed. When she tucked him in she said, "Goodnight, my precious. Sweet dreams," and kissed his forehead. From the shocked look on his face and the way he giggled she realised that that was not something he was familiar with.

Later, downstairs in the servants' hall she asked to speak to Miss Bannister and was directed to the parlour she shared with the housekeeper.

"Ah," Miss Bannister said. "I hope Master Robert didn't cause you too much trouble. He's usually fine once he's in bed asleep." She smiled. "Come with me and I'll introduce you to the other staff. You can have supper with them and use the servants' parlour if you want to do any reading or sewing. The fire will be lit and it will be quite cosy in there."

"Thank you," Nell said. "But before we go could I ask you about Robert's routine."

"Yes?"

"Well, I can't see any time set aside for lessons, visiting his family or going outside to play. Surely his family will want to see what progress he is making and in this house, with its beautiful gardens, he should be out learning about the trees and plants. It seems a sin to keep him indoors. Even in the workhouse the children were taken outside for some fresh air. The Matron thought it essential for their health."

Miss Bannister glared at Nell at the reference to the workhouse children and the allusion they were better treated than Robert. "Well, of course you may take him outside if you feel it necessary," she said, a sharp edge to her voice. "But only around the kitchen garden, the orchard and the back of the house." She pulled herself up to her full height. "I will inform the family should he make any progress."

She was about to walk away when she turned and said more softly, "If you ask the gardener I think there may be some toys in a shed in the grounds, tricycles or a pull along horse he can ride on. But you must never let him out in the front or around the stables. It's far too dangerous and he'd only get in the way."

Nell swallowed. "Yes, of course."

"Come along then, I'll introduce you to the rest of the staff."

Jenny was among the maids milling around in the servants' hall. Miss Bannister clapped her hands and everyone stopped what they were doing. "This is Nell Draper, Master Robert's new nursemaid. I hope you will make her feel welcome."

The footman stepped forward, an evil glint in his eyes. "As welcome as the flowers in spring," he said and took Nell's hand, lifting it to his lips. "Thomas O'Leary at your service."

Nell pulled her hand away. She'd never experienced such forward behaviour and wasn't sure if she should be flattered or offended. He laughed.

"Take no notice of him," Jenny said when he'd gone. "Thinks too much of himself that one."

Alice, the upstairs maid agreed. "I wouldn't be surprised if he's the reason the last nursemaid left," she said. "Always hanging around her he was, making remarks. Thinks the female staff are perks of the job."

"Well, he'll soon find out different if he tries it on with me," Nell said. She was used to speaking up for herself. You had to in the workhouse.

Nell stayed downstairs talking to the other staff for the rest of the evening. She got the impression that this had once been a happy house but recent events had brought tension and bitterness among the staff. She wasn't about to make herself unpopular by asking too many questions, but she had a feeling that the disquiet was something to do with Robert. She'd bide her time but was determined to find out what lay behind the façade of warmth and friendliness of the downstairs staff.

Chapter Three

The next morning when she awoke she saw Robert's bed was empty. She jumped up and pulled the curtains back to find him standing staring out of the window. Outside the sky was blue with pale sunshine. Blue sky always made her think of her mother, Rosa. She touched the piece of blue silk pinned to her vest beneath her nightdress.

Rosa had been a milliner and, in happier days, always surrounded by rainbows of fancy ribbons, acres of lace, colourful silks and huge feathers to adorn the magnificent hats. Her nimble fingers twisted fabrics into roses, begonias, carnations or gardenias in every colour under the sun.

Whenever the sky clouded over or the day was particularly dull or cold Rosa would take Nell to the window to look at the sky. "Look for a patch of blue," she'd say. "As long as there's enough blue to make a baby's bonnet the rain clouds will disappear and the day will be fine." Somehow they always managed to find a little patch of blue.

One day Rosa was making a silk flower the colour of the sky. She cut out a patch of silk and pinned it to Nell's vest. "There," she said. "Now you have your own little patch of blue so you never need to be sad when the rain clouds appear." As a child Nell had loved her little patch of blue.

When Rosa died everything they possessed had been sold and Nell had been taken to the workhouse. Her little patch of blue had been covered by rough hessian workhouse uniforms, but she never forgot. Whenever she was sad or lonely she'd touch the patch of blue silk and the day seemed to get brighter. The blue had faded and the silk frayed, but she still kept it pinned to her vest with her mother's silver bar brooch. That way she kept the memory of mother close to her.

She glanced at Robert. He would have no memory of his mother. She took him by the shoulders and turned him around. "Good morning, Robert," she said. "Come and get dressed and today we'll go out and explore the grounds."

Next to the playroom was a small kitchen area where she could make tea and light snacks if required and next to that a bathroom where she could bath Robert and wash his clothes.

She washed him quickly and dressed him; then opened the cupboard to find the uniform she'd been told to wear. She put it on and realised she'd need to take it in a bit, but just for today she could tie the apron tight and it should pass muster. She splashed her face and brushed her hair, tying it neatly into a bun. Robert tried to grab the brush when she brushed his hair, so she made it into a game and soon had him giggling.

Jenny arrived with their breakfast at the same time as Alice appeared. There was ham, eggs and toast for Nell and a cheese sandwich for Robert.

"Is it all right if I do the bedroom now, and tidy the other rooms?" Alice asked, a worried look on her pale as ivory face. Her fair, neatly tied back hair and delicate features reminded Nell of the china dolls in the cupboard.

"Of course, it is," Nell said. "We're going to be enjoying our breakfasts, aren't we, Robert?"

Alice nodded and disappeared into the bedroom. When she returned Nell offered her a cup of tea. "Oh, no, Miss, I couldn't," Alice said. "I had mine downstairs with the others."

"Well, I'd like some company," Nell said. "It gets a bit lonely up here on my own and Robert's hardly going to tell anyone is he?"

Alice smiled. "All right," she said, "but I can't stay long. I've got all the other rooms to do."

Nell handed her a cup of tea. "How long have you worked here?" she asked.

"Me? I started in the kitchen when I was ten. Came from the village see. Worked my way up."

Nell guessed her to be about seventeen or eighteen. "You must have seen some changes then," she said.

"I'll say," Alice said. She looked as though she was about to say more but discretion got the better of her.

"Tell me about Miss Bannister, has she been here long? She seems very efficient."

"No," Alice said, looking relieved at having the subject moved on to someone else. "She only came after the new Mistress arrived last year. Everything changed then."

"The new Mistress? Do you mean the Master's second wife?"

"Yes." Alice put her cup on her saucer. A wry smile fitted across her face as though she was about to impart a piece of most delicious gossip. "She's American. He met her while travelling, fell in love and married her in Paris. We only heard about it when the Master brought her home as his new bride. Rum do if you asks me."

Nell pouted. It seemed there was no love lost between the staff and the Master's new bride. "What's she like?"

"It's not for me to say," Alice said. "All I know is that when she came, the pictures of Lady Caroline, the Master's first wife, were taken down and put in the basement. Her picture in every room he had, the Master, until she arrived."

"And what about Robert? Did the Master used to see Robert before the new Mistress came?"

"See 'im? Well, yes, I suppose he did. When he was first born, like. Before he went, well you know, couldn't talk and that." Sadness filled her face. "His first nurse was from the village. Very experienced she was, you couldn't ask for better. But when the doctor came and said... well, what he said, they sacked her. Wasn't her fault, but she got the sack just the same." Nell heard the bitterness in her voice. "Wasn't right that, sacking old Mrs Cooper."

Alice lapsed into silence. Robert broke the silence by picking up his glass of milk and dropping it on the floor. The crash as the glass shattered made them both start.

Alice jumped up. "Oh, you little rascal," she said. "Now I'll have to clean that up."

"I'll do it," Nell said. "I've kept you long enough. Thank you for staying. I appreciate it."

Alice nodded, scowled at Robert and made her way out of the door.

Nell heaved a sigh and went to fetch a dustpan and brush from the kitchen to mop up the spill. When she returned she found Robert bent over, trying to gather up the broken glass. "No! Leave it!" she yelled, afraid he might cut his hands.

Robert glared at her, then rushed at her his arms flaying. She dropped the dustpan and brush and caught his arms, pinning them to his sides to stop the onslaught. She twisted him round with his back to her and held him in a bear hug while he kicked and wriggled to try to get free. Her long skirt softened the blows from his feet. He was having a tantrum. Nell was all too familiar with childish outburst of temper from young boys unaware of the strict regime of the workhouse.

Once they learned the consequences and futility of rebellion the tantrums soon stopped.

She held him in a bear hug until his temper subsided. Breathing heavily she put him gently down. He proceeded to run around the nursery, overturning all the toys and pulling everything off the shelves.

Nell stood aghast. So this was what they meant about him being 'difficult'. When everything was tipped over and the nursery a mess he stood, staring at Nell, his eyes shining with defiance. His lips quivered. He looked so small and helpless she couldn't find it in her heart to chastise him but guessed this was the sort of occasion Miss Bannister had referred to when she talked about punishment. He looked as though he expected to be punished. He was daring her to report him to Miss Bannister. She'd seen the harshest and most brutal punishments handed out to boys for the most spurious of reasons. In her experience it only built resentment and hatred.

She crouched in front of him. "I'm sorry I shouted," she said. "I thought you might hurt yourself on the glass."

She waited for the next violent onslaught. It didn't come.

She picked a book up from the floor. "If you've finished we could have a story," she said. "Would you like a story?" She went and sat in the chair and started to read out loud. He came over and climbed on her lap. He turned the pages as she read. It was as though the tantrum had never happened.

When she came to the end of the book she said, "Now we have to tidy up." Robert appeared surprised that the toys were strewn about. He clearly had no idea he was responsible for the mess, but he happily helped Nell put the toys back in their proper places, treating it as new game she had invented. She swept up the broken glass and the milk.

When she'd mopped everything up Nell went and fetched their coats. She decided to take the dishes down herself instead of ringing for Jenny. It would give her a chance to see the kitchen, speak to the cook, Mrs Hewitt, and find out more about Robert's meals. The woman she'd met last night seemed welcoming and she hoped to make another friend.

She carried the tray of dishes down the back stairs and made her way to the kitchen. The kitchen was hot and steamy. Mrs Hewitt was bent over a pan of stew while Elsie, the kitchen maid, peeled and chopped carrots. She turned when she saw Nell and Robert and rushed to take the tray from Nell.

"Why it's the little 'un," Elsie said, placing the tray on the table. She gazed at Robert. "He's shot up since I saw 'im last. A right little cherub he looks." She bent down, a broad smile on her face. "How are you today, Master Robert?"

Robert responded with one of his magical smiles and chuckled. "I'm afraid I've yet to teach him manners," Nell said, "but I'm sure he's delighted to see you."

Mrs Hewitt realised their presence. "You shouldn't be bringing him in here," she said. "Not a place for children." She waved them both out of the door back into the hallway.

"I'm sorry," Nell said. "I just wanted Robert to see where his meals are cooked and thank you for the wonderful breakfast. I brought the empty dishes back."

"Well, that's as maybe, but I'd be blamed if he had an accident or got burned. There's hot pans and all sorts in there. Doesn't bear thinking about."

"No, you're right, Mrs Hewitt," Nell said. "I'm sorry, I didn't think."

Mrs Hewitt huffed and folded her arms.

Nell braced herself and said, "He had cheese sandwiches for tea last night and again for breakfast this morning. I wondered what he was to have for lunch?"

"The last nursemaid said it was all he'd eat. She said he was a picky eater. Lots of children are at that age." Mrs Hewitt sighed. "I tried giving 'im a good variety of different food but everything always got sent back."

Nell frowned. Picky eaters? She'd never come across any picky eaters in the workhouse. There your only choices were to eat what was put in front of you or go hungry.

"I'm sure you did, Mrs Hewitt, and you cook such delicious meals too. It'd be shame if Robert never got to eat any of them."

Mrs Hewitt laughed. "Well, I'll say this for you, girl, you've got nerves. Only been here a day and already querying his diet." She leaned back to survey Nell. "I'd like to see 'im eat more than sandwiches an' all," she said. "I don't know how he survives. Didn't drink his milk neither I heard."

So Alice reported back to Mrs Hewitt. Nell wondered whether Jenny did the same.

"Miss Bannister said as how you'd worked with children like Robert. You came highly recommended. I 'ope you can help poor little mite," Mrs Hewitt said.

Nell smiled and warmth for this big brash woman flowed through her. "I'll do my best," she said.

"Aye. An' I'll do all I can to 'elp. I'll give 'im a few diffent things to try along with his sandwiches." She raised her eyebrows. "I've got a bit of that cottage pie left. I'll try that for 'is lunch."

"That would be lovely," Nell said. "It was delicious."

Mrs Hewitt beamed. "Personally I reckon it's a poison chalice they've given you," she said. "You can't win. You'll get blamed for all the little 'uns short-comings an' there's plenty of them. I wouldn't have your job for all the tea in China."

Relief washed over Nell. Here was someone on her side, who understood her difficulties. She wouldn't be alone and felt she'd made an ally as well as a friend. She pulled Robert closer to envelope him in her skirts. "I don't know," she said. "The job has its compensations."

Mrs Hewitt frowned. "Trouble is nursemaids don't last long around here". She glanced at the boy nestling in Nell's skirts. "It's the little 'uns that break your heart, ain't it?" she said.

Chapter Four

Behind the kitchen a short hallway led to a back door. Outside the kitchen garden was bathed in bright sunlight. Beds bursting with every kind of vegetable filled the centre of the garden while apple, pear and peach trees lined the surrounding walls. Bees buzzed and butterflies flitted from plant to plant. Nell watched a robin pecking in the mud. The garden seemed to give off an air of peaceful tranquillity. Nell turned her face to feel the sun's warmth and breathe in the fresh air.

Robert squiggled his hand away from hers and ran to the iron gate set in the wall. His hands clenched the bars and his head rested against the metal struts as he stared out.

"Come and look at the garden, Robert," Nell called. She started to walk along the paths around the vegetable beds, hoping Robert would follow. When he didn't she went and took his hand. Reluctantly he turned away from the gate. "Shall we see if we can find some apples?" she said.

He frowned, but made no resistance as she led him around the garden. She stopped and pointed out the various vegetables already planted but Robert showed no interest. Then she recalled what Miss Bannister had said about some toys in a shed, so she opened the gate and went to find a gardener.

Next to the walled kitchen garden Nell found herself in another garden, beautifully set out with a sweeping herbaceous border around a paved terrace. A wooden bench at the edge of the paving sat beneath the spreading branches of a spectacular magnolia tree filled with pink and white blossoms. The bench had been placed in the spot most likely to get the morning sun and be shaded from the heat at midday and for the afternoon. It looked magical and Nell couldn't help wondering who sat here in this stunning place.

The garden stretched around the corner of the building so, with Robert holding her hand, she walked around it and saw a young man planting out the beds.

"Good morning," she called.

The man glanced up. He looked surprised to see her, and even more surprised to see Robert. "Good morning," he said. He nodded at the child. "Not often we see young Master Robert out here."

Nell's heart fluttered. If the gardener knew Robert he must have been out here before. So, when did that change and why was Nell discouraged from bringing him into the garden?

"No," she said. "So I understand, but it's something I find quite strange."

"Not the only strange thing around here," he said so quietly that Nell barely heard. He rammed the fork he was digging with into the ground so hard it stood there. He ran his fingers through his unruly mop of dark curls. "Sorry. You're new and I shouldn't be blaming you for what goes on."

"No, but I'd like to know a bit more about what does go on here," she said. "Especially if it concerns Robert. I've been hired to take care of him but it seems no one cares whether I do or don't. But I care. I care a lot."

He shrugged. His face softened. "Don't be too hard on the staff here," he said. "They've a lot to put up with. They're all good people, but there's not much they can do to help if the Lord and Master decrees otherwise."

"But why would he? That's what I don't understand. Robert is his son. Surely he wants the best for him?"

"You'd think so wouldn't you? Although, I suppose, in his position..."

Shock sent Nell's heart spiralling. A swell of anger formed inside her. It rose rapidly to her throat and exploded from her mouth. "His position! I can't think of any position that would justify a man turning his back on his son. His own flesh and blood! I could name a hundred men who'd give everything they owned to be able to look after their children. Poverty and destitution stop them, but as far as I can see there's nothing like that around here." Tears welled up in her eyes as the vision of the families in the workhouse, split up and never seeing their children, filled her mind. Life in the workhouse was cruel. Families were broken up. The Lord of the Manor had no excuse for not looking out for his child.

"I'm sorry," the gardener said, seeing her distress. "My name's Ethan. I'm the under gardener here and I've no right to judge other people, but if there's anything I can do..."

"You can explain to me what happened when Robert was born to make his father so bitter."

Ethan nodded. He picked up his canvas bag and led Nell to the bench. Robert had already found his way there and sat playing with the horse and carriage he'd brought down from the nursery. "I'll tell you all I know if you'll share a cup of tea and bite with me." He took a flask and a tin box out of his bag.

Nell smiled. "Thank you," she said. She was conscious that her heart had quickened and sent her pulses racing.

Ethan poured tea into a tin mug and handed it to her. It felt warm and comforting. Even in his rough overalls Ethan looked smarter than anyone she recalled seeing before. Dark curls fell over his brow and his brown eyes shone with kindness. He stretched out his hand to squeeze Robert's leg which made Robert giggle. Her instinct told her this was man she could trust.

"He was born before his time," he said. "My ma's the local midwife. She was called too late to save his ma." He shook his head sadly."His ma, Lady Caroline was the lovliest lady I ever met. She used to come out to this garden and sit on this bench. Beautiful she was. She called it her secret garden. I planted the borders especially for her with her favourite lilies. She loved lilies. Well, when she died..."

He paused and swallowed. "Worst day ever," he said. "It was as though someone had switched the sun off. Course it wasn't the boy's fault, but the Master was devastated. The house went into mourning." Sadness filled his eyes. He took a swig of tea from his flask. "A woman from the village came as his nurse. She looked after him well enough. Good as anyone could have." He glanced again at the boy. "He wasn't a bad kid, not then. Good as gold he was. Never cried, not even when he fell over. I suppose we should have known then that something was wrong."

"So what happened after that?"

Ethan sighed. "He used to come out here to play. Everything was fine 'til he was about two, then he started falling behind. He began forgetting things he'd learned and no matter how hard she tried his nurse couldn't get him to utter one single word. Everything seemed sort of awkward for him. When he hadn't improved by the time he reached his third birthday they called the doctor in.

Specialist from London he was. Nothing's been the same since."

It was pretty much the story Miss Bannister had told her.

"The Master brought in all sorts of specialists, but no one could make him speak. From what I gather doctors said he wasn't quite right in the head." He shrugged. "The Master was furious. It was a right to do. He sacked the nurse and the staff weren't to utter a word of it to anyone. It's like the Master blamed him. I've not seen owt of him since. That's all I know. Doesn't look like he's got much to look forward to, poor mite."

"Well, we'll see about that," Nell said, her heart pounding with rage. In the infirmary she'd nursed people who had been described as 'not quite right in the head'. She'd found they could learn things if you spent enough time teaching them and they all made some sort of a contribution to the running of the place, even if it was just standing in the laundry turning the handle of the mangle, or helping with the cleaning. All jobs that had to be done by someone. She saw no reason Robert should be any different.

Then she remembered what Miss Bannister had said about the toys. "I understand there are some toys kept in a shed somewhere," Nell said. "Do you know where I might look for them?"

The gardener pouted. "Don't know about that," he said. "I just do the planting and look after the beds. Don't know anything about toys. I'll take you to see my pa, Harvey Baines, he's the head gardener. He should be able to help you."

Nell thanked him for the tea, gathered up her skirts and stood up. She lifted Robert off the bench. "Come on, Robert," she said. "Let's go and find these toys."

They found Harvey by the greenhouses potting up seeds. He too seemed surprised to see Robert out with his nurse. He rubbed his chin. "Not sure you ought to be out here with the little lad," he said. "Master won't like him running about the place."

Nell was shocked. "And why shouldn't he be running about the place? It's his home. If anyone has a right to be 'running around the place' it's him."

Harvey shrugged. "If you say so," he said. "I just thought..."

Nell never did find out what he thought. "Lady said something about some toys in a shed," Ethan butted in. "I thought you'd be best person to ask."

Harvey thought for a moment, his weather-beaten face creased into a frown. His eyes narrowed. "There were some in the outbuildings next to the potting sheds," he said. "Not sure if they're still there."

"Can we go and look?" Nell said.

Harvey wiped his hand down his brown canvas apron. "Foller me," he said.

In the shed Nell found a selection of pull along toys, a stuffed giraffe, a horse and several other unidentifiable animals. There was also a pony carriage and a couple of rusty tricycles.

"Used to belong to the girls," Harvey said. "They used the carriage to ride around the grounds pulled by one of the ponies."

Nell picked up the better looking of the two tricycles. "What about this?" she said. "If we clean it up I think Robert could ride it."

Ethan took it from her. "I'll give it a clean and some oil and bring it to you in the garden," he said. Nell didn't miss the smile and glint in his eye when he said it either.

She found a ball and some skittles dumped in the corner of the shed. She picked them up, brushed them down and took them with her. She played skittles with Robert until Ethan, true to his word, brought her the tricycle, restored to a reasonable condition. He'd even wrapped cotton strips around the handles to make them more comfortable to hold.

He watched as Nell put Robert on it and pushed him around the garden. Robert laughed and giggled as they went along with his legs stuck out. She tried to get him to use the pedals but he couldn't get the hang of it. Give it time, she thought, but at least she'd managed to get him outside and on the tricycle. It was a start.

Chapter Five

Over the next few weeks Nell spent most of her time with Robert getting to know him and his ways. It became clear to her that Robert's tantrums were usually triggered when she tried to stop him doing something he'd set his heart on. Like summer storms they blew up out of nowhere and disappeared just as quickly as they had come, leaving Robert completely unaware of what had happened. Mostly his outbursts were short-lived. She'd hold him close while he hit out and kicked her and then carry on as though nothing had happened. She sensed his frustration when things didn't go his way but found it easier to distract him with something new, rather than battle with him. When he did lash out she never felt the need to refer to Miss Bannister.

She tried to bring some structure to his day by sitting him down after breakfast with some books, reading to him and counting, either on his fingers or with some bricks. She found he'd be fine for a short while, but soon got sidetracked, then he'd run to the window to stare out, or play with his toys and all her appeals to pay attention to the books fell on deaf ears.

He behaved strangely too. Sometimes he'd stomp around like a dark cloud threatening rain, waving his hands as though talking to someone she couldn't see. Then he'd laugh at nothing.

He had an intensity of purpose that she'd never seen in a child before. The fact that he had no words appeared to be as natural to him as breathing. Perhaps because he'd never had a voice, she thought. He'd always been a silent boy. Still, even without words he made it clear what he wanted.

"I've never seen a child able to express so much with a look or a glance," Nell said to Jenny one day. "And far from being feeble-minded as his silence might suggest, he's very determined."

Jenny agreed. "He certainly has a way about him," she said clearing away the dishes.

"He's not stupid either," Nell said. "No matter what everyone thinks."

Nell soon came to understand the strict routine and nature of the house and the people in it. She learnt that Jenny had a great sense of humour and

Alice liked to gossip. Mrs Hewitt was a kindly soul but she ran the kitchen maids, Elsie and Sarah, ragged. All the female staff shuddered in the presence of the housekeeper, Mrs Grindley, although Miss Bannister and Miss Lorimer, the lady's maid, reported directly to the Mistress. The butler, Mr Maybury, oversaw the male staff and was a stickler for rules.

She also learned something else one morning when a sullen Thomas O'Leary brought breakfast for Nell and Robert.

"Jenny's sick," he said. "Double duties for the rest of us."

Nell said she hoped Jenny would soon feel better.

"Hmmph," Thomas said. He ran a speculative glance over Nell. "Well, I must say you're an improvement on the last girl. Lump of lard she was." He placed the breakfast tray on the table. "How are you getting on with the idiot child? Has he bitten you yet?" He nodded to Robert who was staring out of the window.

Nell's hackles rose. "He's not an idiot child. In fact he's quite bright," she said.

"Oh yes, bright as ditchwater he is." He tapped his head. "Got a slate missing you know. Why else would they employ you, a workhouse girl, to look after him instead of a proper nurse from London like they had for the girls?" He winked at Nell. "Me? I'm glad it's you not one of them. Better for me."

"What do you mean?"

He stepped towards her. "Come on. I know you workhouse girls. Always up for a bit of a romp and some slap and tickle."

Nell was aghast.

"Not like them tight-arsed London nurses," he said moving closer.

Nell edged around the table.

"Playing hard to get?" he said with a grin.

Nell picked up the hot teapot and removed the lid. "Come any closer and you'll get this all over you," she said.

He grimaced but backed away. He laughed. "Let me know when you change your mind," he said. "You'll soon get fed up with only that retard for company." With that he left the room.

Nell sank into the chair. She felt as though she'd been hit by a runaway train and all the air knocked out of her. Was that what everyone thought of her and Robert? Two misfits who deserved each other?

Well, Robert couldn't speak up for himself but she could. You had to in the workhouse. No one else would, except old Flossie. Flossie had taken Nell under her wing when she first arrived. She didn't know how she'd have survived if it hadn't been for Flossie speaking up for her. When Flossie got sick Nell was the only one who'd nurse her. All the others were frightened of catching the fever, but Nell didn't care. Flossie had been kind to her when no one else was and, as Flossie herself said, "When you've got nowt you can't fear losing it." Nell sat with Flossie and held her hand as she died.

"Don't worry about me, love," Flossie said. "I'm going to a better place." Nell remembered thinking that any place would be better than where they were. Now she remembered something else Flossie had said. "Stand tall," she used to say. "Don't let 'em see you cry. When you reach rock-bottom the only way is up." Well, she didn't care what Thomas O'Leary thought. Or any of them for that matter. She'd speak up for herself and for Robert. She wasn't going to let them see her cry and she'd prove them all wrong. She'd show them.

The best part of the day and the thing Robert loved most of all was going outside to play in the sunshine. As the weather improved Nell was able to take him out more often. She'd regularly take him to see where lilies and poppies filled the garden with their striking, colourful blooms. A large magnolia provided shade and roses, lavender and orange blossom scented the air.

One fine morning, when the May sun was at its brightest, Nell decided to go as far as the orchard so Robert could run around and they could play hide and seek between the fruit trees.

Robert ran ahead of her as she strolled along enjoying the warmth of the sun. The blossom on the trees appeared like fluffy clouds in a summer sky. She breathed in the scent of the freshly cut grass and watched the bees flitting between the branches. The day felt idyllic. It was the perfect place to sit and read to Robert, or play between the trees. She made her way to the bench where they usually sat. A young girl sat there reading a book.

"Good morning," she called. "You must be, let me see, Ellen isn't it?" She guessed the girl to be about nine. "I'm Nell, Robert's nursemaid."

The girl look startled. "Oh," she said, wriggling uncomfortably. "I just thought I'd come out and revise. I have to learn this poem to recite to Papa this afternoon and it keeps slipping from my mind. I told Miss Bannister I was going to change my dress but came out here instead. You won't tell anyone will you?"

Nell felt a sharp shock as she realised that she was speaking to Lord Eversham's daughter and that she was privileged, not only to see her father, but also to demonstrate her learning with recitations. She smiled. It wasn't the girl's fault and she was obviously distressed at being discovered in the orchard when she was supposed to be elsewhere. "No," she said, "I won't tell, and Robert can't, so you may rest easy."

Ellen breathed a sigh of relief. "Thank you," she said. She looked at Robert. "He's grown since I last saw him. Hello Robert, I'm Ellen, your sister. Do you remember me?"

Robert smiled then looked uncertainly at Nell.

"It's all right," Nell said. "He's probably wondering why he hasn't seen more of you."

Ellen blushed. "We're not supposed to play with him," she said. "Miss Bannister would be most displeased. I must go. Sorry." She picked up her book. "Poor Robert, whatever will become of him?" she said before dashing off.

Well, Nell thought. Not supposed to play with him. Honestly, anyone would think he was a monster instead of the brightest, loveliest, most darling little boy she'd ever met. And what did she mean, whatever will become of him? Did she know something Nell didn't?

Soon the house was thrown into a fury of commotion as Lady Eversham arranged a host of parties, balls and events inviting the cream of society.

"She certainly wants to make her mark," Mrs Hewitt declared after having been asked to cater for 900 guests at one summer ball. "Couldn't find anyone more different to Lady Caroline," she said. "This one's more interested in being seen in elevated circles than caring about the tenants, farmers and locals. It'll end in tears, you mark my words."

Most of the staff agreed with her. One evening, the warmth of the June sun lingered and being indoors felt stuffy and hot. Nell went out to sit in the garden where she'd seen Ethan watering the flower beds. He came to sit with her on the bench. "Everyone's all fired up about the ball," he said. "Jenny's been talking of nothing else for weeks."

"I know, the whole house is in uproar," Nell said. "But it puzzles me. What sort of people care more about their social standing than the wellbeing of their children? They don't care about them at all. As long as their summer ball is the talk of the county and the highlight of the season their happiness is complete." Her shoulders slumped.

Ethan shrugged. "That's the nobility for you," he said.

Over the next few weeks Nell often found she was left to fend for herself and Robert when it came to their meals as everyone was kept busy and had little time left to worry about them. Extra staff were brought in to cope with the ever increasing demands of the Mistress's social calendar.

Every day Jenny regaled Nell with the comings and goings of the house. "The dressmaker's coming today to measure the girls for their new dresses," she said one day. "They're to have new outfits for the balls and they're going to perform for the guests."

"Perform for the guests?"

"Yes, you know, on the piano and the violin. They're having extra lessons in the music room every afternoon, and learning to dance. Honest, they're so excited they can hardly keep still." She laughed.

"And what about Robert?" Nell asked.

Jenny's face fell. She shrugged. "Same as usual I suppose. Keep quiet and out of the way."

Fury, sharp as a knife, struck Nell's heart. It was so unfair. Nothing was Robert's fault, and yet another part of her knew that this was the way it would always be. He was a casualty on the battlefield of broken dreams. Being less than the perfect son and heir would make him invisible to anyone who mattered.

Nell approached Miss Bannister. "Will Robert be getting some new clothes when the dressmaker calls?" she asked.

"New clothes for Robert? Why? Has he grown out of his old ones?"

"No, for the ball," she said.

Miss Bannister frowned. "He won't need anything. He's far too young to be allowed to stay up like the girls."

So Nell decided to try something else. "As the schoolroom is not used in the afternoons could I take Robert there to teach him his numbers and letters? I think a change from the nursery would improve his concentration. In the workhouse..."

"We are NOT in the workhouse!" Miss Bannister barked, her eyes blazing. "But if you don't take care you may end up back there." Nell's constant references obviously infuriated her, but Nell had discovered that allusions to the workhouse offering a better environment for Robert than that currently allowed usually resulted in her getting everything she wanted. She was determined to speak up for him, but she didn't want to risk losing her place.

Miss Bannister let out a long breath. "You'll be wasting your time. Lord Eversham put aside any ambition he had for his son some time ago. Still, I suppose it will be all right," she said eventually. "Just as long as there's no mess, nothing broken and everything put away in perfect order. If you think you can control him."

"You won't even know we've been there," Nell said. It was another step forward in her efforts to get the rest of the family to include and acknowledge him but resentment still hardened her heart. How different it was for these people who had no idea what it was like to have to beg for everything they so easily took for granted.

After that Robert spent two hours every afternoon with a slate learning to write his letters and count his fingers. Nell saw his sisters' drawings on the wall. They'd drawn the house, the stables and the horses. They were very good. It appeared they had talent, so perhaps Robert did too. She gave him a pencil and paper. "Can you draw a horse, Robert?" she said. "If you do I'll put it on the wall with the other pictures."

Bewilderment filled Robert's eyes as he stared at the pencil in his hand and then at the paper. First of all he scribbled over the page. She took it away and gave him another. He scribbled over that. Then she showed him the pictures the girls had drawn.

"Can you make pictures like that, Robert?" she asked. He looked at her, then at the paper and pencil, then, his little face puckered with solemn concentration. He scribbled an outline just about recognisable as a face with dark curls of hair protruding from a nurse's cap. Nell gasped. It wasn't a horse, but it was what he saw in front of him. Her heart sang.

"Well done! Clever boy," she said and gave him a hug. She put his drawing on the wall with the others and put a small sketch pad and pencil in her pocket. Perhaps, if he could learn to write and draw he'd be accepted by the family and his future would be more secure.

When they returned to the schoolroom the next afternoon she noticed Robert's picture had been taken down.

Chapter Six

Whenever the weather was fine enough Nell took Robert outside. They played in the orchard for a while, with Robert hiding, then laughing and giggling when Nell found him and tickled him. Her heart lifted at his laughter and the magical transformation from the solemn, silent boy to a wriggling, giggly one. There were tears too, when he struggled to do something or make himself understood, but they were soon wiped away, replaced by smiles and laughter. His happiness brought her more joy than she had ever known. It was so rare and precious it made her heart burn with love for him.

She tried to interest him in the trees and different grasses growing all around, but he would just run and hide behind a tree again waiting to be found and tickled. Then she let him ride his tricycle up and down, ringing his bell as he went, until lunch time.

"Come along in, Robert. We'll have some lunch then we can do some lessons," she said.

Robert obediently followed her in.

There was an empty store-room under the stairs where Nell kept his outdoor toys. She opened the door to put the tricycle away when she felt a pair of hands on her back. A mighty push sent her sprawling into the cupboard. She only managed to stop herself landing on the floor by raising her arms to bang up against the wall in front of her. She spun around. Thomas, the footman leered at her. "Well, this is nice and cosy isn't it?" he said. "Time for us to get better acquainted."

He stepped closer, a wide grin spread across his face, lust lit up his eyes.

"Get off me," Nell said. "I've heard all about you and your loutish ways. Well, you'll not be making a fool of me."

He placed his hands either side of her head against the wall behind her, and pressed his body into hers. His hot, beery breath warmed her cheek.

"Give us a kiss, then. Come on you know you want to."

Nell's eyes widened as a molten fury exploded inside her. "No I do not," she shrieked and struggled to push him away. He was much stronger than her and his throaty laugh showed how much he was enjoying the confrontation. Boiling blood ran through her veins and flushed her face.

She struggled to free herself and lift her knee so she could ram it into the soft part of his groin. Suddenly he let out a howl and spun around. Nell saw Robert standing behind him his little face sombre, his blue eyes saucer wide staring at them.

"Little beggar bit me," Thomas yelled grabbing his calf. He raised his hand to hit the child. Nell gasped. Before he could bring his fist down another hand grabbed his arm and held it.

"You forget yourself," Ethan said. His eyes blazed. "Don't even think about hitting the young Master or I might forget my place too." He grabbed Thomas's tunic with his other hand and forced him into the hallway. "And don't ever treat anyone like that again or you'll have me to deal with." He gave Thomas a final push in the direction of the kitchen and watched as he slunk away.

"Some people are best avoided," Ethan said when he returned.

"I know," Nell said. "But I don't think he'll try again with Robert here to protect me." Ethan chuckled. "I was just outside. Thomas's yell brought me running," he said. "So I guess we can thank young Master Robert." He ruffled his hair. Robert chuckled and clapped his hands. They both laughed, although Nell felt sure Robert had no idea what was going on.

"If he bothers you again let me know," Ethan said. "We gardeners have ways of dealing with worms like him."

Nell thanked him. She was still shaking but she had the distinct impression that this would not be the last she'd hear of Thomas O'Leary.

A couple of days later Nell was going through the clothes in Robert's chest of drawers, making a list of anything that needed mending, or replacing when she found a gold locket, silver Christening cups, cutlery and several other silver items. They'd all been stuffed to the back of the drawer. She asked Jenny about them.

"They were his mother's," Jenny said. "Gifts from the family when he was born. The photo in the frame is her and the picture in the locket. The Master gave it to her to celebrate the birth of a son. When she died he couldn't bear to look at it, nor any of the other things. That's why they were all put away in a drawer. They remind him of her and his loss."

One of the cups had Robert's name and a date engraved on it. "What about the date here on this cup?" she said. "It's next month."

"Robert's birthday, although it's never celebrated. The house goes into mourning. I suppose it might be different this year, with the new Mistress an' all. Still, I expect we'll all have to go to the service in the chapel. We do every year."

The next morning she took Robert out to play in the garden, hoping to run into Ethan. Over the months she'd run into him several times and always found him willing to sit and chat, or tell her about things while he worked. He'd talk to Robert too, and treat him the same as he would any other child. Robert always seemed happier when he spent time with Ethan, it was as though they had formed a special bond. The sort of bond he should have had with his father, Nell thought, but pushed the preposterous thought from her mind.

"I doubt they'll be draping the rooms in black this year," Ethan said when she asked him. "Not with the new Mistress taking Lady Caroline's place. They'll still have the service in the chapel though, for the girls."

"For the girls?"

"Yes. It's a Memorial Service for their mother."

The familiar bitterness curled in Nell's stomach. "She was Robert's mother too," she said. "Although that seems to have escaped everyone's mind. I don't suppose he's to be invited."

"He never has been," Ethan said. He hung his head. "I'll say a prayer for him," he whispered. "And for you too."

When the day arrived bright, sunny and cloudless, Nell watched Lady Eversham leaving in the coach to visit friends in town. Once she'd gone all the curtains in the house were drawn, plunging it into darkness. The clocks were stopped, the mirrors covered. Talking above a whisper was banned. It felt as if they were living in a mausoleum. At eleven o'clock the Master would lead his daughters, guests and staff to the chapel for the Memorial Service.

Nell wasn't to be so easily defeated. She found Miss Bannister in the schoolroom draping black cloth over the tables. "Should Robert wear his best suit?" she asked.

"His best suit? Whatever for?"

"For the memorial service for Lady Caroline. I understand everyone is expected to attend. Surely that includes her only son? She was his mother too."

Miss Bannister took a deep breath, her face contorted. "I really don't think it appropriate for him to attend. He's far too young and would never understand the service, let alone the reason for it. No, it would be in his best interest to stay indoors where his routine will be familiar and avoid any upset." With that she stormed off. What else did Nell expect? She was a girl from the workhouse and he was the imbecile son, neither worth any genuine consideration.

At quarter-to-eleven she watched the procession making its way along the drive. She sat Robert down and showed him the photo of his mother in a silver frame. Then she showed him the locket. "This is your mother," she said. She wrote the word 'Mother' on his slate. She stroked his cheek. "You have her eyes and fine as silk, spun-gold hair," she said.

Robert stared, his eyes empty of emotion. Nell touched the picture, then touched his chest. "Keep her memory here in your heart," she said. It was where she kept her own mother's memory.

Robert touched the picture and then his chest. Was he merely copying her actions, or had he understood? Nell didn't know, but she felt heartened.

It was his birthday. Something that should be an occasion for celebration, she thought, even if it were only the two of them. She lifted his hand and spread his fingers, counting one, two, three up to six. "You're six years old today," she said. "Let's have a party."

Flossie had taught her to sing when she was sad to dispel the perpetual, all enveloping misery of their lives. She'd taught her music hall songs that were popular in her youth, songs that always made Nell laugh. It was what they needed today, something to raise their spirits.

She hummed as she took him downstairs to the kitchen to pick up a picnic to take to the orchard, away from the house and its dismal show of mourning. The kitchen was empty and eerily silent. She laughed and danced Robert around the table, singing. Robert laughed and danced around with her and the overwhelming gloom pervading the house faded away.

In the larder she saw the luncheon prepared for the Master and his guests when they returned. Next to the luncheon she saw a small cake iced with Robert's name. Mrs Hewitt must have made it especially. Nell smiled. At least someone cared. She put it, with some of the choices delicacies from the luncheon, into a basket.

The late July day was bright and warm. Nell skipped along swinging Robert's hand as they made their way to the orchard where shadows dappled beneath the trees. She set the basket down and spread a blanket on the ground. Then they played hide and seek; Robert's favourite game. Whenever Nell found him she'd tickle him just to hear him giggle with glee. The sun shone and insects buzzed in the air, while crickets chirped in the long grass. They played skittles on the manicured lawn next to the orchard. After that, when they were both tired of the game, she pushed him on the swing hanging from the branch of a sturdy oak Ethan had fixed up for him. She sung to him and showed him how to clap along to the nursery rhymes her mother used to sing to her. At lunchtime they sat in the grass and ate their picnic. She gave him a piece of the cake, but sadly he refused to eat it.

Later, in the afternoon when everyone had returned from the church service and Nell and Robert were in the secret garden, Ethan appeared. Nell was sitting on a bench and he sat down beside her.

"So, how was the service," Nell asked, a little more spikily than she intended.

He shrugged. "Shorter than usual," he said. For some reason she couldn't understand Nell was glad of that.

"I've a present for Robert," he said. "I hope you don't mind."

Mind? Nell was delighted at his thoughtfulness. It would be the only birthday present Robert was likely to receive. He pushed a brown paper bag into her hands. "It's just something I made," he said.

Nell called Robert. "Come and see what Ethan has brought you," she said.

Robert came and Nell pulled the carved horse out of the bag. It was made of polished wood stained to resemble the Master's favourite stallion. "Well, what do you think of that?" Nell asked Robert.

A broad smile lit up his face as he took hold of the horse. Still grinning he climbed on Ethan and gave him a hug.

Nell's heart swelled. Who needs words, she thought as Robert's delight was obvious. Ethan was grinning too. It was a moment she vowed she'd never forget as she watched Robert gallop the horse around the terrace.

Chapter Seven

August brought the season of weekend shooting parties when the house was again thrown into busy actively. Lord Eversham hosted the annual shoot, a grand affair with visitors from all over the county. Women wore their best dresses and men turned up in their best carriages. The shooting party would go out to the fields first, to be followed by the women driving out to watch. Food and wine flowed. Lady Eversham fussed around making sure everything was perfect for her guests. It was the busiest Nell had seen her. Once she even asked Nell to mind two of her guests' infant offspring so they wouldn't disturb the shooting party.

Nell took them up to the nursery where they played with Robert's toys. In the afternoon she put them down for a nap in the bedroom she shared with Robert, him having given up his afternoon nap at Nell's insistence. "He's old enough to be awake all day," she'd said to Miss Bannister. "The boys in the workhouse…"

Miss Bannister huffed. "He's in your charge, you may do as you please," she'd said, before stomping off.

The weather was exceptionally hot and all the windows in the house were open although the air was still and heavy with heat, barely stirring the leaves on the trees. When Nell returned to the nursery she saw Robert standing by the window. He'd been playing with his toy soldiers on the floor. Now he had them stood on the windowsill and was flicking them out, watching each one as it arched onto the terrace below. Some fell in the bushes, while others reached the paving.

"Oh no, Robert," she said, and dashed over to close the window. Robert screamed at having his game interrupted and threw himself onto the floor in a tantrum. She'd seen worse in the workhouse and had by now become used to Robert's efforts, which were intense but usually short-lived. She laughed. "Well, I know someone who isn't going to have one of Mrs Hewett's fruit scones with jam this afternoon," she said, and carried on preparing their nursery tea.

Robert, realising that he wasn't going to get the attention he desired, laughed too. That was what she loved about him, his moods were fleeting, he was easily distracted and his sunny disposition quickly restored.

When she'd calmed him down she left him playing and went to retrieve the fallen soldiers. They'd landed on the terrace that led off the dining room, a place she was forbidden to take Robert, but as she was alone she didn't think it would matter.

She went through the kitchen garden and opened the gate onto the terrace. As she passed the open dining room window she heard voices she recognised as Lady Eversham and her brother, George, one of the weekend guests.

"What good fortune," he was saying. "A wealthy belted Earl with only daughters. The future does look promising."

"He does have a son," Lady Eversham said, "but he's hidden away. Poor soul is half-witted. "

Half-witted? A flame of anger flickered inside Nell rapidly growing into a furnace of rage. 'He's not half-witted,' she wanted to scream. 'He may be a bit behind in his learning, but his mind is as bright and sharp as anyone's'.

"Half-witted? Not fit to inherit then? We'll need to make sure of that," George said.

"Yes, I plan to," Lady Eversham said.

"What on earth are you doing here?" Miss Bannister's steely tones rang out, dousing Nell's rage like water on embers. "And where's Robert and the two little ones? You haven't left them alone have you?"

Flustered, the colour rose in Nell's cheeks. "No. The little ones are taking a nap and Robert is playing. I just came down to retrieve some of his soldiers that fell out of the window in the breeze."

Miss Bannister looked up.

"I've closed the window now," Nell said and held out the soldier she'd picked up to show Miss Bannister.

"You should have asked one of the outdoor staff," Miss Bannister said with an edge to her voice Nell hadn't heard before. "That's what they're there for." She huffed. "Well hurry up and get back. I don't like Master Robert being left unattended." She paused. "I understood you were able to follow orders. If you don't learn your place you'll soon be looking for another position."

Nell's face flamed. Her blood boiled. She finished picking up the soldiers under the shrubbery and hurried back to the nursery. A thousand questions buzzed through her mind.What did Lady Eversham mean? A cauldron of anger burned inside her.

The next day dawned warm and sunny so Nell took Robert out into the garden hoping to find Ethan attending to the beds. She took a snack and a drink for them so they wouldn't have to hurry back. The day always appeared brighter when she ran into Ethan and things didn't look so bad for Robert either as Ethan always chatted to him, undaunted by his lack of response. She felt a flutter of excitement and her heart lifted when she saw him digging out some faded lilies. It wasn't long before he left his work to sit on the bench with Nell.

"How's he doing?" he asked.

"Well, he is as he is," Nell said. "The brightest, happiest, sunniest little boy I've ever known." Then she told him about the conversation she'd overheard at the shoot, which had been playing on her mind. "He's not half-witted. He's bright as a button, just different, that's all. What do you think Lady Eversham could have meant? Having plans?"

His brow creased into a frown. Nell knew how concerned he was for the boy. He shrugged, but from the look on his face Nell knew he was thinking more than he dared say.

"Perhaps I'm blowing it out of proportion," she said. "After all, what can they do? Robert is Lord Eversham's eldest son. Nothing in the world can change that can it?"

A couple of days later Jenny came into the nursery with Nell and Robert's tea. "Miss Bannister said I was to stay and mind Robert. She wants a word with you in the school-room."

She put the tray down. "Trouble if you ask me. She didn't look too pleased when she said it."

Nell's heart sank. What was it now? Miss Bannister had been watching her more closely than she was comfortable with ever since the episode on the terrace. She'd been so careful not to upset anyone too. She'd even helped Alice with a dress she was making. Heart hammering she made her way to the schoolroom.

"Jenny said you wanted a word," Nell said. "If it's about Robert's lessons I was going to ask you..."

"No. It's not about Robert." Her icy gaze washed over Nell. She took a deep breath, as though hesitant about what she was about to say. "I hate gossip," she said eventually, "but unfortunately in a place like this it can't be avoided."

Nell frowned. She often chatted with Alice and Jenny but could think of nothing she'd said that might have offended Miss Bannister.

"I hear you've been spending your time in the garden canoodling with the under gardener," Miss Bannister said. "The Master won't tolerate the person responsible for his son's welfare fraternizing with the lower orders. You need to realise you have a privileged position here. It is a position that requires a great deal of responsibility. I thought you were up to it, but it appears that I was mistaken."

The shock stung like a sharp slap. She couldn't have been more surprised if the wall had opened up and a bird flew out. What on earth was Miss Bannister talking about?

"Canoodling? That's a lie. I've never canoodled as you put it with…" Ethan. She meant Ethan. Her breathing deepened as she tried to contain her anger. "I fully realise the importance of my position here and I'd never do anything to hurt Robert. Yes, I did ask the under gardener, Ethan I believe is his name, to help with Robert's tricycle. It had a squeak, you could hear it for miles. He was kind enough to oil it and also restore some of the other toys from the shed." Gradually her anger subsided as she realised the stupidity of the accusation.

"You did say to ask the outdoor staff if I had a problem with Robert's outdoor toys. I was merely following your instruction."

Miss Bannister sniffed. "As I said, I hate gossip especially malicious gossip which this patently is. However, it's a warning. As Robert's nursemaid your behaviour must be beyond reproach. If I hear any more of such goings on with the male staff you will both lose your jobs."

Miss Bannister dismissed her and she went back to the nursery to ask Jenny if the staff were talking about her.

Jenny shook her head. "Not that I've heard," she said. "But I wouldn't put it past Thomas O'Leary to be spreading rumours. I think he's got it in for you. I wouldn't trust him further than I could throw him."

That made sense. Nell thought about it. The prospect of losing her job, and Ethan losing his, just because she'd spent a few precious hours in the garden talking to him, seemed beyond reason. Still, Miss Bannister was right. Her position in the house depended on absolute discretion and prudence. Any sort of improper behaviour could easily see the end of it.

Over the next few weeks she made sure only to sit in the garden with Robert when Ethan was absent. If she saw him there she'd take Robert out to the orchard or along to the woods.

The thought of losing her job and thereby losing touch with Robert made her heart crumble to dust. Since being his nurse she'd become closer to him than anyone in her life before. Seeing his cheery face and enjoying his sunny disposition every day had become as essential to her as breathing.

Sadness wrapped around her. It would take the force of a hurricane to wrench this small boy from her heart.

Chapter Eight

The weeks up to Christmas came as a brief respite for Nell and the rest of the staff. The family undertook a round of visiting and found their amusement elsewhere. The girls went with their father to visit their grandparents and Lady Eversham spent several days visiting friends.

While the girls were away Miss Bannister stepped in to see to Robert so Nell could visit her friends in the workhouse on Christmas Eve. Mrs Hewitt made up a hamper of food for her to take. "I've put in some meat pies and small cakes for the little ones," she said. "Don't suppose they get pies and cakes very often."

You don't know the half of it, Nell thought as the memory of bowls of gruel or thin soup rushed through her mind. Miss Bannister agreed to her taking some toys the girls had grown out of and she was allowed the use of the spare carriage for the journey.

The day started frosty and Nell was glad of her coat and boots. It felt strange travelling in the carriage, properly dressed and carrying gifts on her way to the place where she'd spent so many years struggling to survive. She remembered previous Christmases. It was the one time of year when work could be put aside, visitors were welcomed, usually the clergy and the grand and good of the county, and the food on the table was actually edible. Everyone attended the church service to give thanks for the kindness and generosity of the benefactors and the Board of Guardians handed out Christmas biscuits to the children. Although the surroundings were drab and uninspiring, Nell always loved the Christmas service with the hymns and carols and the one day in the whole year she didn't have to worry about a beating for some imagined misdemeanour.

When she arrived she was greeted by the Board of Guardians and recalled Miss Bannister saying that her brother was on the board and had recommended her. I must thank him, she thought as she got out of the carriage. Looking after Robert had brought her more joy than she could ever have imagined.

Walking into the workhouse the smell of carbolic permeating the walls almost overwhelmed her. Memories flooded her mind. Did she really spend her life here? It felt a world away from her life today. She gave thanks to God for allowing her to escape and wished she could help the others escape too.

Inside, her mind muddled with confusion. How odd it was to be treated like a guest and sit at the top table in the dining hall. Her heart flipped when she saw the pallid faces of the men and women sat in rows, sullen and silent, their eyes reflecting the soulless misery of their lives. They'd be consigned to remain here for the rest of their days unless, by a stroke of good fortune such as she had had, they could find work elsewhere.

A maelstrom of emotions swirled inside her when she walked into the children's room to share out the toys she had brought. She'd only been away for a few months but she'd forgotten how noisy a room full of children could be, especially these children suddenly released from the oppressive discipline that ruled their lives.

One little girl was so entranced she clung to Nell's skirt and wouldn't let go. Blonde curls danced around her face, but Nell saw a depth of wisdom far beyond her years reflected in her soft blue eyes. The label hung by a string around her neck proclaimed her to be 'Girl no 126'. "Hello, what's your name," Nell said.

"My name's Kitty and I'm five," Kitty said.

A year younger than Robert, Nell thought, but so much more lively and sociable. Nell helped her undress the doll she'd been given and dress it up again, brushing its hair with a small comb.

"She's so beautiful," Kitty said. "I wish I could keep her."

"Of course you can keep her," Nell said, then remembered that, in the workhouse, everything had to be shared. Nothing belonged to anyone. Personal possessions weren't allowed. "She'll stay here and you can play with her when you've finished work." Nell's heart dropped several notches when she realised how rarely that would be.

"So, tell me what else you like to do," she asked trying to get Kitty's mind off the doll.

"I like dressing up," Kitty said. "Or I did, but all the dressing up cloths were ragged and dirty so Matron threw them out. We don't have any now." She looked sad.

Nell grimaced. She recalled the huge hamper of dressing up clothes sitting unused in the nursery cupboard. What a delight it must be for these children to put colourful clothes on over their drab workhouse uniforms and pretend to be other people, even if it was only for a short while. "I'll send you some," she said. That was the least she could do.

Kitty went on to tell Nell about the broken toys they usually had to play with. "But most of the time I have to pull oakum with the others."

Nell remembered the hours she'd endured unpicking fibres from old ropes to be sold on to ship-builders for waterproofing the boats before she moved to the nursery to look after the younger children. She shuddered at the memory and at the thought that this bright, intelligent girl would have to be doing it until her fingers bled for many years to come. She got up to move away.

"Please can you stay and play with me?" Kitty said.

Nell smiled. "I have to play with the others too," she said.

For the rest of the afternoon Kitty followed her around the room. Nell tried to involve her in the other groups playing together with the games she'd provided, but Kitty persisted. She never stopped chatting either, which brought home to Nell how different and vulnerable Robert was from these other hardy, more stoic children, who had nothing but their own ability and fortitude to rely on. They managed to put up with whatever life threw at them and still retain a level of resilience that amazed her. How would Robert manage without the skills necessary to stand up for himself?

Kitty turned to stare at Nell, her blue eyes wide as a summer sky pleading, "Are you going to stay here forever?"

"I'm sorry but I have another little boy to look after."

"Can you take me home and look after me too?" Kitty asked. Hope shone in her face and Nell swallowed the lump rising in her throat. It was every workhouse child's dream to be taken home and loved by a new family.

"I'm sorry," she said, but part of her ached to do something to help these children whose lives wouldn't be any different from her own.

In the evening the carriage returned to collect Nell and she bade farewell to the Board of

Guardians, making sure to thank Miss Bannister's brother for the recommendation. He was pleased to hear of her excellent progress. "It gives us hope for the others," he said. "A good example beats a thousand words of promises."

As the carriage drove away Nell's thoughts returned to Robert. She recalled seeing the boys in the workshops where some were too traumatised to speak and others forbidden to do so. They used signs and signals to let the others know what they wanted or what they were doing. They even managed to make each other laugh with their antics. If signs and signals worked in the desperate environment they inhabited, perhaps she could show Robert a few. In any event she was determined to spend more time with him at his lessons, teaching him to read and write so there'd be a least a sliver of hope for him in the future.

That evening all the staff were called into the ballroom where a huge, decorated Christmas tree stood with brightly wrapped parcels beneath it. Lord and Lady Eversham handed a gift to each member of staff, calling out their names to come forward. Nell's name wasn't called; there was no gift for her.

"They don't know you exist," Jenny said as they left the room. "And they wish Robert didn't either."

The truth of that hit Nell like a dagger in her heart. Tears filled her eyes as she turned and made her way back to the nursery.

On Christmas Day the family all sat down together for a lavish Christmas lunch, all except Robert, who was considered too young to join in the celebration. The same lavish fare was served to Nell and Robert in the nursery. When Jenny brought the tray up Nell saw several packages on it. "I don't know who they could be from," Jenny said with a grin. "They just appeared on the tray."

Nell knew better. She opened the first one. It was a box of coloured pencils for Robert from Jenny.

"You shouldn't have," Nell said, but her voice showed how much she appreciated it. She opened the second parcel for Robert. "I wonder who this could be from," she said. As the paper fell away she gasped. In her hand she held a book filled with drawings of every type of tree on the estate, together with the name of the tree and where it could be found. It must have taken Ethan months to complete and he'd given it to Robert. His kindness took her breath away. "Oh how wonderful," she said and showed it to Robert. "Please tell him thank you," she said. Jenny's smile stretched from ear to ear.

"Now open yours," Jenny said, bubbling with excitement. So Nell did. Jenny had bought her a tortoiseshell comb.

"It's beautiful. Thank you," Nell said.

"Now the other one," Jenny bounced on her heels with excitement.

Nell laughed. "I swear you get just as much pleasure sharing our gifts as you do opening your own."

"More," Jenny said, her eyes sparkling.

Nell pulled the paper apart and found a small box. She opened it and her jaw dropped. A silver brooch in the shape of a lily glistened inside. It was stunning.

Jenny clapped. "Ethan went to town specially to buy it. Saved up all his wages he did" she said. "He thinks a lot of you. He's always talking about you."

Nell's face flushed with pleasure. Of course Jenny would know, she was his sister after all.

In accordance with tradition a party for the Manor staff was held on Boxing Day in the ballroom. Food and drink, beer for the men and lemonade for the ladies, were set out on a long table. A trio of musicians from the village supplied the music. Mrs Hewitt offered to sit with Robert for the evening so that Nell could go.

"I'm too old to bother with prancing about at my age," she said. "Dancing's best left to the young. My old bones prefer to sit quiet and I might as well sit in the nursery as anywhere else." Nell couldn't thank her enough. She'd never been to a dance and anticipation bubbled inside her. She fussed about what she would wear and spent a good deal of time making a suitable dress from a piece of pale blue material she'd been given to make new tablecloths for the nursery. As the old tablecloths were hardly worn Nell thought she could make better use of it. The dress she made was simple and quite plain but from the cuttings she made small roses to sew to the neckline and sleeves, with a larger one sewn to the waist. Then she pinned a darker blue ribbon to the bodice with the brooch Ethan had given her. She also pinned blue roses into the curls of her chestnut hair. Looking in the mirror she was pleased with the effect.

"You look amazing," Jenny said when she came to collect her for the party. "My brother's eyes will pop right out of his head."

Nell blushed but her heart raced a little faster.

At six o'clock they all assembled in the ballroom. Lord and Lady Eversham made a brief appearance before they disappeared and the staff were left to enjoy the party. They hadn't been in the ballroom long before Thomas strode up to them. It was obvious from his demeanour that he's been at the drink well before the party started.

"Well, Miss Snooty-Nose," he said grabbing Nell. "Don't' tell me you don't dance." He pulled her onto the floor. Crushed in his embrace she had little option but to dance around the floor with him. He laughed at her helplessness and danced them into a corner where Nell feared the worst. Before she could get her breath a hand appeared on Thomas's shoulder.

"I believe I booked this dance," Ethan said.

"So you did," Nell said sighing with relief at his intervention and once again Nell was whisked into the centre of the floor, only, this time she didn't mind at all. The dancers whirling around the floor were less glittering than those who danced at the summer balls, but to Nell the music, the elegance of the grand hall, the thousand specs of shimmering light from the chandeliers and being held in Ethan's arms made it perfect.

She wished the dance would go on forever. When the music stopped Ethan led her to a seat to get her breath back. He got them both a drink. In the background the music started up again but Ethan made no move to go back on the floor. "I have something to tell you," he said. "But it's difficult to find the words."

Nell's heart raced.

He bit his lip. "I've been offered another job," he said. "In London."

The blood drained from Nell's body. A sickening dread filled her stomach. "London?"

"Yes. A couple who came for the Summer Ball. They admired the garden and Dad told them I'd laid it out and planted it." He looked at Nell. "They have a house in London and an estate in Kent. They want me to be their Head Gardener. It's a chance I'd never get here, well, not while Pa's alive." He lowered his head and waited for Nell to speak.

Thoughts rushed through her head like coursing hares. It was the chance of a lifetime for Ethan. He was right, he'd have no real future here. "I don't know what to say," she said at last. How could she tell him how devastated she'd be? People like her and Ethan had to grab the wheel of fortune if ever it spun their way. No one could blame him for wanting to better himself. Isn't that what everybody wished for?

"I wanted you to be the first to know," he said. "I haven't even told Jenny. What do you think?"

Her heart skittered. She longed to tell him to stay, to say how much she'd miss him and how her life wouldn't be the same without him. "Of course you must go," she said. "It's what you deserve. A step up, something better." Her voice faded away. She could hardly speak.

"I'll miss you," he blurted, colouring to the roots of his dark as night hair.

She managed a smile. "I'll miss you too," she said, "and so will Robert."

At the mention of her young charge's name he became suddenly serious. "You've been good for him. You've brought him out when no one else could and done more for him than anyone. You've succeeded where others have failed. Always remember that," he said, his voice filled with tenderness.

The gaslight flickered on his face and shone on his hair. Nell's heart ached. She wanted to beg him to stay. "When do you leave?" she asked.

"Day after tomorrow," he said. "I'll start in the New Year."

"I wish you well," she said, a catch in her voice. "I'll always remember your kindness and how you treated Robert."

He took her hand and raised it to his lips. "I won't forget you," he said.

"Nor me you," she replied.

Chapter Nine

That January was particularly cold. It had snowed for several days and Nell hadn't been able to take Robert out. The confines of the nursery were suffocating, but she did her best to keep Robert amused. Alice was doing her usual morning cleaning on the nursery floor when she told Nell about the Master's plans to travel abroad. "Lady Eversham was adamant," she said. "I overheard them arguing when I went to clean their room. She said she wouldn't spend another winter in this country when the Continent offered better weather." She eyed the piece of toast Nell had spread with marmalade. "Are you going to eat that?"

Nell was, but she wanted to hear more about Lady Eversham's plans and chatting to Alice, which had become a regular part of the day, brought the only relief from her isolation. "No, you may have it," she said. "I've had sufficient."

Alice sank onto the chair opposite Nell and picked up the toast.

"Would you like some tea too?" Nell asked. She poured a cup for Alice. "Please tell me more about Lord Eversham's plans."

"Well, I heard that they'll be away for months and the whole house is to be thoroughly cleaned, new curtains, upholstery, redecorated, the lot." Her eyes widened like flowers opening in spring as she spoke. "It's got Mrs Grindley in a fine tear, it has. Don't know whether she's coming or going she don't."

Nell smiled. With the Master away and Mrs Grindley up to her eyes overseeing the redecorations there may be more opportunities for Nell to take Robert out of the nursery.

"What about the girls? Are they going too?"

"The girls? No. They're to visit their grandmother. Leastways, that's what I heard. Miss Bannister'll be going with them." She sat back, shook her head and let out a sigh. "This place'll be like a morgue," she said, "with them all going away."

So, Martha and Ellen were to go to their grandmother, but not Robert. The familiar pang of rage curled inside Nell. She took a deep breath to calm her fury. It was so unfair. The girls' grandmother was his grandmother too. Didn't she care about him?

"Would that be his grandmother on his father's side?" Nell asked.

"Oh yes. We haven't seen his other grandmother since the new Lady Eversham arrived." She pouted. "I don't think they have much time for the Lady Caroline's family, not with her… you know… and him…" She nodded at Robert.

Nell nodded, but a volcano of fury swirled inside her.

She tackled Miss Bannister about the trip. "Will Robert be going too?" she asked.

The governess grimaced. "No. It's been decided that the change would be too difficult for him. He needs routine. Doctor's orders." And that was the end of that.

Packing the house up ready for the redecoration took longer than anyone expected. Nell used the opportunity of the upheaval to take Robert out into the garden as often as possible. That's when she missed Ethan the most. She found an old sled in one of the outhouses which Harvey Baines restored for her so she could pull Robert along on it, laughing and giggling. He loved to be moving and didn't seem to feel the cold at all.

The next three months were the happiest Nell could remember. She even managed to take Robert into town. She told Mrs Grindley that she had some urgent errands to run. Robert needed to be fitted with new shoes and she wanted to buy some material for a new dress.

"Miss Bannister usually sees to the ordering of new shoes for the children," Mrs Grindley said when Nell spoke to her. "The boot-maker calls here. No need to take the child to town."

"I need to go to town for my purchases," Nell said. "Should I leave Robert with you?"

Mrs Grindley scowled. "Think I haven't got enough to do?" She huffed. Leaving him with one of the parlour maids would mean she'd have no one to clean the rooms and anyone else would be totally unsuitable to be left in charge of him, so she had no option but to let Nell take Robert with her. "Well, I don't suppose it'll hurt, just this once. But mind you keep a close eye on him. Buy what you need and be sure to be back by lunchtime."

Nell took the spare carriage into town, the best one being used for Miss Bannister and the girls visiting their grandmother. Although the day was cold the sky was blue and clear. Nell touched her piece of blue silk and thought of her mother. How she would have enjoyed being out and about on a bright clear day like this.

In town Nell held Robert's hand as they went around the different shops. No one made any comment about the small boy with his nursemaid. The only raised eyebrows came from the boot-maker's where Nell ordered Robert's shoes to be delivered and put on Lord Eversham's account. "Don't often see young Master Eversham around here," the cobbler said. "If it wasn't for the shoes I send to the Manor you wouldn't even know Lord Eversham had a son."

Nell smiled, but her heart clenched at the familiar story. Was his confinement in the Manor a way of denying his existence? To what end? Memories of Lady Eversham's conversation with her brother and the surprise of the outdoor staff at seeing him cascaded through her mind. The fact that the girls were often seen about town, paraded for visitors to admire their various talents, only hardened her conviction that any plans Lady Eversham had for Robert would, without doubt, be to his detriment.

Once she'd completed her purchases Nell called into the tea shop. She made a point of telling the girl she was accompanying Master Eversham, Lord Eversham's son. It didn't improve the service, but Nell felt that she had at least made Robert's presence known and if the girl gossiped as much as most girls her age, then the news would spread around town and Robert's existence would be noted.

After tea Nell walked around the town admiring the shop window displays and watching the people hurrying by. This was a part of life she'd not seen before, ordinary people going about their ordinary jobs. This was how most people lived, she thought, a world away from the suffocating atmosphere of the Manor with its manicured lawns, perfectly placed rooms and immaculate service. Why shouldn't she and Robert enjoy these ordinary things? She vowed to take advantage of Miss Bannister's absence and Mrs Grindley's too-busy-to-be-bothered attitude to take Robert out more often.

Miss Bannister returned with Martha and Ellen at the end of February and they were immediately whisked into a whirl of engagements. The dressmaker came to measure and fit them for their summer wardrobes, a new music tutor was engaged as well as an instructor of dance. New books were ordered for the schoolroom and an intense curriculum of learning set out for them. It soon became clear to Nell that the freedom she'd enjoyed over the last two months would be curtailed. She would once again be restricted to the nursery, except for the days the weather was fine enough to take Robert out to play in the garden or the orchard.

By the time Lord and Lady Eversham returned in March fierce winds rocked the trees but daffodils nodded their heads in the shelter of the walled garden. It had become Nell's favourite place to sit and read to Robert or watch him play.

She often recalled the first time she'd sat on the bench with Ethan. Could it really be a year ago?

The redecoration of the house was finished, curtains replaced, rooms refurbished, everywhere cleaned from top to bottom, but not everyone was happy. Alice told Nell she'd overheard Mrs Grindley complaining to Mr Maybury, the butler, that it wasn't in keeping with the history of the house. "Mrs Grindley called the Mistress 'a typical American' and said her taste was 'all in her mouth'," Alice reported with a chuckle. "She said the bedroom looks like a bordello and the reception rooms like some high class brothel." She paused. "Don't ask me how the old harridan knows what a bordello looks like, nor a high class brothel come to that. I doubt she's ever been in one."

Nell laughed. "Perhaps there's more to her than we know," she said. "Everyone has their secrets." The look on Alice's face kept Nell amused for the rest of the day.

Jenny still brought Nell and Robert's meals and collected the dishes. Nell asked her whether she ever heard from Ethan. "Oh yes," she said. "He's doing very well. He's moved to the Duke's estate in Kent. They're ever so pleased with him."

"Send him my best regards," she said. "I'll always remember his kindness."

Jenny paused in clearing the dishes. "I doubt he'll forget you either," she said. Then she hurried away and Nell had to be satisfied wondering if he thought about her as often as she did him.

The Evershams had only been home a few weeks when the announcement was made. The butler, Mr Maybury, and Mrs Grindley were the first to know. The doctor was called and a nurse/midwife engaged from London.

"They're not trusting old Mrs Baines again," Alice said, when the news permeated through the household staff. "Nor Mrs Cooper, Robert's nurse. Not enough for Lady Muck. She has to have people from London."

Over the months the house was again thrown into a flurry of actively, but the balls and engagements of the previous summer were scaled down to accommodate Lady Eversham's condition, which didn't stop her being increasingly demanding. Nell even heard Mrs Hewitt complaining about her constant instructions relayed to the kitchen by a glowering Thomas.

"Can't eat this, won't eat that! Al'as fancying som'at else then leaving it. Says she feels sick." Her eyes blazed brighter than the sun. "My food ain't never made anyone sick," she said.

Nell's stomach churned at the growing discontent in the house. Some days the tension felt like a kettle coming to the boil, ready to let off steam. "Weren't like this in the old days, before Lady Muck came," Alice confided over morning tea in the nursery. "Weren't like this at all."

As time passed Nell became more and more aware of Robert's isolation, isolation made more obvious by the actions of Lady Eversham. She no longer rode out with her husband in the mornings but preferred to sit in the walled garden, declaring that, being nearer the house, it was more convenient than the formal garden she usually enjoyed. It was the best place for her to enjoy the sun, she said. Nell was banned from going there and had to content herself with taking Robert to the orchard or the kitchen garden if she wanted him to play outside.

Even the memorial service for Lady Caroline was scaled down to a short service attended only by the family. "Out with the old, in with new," Mrs Hewitt said when she heard, but Nell felt a glow of warmth and appreciation when she saw the cook had added a small cake iced with an 'R' and a number seven to Robert's tea.

If they had visitors, which became a more and more frequent occurrence, she was confined to the nursery.

She could no longer take him to the schoolroom either. Miss Bannister said the girls' lessons were more important now they were older, and she needed to sit in the schoolroom preparing them while the girls rode out or had lessons in the music room or the library.

"I think she's got it in for 'im," Alice said when Nell told her about the restrictions placed on her by Lady Eversham. "Don't want 'im anywhere's around she don't. Wait 'til she gets her own little lad. Let's see how different things'll be then."

Nell blanched at the thought. She recalled the conversation she'd overheard at the shoot last August. Fear curled in her stomach. As the pregnancy progressed Nell experienced a strange feeling of foreboding. If Lady Eversham had a boy, as she hoped, Robert's future would hang in the balance.

In the morning of 24th September Lady Eversham went into labour. The house was in turmoil. Lord Eversham insisted on the best care for his wife. No chance should be taken 'this time', he said. The doctor was in attendance with the help of the nurse/midwife and at four o'clock the following afternoon, after a long and arduous labour, Lord Eversham's second son was born.

Chapter Ten

The train pulled into Kings Cross station with a grinding of wheels, an ear-splitting hiss and a belch of smoke. Nell looked at the small boy staring out of the window, his face bright with innocence, and her heart ached. He'd been so excited, jumping about and clapping, when she'd told him they were going on a trip. "We'll be taking the train," she'd said, hoping her voice didn't betray the despair in her heart. She'd spent the whole journey in a turmoil of emotion. An overwhelming sense of betrayal engulfed her. Ever since she first saw Robert that day in the nursery, every instinct had been to protect this small vulnerable boy who couldn't speak up for himself. Now every fibre of her being cried out to her and a powerful surge of emotion propelled her into action.

She bit her lip and tried to still her racing heart. "Come on, Robert," she said. "We're here and we're going to play a game."

He grinned and touched his fingers to the sides of his lips in the sign she'd taught him meant 'fun' or 'game'. A familiar rush of delight flowed through her at his sharpness. He was always doing unexpected things that amazed her, but no matter how often or how enthusiastically she reported his progress to Miss Bannister her stance remained the same. "It's such a shame," she'd say. "He'll never amount to anything, well, nothing his father could ever be proud of." Well, now he had a second son and Nell had no doubt that he'd be proud of him, Lady Eversham would make sure of it.

It hadn't taken the new mother long to persuade her husband that Robert should be sent away. "It's for his own good," she said. "He'll get the best care." Of course that was far from true, but Lord Eversham, having been newly presented with a son, one who, with luck, would be more acceptable to society than Robert, was easily convinced. Even Miss Bannister shuddered when she told Nell of the plan.

"They may be able to help him more than we can," she said, turning her face away so Nell couldn't see the deceit in her eyes.

It was Mrs Hewitt who said it best. "Out with the old, in with the new," she said to Nell. "He's to be thrown out like the old curtains, you mark my words, no good'll come of it."

"It's a hospital," Miss Bannister told Nell, when giving her directions.

"An asylum more like," Mrs Hewitt said.

A hospital where he'd be locked away, out of sight for the rest of his life, was the way Nell saw it. But it was no use arguing. All the time she'd spent trying to get Robert accepted for the smart, cheerful spark he was, had been to no avail. Her powerlessness to change anything overwhelmed her. She thought she'd experienced misery and hopelessness in the workhouse, but it was nothing to how she felt when she heard of their plans.

Sickness and disbelief swirled inside her. She'd heard rumours about asylums where inmates lived in the worst possible conditions, not only locked up but manacled as well. How they slept on straw mattresses in damp cells, never seeing the daylight. Is that what Robert's father wanted for him? At least when Nell had gone into the workhouse she'd known the reason why and what was expected of her. She'd had enough wit to keep out of trouble, make herself useful and avoid punishment. Robert would have no understanding of what was happening to him. No defence for it either.

She couldn't believe a man could be so cruel and heartless to his own flesh and blood, then she recalled what Ethan had said: 'That's the nobility for you'. Well she wasn't noble and she wasn't about to sacrifice this young boy to their callousness. She'd never subject Robert to the sort of humiliation they proposed for him. Robert wasn't an imbecile like they said, but if he spent any time in an asylum he soon would be.

Boiling with rage she took her carpet bag down from the luggage rack, and took Robert's hand.

"One, two, three jump," she said, and together they got off the train to join the bustling throng heading towards the station exit. Black smoke from the steam engine filled the air, the grime settling on their clothes as they walked. Porters wheeled wooden trolleys laden with suitcases of every hue. People jostled and hustled around her. Robert stared, his startled eyes darting from one unfamiliar sight to another. The platform was chaotic, dirty and noisy. Bewilderment paled his face. Nell clung to his hand as they were swept into the pushing and shoving mass.

She had only the one bag and they made their way slowly out of the gate. Outside the station hansom cabs, hackney carriages and carts lined the pavement, vying for fares. An endless parade of carriages, carts and cabs rushed past adding to the noise and confusion.

Nell's heart pounded. She held tightly to Robert's hand and made her way past the hansoms. She gritted her teeth as a rock of determination hardened inside her. She'd tried everything to get Robert accepted for the extraordinary, delightful child he was and argued that his disability shouldn't be allowed to hold him back. Now she'd have to prove it.

One of the hackney drivers was brushing his horse's mane. He looked approachable.

"I'm looking for lodgings," she said, her voice several octaves higher than usual. "Respectable and clean, but not too expensive for a nursemaid and her charge. Do you know of anywhere that might suit?"

He turned to survey her and Robert. He nodded and a small hollow-eyed boy in ragged clothing rushed to open the carriage door. Nell pushed Robert inside and climbed in herself. She handed the boy a penny.

"You'll only encourage them," the driver said, but the boy had run off.

During the short drive she looked out at the noisy, teeming, wind-rattled, streets. The carriage bumped over cobbles in the narrow thoroughfares as they passed dingy houses, crowded together in grimy rows. It was a million miles away from the grassy, tree filled estate where Robert had lived all his life. A stone of dread settled in her stomach. She'd taken this small, vulnerable boy from the cosseted comfort of his home and brought him to this gloomy, grey, treeless place. How would he cope? She'd no experience of independent living, having her own place and looking after the boy on her own. No experience of living in a place like

London either come to that. What on earth was she getting them into?

Then she thought about the alternative and her resolve stiffened. She'd have to have strength enough for both of them.

The hackney pulled up alongside a row of terraced buildings in front of what Nell saw was a coffee shop. Its windows were steamed up but she could make out the sign that said, '*Room to Let*'. Another sign said, '*Breakfast 2d.*'

She climbed down to the pavement and glanced up at the windows above the shop. They looked clean enough with the light of the afternoon sun glinting on them. Next door but one was a greengrocer. A chandler's store stood at the end of the street. Nell was taken aback by the choice, expecting to be taken to a lodging house but, glancing around she thought perhaps this would suit her better.

"This is Lottie's Place," the driver said jumping down from his seat and looping the horse's reins around the brake handle. "Respectable and reasonable, you said. Well, she'll see you all right. You'll not do better than Lottie for fairness." He pushed the café door open and called out, "Customer for you, Lottie. Lady and lad wants a room."

A woman in a white apron rushed towards them. A white cap covered her hair and beneath the apron Nell noticed a dark blue cambric dress similar to sort favoured by Mrs Grindley. She smiled to herself but decided that was insufficient reason to doubt Lottie's good intentions.

"Good afternoon," Lottie said, wiping her hands down her apron. "Come about the room have you?" Without waiting for an answer she hurried past them. "Foller me," she said and led them to a front door next to the shop.

Nell squeezed Robert's hand as Lottie opened the door and led them up the stairs. She showed them into a large room at the front of the building. A fire was laid in the grate but not lit. A tall pot stand stood next to it with a pot suspended from an arm that could be swung across the fire to heat up food or water. Two armchairs stood either side of the fireplace, a table and two dining chairs were placed beneath the window which overlooked the road. Behind an over-stuffed sofa a red velvet curtain hid a bed large enough to comfortably hold two people. A wash stand with a bowl and water jug stood beside a chest of drawers in the curtained off section of the room. A dresser occupied the wall opposite the fireplace. As well as a lamp on the dresser Nell noticed gaslights in alcoves either side of the fireplace.

"Best room in the house," Lottie said. "Six shillings a week, a month in advance. You share the wash house out back. Gas and coal included. Do your own laundry."

Nell walked around the room, a fist like grip squeezing her stomach. She glanced in every corner, nook and cranny. The room was tiny compared to the spacious nursery at the Manor, but it was clean and provided every necessity. A month's rent in advance would take most of her money and she still had to feed them both, but at least they'd have a roof over their heads.

"Does that include breakfast?" she asked.

Lottie laughed. "You're a cheeky one," she said, but her eyes sparkled. Her face softened when she looked at Robert. "I suppose I could stretch to a couple of breakfasts."

"Then we'll take it," Nell said. At least she'd managed to secure them a place to stay and something to eat each day. It was a start.

She dug the rent money out of her purse and handed it to Lottie. Miss Bannister had given her some money for her return ticket and incidental expenses, plus she had the little she'd managed to save from her wages, but that wouldn't last long. She swallowed at the dwindling of her resources but that would be the least of her problems.

"I'll get you a receipt," Lottie said. "Always like to do thing properly, then we know where we stand." She grinned. "Everyone calls me Lottie and you'll find me in the café any time you need anything. I'll need your name for the books."

Robert had run to the window to look out. Nell turned Lottie away and dropped her voice to a whisper. She hoped the noise from the road would drown out her words. "I'm Lily, Lily Drummond," she said. She'd seen the name Drummond carved on some wooden barrels at the station, it was the first name that came into her head. "The child is my nephew Bobby, my sister's boy. I'm his guardian. His parents were killed in an accident last year. I fear neither of us have fully recovered from the shock."

"Oh, how tragic," Lottie said and, for a moment, Nell worried that she might move to console Robert. Thankfully she must have thought better of it. "I'll leave you to settle in then," she said. "But don't forget, if you need anything I'll just be downstairs."

"Thank you," Nell said, breathing a sigh of relief as Lottie left and she heard her footsteps descending the stairs.

Robert was still staring out of the window. She went and stood behind him. The road outside teemed with horse drawn vehicles. The noise enveloped them. Nell felt a brief wave of relief wash over her, but it was short lived.

She took Robert by the shoulders and turned him towards her. His solemn little face was etched with sadness and confusion. Her heart swelled with love for this remarkable child with the face of an angel. He put a finger to each side of his mouth. "Game?" The question shimmered in his eyes. He looked so innocent, fragile and heartbreakingly vulnerable and now his future depended entirely on her.

She forced a smile and a lightness she didn't feel into her voice. "Yes it's a game," she said. "I'm to be called Lily and you are Bobby. Can you remember that?"

He nodded, his eyes still filled with questions.

Her heart faltered. "You know I would never do anything to hurt you don't you?" she said. "Whatever happens I want you to know that I'm doing it for the best."

He half-smiled and turned away again to gaze out of the window.

She sprang up. "I bet you're hungry," she said. They'd eaten before they left but that was hours ago. She went to the bag and unpacked a tin of Robert's favourite cheese scones and sandwiches which Mrs Hewitt had prepared for their journey. A sudden memory of the warmth and luxury they were leaving behind struck her, making her pause. This was probably the last time they would enjoy such luxuries. "Teatime," she said more brightly than she felt. "It's your favourites."

She took some plates from the dresser and found some cutlery in a drawer. She set the plates of scones and sandwiches on the table. Mrs Hewitt had also included milk for Robert and a flask of tea for her.

"It's just like a picnic," she said. "You remember our picnics in the woods? They were fun weren't they?" Somehow, she thought, this just doesn't compare, but she'd put on a brave face and deal with anything that came their way. In fact she'd do anything to prevent Robert ever finding out the truth.

The memory of those picnics ran through her mind as she bent to light the fire to get a little warmth into the room. Once outside he'd been a different boy away from the confines of the nursery. He'd run off his energy while she did her best to chase him. They played hide and seek in the woods with him laughing and chuckling when she found him and tickled him until he collapsed giggling on the ground. Playing outside he became calmer, his early tantrums lessened. Would they return once he was restricted in these very different surroundings?

After they'd had their tea Nell stoked the fire with the coal Lottie had kindly left for her. She drew the curtains across the window and lit the gaslights as the sky darkened. The dull glow gave the room a cosy feel. She sat on an armchair near the fire and Robert squeezed in beside her to listen to her reading from his favourite story book. With her arm around him and his body pressed against hers she again felt the strength of the familiar bond between them. Nell read the words while he turned the pages. These precious moments together had always been the most treasured part of her day.

After the story Nell warmed some water from the water jug over the fire for him to wash. Behind the curtain he changed into his nightshirt. As Nell folded his clothes to put in the chest of drawers she couldn't help but notice how different they were from the clothes of the hollow-eyed boy who had rushed to open the carriage door. How long would it be before Robert's clothes were ragged too? She pushed the thought to the back of her mind and carried on unpacking her bag. She'd brought little enough with them, but she'd have to make the best of every item if they were to survive.

Lord Eversham had no interest in keeping anything that reminded him of Robert's birth and the loss of his first wife. Miss Bannister told her to take everything that might remind him of Robert. Nell had wrapped Robert's things in one of his shirts and put them in the bag. As well as a few of Robert's books and favourite toys there were the gifts of silver from his family: christening cups, cutlery, a candle-holder, a small, ornate dish, slender specimen vase, the framed picture of his mother and the gold locket and chain given by Robert's father to his wife on the occasion of Robert's birth which also contained a picture of his mother.

Nell pushed the articles into a drawer in the dresser. If worse came to worst she'd have no trouble selling them to get by.

Once Robert was safely tucked up in bed Nell sat by the fire contemplating the decision she had made and the path she had taken. It had been an impulse that made her walk past the hansoms and find lodgings for herself and the boy. She wasn't sure what she was going to do now, only that she would give her life for the boy if that's what it took, and that was all she needed to know.

Nell shuddered as she thought of the far-reaching change she'd brought about by her actions. She'd taken him away from all that was familiar, his family and his comfort. How would he react to losing his home, the people he knew and the places he recognised? All she could offer in their place was uncertainty, probable hardship and possible hunger. Her heart ached for him.

She recalled how her world had been turned upside down when her mother had died. She'd lost everything she cherished when she went into the workhouse.

She sighed. It was no use regretting the past, what was done was done and couldn't be undone. Now they had to make the best of it. They'd been lucky finding the room. She was surprised how comfortable, clean and cosy it was. It wasn't the most luxurious but as long as she and Robert were together everything would turn out all right.

Tomorrow she would go out to look for work, but it would be something of her own choosing and she would insist on taking Robert, or as he was to be called, Bobby, with her.

Sitting by the fire watching the dying embers she felt a sense of peace she'd never experienced before. This was the first time in her life she wasn't accountable to anyone. No workhouse Master beating her for some imagined misdoing, no governess constantly criticizing her efforts to teach Robert to read and possibly to write. She was free to make her own decisions. Their future rested in her hands alone.

Chapter Eleven

The next morning Nell was woken before dawn by the hammer blow of horses' hooves and the clatter of wheels rumbling over cobbles as they rattled past the window. She hadn't slept well, dozing only intermittently. The streets were never quiet. She'd heard the watch calling the hour, the noisy babble of revellers making their way home from the night's entertainments and the cacophony of the costers' cries and early morning traders making their way to market. She hadn't realised how noisy living in town would be. Mornings at the Manor were so silent you could almost hear the grass grow.

She sat up and listened to the clatter coming in from outside. Memories of the day before, leaving Inglebrook Manor, the train journey and eventually deciding to find them a room, flashed through her mind. The enormity of what she'd done brought a sudden chill to her bones. She may have done it with the best intention, but she'd disobeyed Lord Eversham's orders. What would he do when her failure to arrive at the hospital was discovered? Kidnap was a hanging offence.

She bit back the doubt rising inside her. She'd made the decision, now she had to make it work. She had to find a new life for both of them. She took a deep breath. She was on her own – with Robert. There'd be no Jenny coming to bring breakfast and clear the dishes, no Alice to clean the room and stop and chat, no Mrs Hewitt making Robert's favourite dishes. An agony of despair washed over her as she realised how much she'd miss them. They'd been her only friends but contacting them was out of the question. She didn't know how long it would be before Robert's family discovered he hadn't arrived at the hospital as planned, or whether they'd even care, but she couldn't take any chances.

She wasn't afraid of hard work. The years in the workhouse had hardened her to life's realities. From now on it would be Lily Drummond and her nephew Bobby. There was no reason anyone need know any different.

Robert was awake and up even before her. She found him, already dressed, standing by the window staring out. The lively activity in the street below held him entranced. It seemed to amuse him. He pointed excitedly when he saw Nell and grinned. Her lips twitched into a smile. He didn't seem any different, despite the gigantic change to his living conditions.

She hugged him, kissed his forehead and said, "Good morning, sweetheart."

She washed, dressed and brushed her thick chestnut hair, plaited it and coiled it into a bun at the nape of her neck. She gave Robert his coat and signed to him that they were going downstairs to eat. He looked bemused, as though he didn't quite understand, but Nell was confident that at least he'd be hungry enough to eat whatever was put in front of him.

She put her coat on, tied her bonnet under her chin and, once they were both ready, took Robert's hand to take him downstairs to the café for breakfast.

The steamy warmth hit them as soon as she opened the door. It took her a moment to focus through the fog of smoke and steam. The smell of cooking, sweat and tobacco smoke greeted their entrance. Tables, set out in rows, were occupied by men puffing away at pipes or the occasional cigarette, their heads bent over random pages of the morning newspapers while they ate their breakfasts.

At the far end of the shop she saw Lottie behind the counter where a queue had formed. She was handing out large cups of tea and coffee while an elderly man behind her sliced a steaming ham. A noisy hubbub of raucous voices filled the air. Nell spotted a space on a bench as two men got up to leave. She pushed Robert into it. "Do you mind if we join you?" she asked the other occupant of the table.

He glanced up, surprised. She realised that these men, all familiar with each other, were unused to strangers striking up a conversation. Most of the newcomers grunted or nodded to their companions before joining them. The lively debates started after the breakfasts had been eaten.

He grunted and returned to his paper.

"Wait here, Bobby," she said. "I'll get us something to eat."

Robert's eyes rounded at the unfamiliar name. Then a slow smile crept across his face. He put his fingers to his lips in the way she'd taught him to say "Game?"

"Yes," she whispered and squeezed his hand. The 'game' couldn't go on forever, she thought, but the alternative of telling him the truth was out of the question. This was going to be more difficult than she had supposed. She gave Robert his sketch pad and pencil to keep him occupied while she went and queued for their breakfasts. He drew what he saw. It was as though it was his way of communicating and he was good at it, so Nell was happy to leave him to it.

She sighed and went to the counter.

Lottie recognised her immediately. "Good morning," she said. "I hope you found the room comfortable."

"Very, thank you," Nell said. "If a little noisy."

"You soon gets used to that," Lottie said. "Now, what can I get you for breakfast?"

The choices were sparse compared to what Mrs Hewitt dished up every morning. Nell decided on bread, cheese and a slice of the boiled ham with coffee for them both. Robert had never had coffee before, but if he was to survive the day he'd need something hot and strong inside him. She'd noticed boys outside all queuing for their penn'oth of coffee before they started their morning's work. The sight of them brought home to Nell the fact that most boys Robert's age worked to support their families. Life here would be much harder than the easy, idle life they'd had at the Manor. The knots in her stomach tightened. She wouldn't be defeated at the first hurdle. She squared her shoulders and stiffened her resolve.

"Here you are, luv," Lottie said handing her two plates each with a thick slice of the still steaming ham, cheese and even thicker slices of bread. Nell picked some cutlery from the tray at the end of the counter and took the plates back to the table. Then she returned for the mugs of coffee.

They ate their breakfasts in silence. Robert started by picking at his and Nell was afraid he'd refuse to eat it, but to her delight he left only the crusts of bread. He turned his nose up at the coffee. Nell showed him how she was drinking hers, so he sipped it again. Then he nodded and finished it. She put her arm around him and gave him a hug. "I'm so proud of you," she whispered. "You're amazing."

His eyes shone as he looked at her and he gave a dazzling smile. Her stomach churned as she thought about what lay ahead of them that day, but she was determined not to let Robert see it.

"Come on," she said. "Let's go out and explore the neighbourhood."

As they stepped outside a cacophony of noise and bustle assailed them. The city was coming to life. Carts, carriages and hansoms clattered past pavements crowded with people rushing to their work. Costers called their wares from stalls in the street and street sellers called theirs trying to out-shout them. People jostled past, heads bent and unaware as they hurried along. Nell breathed it all in. She felt out of place in this busy, bustling road, so very different from the quiet lanes around the Manor.

Robert gripped her hand. What must he make of the noise, the hustle, the people? It was more crowded, noisier and dirtier than she had ever imagined. At least in the pulsating vibrancy of the city there were bound to be opportunities and it would be easier for them to disappear into obscurity. She glanced down at Robert. Although his little face was serious and his eyes sunflower wide, they brimmed with trust when he looked back at her. That made her feel a little better.

They walked together for a while. Then, as they neared the river Robert ran on ahead. Nell watched him stop and gaze out over the flowing water. He seemed entranced by the boats, barges and lighters making their way to and from the docks. October sun glittered on the water but it wasn't long before a cold breeze forced them to move on. Nell found a coffee shop where they could get out of the wind and bought them each a mug of hot chocolate. This was the first day, and probably the only one they'd have the time to spend so leisurely. With the money in her purse rapidly dwindling she'd have to find work and find it soon.

On the way back Nell decided to see if she could find work in the local area. She wasn't fussy what she had to do, the only thing she was determined about was that she'd keep Robert with her. If she found nothing there then she'd travel into the city or the West End trying for shop work.

Of course taking Robert with her might cause some difficulty, but she couldn't leave him. Ideally they'd find work together.

As they walked back to their lodgings she kept an eye out for cards in shop windows offering work. There were one or two cleaning jobs advertised and bar work in a pub. She went in, but as soon as they saw Robert the man shook his head.

"It's evenings, all night 'til early morning some times. Can't 'ave a nipper in. Give the wrong impression that would."

By the time they got home she'd unsuccessfully tried several places, but, given that this was a huge city, she wasn't downhearted.

"Don't worry, we'll find something," she said to Robert as they had their tea. She wasn't sure he even understood, but telling him what was on her mind always made her feel better.

After tea they sat by the fire while she read to him from one of his books. She settled him into bed and kissed him goodnight. Then she sat and again pondered the wisdom of what she'd done. It felt right, but if she couldn't find work, what would they do then?

The next morning Nell set out again with Robert, determined that today she'd do better. After all, everybody seemed to be hurrying to their jobs, so there must be somewhere she could find work. She'd do anything, she wasn't fussy.

The first place Nell tried was a milliner's in a row of shops along a street with a collection of drapers, fabric and costume shops. Here she could get ribbons and silk if she needed to make trimmings for hats, just as her mother had done before she became too ill to work. They could work in a backroom and Robert could help her. That way they'd still be together.

"No, I'm afraid we have no vacancies," the haughty lady in the shop said, eyeing Robert suspiciously. "I trim the hats myself. Perhaps you should try further along the street."

So Nell tried every shop the full length of the street where haberdashers and dressmakers made their livings. She got a slightly warmer welcome in most, but again no work was available. "We've little enough work for ourselves," the lady in one shop said. "It's a family business and I have to put my own folk first."

It was the same all along the street. Wherever Nell tried she was turned away as soon as they saw Robert in tow. By the end of the day she was exhausted and disillusioned. Her jaunty, optimistic mood of the morning had completely evaporated, but more worrying was the effect it was having on Robert.

He ambled along beside her and stood patiently while she made enquiries in each of the places she tried, but he wasn't stupid. It was soon clear to Nell that he understood completely what was going on. At each rejection he would tug at her sleeve as if to drag her out of the shop to avoid further humiliation. The hurt in his eyes brought the familiar twist in her heart. It was only the thought of what his family had planned for him that steeled her resolve to carry on. Whatever hardships they encountered would be nothing compared to the alternative.

"Why don't you try Delaney's Factory, at the end of the street," one woman said to her. "They're always looking for help and not too fussy who they take on."

Nell smiled. "Thank you, I will," she said.

When she got to the place the woman had pointed out she saw the sign on the door of what looked like little more than an old wooden barn. There were no windows but she could hear the hum of the machines inside.

"Wait here," she said to Robert. "I'll only be a moment." She wasn't prepared to subject the poor boy to any further degradation.

The musty smell of fabric, the noise of the machines and the claustrophobic atmosphere struck her as soon as she opened the door. Men and women sat in rows, heads bent over their machines feeding endless piles of material into them to make trousers, jackets, caps and coats for sale in the nearby market. It didn't take Nell long to make up her mind about the conditions the men and women were working under. It was even worse than the workhouse.

This place wasn't fit for animals, she thought, and no matter how desperate she got she'd find something else. She'd find something she could do at home, even if it meant working her fingers to the bone.

She decided they'd had enough for the day anyway. The night was drawing in and the cold and damp penetrating her thin woollen coat. Robert would be cold and hungry, so they made their weary way home.

Chapter Twelve

The next morning after breakfast, before setting out, Nell took the things from the drawer and laid them on the bed along with her own small bits of jewellery. She'd noticed a pawnbroker not far away yesterday. These were quality items and should fetch a good price, even in this run-down part of town. Robert picked up his mother's locket. The look on his face, sadness mixed with defiance, wrung her heart. He put the locket back in the drawer. He picked up the bar brooch that had once belonged to Nell's mother. It wouldn't be worth much anyway. She'd only kept it because it had pinned her little piece of blue to her vest when she went into the workhouse. It was all she had left of her mother. He put that in the drawer along with the silver lily brooch Ethan had given her.

Nell picked up the candleholder. "This could be useful," she said and put it on the small table next to the bed. It might help Robert feel more at home if he had his own things around him. She picked up the cutlery, christening cups and silver dish. One of the cups was engraved with Robert's name and date of birth. She put that back in the drawer but the others, beautifully engraved with cherubs and candles, she left out.

"These should bring enough to keep us for a while," she said. She crouched down next to Robert so her face was level with his. "It's for the best. Please believe me. I wouldn't be doing this if I didn't have to."

He pouted and nodded, showing his understanding. Nell smiled and put the things into her bag. She put the vase and framed photo back in the drawer. She could sell them later if she had to. Then, wrapped up against the cold, they set off.

Nell was surprised at how much the items fetched at the pawnbrokers. The pawnbroker's eyes lit up when he saw them and he made her a generous offer. "Not every day I get such quality goods," he said. "I won't ask where they comes from, but trust you have the right to sell them."

"Oh yes. They belong to my nephew here. We have no further use for them."

The pawnbroker nodded and handed over the cash. With the money safely in her pocket Nell felt a lot happier.

As they passed the market Nell bought a muffler and cap for Robert. She wrapped the muffler around his neck and pulled the cap low over his face. Her heart ached with love for him.

"Come on," she said. "We're bound to have better luck today."

First of all she tried the local shops, the butcher, the baker and the candlestick maker but all to no avail. Then she travelled further afield, walking along Holborn and down to Temple Gate. This time she left Robert by the canal watching the boats. By the end of the day her feet ached, but not as much as her heart. Once again she wondered about the decision she had made but in her heart she knew she had no option. The alternative was even worse.

The next morning she asked Lottie if she knew of anything. "You could try one of the costers or traders," she said, "but only for the boy. They don't take women."

Nell shook her head. Even as a last resort that was out of the question. Either they'd get something together or not at all. At least the breakfast was paid for so she made sure that she and Robert made the most of that. The days were getting colder. Perhaps she could earn some money buying from the market and selling on the street. It wasn't a very welcome idea, but she was getting evermore desperate.

After breakfast she went with Robert to the local market. The stalls were crowded, people yelling out their wares. Although the stallholders seems cheery enough as they wrapped their goods and took the offered money, it felt cold and the wind was bitter. She tried to imagine herself here with a stall, but the vision faded as she realised how hopeless that would be. The traders were hardy, robust and used to being outside for long hours in all weathers. It would be a precarious way of making a living too, with no guaranteed income. She recalled the long hours her mother worked for a pittance. No, she'd have to think of something else, anything else.

After that, she bought a newspaper every morning and, while they were having breakfast, went through the advertisements. There were openings for domestic servants, cleaners and shop girls. Most were for live-in staff which she discounted as they'd never take Robert. She made a list of one or two possibilities, but her heart wasn't in it. She'd been in domestic service and, even as a last resort, it wasn't something she wanted to try again.

As she pondered, the man sitting opposite finished his meal, picked up his hat, which had been lying on the table beside his plate, and left. His place was taken by a much younger man. Clean shaven he had a boyish face, fair hair and cornflower blue eyes that sparkled like faceted gems. He put his battered, rust colour hat on the table next to his breakfast. "Morning," he ventured.

Nell swallowed the bread that almost stuck in her throat. "Morning," she said.

She recalled seeing him on previous mornings, chatting to the other traders or talking to Lottie. He appeared to be very popular if the laughter accompanying him around the room was anything to go by.

He grinned. "Not often I get the chance to have breakfast with a pretty lady." He nodded to Robert. "The boy. He with you?"

"He is."

"He looks a likely lad. A bit skinny but smart. Lottie mentioned a lass and a lad looking for work. That you?"

"Maybe."

"I've got stall in the market. I could use a smart boy, especially if he came with the promise of an acquaintance with his ma."

Nell coloured at his familiarity, but she had to admire his cheek. "I'm his aunt, not his ma," she said.

"Even better." He shifted his gaze to Robert who was looking bemused. "Course you needs to have good lungs to call out the prices. Give us yell, boy. Loud as you can."

Robert turned to Nell, his eyes stretched wide. She put her arm around his shoulders. "We're aiming for something better than a stall in the market," she said. She stood to leave. "Come along, Bobby, I think we're finished here." With that she picked up Robert's sketch pad, shoved it in her bag and strode to the door, her heart in her mouth.

Outside she stopped to gather her thoughts. The encounter had rattled her. She hadn't contemplated the problems of passing unnoticed with a boy who couldn't speak. She'd become so used to his silence she'd stopped being aware of it, but now realised is must be obvious to anyone watching them that she was the only one talking.

She sniffed the dampness of the air as she pulled her gloves on and blinked back the tears forming in her eyes.

The café door opened and the man came out. "I'm sorry," he said. "I didn't mean to upset you, but I couldn't help noticing how one-sided your conversation was. Most of the lads around here could talk the head off a penny. I saw straight away that your lad was different."

Different! That was a label she'd been fighting for the last two years. The label that would see him threatened with what she considered to be a fate worse than death. She bridled at the man's interference. She glared at him.

"Whoa there," he said, putting his hands up to defend himself. "I only meant..."

"I'm quite aware of what you meant," she said. "Now if you'd kindly leave us alone..." She went to walk away but her feet wouldn't move. This man was only trying to help. He had a kind face and gentle voice. She immediately regretted her comment.

"I was only going to suggest that if you was looking for work you try Bradley's Funeral Parlour in East Street. He's always looking for lads, and lads what can't talk would be right up his street." He chuckled. "There's none so silent as the dead and there's always a call for funerals. Death never goes out of fashion does it?"

Her heart sighed with relief. She even managed a smile. "That's very kind of you," she said. "I'll give them a try. And I'm sorry about before. I didn't mean anything by it, you know the remark about the market stall. I'm sure it's a very honourable profession."

"'Tis indeed," he said with a grin. He put out his hand. "Name's Josh," he said.

"Lily," Nell replied thankful that she'd remembered what she told Lottie. "And this is Bobby. We're in the room above the café."

"I know," Josh said. "Lottie told me." He grinned. "Can't blame a chap for wanting to know about the prettiest gal he's seen around here in a long while. I hope we can be friends."

Nell was taken aback. Ethan was the last man who'd wanted to be her friend and she'd valued that friendship more than she could say. "I'm sure we will be," she said.

He gave her directions to the funeral parlour. "Ask for Mr Bradley himself," he said. "He'll see you all right."

"Thank you I will," she said and bade him goodbye.

Chapter Thirteen

It was a good half-hour walk to the address Josh had written down for her. An early morning mist hung in the air, sending a chill through her body. They walked along twisting streets lined with tall buildings. Nell almost got lost. She had to stop twice to ask the way. It was all very different from the wide open fields around the Manor. Robert ran ahead of her, his hands in his pockets, kicking at stones or tin cans lying in the gutter. She mulled over the brief conversation she'd had with the market trader and realised she knew nothing about him. Perhaps she'd ask Lottie. Lottie had told him about her so she must think him all right. She hadn't realised what a close-knit community the market traders were. That too was very different from Inglebrook Manor.

As they neared East Road the buildings became less crowded and more impressive. She guessed it was far enough out of town to cater for the more well-to-do clients, but not so far as to be out of the reach of the poorer parts of the city.

When she arrived she stood on the pavement staring at the double fronted façade. A sign above the door declared it to be *Bradley's Funeral Parlour*. Beneath the gold lettering a small sign read: *'Memorials our Speciality – All Tastes Catered For'*. The windows were draped in black cloth, a bouquet of silk flowers in a brass vase stood in one window, while a neatly arranged selection of black-edged notepaper and envelopes were displayed in the other. A small, discreet notice informed passers-by that all the requirements of mourning could be obtained within. A shiver went down her spine. She stood for a few moments gathering her thoughts. She wasn't sure whether to go in or maybe come back tomorrow after she'd spoken to Lottie about it. After all, she knew nothing about this 'Josh' although he'd seemed friendly and Lottie had told him about her and Robert, so perhaps he could be trusted. Well, there was only one way to find out, she thought.

She squared her shoulders, breathed deeply and rehearsed in her mind what she would say. The establishment looked wealthy enough and she'd only take a job if they had employment for them both. She wasn't willing to send Robert to work alone. If Mr Bradley wouldn't take both of them she'd find something else.

When she'd thought about getting work to pay for their keep she'd imagined finding something like Rosa, making hats and working from the room they now called home. Of course being shut up in the room they lived and slept in wouldn't be ideal. The pay would be dire and the hours long, but she could at least keep Robert with her. Perhaps the funeral parlour would offer a better alternative.

She crouched down, her face inches in front of Robert's. "Now remember," she said. "You are named Bobby and I'm Lily. They either take both of us or neither." Confusion filled his eyes. She ran her fingers through his hair and brushed a spattering of mud from his trousers. She fished in her bag and brought out a candy bar for him to chew. She didn't miss the reproachful look he gave her as he pouted before tucking into the candy bar. Her heart squeezed. He was too young to understand what lay ahead of them, or her reasons for what he must consider the oddest behaviour, but sometimes he had a level of perception that scared her. She was relying on his trust and thankful that, at least, that was something she could depend upon.

A muffled bell rang when she pushed the door open. She gazed around. The walls were hung with pictures depicting various modes of transport. She assumed they were hearses. Two red velvet upholstered chairs stood next to a small table. The lobby was thickly carpeted so no footsteps would break the silence, in fact the whole atmosphere was one of hushed reverence. Behind the desk she saw piles of papers all awry.

No one came in response to the bell. She thought to call out, but hesitated. She opened the door again and closed it. The bell rang again. Again no one responded. She was just about to call out when a man appeared from behind a curtain across the doorway behind the desk. Tall and slightly bent, he had the look of a caricature. Worry lines etched deep in his face made it appear grey to match the sparse tendrils that curled around the indentation of hair crushed by the frequent wearing of a tall hat. Nell wondered whether his sorrowful look was caused by his trade or the reason he chose it.

He paused when he saw Nell and Robert. He seemed unable to make up his mind what to say next. It looked as though the presence of a young lady with an even younger boy had unnerved him. It was the last thing he'd expected to see.

"Oh, my dear," he said at last. "To be bereaved so young. It's a terrible thing. I'm sorry for your loss and that you find yourself in need of my services. Please take a seat, I will be with you shortly and I assure you that I will do everything in my power to alleviate your suffering."

Nell's heart pounded. "Oh no," she said, trying to recover from the shock of his misunderstanding. "I haven't come for a burial. Oh dear, I seem to be doing this all wrong. I'm sorry, perhaps I should have written first, but when Josh said..."

His brow furrowed. "Josh? Josh from the market sent you?"

She blushed. "My name's Lily and this is my nephew Bobby. Josh mentioned that you might be looking for a lad to help in the workshop. Bobby doesn't speak. Josh mentioned that might be an advantage."

"Doesn't speak, ay? Mute?" He gazed at Robert, seizing him up. "He's smart enough. Good looking too. A silent boy would be in demand to walk behind the coffin at children's funerals. Do you think he could that?"

"Yes. He's very bright. He can do a lot more than people give him credit for. Just because he doesn't speak doesn't make him stupid." She was getting angry now. Angrier than she'd ever been. Even more angry than she was at the intransigent people at the Manor who'd sentenced him to a life locked away in the nursery. Her eyes sparked fire.

She was about to turn and walk out when Mr Bradley spoke.

"I'm sure he'll be fine," he said. "Most people talk too much anyway. Empty vessels they are. Can he do woodwork and carpentry? That's what I need in the workshop."

Nell relented. "He can do whatever you ask. He just needs to be shown once. Picks things up quicker than a frog flicks flies."

"Show us your hands, boy," the undertaker said.

Robert held out his arms. Mr Bradley turned his hands over. "Hmm. These aren't the hands of a working lad," he said. "Done any work before, boy?"

Robert stared at him.

"Like I said," Nell told him. "He doesn't speak."

The undertaker smiled. "He can start sweeping the floors, then we'll see about teaching him woodworking." He turned to Nell. "And what about you? I'm guessing Josh made some suggestion that I might find a place for you as well."

She blushed. "Well, he did mention…" Nell glanced at the paperwork cascading over the desk. "I could sort out the books for you, do the paperwork, help with the orders, even produce many of the necessities of mourning you provide. I take it that includes wreaths, ribbons, mourning dress, hats, widow's weed, jewellery…"

He chuckled. "It does," he said. He nodded at the paperwork. "The missus used to do all that, and the other stuff. It's piled up a bit since she's been taken ill. I've been meaning to get someone in for a couple of hours in the mornings to do it. Told Josh that an' all." A look of resignation came over his face. "If Josh thinks you're all right, that's good enough for me."

He held out his hand. "Six shillings a week for the both of you. Seven o'clock start, finish at noon. An extra shilling when he follows the coffin when we lay little 'uns to rest. Can't say fairer than that."

"And the mourning wear, jewellery, wreaths…"

"I'll pass on any requests or orders."

Nell shook his hand. "We won't let you down," she said.

"See you in the morning then," he said. "Don't be late." He shuffled out the way he'd come in.

All the way back to the café Nell's heart sung. A light breeze blew and clouds scudded across the sky. She looked up and, sure enough, she saw a patch of blue. "Look, Robert," she said, just as her mother had said to her. "There's a little patch of blue. As long as you can see that you know the day will eventually turn fine."

He stared, but nothing registered on his face. In fact he looked just as lost and confused as he had that first day she saw him. She sighed.

On the way they passed a market so Nell decided to go and see if she could find materials and trimmings for the bonnets and mourning outfits she'd mentioned to Mr Bradley. She'd also need a more sober outfit to give the right impression. Her navy suit would do if she replaced the white frilly blouse with something darker. She could get one for a few pence from the second-hand clothes stall. She could also get some black material to make a sash to wear over it to add the finishing touch.

"Wait for me here," she said to Robert, aware that he'd be bored with tagging along beside her while she picked over ribbons, silks and various other bits and bobs. She hummed as she wandered around the market, picking up a bit of black ribbon here, a piece of black silk there, a bonnet she could trim plus a reasonably priced workbasket containing cottons, needles and scissors. Engrossed in her shopping she lost track of time and it was only as the street began to darken she remember she'd left Robert waiting along the road. He'd be tired and hungry by now and she'd left him alone for far too long.

She raced to the entrance of the market where she'd left him. He wasn't there. She ran up and down, looking along the street. Her heart raced. He was nowhere in sight. She thought back to the games of hide and seek they used to play in the woods near the Manor. That was fun, this was entirely different. Would Robert have thought of the game as he was left on his own, or had he been enticed away by someone or something else?

She started calling his name. "Bobby, Bobby, where are you?" Then she realised how stupid that was. He wouldn't recognise the name, so, in desperation, she started calling "Robert, Robert, where are you?" Of course he couldn't reply. Her heart flipped. He was a young, vulnerable boy on the streets alone without the means to let anyone know who he was or where he lived. The sheer horror of his predicament washed over her. Terror ran through her veins. Anything could have happened to him. "Come on, Robert, this isn't a game. Where are you? You're frightening me."

She was running now, up and down the street where she'd left him, around the other streets, back and forth, calling, calling. If he was hungry would he have gone to find something to eat, or perhaps back to the café? Would he know his way home? Would he be able to retrace the steps they'd taken today? A thousand thoughts ran like hares through Nell's mind. Should she stay here and hope he returns, or go home and hope he turns up there? She thought for a while. It was no use her waiting here. She'd looked everywhere around the streets. But what if she left and he came back and she wasn't there...

She saw a group of boys near a crossing on the main road. Huddled in a group with their brooms she guessed they were crossing sweepers, looking out for ladies or gents who may want to cross the road. They'd sweep a clean path through the mud and horse droppings to the other side and hope to get a ha'penny for doing so.

"Have any of you seen a young boy hereabouts?" she asked. "I left him standing by the market square, now he's disappeared. Have any of you seen him?"

They looked at one another, shaking their heads and shrugging.

"He was wearing a navy coat and a matching cap," she said as though that made any difference. "We've only just moved here and I'm afraid he may have got lost." Tears welled up in her eyes at the enormity of what had happened. Her poor lost boy was now lost completely and it was all her fault. Fear and anxiety wrung her stomach.

"What's it worth if we finds 'im?" the tallest boy, who seemed to be in charge, said. "Worth our going looking is it?"

Nell dug into her reticule and pulled out a sixpence. "This now and another if you find him," she said.

The boy took the money. "A navy coat and matching cap, you say?"

"Yes. His name's..." she hesitated. Now she was being ridiculous. What did it matter if they knew his name if it made it easier to find him? "Robert. He's seven years old, small for his age... not as tall as you... he has blue eyes and blonde hair, very fine, and his face is thin and..." A huge wave of panic welled up inside her as she thought how Robert might look to these ragged boys who were skinny as bones and between them wouldn't have had enough material in their worn-out clothes to make a decent shirt. "He's wearing good shoes..." she added as her voice faded away.

"Where should we bring 'im if we finds him?"

Visions of them finding him and Robert being so scared as to run away flashed through her mind. "If you see him he may be frightened. Tell him Nell's looking for him." She hesitated to use her real name too but, on balance, decided, for Robert's sake, to throw caution to the wind. "He can't speak," she blurted.

The boy looked at her and shrugged. "Dumb mute eh? Not to worry, we'll find 'im."

Nell's heart lifted. Perhaps these boys were honest and meant well enough. "Do you know Lottie's Place in Clerkenwell Road? We're staying there above the shop."

The lad grinned. "Everyone knows Lottie's Place." He shoved the money in his pocket. "He's probably gone there already, but if we sees 'im we'll be sure to bring 'im 'ome," he said.

All the way home she worried whether she'd done the right thing. She'd ached to ask them to take care and be kind to him but then thought better of it and only added, "There's no payment if he's hurt," hoping that would ensure his safety, from these boys at least.

Panic hastened her steps. She forced herself to think about making tea and getting Robert home in the warm again. One thing was certain; once she got him home, she'd never let him out of her sight again.

As she turned the corner into the road she saw him sitting on the doorstep eating an apple. He'd found his own way home. Relief, tinged with disbelief, flooded over her. She ran up to him and hugged him. "Where were you?" she said, unable to believe her eyes. "I thought I'd lost you."

He stared at her and grinned, his eyes sparkling.

She ushered him inside and up the stairs to their room. "Well, I don't know how you did it," she said. "Finding your way home like that, but I'm really pleased you did." Another wave of relief flowed over her. He wasn't stupid, she now realised he'd always be able to find his way home. He had a phenomenal memory, she'd forgotten that.

Chapter Fourteen

Nell spent a restless night worrying about what she'd done. She went over the day in her mind, the meeting with Josh, the chance of finding work and then Robert's horrifying disappearance. He'd returned home alone with a couple of apples he'd picked up. She worried about that too. Where had he got them? Had he stolen them, if so he could get caught and either deported or jailed.

When she'd confronted him he'd glared at her, puffed up with anger. Not being able to speak didn't mean he couldn't show his feelings in different ways. Then he'd placed the remaining apple on the floor and acted out surprise at finding it and picking it up to eat it. His antics made her laugh, mainly with relief, but also with joy. She'd underestimated him, just like everyone else. It was something she vowed she'd never do again.

She looked at his sketch pad and saw an expertly drawn picture of Josh. Robert must have done it while they were having breakfast. She smiled and tore the picture out. She wasn't sure why, just that she'd like to keep it as a reminder of his kindness in case she never saw him again.

Robert, as usual, was up and dressed before her. He'd already been to the wash house for hot water and was standing at the window looking out. Not for the first time she wondered what was going on in his head. What did he find so fascinating outside that he could stand and stare at it for hours?

She put the thoughts behind her and got up. She dressed with care, wearing the navy blouse she'd bought in the market. She folded the black silk sash she'd made to wear over it and put it in her bag to put on when she got there. She'd also made a black silk flower she could pin onto her suit jacket to reflect the respectful nature of the place where they would be working. It wasn't perhaps the best choice of occupation for her and Robert, but it would have to do until something better came along. She reminded herself to be grateful, after all, if it hadn't been for Josh...

Breakfast that morning was a hurried affair with the café busy, noisy and crowded, so Nell didn't get a chance to ask Lottie about him. She just collected their breakfasts and bought them each a pie they could have for lunch. Then they set off on their journey to the first day of Robert's working life.

Mr Bradley greeted her when she arrived.

"You came then? Wasn't sure you would." He smiled.

"I said we'd not let you down," she reminded him.

"Well, best get started then," he said. "I'll deal with the clients. Anyone comes in you call me. I'm just out here in the back. You need to go through the paperwork." He indicated the papers cascading over the desk. "You'll find bills that need chasing up and some that need paying. Just separate them into piles and I'll deal with them later. Linus Frumley is in charge of the workshop. I'll take the lad and introduce them. No need for you to bother."

"It's no bother," Nell said quickly. "I'd like to see around the workshop, give me a better idea of what we offer." She smiled briefly and put her hand on Robert's shoulder.

"As you please," Mr Bradley said. "Although I doubt you'll find it of interest."

On the contrary, Nell thought. I've every interest in meeting the people Robert will be spending time with. And seeing what will be expected of him.

Nell followed the undertaker through to the back of the shop. The workshop was a depressing place, filled with half-made coffins. It smelled of sawdust and wood chippings. Planks of wood in various colours and sizes leaned against the walls. A heavy set, swarthy featured man, with dark hair falling onto the grubby collar of his work-shirt, stood at the bench, chisel in hand, carving a wooden scroll.

"Ah, Linus, I have a new boy for you. A mute, so he won't cause much trouble. He can start with sweeping the floors, then I want you to show him how to cut and plane the wood to size for the parish coffins."

The man scowled.

"The more expensive coffins are made to order by outside craftsmen," Mr Bradley explained. "We just finish them here with linings, handles, scrolls, plates, etc. Coffins for the parish are made here. No finish on those."

Nell shuddered at the memory of the workhouse where parish coffins were provided for burials in paupers' graves around the edges of the cemetery. She guessed the same thing happened here. Only the wealthy would be able to afford anything other than the simplest funeral.

Linus turned and glanced at Robert before stretching his hand out to pick up a broom. "'E don't look to me like he'll last the day," he said, holding the broom out in Robert's direction. "Start over there." He pointed to the far side of the workroom where another bench littered with tools stood next to the wall.

Robert stared at him, his eyes filled with tears that threatened to spill over.

Nell grabbed the broom. "Come on, Bobby, I'll show you," she said, grabbing his arm and pulling him to the other side of the room. She put her arm around his shoulders and crouched beside him. "I'm sorry. I know this is not what you expected but it's only for a short while. Please, do this for me and I'll find something else as soon as I can. I promise." Tears filled her eyes too but she blinked them away. What had she done? Why had she ever thought this a good idea? "If you really can't stand it we'll go home. I won't make you stay," she said, although in their current situation they needed the money and she could think of no alternative. Josh had recommended it. Surely he wouldn't have suggested it if he'd thought it a bad idea.

Robert grabbed the broom, turned away and started sweeping the floor so vigorously she thought the broom would break in two.

"He'll be fine," she said, forcing a smile for the two men who were watching her. "Just takes a bit of getting used to."

That set the tone for the rest of the morning. Nell's stomach churned the whole time as she thought of young Robert left with the overbearing Linus. Still, there wasn't much she could do about it. They'd just have to put up with it until she could find something better. At least it was only the mornings; they'd have the afternoons free. That was something she could hang on to.

Sitting behind the desk she tried to concentrate on the papers strewn over it. The undertaker's wife must have been ill for some time, guessing by the amount of paperwork piled up. Some bills dated back over six months, although the invoices for funerals still outstanding were fewer. Gradually she managed to sort them into piles. The hours flew by.

The first caller to the shop was a coster with a barrow load of brass handles. Did they want to buy any? Nell didn't know so she had to call Linus. He appeared through the workshop doorway scowling, which Nell soon came to realise was his most used expression.

He glared at her. "You should've sent 'em round the back," he said, none too pleased at having his work disturbed. "Down the alley and round the back," he said to the coster. "I'll take a look but can't promise nowt." He disappeared back behind the curtain.

Nell felt suitably chastened. Why hadn't she realised there'd be a back entrance to the workshop. She went out to see for herself. In fact there was a considerable sized yard out the back, which she hadn't noticed before. Robert was out there sweeping it. Her heart turned over. An open shelter ran the length of one side of the yard. Beneath it a lad, bigger than Robert, was polishing the panels on an already gleaming hearse. Another cart stood alongside it, smaller and rougher in finish. Three wooden sheds stood the other side of the yard, which Nell guessed would be used as storerooms. The place was altogether much bigger than she had supposed.

She sighed and went back to her post in the front of the shop. She spent the next hour making an inventory of the bills outstanding for wood, screws, tacks, and other ironmongery items that had been delivered. The hands on the clock on the wall came round to twelve noon and she started to pack her things away. She was about to call Mr Bradley to say she was ready to leave and take

Bobby with her when a man, a labourer from the look of his clothes, came into the shop. He stood turning his cap in his hands, an anguished look on his face.

"Can I help you?" Nell said as cheerfully as she could.

"I come to see Mr Bradley," he said. "It's about our boy, our youngest. Got took in the night. Mr Bradley said..."

Before Nell could find out what Mr Bradley had said the man himself appeared next to her. "It's all right, Miss Drummond," he said. "I'll deal with this. You get yourself off and take the lad with you. Come again tomorrow."

Nell didn't need second telling. "Thank you," she said and rushed out the back to find Robert. "Bobby, Bobby," she called. "Are you ready? We can go now."

"He's out in yard," Linus said. "No use calling 'im. Deaf as well as mute he is. Don't answer no matter how loud you call."

Nell swallowed. Of course he wouldn't answer to the name of Bobby. Still, she thought, letting Linus think him deaf as well as dumb mightn't be such a bad thing. Better than letting him know more of their business than need be.

With great relief Nell stepped out into the late October sunshine with Robert at her side. She decided to take him down to the river to see the boats. He'd enjoy that, and it was a chance to make up for the horrors of the morning. She took the pies she'd bought that morning with them so they could have a picnic.

Robert, happy at his release skipped along beside her. It was a good hour's walk to the river, but the afternoon was pleasant. Nell pointed out the buildings to Robert as they went.

Walking in the sunshine, holding Robert's hand, didn't quell the anxiety churning inside her. She'd never been so touched as she was seeing the young man's anguish that morning. He'd lost his youngest son. How terrible that must feel. She'd lost both her parents when she was young. Too young to remember her father's passing but memories of the confusion and swirling emotion she'd felt at the loss of her mother welled up inside her bringing tears to her eyes.

She wondered how old the boy was. Mr Bradley seemed to know about him, the man had mentioned speaking to him earlier. Was that to make arrangements for what he knew was bound to happen? How sad. The thought brought a lump to Nell's throat. She'd never considered that part of the business, meeting the bereaved, dealing with loss and the effects of it on families.

She'd seen death in the workhouse, infants more often than adults. Faces she'd known flicked through her mind at the memories of their passing. At the time she'd thought no more about them than to be thankful for a happy release from the misery of their lives and illnesses. The Matron told her that a better place awaited them, and she never doubted it. Any place would be better than where they were. She'd never given any thought to their families. Most of them didn't have families to grieve for them anyway.

That thought brought her back to Robert. He was lost to his family. Did his father grieve for him? Or was he still so mired in grief and anger that he wouldn't feel the loss of the child who'd robbed him of his first wife? Did the fact that he'd turned out to be mute and ran amok in the nursery as soon as he was able to walk, compound his view that the boy was possessed of the devil? Was that why they wanted him locked away?

A shiver ran though her. She shook the thoughts away. Robert walked ahead of her, his interest caught by his surroundings, the boats on the river, the carriages dashing past on the road and people hurrying against the breeze. She smiled. When they got near to the pier at Blackfriars, Nell bought them both a cup of hot chocolate from a street vendor. They found a bench where Robert could watch the boats coming along the Thames and had their picnic. He may not be surrounded by the wealth he was born to, but she was convinced that he too was in better place.

Chapter Fifteen

When they arrived home Nell took Robert to the café and bought them each a cup of Lottie's homemade soup to keep out the cold and a bun to go with it. Robert made the sign for 'trains' showing Nell he was eager to go to the end of the road where he could lean over the fence and watch the trains rush by as they made their way to Waterloo station. He'd only ever seen trains in picture books before they travelled to London on one. He was fascinated by them. In fact he was fascinated by anything that moved, from the boats on the river to the carriages and cabs that thundered past the window of their tiny room. Just like any boy, Nell thought, which to her mind was a good sign.

She gave him his sketch pad and let him go out. "Come back as soon as it gets dark," she said, which would be in about half an hour. The nights were closing in and they'd had several days of frost. He nodded his understanding and rushed out.

As the café was quiet Lottie came to join her, just as Nell had hoped. She wanted to ask her about Josh and was glad Robert was out of earshot. He didn't miss a thing.

"Been rushed off me feet this morning," Lottie said. "Them street kids need more than the coffee they get with their ha'pennies."

"I noticed them crowding round the hatch before dawn," Nell said. "Is it always so busy?"

"Most days. I give 'em yesterday's leftovers, that's why there's so many of 'em come here. Dad bakes fresh overnight, so we always have plenty. Poor mites. I feel sorry for 'em but what can I do? Can't take 'em all in can I?"

"Don't they have homes?"

"Most of 'em do," Lottie said, "but that only gives 'em a bed to sleep in. No one sleeps on the street from choice. It's hard, but better than the alternative."

Nell guessed she meant the workhouse. She could understand that. They were free from the stifling discipline, the hard physical labour and the frequent beatings. Since she'd grabbed at freedom, however poverty-stricken they may be, there was pride in taking one's own decisions.

"Josh not in today?" she asked as casually as she could manage. "I didn't see him this morning and I wanted to thank him for his suggestion that I try the funeral parlour. Mr Bradley took us both on and I'm grateful for the work."

"Josh Bradley? No he's a trader and travels to markets all over the country. He'll be back in a couple of weeks I expect, bursting with tales of his adventures." She smiled. "Got itchy feet that one. Always brings a bit of life to the place. Most of the other traders would crack their faces if they raised a chuckle. Not Josh though. He's a live wire all right."

Nell frowned. "Bradley? Did you say his name was Bradley?"

"Yes, that's right. The funeral parlour is his father's place. Amos Bradley used to be a carpenter years ago, that's how he started out – making coffins. He uses the old yard for his workshop. There's a mortuary half a mile away next to the chapel of rest where people can visit their loved ones, well, those as can afford it."

Nell had wondered where they kept the bodies. She hadn't seen any and thankfully neither had Robert. She thought it would upset him too much. So, the shop and the yard were just a small part of the business. She was glad of it.

"Amos found there's more money in funerals than furniture," Lottie said, wrinkling her nose.

"I'm not surprised," Nell said, "judging by the bills I've seen. The costs are incredible."

"People like to pay a lot," Lottie said. "Makes 'em feel better. Since Prince Albert died deep mourning and no costs spared funerals have become very fashionable."

A paper boy popped his head around the door. He winked as he tossed the evening paper onto the table.

"Thanks, luv," Lottie called after him as he disappeared out of the door. Nell raised her eyebrows. "I sees 'im all right," Lottie said and proceeded to tear the paper into pages which she put on the counter. Nell recalled seeing the men reading pages from the newspaper while they ate the first time she and Robert had breakfast in the café.

She didn't have time to question Lottie further as a customer came in and Lottie was called away.

The next morning Mr Bradley asked Nell to visit the family of the man who'd called about his son's passing. "His name's Henry Gibbins. It's his wife you want to see. See if you can provide her with something appropriate at moderate cost," he said.

He gave Nell the address. "Go this afternoon and give the bill to me."

Nell realised that her bill would be added to the cost of the funeral. She wondered how the Gibbinses would be able to afford such lavish arrangements.

She worked her way through the paperwork, swept the office and tidied the window display. She popped out into the yard several times to check on Robert. Linus Frumley was the most uncivil, thuggish person she'd ever encountered and she wanted to make sure he wasn't picking on Robert. As it happened Robert had made friends with another boy, who said he was called Goose. Goose was happy to show Robert where to put the wood shavings he swept up and how to clean and polish the hearses, paying special attention to the wheel axles.

"They 'ave to be greased to make sure they run quiet," he said. "Can't 'ave a squeaky wheel. That won't do at all."

When twelve o'clock came she collected Robert and together they made their way to the address Mr Bradley had given her. She found Mrs Gibbins upstairs in the three roomed home the family rented in a house shared by several tenants. The three eldest of her children, aged between seven and nine, had been sent out to see what they could earn helping the stallholders in the market. The youngest remaining two were at home, sitting on the floor while Mrs Gibbins tackled the pile of ironing she'd taken in. Clothes horses full of wet washing stood around the open fire. The room was steamy, hot and suffocating. The only window closed. Nell shuddered at the realisation that the body of the deceased would be in the other room, his coffin covered by the pall Mr Bradley had provided. It would be carried out of the house on the day of the funeral.

"Henry's had to go to work. Can't afford to miss a day's pay. It's little enough as it is," she said, when Nell mentioned where she was from.

"It's you I've come to see," Nell said. "Mr Bradley mentioned that you may require some mourning wear. A bonnet or mantle to put over your shoulders perhaps?"

"Oh that's everso kind of 'im," Mrs Gibbins said. "Just a bonnet to wear for the funeral, luv. I can return it after the... you know..." Her eyes shone with unshed tears.

Yes, Nell did know. She glanced around. The room looked very poor indeed and the thought of mother, father and the children sharing such humble livings made her wonder again how the funeral would be paid for.

In the end Nell agreed to make a bonnet and mantle for Mrs Gibbins which she would drop off before the funeral which was to be held at the end of that week.

On the way home she picked up the material she would need. She could make the bonnet and mantle that evening after Robert was in bed and have it ready in plenty of time.

Nell arrived early on the day of the funeral to see to the arrangements. It wasn't the only funeral of the day, and not by any means the grandest, but it was the one closest to Nell's heart. She worried about Robert's role in it. It was something he'd never done before, but over the last few weeks their lives had changed beyond recognition. She wondered what he thought of it all. The visit to the bereaved household had shocked him, she saw it in his eyes. Death was something new to him, although not to her. She'd become accustomed to it but for him it was different. Was he too young to be made aware of it? It was part of life and, working where they did, it was unlikely she could protect him from the realities of it.

She showed him the top hat and black coat he'd be expected to wear and explained to him that he was to follow the coffin. His eyes shadowed with misery. His face set into a grimace. It was clear he hated the idea. He grabbed the coat and hat, threw them on the ground and gave her a rebellious stare.

Her heart stumbled. How could she explain to him what it would mean to the family to have their son buried with all the accepted ceremony and ritual that accompanied respectable funerals.

"You remember the lady we visited, who'd lost her son? Your presence at his funeral will bring her comfort," she said. "It will help her to remember the solemnity of the occasion and the joy that her son's short life gave her."

Robert stood motionless, staring. Then tears splashed onto his cheeks. Nell pulled him into her arms and held him, shushing in his ear while she stroked his head. She closed her eyes. Knots tightened in her stomach. What on earth was she doing? What right had she to subject this small naïve boy to such things as they were having to experience? How could she expect him to understand? Then she recalled the alternative and the knots unravelled.

She held him at arm's length. "You don't have to if you don't want to," she said. "I'll tell Mr Bradley no."

Slowly, glaring at her, he picked up the hat and put it on his head. Nell helped him into coat, her heart almost bursting with pride.

Nell walked along the road alongside Robert, watching his every move. He seemed to be in a daze, lost in another world, his face sombre. He performed his role perfectly.

Afterwards Henry Gibbins made a special effort to thank Nell. He showed her the black-edged mourning card Mr Bradley had given him. It bore a picture of the boy, with the words *'Barney Gibbins, At Peace'* and the dates of his birth and death written beneath it.

"We didn't have him long, but he was loved," Henry said. "And this is to remind us how blessed we were to have him, even for such a short time. I'll al'as be grateful to Mr Bradley. If it weren't for 'im letting me pay what little I can afford when I get paid now and then our lad'd be in a pauper's grave." He wiped a tear from his cheek.

Nell recalled the fear of the pauper's grave that haunted the workhouse. Flossie bore the hardships, pain and misery that her life entailed, but she dreaded the indignity of a pauper's funeral. It was her one regret in life, often voiced to Nell as she was dying. "I'll be buried under the hedge with nowt for anyone to remember me by," she said. When Nell assured her that she'd remember her, she'd patted her hand and said, "Get out of here, luv. Soon as you can and don't never come back."

"It's not everyone who'd be as kind as Mr Bradley," Henry Gibbins said. "Our Barney will make sure there's a place in heaven for 'im." He smiled and gazed at the card in his hand. "Least Barney could do."

Nell recalled the grave a few feet away from the hedge where the paupers were buried. Barney Gibbins wouldn't be the only child buried in that grave, but the fact that there was a place where he could rest in peace brought comfort to his parents.

Nell made sure Robert, who still refused to answer to the name Bobby, was given the shilling he'd earned. He did at least smile when she told him it was his to keep and spend on whatever he liked. In the end he spent sixpence on some chocolate, a new sketch pad, coloured pencils and two meat pies. He saved the other sixpence for another day.

Doing the books the next day Nell realised that the cost of Henry's son's funeral, including the bonnet and mantle Nell had made for Mrs Gibbins, had been added to the bill for the much grander funeral that had taken place that morning. Over the next few months she noticed that the costs of all the poorer clients' funerals had been added to the costs billed to those who could better afford it.

Chapter Sixteen

Nell and Robert soon dropped into the routine of breakfast in the café before going on to work at the funeral parlour. Lottie took a shine to Robert. She called him Bobby and one morning she asked Nell about him. Like Josh she'd realised he never spoke. "Poor little mite," she said. "I expect he misses his mother."

"We both do," Nell said. As she said it she thought of her own mother. She missed her still, but she felt sure that her mother would be proud of her for striking out on her own, being her own boss and finding her independence.

"It's good of you to take 'im in," Lottie said. "It's not everyone as would, 'specially with his... you know... not talking an' that. Strange what tragedy can do to a person."

Nell had to agree. She saw plenty of tragedy working where she did. Although she wasn't happy about Robert working in the yard there was little she could do about it. She often heard Linus Frumley bellowing at the lads and feared he'd take his rage out on Robert, him being the youngest and most vulnerable. Anxiety curled in her stomach whenever she thought about Robert's future. He deserved better than she could do for him, but the alternative his family had in mind was even worse.

Some of the other boys went to a nearby ragged school, but it would be no use sending Robert there. He'd soon be overwhelmed by the other boys and without Nell's support to help him he'd be beyond bewilderment.

Whenever she got the chance she'd pop out into the yard to look for him. She'd often find him hiding behind the hearses he was polishing. When she found him his little face would light up. It reminded her of the games of hide and seek they'd played in the orchard in the summer. Nell stomach churned at the memory.

Nell was glad that at least they had a hot breakfast before setting out to walk to work. One day at the counter she chanced to glance at the newspaper pages set out for customers to help themselves to read over breakfast. After breakfast the pages would be returned for someone else to read. Her heart almost stopped when she saw the headline. It said 'Lord Eversham's Son Kidnapped.' The air punched out of her lungs. She struggled to suck it back in. She glanced around, picked up the page, folded it and put it in her bag. "Come along, Bobby, we don't want to be late," she said hurrying him out of the café.

In the office her hand shook as she took the page out and read the story. She examined it carefully. It said: *'The police are interested in the whereabouts of Miss Nell Draper, his nursemaid, last seen with Robert Eversham boarding a train to Kings Cross, London.* There was a description of Robert and the clothes he was wearing together with a description of Nell.

Her heart pounded. She'd fitted Robert out in second-hand clothes from a stall in the market. She was glad now that she hadn't sold his old ones but kept them folded up in a drawer as they might easily be recognised. She read the story through twice. There was no mention of Robert's lack of speech or his perceived mental incapacity. Neither was there any mention of the silver articles she'd taken from his drawer in the nursery and sold to the pawnbroker to pay for their keep. That at least was a relief. She guessed they hadn't even bothered to check what else she may have taken. All they were concerned about was that he should be gone, all his things should be cleared away and the place left clean so the new baby could take his place.

Now, according to the story in the paper, he was missing. No mention was made of the appointment with hospital psychiatrist who would certify his incapacity and see he was locked away, out of sight, forgotten. That apparently hadn't been thought worthy of mention. Cold fury raged inside her. There was an address for information to be sent and a small reward was offered. They didn't even care enough to make it a significant sum.

Fear and fury raged inside her. She remembered the hackney carriage driver at Kings Cross. Would he remember a woman with a child looking for lodgings? She recalled telling him she was a nursemaid. Would he put two and two together? Her heart sank as a ball of lead formed in her stomach. 'Kidnapped' the paper said. Kidnap was a hanging offence.

She refolded the paper and put it back in her bag. She'd have to be careful who she spoke to when taking him out and be sure to emphasise the relationship she'd invented by calling him her nephew, but hopefully no one would take the small, badly dressed child with its aunt for the son of an Earl. After that Nell made sure to buy a newspaper on the way to work so she could check for any further mentioned of Lord Eversham or his missing son.

The week before Christmas the weather turned cold. Pavements were icy with frost and snow turned to slush as the carriages and cabs rushed along the road. The cold weather brought a sudden influx of business to the funeral parlour and Nell was kept busy in the shop. She worried about Robert, fearing what might happen to him when she couldn't be there to look after him. Thankfully Robert had taken to Goose and followed the older boy around until Goose set him to work sweeping or polishing.

"Don't worry about 'im, Miss," Goose said to Nell. "I'll keep an eye on 'im and keep 'im out of the way of Mr Frumley's temper. 'E's fierce when 'e gets a tear on. Saw 'im beat up a lad so bad once 'e didn't come in agin for a week."

The thought made Nell shudder.

One day she'd gone into the yard to look for Robert to take him home. When she couldn't find him she'd asked Linus. He'd glowered. The look on his face pure evil. "Probably off skiving with the other lads," he said. "If I finds him he'll be in for a belting. Little guttersnipe."

Nell's heart crunched. The thought of what this evil man might to do Robert haunted her. The sooner she could find another job the better. She was grateful to Mr Bradley for taking her on in the first place, without references or knowing anything about her, but it clearly wasn't the best place to bring up a sensitive child like Robert. Little did Linus Frumley know that the guttersnipe he referred to was in fact the eldest son and heir of Lord Eversham. Still, it would be far worse if he ever found out.

She didn't trust Linus Frumley. Time and again she found him talking to unsavoury characters in the yard, characters who had no business with the funeral parlour. She guessed he was running some sort of business of his own. Discretion, the fear of losing her job and fear of what he might do to Robert kept her from expressing her opinions, but still the thought lingered at the back of her mind.

As Christmas approached the weather grew gradually worse. Snow fell most days and the sleeting wind was bitter. Nell bought Robert a thick coat and cap the same as the other boys wore, so he would fit in better and a thick cape for herself. She was able to make a surprising amount of money selling the black silk roses she made. Many of the bereaved families bought them to place in vases alongside pictures of their loved ones. The poorer clients bought bonnets and mantles and the more wealthy paid considerable amounts for the lavish creations in black silk and feathers she fashioned into hats with fetching half-veils. She also had a chance encounter with a woman on the market who sold millinery. When she saw the silk flowers Nell made she said she'd buy them to adorn her hats and bonnets so Nell soon found she had a steady income.

As her finances improved so did her mood. She hummed as she decorated their small room with paper-chains, holly wreaths and candles. She bought a music box in the market. Robert adored it and would sit for hours turning the handle to make it play. She bought gifts. Toys, books and games for Robert, lavender oil for Lottie and an almanac for Ernie, Lottie's father. For the first time since she left the Manor she felt that perhaps life had taken a turn for the better. She was managing and Robert was happy, his sunny disposition had returned. The evenings, sitting by the fire reading to him and helping with his lessons was still the best part of the day.

There was no shortage of coal for the fire to keep them warm or to heat up soup or cook toast or potatoes. The thing she missed most of all was company. She missed the morning chats with Alice and Jenny and, she had to admit, with Ethan. Especially with Ethan. She missed the rush of excitement when she saw him and the catch of her breath when he came and sat with her on the bench. She often pictured the garden with its colourful flowers and heavenly scents. Then her heart would stumble. The dusty, grim, smoke-filled streets of London could never replace those treasured memories. Nor would the surly conversation with the traders in the café over breakfast ever replace the memory of the lively, gossipy tête-à-têtes with the housemaids.

When Lottie heard Nell had no particular plans for Christmas Day, she insisted they spend the day with her and Ernie. "It won't be much," she said. "A goose, and veg from the market, but the company will be lively and you never know who might pop in. We get all sorts."

"In that case I can hardly refuse," Nell said, laughing.

On Christmas Eve she left the shop early. She'd overheard two women in the market talking about the pond in Regent's Park which was frozen over.

"There's people skating and dancing on the ice," one woman said. "There's coffee stalls and roasted chestnuts. Like a proper fair it is."

Nell decided to take Robert that afternoon to see the spectacle. They walked to the park along roads heaving with life. Every shop window was lit with a Christmas display and music from barrel-organs played as they walked along. Even Robert seemed to catch the festive spirit. He had a glow on his face that made Nell's heart melt. The fairground atmosphere continued in the park where street sellers had set up their stalls selling everything from rattles, snow-shoes, mufflers and buckets to figurines of skaters and dancers.

Nell bought them each a mug of hot chocolate and sat to watch the dazzling displays. Robert got out his sketch pad to capture the scene. It was magical, but Nell couldn't help her mind wandering back to last Christmas at Inglebrook Manor, the visit to the workhouse and meeting Kitty. She wondered how she was getting on. The small child with a halo of blonde curls often popped into her mind. She wished she could do something for Kitty, but in her heart she knew she never could. All she could hope was that the Christmas spirit would enter the workhouse and all the children would have a chance to play and be well fed for once.

Perhaps one day she'd be adopted by a new family but Nell knew the chances of that were very small indeed. The best she could hope for was to learn a trade so she'd be able to support herself when she left Salvation Hall House.

She thought about the Christmas Ball and the much less costly party for the staff. She remembered the kindness of Alice and Jenny and the gift Ethan had bought her. How different this year would be. Not so lavish and luxurious but this was the first Christmas in her life when she'd have the freedom to choose how to spend it and who to spend it with.

After the skating as darkness fell, they walked back along the brightly lit streets all festively decorated. The hurdy-gurdy music from the barrel-organs filled her ears. She gave pennies to each of the entertainers and wished them a Merry Christmas.

The smell of mince pies, roasting chestnuts and rich puddings filled Nell's nostrils. She went into the shop and bought some for their tea, although it was doubtful that Robert would eat them. He'd taken to only eating cheese sandwiches for tea with scones. It was as though he'd reverted back to the tea Mrs Hewitt used to prepare for him. Nell was only glad that he at least ate the hearty breakfast Lottie prepared and the pie she'd buy for his lunch.

Christmas morning Nell put on her best dress and dressed Robert in his second-best suit. His best suit remained folded up and pushed to the back of the chest of drawers. She pinned her hair up and adorned it with a slide decorated with feathers. Downstairs the café was steamy and warm. Outside a crowd of boys hung around the hatch, despite the café being closed. Lottie gave them each a hot drink before sending them on their way. The calls of "Thanks, Missus," and "Merry Christmas" echoed in the rapidly emptying street.

"Pastor Brown's giving 'em all dinner in the church hall after the service," she said. "Probably the only day they'll see the inside of the church." She laughed.

Nell had asked Lottie about the Christmas Day church service. She wanted to take Robert. He'd never been to church or even to the Manor chapel. The only services he'd ever attended were held around the graves of the children whose coffins he followed. She thought it about time he saw a different side to the church, one a bit more joyful and full of hope. She'd found the regular Sunday services all the workhouse children attended an uplifting experience. She hoped it would be the same for Robert.

By the time they arrived the church was crowded but they managed to find seats at the back. Robert gazed around as though taking everything in. He sat with his hands in his lap and, even at the end of the service Nell couldn't tell whether he'd enjoyed it or not. His little face was set, his mood passive. She sighed. She'd done her best and at least he'd been.

"We'd best get back and start the dinner," Lottie said as they hurried out. Nell was glad they weren't hanging around. She'd enjoyed the singing which brought back memories of the Christmas services in the workhouse, but she wasn't so keen on the sermon.

A light drizzle dampened the air as they made their way back to the café. When they arrived Nell was glad to get back into the warmth. By midday the street outside was empty. The only sound the occasional carriage or cab taking latecomers to their lunches.

Ernie pushed two tables together before he disappeared into the kitchen with Lottie. Nell spread cloths on the tables and set out the cutlery. Lottie produced an arrangement of holly and candles with bright red ribbons tied in bows as a centre-piece. She brought out glasses and a couple of carafes of wine.

Several men Nell recognised as traders from the market joined them, each of them giving Lottie a hug in thanks for the invitation. They'd brought a small keg of beer too.

"Wouldn't be Christmas without a few pints in good company," one of them said. The others all agreed. Nell smiled. This Christmas certainly would be different, she thought.

The smell of roasting goose filled the air as they all started on the drinks, toasting one another and wishing, "Good Health and Happiness to all." Nell was laughing with a young lad called Harry when the door opened again and Josh walked in.

"Well, hello, stranger," Lottie said. "I wondered when you'd be back."

"Couldn't keep away could I?" Josh said, sweeping her up and spinning her around. "Not when the best cook in London's doing dinner."

"Get away with you," she said when he put her down, but Nell didn't miss the look of pure joy that lit up her face.

"And how's my favourite girl and the little one?" he said turning to Nell. "I hear you're queen of the mourning wear. Glad to hear you're making something out of it. Pa isn't the most generous employer, but he speaks well of you."

A warm glow washed over her at his compliment. "I do well enough," she said.

"And Bobby?"

Nell laughed. "See for yourself." Robert was enthralled watching Ernie playing with a clockwork drummer boy. He'd wind him up and set him off and the boy would keep drumming until the spring wound down. Then Ernie would wind him up again. The look on Robert's face was pure delight.

Dinner in the café was eaten accompanied by a confusion of noisy enjoyment. Laughter filled the café, mostly Nell thought, due to Josh's presence. He had a way of making everyone feel at ease and the hours spun away.

After dinner, when Nell and Josh had washed up and the table had been cleared, they all adjourned to the tap room of the nearby Crown and Anchor where a raucous sing-song went on until the early hours of the next morning.

Nell was afraid it would be too much for Robert. He became agitated and alarmed at loud noise, so, just after midnight she said her goodbyes and went to take Robert home.

Outside the night air was frosty and the earlier drizzle turned to ice. Josh insisted on walking her home. He offered his arm in case she should slip on the icy cobbles. Robert walked slightly ahead of them. "I've never seen you looking so bonny," Josh said. The lamplight glistened on the pale sweep of his hair as they walked beneath its amber glow. "The London air must agree with you."

Nell felt the blush rush to her face. She hoped Josh wouldn't see it in the dark. "It's either that or the wine," she said. "I'm not used to such lively company."

"You should get out more," he said. "Go to the theatre, the music hall or the galleries, preferable in the company of someone who appreciates great beauty."

"I'm not sure I'm acquainted with such a person," she said, smiling.

He raised his hat. "Joshua Bradley, at your service, ma'am," he said.

"Why, thank you." They had reached her door. "Well, I'll say goodnight," she said.

"Goodnight, for now," he said. "Until tomorrow comes."

The brush of his lips against hers before he stepped away was so fleeting Nell wondered afterwards if she'd imagined it.

Chapter Seventeen

The next morning Josh had gone and with him a small part of Nell's happiness.

"He'll be back," Lottie assured her. "He has to go where the trade takes him but like the sun in summer and the rain in winter he'll be back."

Nell's heart sunk a little at having to go back to the funeral parlour. She realised Josh had suggested it as a way of earning enough to pay the rent and thereby keep her close, but as a way of making a living... well it was better than the infirmary, she supposed and her presence did bring comfort to the bereaved so that was something.

Over the next few weeks Nell took Robert out as much as she could. They spent afternoons in the museums and galleries if it was cold or, if it was warm enough, for long walks down by the river.

By the end of January the weather had improved, although mist still hung over the cold damp streets in the early morning. One day, while scanning the newspaper for any mention of Lord Eversham, she saw a small advertisement for someone to sit with an elderly lady for two hours on three afternoons a week to read to her or simply to provide comfort and company. The advert said: *'Must have nursing experience.'* It wasn't far away so Nell decided to walk to the address that afternoon to see if the job was still vacant.

She showed the advertisement to Robert. "It's only for a couple of hours three afternoons a week," she said. "You'd have to come with me. What do you think?"

Robert stared silently at her. Of course he'd have no understanding of time or what it meant to have plans for the future. All he knew was here and now. He had a fantastic memory for things he'd seen and people he'd met, but the concept of tomorrow somehow eluded him.

Nell sighed. Given the address she thought it might be well paid and any extra cash she could earn would be welcome, so she thought she'd give it a try anyway.

She managed to leave the funeral parlour with Robert early as it was quiet with only two funerals booked for the rest of the week. She found the house in a well appointed street of tall Georgian buildings. She checked the house number. The portico led up steps to a black painted door with a large brass door-knocker in the shape of a lion's head. She smiled at Robert. "In for a penny," she said. She walked up the steps and knocked. The door was opened by a grey-haired man in a cut-away coat and striped waistcoat.

Nell showed him the advertisement in the paper and he beckoned her inside.

"If you'd care to wait in here I'll tell the master you've called, although I wasn't informed of any appointment."

Nell's heart sank. Of course, she should have written with references and asked for an appointment. She glanced around. A large fireplace dominated the room which overlooked the road. Pictures lined the walls. A rug, she assumed to be Persian, lay in front of the hearth with a well upholstered chair either side of it.

Nell paced the floor. Why on earth had she come here? What had possessed her? She'd worked in this sort of establishment before. She'd forgotten how oppressive the atmosphere could be. This was no place for her and Robert, especially not Robert. He shouldn't be subjected to the sort of humiliation that was bound to be heaped upon them. She was just about to leave when the door opened and the butler asked her to accompany him. "Mr Crosby will see you in the study," he said, leading the way.

Nell followed him to a room at the back of the house, overlooking the garden. Through the window she saw patches of blue sky between the pearl grey clouds.

Mr Milton Crosby, a slim-built man with sideburns and longer-than-was-fashionable auburn hair, sat at a solid mahogany desk opposite the door. His dark blue suit, worn over a matching waistcoat and crisp white shirt, was expertly cut to flatter. The warmth in his face put Nell immediately at ease. He had a grace about him too, and a ready smile that reached his soft hazel eyes.

"So, you want to be a companion to my mother," he said. "Well, you'd better tell me a bit about yourself and how you think you can help her. She's the one needs a companion and nurse."

Nell swallowed. "My name's Lily." She hesitated. "Lily Drummond. I have worked in an infirmary with all sorts of illnesses and in all conditions. I like to read and, if that's what you're looking for, I would have great pleasure in reading to your mother."

"Worked in an infirmary, eh? Good. References?" He held out his hand. Nell blanched. She hadn't any.

"No? Well, have you ever been in service? You'll have references for that."

Nell frowned.

Mr Crosby sighed. He stared at Nell, then at Robert and understanding filled his eyes. "Oh. I see," he said.

Nell realised he'd looked at Robert and thought he was her son.

"This is my nephew, Bobby. I would have to bring him with me."

"Nephew eh?" he said, eyebrows raised and sounding as though he didn't believe a word.

Nell stuck her chin out and said, "Will that be a problem?"

He chuckled. "You've got a nerve, I'll say that for you. Mother would like that." He stroked his chin. "You say you have nursing experience. Tell me, how would you treat an ulcerated leg?"

Nell smiled. Leg ulcers were common in the workhouse. "There are several ways to treat them," she said. "Personally I'd recommend cleaning the wound with a solution of carbolic and then finely crushed charcoal applied with a dressing and changed every two days. The charcoal absorbs the pus and it's an antiseptic."

He nodded.

"Laudanum for the pain," she added.

"Headache?"

"Willow herb can be very effective," Nell said.

"Toothache?"

"Oil of cloves."

He smiled. "You'd better come and meet my mother. I warn you, she's very fussy." From the tone in his voice Nell guessed he'd interviewed several girls his mother had turned down and was now thoroughly sick of it. Perhaps she was giving her son a hard time because he now ruled the house and she wanted to assert what little power remained to her. "She has a bad leg. You will need to change the dressings. Will that be a problem?"

"Not at all," Nell said. It was work she'd done before and she was confident she could manage it.

"Good."

Nell and Robert followed him into the parlour where his mother sat in front of the fire, her legs covered by a blanket. The room was light, airy and warm. Altogether a very pleasant room, Nell thought.

"Been in service before?" Mrs Crosby snapped surveying Nell through half-closed eyes. "I don't want some girl off the streets coming here wasting my time. Bad enough with Mrs Thingamejig faffing around me every morning. Can't be doing with faffing around."

Nell drew in a breath. "I can assure you I have no time for faffing," she said in her best cut glass accent, one she'd picked up at the Manor. "I understood it was intelligent conversation and a little light reading you required. If that's not the case…"

Mrs Crosby laughed a cackling laugh, throwing her head back. "She'll do," she said. "I like a girl with a bit of spirit. We'll get on famously." She glanced at her son. "You can go," she said, dismissing him with distain.

"I have my nephew to look after," Nell said, pushing Robert forward. He'd been hiding behind her skirts during the encounter and Mrs Crosby hadn't noticed him. "I'll need to bring him along."

Mrs Crosby frowned.

"He'll be no trouble," Nell said.

"Well, that's settled," Milton said, as though relieved to have got rid of a problem by shoving it onto someone else. "Bring the boy along. As long as he can sit quietly. Mother is a firm believer in children being seen and not heard. Isn't that right, Mother?"

His mother scowled. She beckoned Robert towards her. He glanced at Nell before stepping forward. "What's your name, son?" Mrs Crosby asked.

"He doesn't speak," Nell said, rushing to his defence. "If it's a problem I'll not take the job."

Mrs Crosby's cackling laugh rang out again. "What can't speak can't lie," she said. "Looks like he's got a wise head on his shoulders. He'll do."

So it was settled. Nell would come to the house Monday, Wednesday and Friday afternoons with Robert. She'd change the dressings on Mrs Crosby's leg and read to her. It was clear both Mr and Mrs Crosby thought Robert, or Bobby as she'd called him, was her illegitimate son, which would account for her being sacked without a reference. Still, what did it matter what they thought? In fact, it might even work to her advantage as it would be less likely they'd discover the truth.

Although the hours were less than at the funeral parlour the pay was just as generous. It meant Nell could treat Robert to some new clothes and several outings. He was particularly fond of visiting the galleries and exhibitions.

As the weather brightened spring flowers appeared in the market and Nell bought bunches of daffodils to brighten up their small room. She made spring flowers in rainbow colours which she sold to Lydia, the woman in the market.

At the funeral parlour things were becoming more and more difficult. Nell kept finding invoices for brass handles, embroidered palls to cover the coffins and ornately gilded scrolls and cherubs that didn't match with any of the recorded deliveries. The suppliers were unknown to her too. She went to see Mr Bradley.

"The deliveries are all checked off by the lads in the yard," she said, "but I can find no record of these items having been delivered." She showed him the invoices which amounted to a considerable amount.

Mr Bradley glanced over them and handed them back. "Best speak to Linus. He's in charge of the yard. I expect the records have gone astray. He's good with wood, but not so good at keeping records. Best ask him."

It took Nell a couple of days to catch up with him, and then he clearly wasn't in any mood to be accounting for how he kept records. When she asked if he had any paperwork that could confirm the deliveries his face grew red and his eyes bulged. "What you saying? Saying I stole 'em? What good would they be to me?" Nell fully expected him to give her a clout, just as he did the boys when they displeased him. "I 'spect you made 'em up to get money from Mr Bradley, that's what I think. Wouldn't put it past you either."

Now it was Nell's turn to get angry. "I didn't make them up. Why would I? I've never even heard of some of these suppliers. You deal with them. You must have records."

He shrugged and turned away to show the conversation was over.

"Well, I'm not going to pay them," she said, rage churning in her stomach. "Not unless the goods can be accounted for."

"We'll lose our suppliers if we don't pay them," he said. "They're bills for things we've used. All gone now. I can't be expected to keep check on everything. Just pay 'em, that's what you're paid for."

Again she asked Mr Bradley. He shrugged his shoulders and said, "Best pay 'em."

She huffed. The costs would be added to somebody's bill that was for sure.

Chapter Eighteen

On Monday Nell rushed through her work at the funeral parlour as she had the afternoon with Mrs Crosby to look forward to. Her mind spiralled back to her time working in the infirmary when she'd tended everyone from the very young to the very old. She'd always found the work fulfilling and the people interesting. They all had their stories. Taking care of people had come naturally to her, if she'd ever been in a position to train as a nurse she would have taken the opportunity. She'd read about Florence Nightingale's School of Nursing in St Thomas's Hospital in London, but that was a dream that seemed as far away from reality as the stars in the night sky. She'd had to content herself with helping the workhouse inmates. At least that was something she could be proud of.

Linus had been out most of the morning and had taken Goose with him so it had been quiet in the yard. Nell found Robert watching one of the other lads carve the scrolls that went on the coffins. She insisted he wash his hands and face before accompanying her to Mr Crosby's house. She brushed his coat and cap and dabbed his face with her handkerchief. "We want to make a good impression don't we?" she said.

Robert stared silently at her. She realised he wasn't at all concerned what sort of impression they might make, nor did he understand the reason for it. He just did as she told him, which was often a blessing.

As they left the building Josh was waiting outside. Nell stopped in surprise, her heart beating a little faster. Then she realised he probably hadn't come to see her at all. "Have you come to see your father?" she asked. "He's in his office. He'll be delighted to see you."

Josh laughed his engaging laugh. "No. It's you I've come to see." He held out his arm. "I'd like to walk you home and, if you've a mind, perhaps we could step out this evening. They've a new pianist at the Crown and Anchor and from what I hear he's in need of a bit help with the singing."

Nell laughed. He really was irresistible and she was flattered, but didn't want to appear too eager. "That's very kind of you," she said. "I'd enjoy the company but I'm afraid I'm not going home. I have an engagement this afternoon in the other direction. Perhaps another day?"

He looked shocked. "An engagement? I've only been away a couple of weeks." He took off his bowler hat and held it to his chest. "Please tell me you haven't given your heart to another so quickly. I fear mine would break if you have."

She laughed at his teasing. "No, but I have another job. I'm to sit with an elderly lady in Bloomsbury who requires my presence to lighten up a dull afternoon."

"But you'd leave me with a dreadfully dull afternoon bereft of your company?"

She started to walk away and he fell into step beside her. "What about this evening? Or have you another engagement?"

She paused. How could she explain that she couldn't leave the boy. It wouldn't be fair on him as much as she'd like to go out with Josh. "I'm afraid it's not possible," she said. "I won't leave Bobby alone. He's my responsibility and one I take seriously. Sorry."

"At least let me walk with you to, where was it?"

"Bloomsbury."

"Bloomsbury." He raised his eyebrows. "Going up in the world are we?"

She laughed. "Not really. I'm employed as a companion. No better than a domestic servant, but glad of the job just the same."

"Oh well, at least let me walk with you," Josh said smiling his irrepressible smile. So the walk to Bloomsbury turned out to be quite pleasant. Josh told her about the different places he visited, the different markets and the people he met. His stories made her laugh and it was with a light heart that she arrived at the Crosby house.

Josh left her at the bottom of the steps leading to the front door. "I'll look forward to seeing you this evening," he said. "In the café."

Inside the house Nell was shown into the front parlour where Mrs Crosby sat by the fireplace. A small table next to her held a tray with a bowl of carbolic solution, bandages, a pot of finely ground charcoal, several vials of medication and a bottle of gin. A half empty glass stood next to the bottle. A tall Chinese screen stood alongside her chair.

"Come on in, girl," Mrs Crosby said when the butler showed Nell into the room. "I understand you've dressed wounds before. Well, let's see how good you are. I hope you know what you're doing."

This was one area Nell felt confident about. Her years working in the infirmary had taught her about the importance of hygiene, the need to avoid infection and how intrusive medical procedures felt to the patients undergoing them.

"I can assure you I have done this before," she said.

"What about the boy?" Mrs Crosby asked, scowling at Robert.

Nell smiled and turned Robert towards the window where a table and chairs almost filled the bay. Robert climbed onto one of the chairs and stared out. She took his sketch pad and his favourite picture book out of her bag and put them on the table with some pencils and a bag of sweets.

"He'll be fine," she said, drawing the screen around the old lady.

She removed the blanket from Mrs Crosby's lap and lifted her skirt to survey the bandages, browned with blood and pus, around her left leg.

She took a pair of needlework scissors from her bag and cut away the stained bandages. Mrs Crosby watched her, sipping gin which Nell suspected had been mixed with laudanum. Nell chatted about the weather and asked Mrs Crosby about her general health as she cleaned the wound and redressed it.

"Nothing wrong with me that losing twenty years wouldn't cure," Mrs Crosby said. She sighed. "Old age is a terrible thing, but I won't go down without a fight."

Nell smiled. At least this woman had something to fight for; a reason to hang on as long as she could, unlike the people in the workhouse for whom death came as a pleasant release. "I'm sure you'll be with us for many years to come," she said.

Mrs Crosby scowled.

Once the new bandages were in place Nell ran a hand over the other leg. "Do you experience any problems with this leg?" she asked.

Mrs Crosby shook her head.

"Well, that's done then, unless there's anything else?"

"No. You'll do," Mrs Crosby said, leaning back in her chair. The pinched look she'd had on her face when Nell arrived had been replaced by a softer more gentle one.

Nell pushed back the screen. Mrs Crosby tugged at the bell rope just within reach and a few minutes later a maid appeared.

"Take this away and bring us tea," Mrs Crosby said, indicating the bowl of carbolic now red with blood and pus and the discarded dressings. "And some of Mrs Tipping's cake," she added.

The maid bobbed a curtsy, picked up the tray and hurried out of the room, to reappear a few moments later with a tray loaded with a silver tea-service, three cups and a cake sliced ready. She placed the tray on the table next to Mrs Crosby, eliciting a barely audible, "Thank you, Polly."

Nell guessed the tea tray had been prepared beforehand and the addition of cake a reward if all went well. A wave of pleasure swept over her. The reward for doing a good job, she hoped.

Mrs Crosby poured the tea and handed Nell tea and cake for Robert, which she took over to the table for him. She took the other chair and placed it next to Mrs Crosby ready to read to her.

"Now, tell me something about yourself," Mrs Crosby said. "I never believed that stuff about your nephew."

Nell reddened. "Not much to tell," she said. "He's my sister's child. Orphaned, so I'm his guardian. I'm looking after him."

Mrs Crosby chuckled. "Whatever you say, my dear," she said, but it was clear from her expression she didn't believe a word. Nell wasn't about to enlighten her further.

"So, where did you learn to dress wounds so efficiently? Workhouse was it?"

Nell swallowed. She didn't mind indulging the old lady with a bit of chat about the weather, but didn't want her prying into her past.

"It's all right," Mrs Crosby said. "Doesn't bother me. My son might have something to say though. Got respectability he has. Got it bad. I never was much one for convention and propriety. Always been a bit of rebel." She glanced at Nell. "I bet you have too," she said.

"I worked in the infirmary, as I said," Nell admitted. "Worked there quite a long time."

She sipped her tea.

"I bet you've some stories to tell then," Mrs Crosby said with a gleam in her eye.

Nell relaxed. All the old lady wanted was to hear the gossip and shenanigans of the workhouse inmates. She could easily supply those. "I came here to read to you," she said. "I presume you have a book in mind."

"Intelligent conversation you said when you came. Let's start with some of that." She rang the bell again and the maid appeared. "Today's newspapers, Polly."

Within minutes Polly reappeared carrying a selection of papers. "Read these," Mrs Crosby said. "Then we can discuss the issues of the day."

Nell picked up *The Illustrated London News* and began to read. The rest of the two hours was spent with her reading snippets from the society pages and Mrs Crosby relishing the gossip.

By the time she got back to the café with Robert dusk was falling. She popped in to see Lottie and get them both drinks to go with the meat pie she'd bought for their tea. She was surprised to see Josh there, waiting for her.

"It's all arranged," he said. "Ernie has volunteered to babysit Bobby this evening so we can go out." His eyes sparkled with mirth. "You don't mind Ernie looking after Bobby do you?"

Nell didn't know what to say. Ernie, Lottie's father, worked night shifts at the bakery, coming home early morning with bread and rolls for Lottie and then staying to cook the breakfasts. After breakfast he slept until midday in the upstairs room at the back next to Nell and Robert's room. She saw him now sitting at one of the tables.

"Ernie," she said. "Are you sure you don't mind?" She guessed Josh had persuaded him. He could be very persuasive and she hated to think he'd been pressed into doing something he didn't want to do, just so Josh could take her out. Going out in the evening wasn't something she missed, never having had the chance to do it before. Socialising wasn't included in the routine of the workhouse nor at the Manor, so she didn't think anything of it.

It was Lottie who spoke for Ernie. "He'd only be sitting in his own room, so might as well sit in yours," she said. "As long as you're back so he can get to the bakery before midnight."

"Ernie?" Nell said, touching his shoulder to make sure he understood the arrangements being made for him.

Lottie pulled Nell away. "He doesn't speak either," she whispered. "Not now. Not since he came back from the Crimea in '56. But he has all his other faculties. He can sit with Bobby and if there's any trouble I'll be here in the café. No reason you shouldn't go out and enjoy yourself for once."

Nell gasped in shock. Why hadn't she noticed that before? She thought back to Christmas, Ernie and Robert playing together with the clockwork drummer and a monkey that climbed up and down a ladder. She'd heard Robert chuckling and giggling, but now realised that she'd never heard Ernie speak in all the time she'd known him. No wonder he and Robert got on so well. They had a lot in common.

Perhaps an evening out with Josh would be fun, something that had been missing from her life since leaving the Manor. "If you're sure," she said.

"I'm sure," Lottie said.

Nell smiled. For the first time in her life she had friends she could rely on, people who felt like a family and something to look forward to. She blessed the day the cabbie had brought her to this place. For the first time ever she felt at home.

Chapter Nineteen

The next morning Mr Bradley asked her to visit a widow whose son was making arrangement for his father's funeral. "Mr Armitage, from the bank," he said. "Very sudden. His son came in yesterday, we're burying him on Friday." He gave her the address. "One of your best hats and an embroidered mantle," he said. "She's quite elderly and frail, so I hope your visit will go some way to help mitigate her loss. You can take the boy, I find young children always bring joy to those whose families have grown and moved away. Young Bobby should bring a smile to her face if nothing else."

It was true, Robert had a way about him, easy charm and the sort of dazzling smile that made everything else forgivable. The fact that he couldn't speak made him appear well mannered too.

That afternoon she took her cloth samples and some sketches of the style of hats she could make. Mrs Armitage lived in a grand house in a leafy road far enough off the beaten track to be fashionable. The butler showed Nell and Robert into a sitting room where Mrs Armitage was having tea.

"Bring another cup," she said to the butler, then, seeing Robert added, "and some milk for the child."

Nell sat Robert on a footstall with his sketch pad and a book while she went through the designs and fabrics, ribbons and veils suitable for a widow in mourning. It was imperative that the widow was seen to be properly grieving, so the hat and mantle were to be quite elaborate.

"Deep mourning," Mrs Armitage said. "I'm to be in deep mourning." She looked quite depressed about the prospect. "Society's rules must be obeyed," she said. "No matter how irritating and inconvenient."

Nell sympathised. The death of her husband meant Mrs Armitage would be unable to receive visitors or venture out to any engagements for at least three months, possibly longer. These days deep mourning had become de rigueur.

Mrs Armitage fingered the fabrics and looked over the designs. She dithered from one to the other as though unable to make up her mind. Nell realised that losing her husband must have been very distressing, so put her inattentiveness down to that.

"This would look good on you," or "What about this one," merely left Mrs Armitage gazing distractedly at the ceiling. Nell felt sure there was something else troubling her. It was as though she wanted to tell Nell something, but wasn't sure how to broach the subject. While they were having tea Nell decided to approach it straight on.

"Is there anything troubling you, Mrs Armitage? You seem a trifle preoccupied."

Mrs Armitage gazed at Nell. Then it all came tumbling out. "I didn't want to say anything, I mean it's not your fault I'm sure, but…" she sighed. "My son said not to make a fuss. He said I'd got it wrong, with the upset and everything, but I haven't, I know I haven't."

Unshed tears shone in her watery eyes. She looked so distressed Nell put her cup down and put her arm around her to comfort her. "Got what wrong? What is it? You must tell me."

"My husband's gold ring and his diamond tie pin. He was wearing them when he..." she paused and wiped a tear from her cheek. "When he... you know... Some men came to take him away. They left his gold watch and chain, but I haven't been able to find his ring or his diamond tie pin. It was his favourite. He always wore it when he went to work at the bank." She stared at Nell. "My son says I must be mistaken, that I've misplaced them. But I know I haven't."

Nell was appalled. It was possible that the ring and tie pin had been taken to the mortuary, but they should have then be returned with Mr Armitage's other effects. If they were busy they may have been overlooked. "Please, don't worry. I'm sure it's some sort of mistake. I'll mention it to Mr Bradley. If your husband's things have been taken I'm sure we'll be able to find them and return them," she said.

"Thank you, dear," Mrs Armitage said. "If you could just enquire. I don't want to accuse anyone but..."

"Don't worry. I'll sort it out," Nell said with more optimism than she felt. "Now, let's get on and chose a magnificent hat to impress your friends and show how deeply you mourn the loss of your loved one."

Mrs Armitage chuckled. "He was hardly that, but he was all I had, apart from my son, who's married and moved away. We rubbed along well enough together, so I suppose it's the least I can do for him."

By the time Mrs Armitage had chosen the style and fabrics for her head covering and short shoulder cape they had finished two pots of tea and a plate of sandwiches. The afternoon had gone in a flash, but Mrs Armitage's claim played on Nell's mind. She'd be sure to mention it to Mr Bradley on her return.

She packed up her things ready to leave when Robert tore off the drawing he'd been working on, an excellent likeness of Mrs Armitage. He presented it to her as a gift, his eyes shining, clearly in an attempt to cheer her up.

Mrs Armitage smiled. "Why that's wonderful," she said. "He's very talented for one so young." She touched his cheek. "Thank you, young man," she said. "I'll treasure it to remind me of the day I met a talented artist."

Robert grinned and Nell's heart swelled.

Nell spent the evening working on Mrs Armitage's mourning wear, but the fact she'd said some jewellery had gone missing was never far from her mind. The next morning she mentioned it to Mr Bradley. "There may have been some mistake," she said, not wanting to accuse anyone. "A mix up perhaps. But I told Mrs Armitage we'd look into it. She was very distressed."

Mr Bradley's face darkened. He glared at Nell. "I can't afford mistakes or mix ups of that nature," he said. "If people start complaining about things going missing it will damage our reputation." If he was trying to conceal his anger he did not succeed. Nell saw sparks of fury in his eyes. "I can't afford to upset people like Mrs Armitage. Any hint of scandal will go round her circle faster than a wheel on a runaway cart." He stormed out of the office into the yard. "Linus," he yelled.

Linus appeared wiping his hands on his woodworking apron, his lumpy face scowling deeper than usual.

"I've had a complaint," Mr Bradley said. "Mrs Armitage. You collected her husband on Monday. What happened to his personal effects?"

Linus stared at Mr Bradley, then at Nell who'd followed him out of the office. "Personal effects? Like what?"

"A gold ring and diamond tie pin he was wearing. Mrs Armitage says they haven't been returned to her," Nell said.

"And she's accusing me!" Linus's voice rose as a red glow climbed up his face. His eyes shot sparks of hatred at Nell. "We'll see about that. Goose, Charlie, come here," he bellowed.

Goose and Charlie came rushing over. "Mr Armitage on Monday. Either of you see a gold ring or diamond tie pin?"

Goose looked at Charlie, Charlie looked at Goose. Fear stretched their eyes. They both swallowed and shook their heads. "Not me, never saw owt," Charlie said.

Goose agreed. "Me neither," he said.

"Woman must've been mistaken," Linus said. "Making wild accusations like that. Probably dreamt it."

Nell wasn't convinced. "She was most insistent, mentioned the items in particular. Said he always wore them."

"Bereavement makes people say the oddest things," Linus said. "Go out of their minds with it some do."

"I think I'd best go and speak to her," Mr Bradley said. "Find out the truth of it. Don't want her spreading ugly rumours about our services do we?" He looked most agitated.

Linus's mouth twisted into a snarl. A bead of sweat ran down his face. "Could have been a mix up I suppose," he said. "I'll check with the mortuary."

Mr Bradley nodded. "Yes. Today please, Linus. Thank you."

Nell saw a vision of a worm wriggling off a hook as Linus walked away.

Later, just as she was getting ready to leave, Mr Bradley came into the shop. His face was white and he was shaking with rage. "Linus found these in a drawer at the mortuary," he said, showing Nell a heavy gold ring and a diamond tie pin. "He said it was Goose put them there. I can't think of any good reason he'd do that. When things go missing it casts a shadow over the whole establishment. I've left Linus to deal with him. It's unforgivable."

So, Nell thought, Goose was getting the blame. When she went into the yard to collect Robert she saw a woebegone Goose collecting his coat. He had a swollen eye and a graze on his cheek. "Goose, what happened to you?" she asked.

Goose turned away. "Nothing," he said. "Slipped and fell."

Nell knew better. She'd seen the difference between injuries caused by falls and those inflicted by fists. Anger swirled inside her. She was sure Linus was to blame, but she had no proof so said nothing. But it was something she'd never forget.

That afternoon, at Mrs Crosby's, she wasn't the only one troubled. Robert stared out of the window and didn't touch his sketch pad or his books. Nell recognised the signs of distress. The incident with Goose and Linus had obviously unsettled him. She hadn't seen him so upset for a long time. She wanted to talk to him about it, somehow put his mind at rest, but couldn't find the words. It wrung her heart all the same.

When she got back to the café Josh was there having his tea so they joined him. She told him about the missing jewellery and her suspicions about Linus Frumley. "If anyone's on the take it'll be him. Goose would never steal anything. I'd stake my life on it," she said.

"Goose?"

"He works at the yard looking after the hearses and carts. He's Bobby's friend, isn't he?" she said to Robert. "He's been good to him and I'm sure he's honest as the day is long."

Josh shook his head. "I'm sure you're right," he said. "I've had my run-ins with Linus Frumley, but I can't interfere in my father's business. It's up to him who he employs."

"It's Goose I feel sorry for," Nell said. "I'm sure Linus blamed him and beat him to keep him keep quiet and not to tell on him. It just the sort of thing he would do."

Josh grimaced. "I can see you're upset about it. I'll have a word with Pa and see what I can do. Leave it with me," he said.

Nell was happy to do so.

The next morning Robert was up and staring out of the window as usual when Nell awoke, but for once he hadn't got washed and dressed. She immediately felt alert. This was so unusual as to be remarkable. It wasn't like Robert to step out of his routine. A dull ache of trepidation squeezed her stomach.

"Not dressed yet, sweetheart?" she said. "We'll be late for breakfast if we don't hurry up."

She went to the chair where she'd left his clothes ready folded for him when she put him to bed. The chair was empty. She opened the drawers where his clean clothes were kept. They too were empty. She breathed a sigh. He'd hidden his clothes because he didn't want to go back to the yard. He must have seen Linus beating Goose and it frightened him. Would he be next she wondered?

She looked under the bedcovers, in the dresser, and under the table. They weren't there but it reminded her of the hide and seek games they used to play at the Manor. She turned him away from the window and made the sign for 'game'.

He shook his head, his little face white with sadness, his cheeks wet with silent tears. Her heart retched.

"Okay, I'll send a note. We won't go today, but we will have to go back tomorrow. I need the money to pay the rent. Do you understand?"

He stared at her his blue eyes brimming with sorrow. Suddenly realisation of the enormity of the change she'd inflicted on this young boy hit her. What had she brought them to? It had never been her intention to put his life or limb in danger, but that is what faced them now.

"I'm sorry," she said. "I'll find something else. I'll tell Mr Bradley I can't stay, not with you in the yard with that horrible man. I'll sort something out, I promise."

Silently Robert went and pulled his clothes out from under the bed where he'd hidden them. He got dressed and they went downstairs to breakfast.

Chapter Twenty

As promised Nell sent a note to Mr Bradley saying she wouldn't be at work today but hoped to return tomorrow. It meant a loss of the day's wage but the order for Mrs Armitage would more than make up for that.

"I heard there was trouble at the funeral parlour," Lottie said as she served Nell their breakfast. "Mr Bradley's got a heart of gold, never sees the bad side of anyone, but I never did trust that Linus Frumley. I hope's as how you're keeping a good eye on 'im."

Nell smiled. "I try to keep out of his way," she said.

While they had their breakfasts Nell studied the newspaper columns for possible openings that didn't mean living-in or domestic service. She had nimble fingers, nursing experience and wasn't afraid of hard work. There must be something she could do to earn enough to keep them without putting Robert in danger. She'd be looking for somewhere they wouldn't ask too many questions either.

After a fruitless search she left the paper for Lottie to add to the pages on the counter for her customers and decided to deliver Mrs Armitage's order personally. The funeral was the next day.

The weather was brightening, the late February sun giving some welcome warmth. She held Robert's hand as they walked, admiring the impressive buildings they passed. They arrived at Mrs Armitage's just before eleven, the perfect time to call.

The butler showed her into a small front room while he went to inform Mrs Armitage of her visit. When he returned Nell and Robert followed him into the parlour where Nell was taken aback to see Mrs Armitage having coffee with Mr Bradley. Her heart sank. How could she explain her non-attendance at work when here she was in perfect health visiting one of his clients during working hours?

"Bring another cup and some milk for the child," Mrs Armitage said and motioned Nell to sit beside her. "Look what Mr Bradley has found." She showed Nell the gold ring and tie pin that had miraculously appeared when she'd mentioned their loss to Mr Bradley.

"A mix up at the mortuary," Mr Bradley said. "Soon sorted. No harm done."

Nell wasn't so sure. Robert glared.

A parlour maid appeared with an extra cup and some milk and Mrs Armitage insisted Nell join them for coffee. "Mr Bradley's just telling me about the final arrangements for the funeral tomorrow," Mrs Armitage said. "My son will be chief mourner at the head of the procession. I'm to travel in a carriage behind the hearse." She clasped her neck, tears sprang to her eyes. "I'm not sure I can face it," she said. "The people, the fuss..."

Nell put her hand on her arm to comfort her. "You'll be fine," she said. "Just think of it as the last thing you can do for your husband. Let other people see the respect in which he was held."

Mrs Armitage sighed. "I'm sure you're right, dear. You're such a comfort." She took a sip from the glass on the side table beside her. Nell recognised the smell of gin. "I don't suppose… no it's too much to ask… silly of me."

"What?"

"I don't suppose you and your boy would be willing to accompany me in the carriage," she said. "I'd feel so much better if I had someone by my side, someone to lean on. Someone to provide reassurance."

Before Nell could answer Mr Bradley leaned forward, put his cup on the tray and said, "Of course Miss Drummond may accompany you. Splendid idea. All part of the service." He looked quite pleased to be able to provide the additional facility.

"Oh, thank you. Thank you so much. I will rest easy tonight knowing I'll have company to see me through tomorrow's ordeal."

"I'll leave you to sort out the garments and the arrangements," Mr Bradley said. "Your carriage will arrive to collect you all at ten o'clock." He stood, bade them good day and left.

Nell didn't know what to say. Riding in the carriage with Mrs Armitage would be easy enough and, on the plus side, it meant that Robert would not have to go to the yard in the morning, so that made her happy.

They spent the rest of the morning discussing the outfit Mrs Armitage would wear. She was thrilled with the fine hat and ornately embroidered mantle Nell had prepared. Nell breathed a sigh of relief as she left the house. She took Robert to the river so he could watch the boats and they could enjoy a cup of hot chocolate together.

Friday morning Nell dressed Robert in a new white shirt and the black mourning suit Mr Bradley had sent round from the funeral parlour. She put on her dark blue suit, funeral sash and a fetching black straw hat decorated with black silk flowers, ribbons and feathers. Then, after breakfast they walked to Mrs Armitage's home arriving just before ten. From the house they were to travel to the chapel of rest and from there follow the hearse to the church. Mrs Armitage would say her last farewells to her husband and then return to her home where the men would join the small gathering after the interment.

"Thank goodness it's not thought proper for us women to attend the actual burial," Mrs Armitage said. "I'm sure I wouldn't be able to bear it."

"Will you be all right?" Nell asked, as they sat in the carriage.

Mrs Armitage smiled. "When this is all over you mean?"

"Yes. It will be quite a change for you living alone. I suspect your husband was a formidable presence."

"Indeed he was," Mrs Armitage said. "A *force majeure*. Yes, I miss him already, but I will adjust as we all have to when our circumstance change so dramatically, as you no doubt appreciate." She bowed her head.

Nell smiled. Yes, Mrs Armitage wasn't the only one who'd had to adjust to changing circumstances. She thought again of the vast change she'd brought about to Robert's lifestyle. Like Mrs Armitage, it wasn't what she wanted, but sometimes fate intervenes, and there is no going back.

After the funeral service Nell and Robert accompanied Mrs Armitage home, then left her to grieve amid her friends and acquaintances. It was Friday and she was expected at Mrs Crosby's that afternoon.

Released from the solemnity of the funeral, Nell and Robert hurried home to change. Nell put on her brightest shawl and bonniest hat in a gesture of defiance at that imposter death. She hadn't known Mr Armitage, but she felt a strange despair at his passing. She supposed it was seeing his widow left so rudderless and alone. A man in that position would have his club, his friends, his business acquaintances and continue to be welcomed in society, whereas a widow is confined to her home and only permitted to meet with her closest female friends. Any pleasures must be severely curtailed lest society be shocked by her outrageous behaviour.

She bought a pie from Lottie for their lunch and cups of coffee, then walked to the park to sit in the afternoon sun. After lunch a brisk walk to Mrs Crosby's quickly dispelled her gloomy mood. Mrs Crosby was always good company and she enjoyed her stories and society gossip. In return Mrs Crosby wanted to hear Nell's tales from the workhouse, so the afternoons were spent in pleasant and often hilarious revelations.

Nell pulled the screens around Mrs Crosby as usual and attended to the dressing on her leg. "This is looking so much better," she said, surveying the ulcer which appeared to be healing over. Does it cause you much pain?"

"Not so much it can't be dulled by a few glasses of gin," Mrs Crosby said chuckling. "But I'm pleased to hear I'm on the mend. You have magic fingers, my dear. I'm very grateful to you for your care."

After finishing the dressing, Nell folded back the screen and Robert came to sit on a footstall while they had tea.

Drinking her tea and chatting to Mrs Crosby, Nell didn't hear Mr Crosby enter the room. Shock stole her breath when she saw him standing there and realised he'd been there quite a while watching Robert as he sketched. Her heart hammered. She'd allowed him to think Robert was her son, but had he now had second thoughts? Had he seen the story in the paper and made a connection between the well mannered boy who didn't speak and the Earl's missing son? She'd told him she'd been in service and it was obvious she'd worked as a nursemaid. Was her carefully constructed charade about to be torn apart?

"Come along, Bobby," she said, emphasising his name. "It's time we went home."

Mr Crosby stepped forward. "Please don't go on my account. I was just admiring your nephew's drawing," he said. "He's captured my mother's expression exquisitely. Look, Mother." He took Robert's sketch pad from his hands to show his mother.

His mother smiled. "A very good likeness," she said. "The boy has talent."

"Is the picture for sale?" Mr Crosby asked.

Nell shook her head. "No. He draws for pleasure not reward," she said. "Come along, Bobby."

Robert stared at her, the look on his face more eloquent than words. He drew a large letter 'R' on the corner of the drawing, the letter he recognised as his initial, tore the page from the pad and handed it to the man. He held out his hand, palm upwards.

Milton Crosby chuckled and put a shilling into Robert's outstretched palm. "Thank you, young man," he said. "I have a small gallery in town, I could exhibit this there." He held the torn out page up. "Yes, properly framed this would be easily saleable. He's signed it with an 'R'. What does that stand for?"

Quick as a flash Nell said, "Robinson. His name's Bobby Robinson. He's my married sister's child. Orphaned. That's why I'm taking care of him."

Robert glared.

"Talent like this should be nurtured, not ignored," Mr Crosby said. "Does he have any schooling?"

"Only what I can teach him," Nell said.

"He doesn't attend school then?"

"He's only seven," she said. "A bit too young yet."

"I see." Milton Crosby frowned. "I know a young artist who could help him refine his skills. If you would allow it of course."

Nell swallowed. Robert tugged at her sleeve, his eyes pleading. "I can't afford..."

"If I could see some of your nephew's other pictures I might find a place for them in my gallery as well. Of course they'd need proper mounting and framing, but I could get a good price for them." He paused. "They'd sell better with a little pastel colouring, something to bring the pictures to life." He hunkered down in front of Robert. "Ever used pastels, Bobby? Or paints?"

Robert stared at him.

"No," Nell said, her irritation mounting at his suggestion. "I'm afraid my budget doesn't stretch to more than pencils and paper and Bobby's always been quite satisfied with those. Come along, Bobby, we have to be going now."

Mr Crosby stood up. "I'm sorry, I didn't mean to upset you, but I think your nephew could benefit from some tuition. It's a shame to let a talent like his go to waste."

"Out of the question," Nell said. "I'm afraid our circumstances..."

"Please, if you would allow it I would like to sponsor him. The lessons would be invaluable and I take considerable pleasure in nurturing talent. If he proves as good a student as I imagine, seeing his improvement would be my reward."

Nell didn't know what to think. Robert tugged at her sleeve again. He stared at her, eyes wide and full of hope. Obviously the chance to sell some of his drawings and learn how to do them better appealed to him. He wasn't stupid. In fact, he was just the opposite. "I'll give it some thought," she said and grabbed Robert's hand. "I'll let you know."

Chapter Twenty One

On the way home Nell thought about what Mr Crosby had said about Robert's schooling. Robert was still seven, but in a couple of months he would be eight. Boys of eight had to attend school unless they were privileged to enjoy private schooling. It was the law. Nell did what she could and felt sure he could read simple texts, count and add up but he'd only learned through constant repetition. Learning with Nell would be very different from learning in a class of rowdy boys who'd laugh and make fun of him. She'd helped teach the little ones in the workhouse and knew how cruel children could be to those weaker or more vulnerable than themselves. The thought of Robert being sent to school, unable to speak and defend himself terrified her. She'd heard that pupils were often beaten if they didn't obey the teacher. It would be a nightmare for Robert. Worse still, they could send him away to a Deaf and Dumb Asylum where he'd have to sew shirts for the rest of his life and she'd never see him again. Tears welled up in her eyes at the thought. She'd die rather than let that happen.

Robert was small for his age and could easily pass for seven for another year. She had no record of his birth, although she was sure there would have been one, but it would be for Robert Eversham, oldest son of Lord Eversham. Nothing to do with Bobby Robinson, her nephew. His birth wasn't registered anywhere. At least that gave her some reassurance, but she wasn't sure how long she'd be able to keep him out of the clutches of the school authorities. It was something she'd have to worry about in the future.

Still, Robert was getting older and she felt guilty that he wasn't learning more. Perhaps she should broaden his education. She decided to go to the market and look out for some books for him. She needed hat shapes and silks in any case and she could see Lydia and pick up some books for Robert. Then they could look at them together.

At the entrance to the market Robert tugged at her dress and made the sign she'd taught him for 'home'.

"Oh all right," she said. She knew he hated the noisy, crowded market. He'd fidget and pull her sleeve to hurry her up when she perused the stalls and did her bits of shopping. Often he'd just stand with his hands over his ears. It was a sign he was getting distressed. If she wanted to avoid a tantrum it was best to move on.

"You can go on home, but wait for me in the café." She gave him the money for a cup of hot chocolate. Lottie would know what he wanted when he gave her the money. He only had to smile his beguiling smile and she'd have given it to him for nothing, but Nell didn't want to feel more obliged to her than she already was.

She was pleased to see a brisk trade going on at the hat stall in the market. Lydia greeted her warmly. "I'm glad to see you today," she said. "I could do with some more of your lovely roses to make Easter bonnets for the ladies. They turn the plain straw hats into something special."

Nell was happy to oblige. It didn't pay that well, but it was steady work and Nell was happy to sit and make the flowers in the evenings. She had nothing else to do once Robert was in bed and the extra money would go towards the books for him.

She bought the coloured silks and thread she would need and then went to look for the books. Most of the editions on the stall were well read and rather tatty. Seeing the state of the books brought memories of the beautiful books in the library at the Manor. While Miss Bannister had been away with the girls she'd had the opportunity to pick books from there, both for herself and to read to Robert. Books were an escape and took them into a different world, a world where lack of speech and being 'different' were no barriers to enjoyment. Miss Bannister had never said she couldn't use the library, but being confined to the nursery made it difficult. She wished now that she'd thought to bring books with them, but of course, destined for the hospital that would not have been possible.

She picked out the best simple arithmetic and spelling books she could find. "Are these the best you have?" she asked.

"For now," he said. "Was you looking for anything particular? I got some nice Dickens coming in."

"Children's books?"

He shook his head. "Nah. Don't get many o' them. Your best bet is the bookshop at the church," he said. "Lots of illustrated children's books there."

"Thank you, I'll give them a try," she said and made a mental note to do so before she made her way home, collecting Robert from the café on the way.

Indoors, while she made tea, she sat Robert down with one of the books, solving sums and counting. Then, after tea she let him choose the book she'd read to him. He chose *Treasure Island*. It was his favourite.

That evening Nell worked on the silk roses, but her mind was never far away from thinking about her work at the funeral parlour and what had happened to Goose. Robert's reaction to it also played on her mind. They'd have to go back in the morning. She relied on the money she earned to pay the rent. She'd have to explain that to Robert, it was another thing she'd taken away from him, the freedom to spend the day playing however he wished. She consoled herself with the thought that his family had planned to take a greater freedom from him, so perhaps she shouldn't feel so bad.

The next morning she was surprised to see Goose sitting in the café with Josh. Josh stood and ushered them into a seat at their table. Robert rushed up and hugged Goose. Goose's expression flitted between embarrassment and pleasure. Nell realised of course that Robert had never had friends before, never learnt how to greet them, or treat them. He had little social grace, but a great deal of spontaneity. Still, the delight on his face filled her with joy.

Josh laughed. Nell sat Robert in the seat opposite Goose, where he immediately got out his sketch pad and started to draw him.

"You're very privileged," Nell said. "He only draws people he likes." She laughed, then thought of the picture of Josh hanging on her wall. A blush rose in her face, but she hid it by going to get their breakfasts.

When she returned to the table with two plates of steaming boiled ham, egg and bread and butter, Josh said, "I've spoken to Pa. He knows Linus can be a bit heavy handed with the boys, and he's got a temper, but he's the best carpenter and carver around for miles. Not right what he did to Goose, but at least he didn't sack him. He could have you know."

Nell nodded. Of course Goose needed the job the same as everyone else. He was the oldest of six boys and his mother depended on his wage. He couldn't afford to leave any more than Nell could.

"Goose will be in charge of the carriages, hearses and carts from now on. He'll work in the yard, not the workshop and Bobby will help him, so neither of them need spend their time in the workshop with Linus."

Nell's heart lifted. "Really? Did you hear that, Bobby? You'll be working on the carriages and hearses with Goose. Won't that be good? I reckon they'll be the shiniest carriages in all of London."

"You can bet on it," Goose said with a grin.

She couldn't tell Josh how relieved she was. "I can't thank you enough," she said. "And Bobby thanks you too."

Josh smiled. "Well there is something you could do for me," he said.

"Yes?"

"I've got tickets to see Marie Lloyd at the Alhambra tonight. You could come with me."

Nell's eyebrows rose in surprise. She'd seen the poster advertising the show at the Alhambra Music Hall, but they came at a price and were hard to get.

"How did you get those?" she said.

Josh winked. "I know a few people," he said, but wouldn't elaborate. "Ernie's agreed to babysit, and tomorrow, if the weather's good, I thought we might take Bobby and Goose to the zoo." Robert looked up from his breakfast and nodded his agreement.

"What about the market?" Nell said. Sundays were the busiest day of the week for the traders.

"All covered," he said.

"Well, I can hardly refuse then can I?" she said.

"See you tonight," Josh said as they were leaving.

Nell nodded. Josh had to go to the market but Nell walked with Goose and Robert. Once Robert knew Goose was going to the yard he was happy to go there too.

After work Nell took Robert to Hyde Park to see the horses and carriages and the gentry displaying their finery. A cool breeze rustled the leaves of the trees where pale sunlight dappled the grass. Nell saw patches of blue between the clouds in a pearl sky. She buttoned Robert's coat and tied his muffler around him against the cold. They watched the horses for a while, then found a café where they had afternoon tea. Nell wanted the day to be memorable for Robert. She had the evening to look forward to.

Josh came to collect Nell at seven o'clock, bringing Ernie with him.

"We'll be back by eleven," Nell said, remembering that Ernie had to get to his job at the bakery by midnight.

Ernie nodded. Nell left him scones, tea and books he could read while Robert slept. She kissed Robert goodnight and tucked him in. She stroked his head. He always looked so angelic when he slept, part of her wanted to stay, but only a very small part.

Butterflies danced in her stomach as she walked along to the theatre on Josh's arm. It was a pleasant evening, the gaslights gave an amber glow giving the street an eerie intimate atmosphere. The last time Nell had been out in the evening was at Christmas when they'd all gone to the Crown and Anchor. She recalled a jolly evening and how popular Josh had been with the ladies. She also recalled the brush of his lips against hers when he said good night. Warmth flowed through her at the thought of what lay ahead.

In the theatre Nell gazed around at the opulent surroundings. The theatre was packed and the Saturday night crowd rowdy, but Nell didn't care. Below the high, domed ceiling, deep crimson drapes, fringed with gold, curtained the ornately decorated boxes set out between gloriously frescoed walls. The stage was brightly lit and she watched enthralled as one after another the singers and dancers entertained.

That evening was the happiest Nell could remember. Marie Lloyd on stage was as saucy as her reputation and Nell laughed until her sides almost split. It was a joyous, uplifting experience, one she realised she'd been desperately in need of. In the atmosphere of the theatre all her troubles melted away and she found herself singing along to the popular songs. She thought of

Flossie who first introduced her to the songs bursting with innuendo, but which could also be sung in all innocence.

She imagined Flossie singing along with her, she'd have been in her element. She recalled the sparkle that filled her eyes when she talked about the theatre, her glory days on the stage and the magic of the performance, and Nell suddenly understood the deep emotion it aroused inside her when she spoke of it. "Once a performer, always a performer," Flossie used to say. It was another world and one Nell was happy to be transported to, even for such a short while. Her face ached from smiling. By the time they left the theatre Nell's head buzzed with excitement.

After the performance Josh bought a plate of oysters to eat as they walked home. Holding his arm it felt magical. When they got to her door he stroked her face. "Good night, Lily," he said.

Nell froze. Her heart stuttered. Of course, he thought she was Lily, the milliner's daughter, guardian of an orphaned boy. She'd been playing the part so long she'd forgotten that no one knew the truth. No one knew who she really was; the runaway nursemaid who'd kidnapped the son of an Earl. A woman who'd be hanged if she was ever found out. How long would she be able to keep her secret from him? What would he think when he found out the truth? She couldn't afford to get involved with him, it would be madness.

"I'll see you tomorrow," he said.

"Tomorrow?"

"The zoo."

"Oh, yes, of course, the zoo."

He bent forward and kissed her cheek. "I'll look forward to it," he said.

"Yes, me too," she managed to whisper as her heart somersaulted into her stomach.

What on earth was she going to do now?

Chapter Twenty Two

The next morning Nell wondered whether to send a note to Josh saying Bobby was ill and they'd be unable to go with him and Goose to the zoo. It would be an easy way out, although Lottie was bound to suspect something and she couldn't keep Robert locked up in the room all day. She'd feel bad about letting Josh down too, especially when he'd gone to so much trouble.

The April sun was shining, the sky was blue, so she decided she'd have to go, but she'd try to keep her exchanges with Josh to a minimum. "Come on, Robert, today we are going to the zoo," she said.

"Won't that be fun?" Meanwhile her heart was pounding.

Josh and Goose were already waiting when they went down to the café for breakfast. Both of them looked smart in their best suits and Josh wore a bowler hat. Goose wore his cap, but it was clear they'd both made an effort. After breakfast Lottie brought them a hamper she'd made up for the picnic. Nell insisted on paying her half which almost led to her first argument with Josh.

"Are you trying to insult me?" he asked when she offered him the money.

"No. I'm trying to pay my way. I don't want to be beholden to anyone," she said, which was a bit rich after he'd treated her to the theatre the night before. "I'll pay for me and Bobby."

"I'll not take your money," Josh said. "I invited you. You'll spoil my pleasure if you don't let me treat you and Bobby."

"It's only lunch," Nell said. "As for the rest…"

Josh shrugged and cast her a quizzical glance, but took the money she offered.

Walking around the zoo in the sunshine Nell felt a different person. She was able to put her worries behind her and enjoy the animals. Whenever she felt Josh getting a little too close she'd run off and look into one of the cages, feigning a sudden interest in that particular animal.

She saw him smiling once or twice at her antics, but he'd turn to Robert and make a fuss of him instead.

She found it easy to walk with Goose and talk to him as a way of keeping a distance between her and Josh. Goose talked about his family and his widowed mother.

"That's how I got the job at the funeral parlour," he said. "Mr Bradley buried my pa and Ma would have been left destitute if it hadn't have been for Mr Bradley taking me on. Mr Bradley saved us from the workhouse. That's why I'd never do owt to hurt 'im." He grimaced. "Wouldn't steal from 'im neither."

"You didn't put Mr Armitage's jewellery into a drawer at the mortuary did you?" Nell said.

"No. Linus took it."

Nell had thought as much.

They stopped and had their picnic, then Josh took Goose and Robert to see the animals being fed. Robert drew an elephant, which Nell guessed was his favourite. She bought them all ice creams, which almost started another argument with Josh.

"You must allow me to treat you and the boys," she said, "or you'll spoil my pleasure."

So Josh relented. She enjoyed the day, but by the time they were ready to go home the sky had clouded over and Nell saw only grey.

Monday Nell put her things into her bag ready to take to Mrs Crosby's. Robert handed her his sketch pad. The question shone in his eyes. She swallowed. It was as though she could read his thoughts. "I don't know, sweetheart," she said. "I'm not sure it's such a good idea." She wasn't even sure Mr Crosby meant it. He could have just been being kind, although he sounded convincing when he'd mentioned the lessons to hone Robert's skill.

Robert continued to stare silently at her until her defences crumbled. "I'll have a look, perhaps one or two…"

Flipping through the sketch pad she saw that some drawings had more appeal than others. Some were brief outlines, but several were quite detailed, like the picture of Mrs Crosby, done in a couple of hours in the afternoon. There were pictures of boats on the river, Goose, Linus and Mr Bradley, all easily recognisable. There were several of her too. He'd made her look beautiful. Warmth washed over her and a broad smile stretched her face, but she removed them. In the circumstance it wouldn't be wise to have her face on the wall of the gallery, lovely as the pictures were. She couldn't afford to take any chances.

In the end she chose a picture of Lottie in the café, one of the boats on the river and another of the skating in Regent's Park at Christmas. "I'll take these and see what Mr Crosby thinks," she said.

She wanted to warn him not to get his hopes up, but the eager look on his face and the hope in his eyes stopped her. He looked so small and vulnerable. Love squeezed her heart. He was too young to realise how cruel the world could be and living as he had at the Manor he'd been sheltered from it. But she hadn't. The harsh reality of years in Salvation Hall House had shown her that deprivation and disillusionment went hand in hand. She'd learned early in life that any hopes or dreams she dared to entertain would soon be beaten out of her. She wanted above everything to shield him from the heartbreak that comes with disappointment.

She waited until tea was served to mention Robert's drawing to Mrs Crosby. "Your son did say..."

Mrs Crosby smiled. "The drawings, yes, Milton was very keen on them. He said young Bobby had managed to capture my personality as well as my likeness. Of course, I'm too blind to see it..."

Nell took the pages she'd selected out of her bag. "Perhaps you could pass these on to him to have a look at."

"He's away until Friday. Why don't you bring them again then? He'll be here and you can ask him yourself."

"Thank you, I'll do that," Nell said, relieved that at least he was willing to look at them. Perhaps it would be all right after all.

For the rest of the afternoon Nell told Mrs Crosby about her visit to the theatre to see Marie Lloyd, although she didn't mention Josh, merely saying she'd been with a friend. Mrs Crosby was always interested in Nell's stories of life in the workhouse, so she told her about Flossie. "She always managed to raise my spirits when things got bad," she said. "She taught me the musical hall songs and made me laugh. I don't know how I'd have coped without her." Even as she spoke the memories of Flossie ran through her mind bringing the sting of tears to her eyes.

Mrs Crosby patted her hand. "It's good to know there is kindness in the world," she said. "We see so much of the other. God rest her soul."

When Nell read the society pages Mrs Crosby added titbits of gossip to each story. It was a happy and uplifting afternoon.

On Wednesday Nell was again at Mrs Crosby's house with Robert. After dressing her leg, which was almost healed, she started to read from the society pages of *The London Illustrated News.* There were articles about outings and events which often involved people Nell had seen attending the balls and parties at the Manor. Nell enjoyed reading these out and chuckled along with Mrs Crosby at the tales she was able to add about the people concerned. She usually had a bit of gossip to impart. 'Things you don't read in the papers' she called them.

Then, to her horror Nell saw a picture of Lord and Lady Eversham with the family standing on the front lawn of Inglebrook Manor. Martha and Ellen were there with Lord Eversham's mother. The caption beneath the picture read: '*Lord and Lady Eversham celebrate the Christening of their son Reginald Arthur George Eversham.'* Nell stared in disbelief. She could hardly breathe.

"Who's that in the picture?" Mrs Crosby asked, screwing up her eyes to try to make it out. "Read it to me."

Nell tried to turn the page, but Mrs Crosby stopped her. "You haven't read it yet," she said. "Read all of it."

Nell had no option but to obey and started to read. As soon as she uttered the words; *Lord and Lady Eversham,* Robert's head lifted from the book he was looking at. He jumped down from his chair and wandered over.

"Lord Eversham?" Mrs Crosby said. A smile lit up her face. "I knew his first wife, you know. Lovely lady. What was her name?"

Nell shrugged.

"Lady Caroline, that was it. She was the daughter of the Duke of somewhere. Where was it now? Lovely lady."

Mrs Crosby closed her eyes and appeared lost in memory. Then her eyes sprang open, her face saddened. "She died, you know. Tragic it was," she said.

Nell's heart hammered. A pain like a tight band squeezed her chest. She wanted to turn the page but Robert's head pressed against her shoulder prevented her. He peered at the newspaper. Surely he wouldn't connect the picture to his past. But then, he did have a phenomenal memory. He tugged at her sleeve. She turned and saw his questioning, blue eyes filled with bewilderment. He pointed to the picture. Confusion creased his brow. He made the sign for 'home' and stared inquisitively at her.

She had no answer for him. Fortunately Mrs Crosby hadn't noticed so she said, "Home, yes, almost time to go home. Collect your things." She closed the paper. "I promised Bobby I'd take him to the park to feed the ducks," she said. "I'll call again Friday. You said your son would be home?"

Mrs Crosby looked cross, but she couldn't see well enough to see the time so Nell felt sure she'd get away with it. She just wanted to get Robert out of there before he demanded a closer look at the paper.

"Yes. I'll mention it to him," Mrs Crosby said.

Nell folded the paper and put it in her bag to read later when Robert was safely asleep. The christening played on her mind. She could think of nothing else all the way home. Was there any mention of his missing son? What else did the paper say? She couldn't wait to find out.

So the new baby had been christened. She wondered about Robert's christening. Had that been a grand affair, featured in the papers' society pages? She recalled the christening cup still in the drawer together with the other gifts. 'Gifts from the family' Jenny had said. Where were those family members now? Had they forgotten about Robert as well? Anger seethed inside her.

The rest of the evening, watching Robert playing with his toys while she worked on the silk flowers she'd sell to Lydia, she couldn't stop thinking about the paper in her bag. The memory of what she'd read smouldered like red hot coals in her brain. She pricked her finger more than once, her mind was so distracted. She daren't take it out, not until Robert was in bed. Even then, she'd wait until she was sure he was asleep.

She prepared their tea and ate it in a trance of despair. While she read Robert a story her mind kept wandering back to it. She only felt able to breathe again when she'd tucked him up in bed and waited until he'd drifted off.

Once Robert was safely asleep, Nell turned up the lamp, opened the paper and read the article. She scanned it to see if Robert was mentioned. He wasn't. No reference was made to Lord Eversham having an older son. His daughters, Martha and Ellen, his parents and Lady Eversham's mother, an eminent American socialite, were all in attendance.

According to the paper it was a joyous occasion, celebrating the safe delivery of a son. What about his first born son? Nell wondered. Did he ever think of him? Was the death of his wife so great a loss that he couldn't bear to look at him? Did he ever love him or care about his wellbeing? Memories of her time at Inglebrook Manor ran through her brain. She couldn't ever remember Lord Eversham asking after Robert, not once did he enquire about his health or any progress he may be making. He wasn't the child Lord Eversham had hoped for. He'd caused the death of his mother. He was 'a difficult child, prone to fits of uncontrollable temper who couldn't even speak'. Worse of all he was 'different'. Even then it was as though he wished Robert didn't exist.

Fury swirled inside Nell. Not so much at the celebration of a christening, which was always cause for joy, but at the way Robert had been erased from the picture as though he had never been born.

A conversation she'd overheard when slipping out through the kitchen garden to retrieve Robert's wooden horse, came into her mind. Lady Eversham was sitting just beyond the gate with her brother.

"We can't allow that simple-minded mute to become the next Lord Eversham," George said. "Not when you have given birth to a son who could take his place."

That was the reason he was to be locked away in what Matron called 'society's dustbin'.

Nell paced the room, her fury mounting. She recalled the impulse that had made her walk past the waiting hansoms at the station, which she'd been instructed to take to the address they'd written down for her. It was merely to save Robert from the future his stepmother had planned for him.

She'd felt sick when she saw the address on the letter she'd been given to take to the hospital. She recognised it. It was an asylum for the mentally ill. She'd read about it in one of Matron's medical journals which had gone on to describe adults and children who were violent, mischievous and incoherent of speech as suffering from 'mania and moral insanity'. She shuddered at the memory.

She knew of women who'd been removed from the workhouse and taken to asylums merely for disobedience and unwillingness to conform to what the workhouse Master described as 'proper moral behaviour'. Matron said asylums were filled with mankind's human debris, the inmates a rag-bag of social misfits, the chronically disturbed or simply those who'd become an embarrassment to their families. Nell guessed Robert fitted into the last category. And because of that this sweet little boy could be certified insane and be locked away forever like Mr Rochester's wife in her favourite novel.

All she'd wanted then was to give him a better life. Now she realised she wanted far more for him. She wanted him to be recognised for the bright, talented, amazing person he was. She wanted him to be able to claim his rightful place in society with all the trappings of the wealthy lifestyle to which he was entitled.

She mused on her ambition. She'd kept his monogrammed shirts, his best blue suit, his mother's locket and the christening cup engraved with his name. All these things could be used to prove his identity, but not before he came of age. Then, and only then, she'd be able to tell him of his past, his family and his entitlement.

If they'd succeeded in having him confined to an institution for the mentally ill he'd have been classified as a 'patient' – an unfortunate who would have no control over his life or the decisions being made about it. If she could keep him from that fate until he came of age no one could make decisions on his behalf. He'd be his own master. He may not be best able to make those decisions now, but in time she was sure he'd grow up and mature and who knew what his future may hold. At least he'd have a chance to find out for himself.

Chapter Twenty Three

Nell tore the page out of the paper, folded it and put it in the drawer with the rest of Robert's belongings. She pushed it to the back of her mind, but it would never be forgotten. There was nothing she could do about it now, but she'd keep it to show Robert when he was old enough to learn about his background and claim his inheritance. It was his birthright and she'd move heaven and earth, if that's what it took, to make sure he wouldn't miss out. She was determined to keep him safe until then.

She put the rest of the paper in the rubbish bag with the blood-stained pieces of silk she'd ruined by pricking her finger, tied the bag closed and took it down to put out for collection.

The next morning everyone at the funeral parlour was on tenterhooks. The two funerals which were to take place were of eminent citizens and would be attended by the cream of society. Mr Bradley himself took charge. Nothing was allowed to be forgotten or misplaced. Goose and Robert would be kept busy in the yard making sure the panels on the hearse and the carriage gleamed, the wheels were spotless and the windows bright. Nell was to prepare the bills, listing all the expenses and Linus and Charlie were dressed in black ready as pall-bearers. At ten o'clock the horses were brought from the stables, harnesses gleaming, to be hitched to the hearse and the carriage.

Tension filled the air and heightened Nell's senses so when she heard Linus shouting in the workshop a swell of dread swirled in her stomach. Was Robert the poor unfortunate feeling the lash of his tongue? She couldn't stop herself dashing out to see what was causing the furore. She breathed a sigh of relief when she saw Linus arguing with an elderly, scraggy man dressed in a brown suit. Wisps of grey hair poked out beneath the stranger's felt hat. The man's pasty, lined face creased into a scowl his eyes shone with spite. Bony fingers jabbed at Linus as the man said something Nell couldn't make out. Linus turned and saw her. A look of pure evil filled his face. He pushed the man away. "You've come to the wrong place," he yelled.

The man shook his head but, seeing Nell, he turned and walked away. "I'll be back," he snarled as he stomped angrily out of the workshop.

Linus turned to Nell. "What do want? Had an eyeful have you? Get out of my workshop. You're not wanted here." Nell was happy to obey. Thank goodness Robert wasn't there, she thought, and once again gave silent thanks to Josh for his intervention.

That afternoon she put the argument out of her head and took Robert to sit by the river where he could draw the passing boats.

Friday morning, Nell put four of Robert's pictures into her bag. Mrs Crosby had said her son would be home and, although butterflies fluttered in her stomach at the thought, she decided Robert deserved some encouragement. He had little else going for him. She'd agree to his lessons too. She had a little cash coming in from the silk flowers she sold to Lydia, so if she had to pay for Robert's lessons she could even do that.

When they arrived at the funeral parlour Nell was relieved to find there was no sign of Linus. One of the other lads was at the bench carving the scrolls and fittings to go onto the caskets for the best customers. Goose had been sent out on an errand, so Robert was set to polishing the hearse on this own. Nell watched as he polished the black panels until they shone, amazed that he took such pride in his work, or was it because he was afraid of falling foul of Linus, that he applied himself so steadfastly?

In the afternoon they went to Mrs Crosby's and Nell dressed her leg as usual. Nell had just poured the tea brought in by Polly, the parlour maid, when Mr Crosby arrived. He rang for Polly to bring another cup and joined them. Nell thought it a good opportunity to mention Robert's drawings. Her hand shook as she took them out of her bag.

"You did say you might be interested in some more of Bobby's drawings," she said, passing them to him.

He smiled as he looked at them. He put the two portraits on one side, then looked again at the scene of the river and the ice skating.

"These are excellent," he said, "but as I mentioned before, a little colour would bring them to greater life. That can be arranged if Bobby could go to my artist friend's studio tomorrow morning. He'll show him how to apply the colour sparingly, just enough to add a little sparkle." He picked up the portraits. "A little blush on the cheek, a speck of blue in the eye and a dash of colour in the hair would work wonders. Do you think Bobby could do that?"

"Saturday morning?" Nell said. She was just about to say she had to work when she saw Robert's face. His unblinking stare and reproachful frown said more than words. He'd never forgive her if she let him miss this opportunity.

"Of course," she said. "He'd be delighted. Where and at what time in the morning?" It would mean the loss of a day's pay, but that was a small matter beside Robert's happiness.

"Champion," Mr Cosby said. "You won't regret it." He wrote the address down for her. "It's not far. The studio is run by Max Pemberton, a friend. Max will look after him. I'll send him a note to expect you. You have no need to worry. Eight o'clock?"

"Eight o'clock," she said. "About the payment..."

"No need. As I said, I'm happy to sponsor him. Seeing him improve and become a great artist will be reward enough."

He hunkered down beside Robert. "Take these with you," he said, handing Robert the drawings, "and show them to Max. He'll show you how to add colour and bring them to life. Then I'll pay you five shillings each for them. What do you think?"

The smile on Robert's face told them what he thought. He nodded his head. Five shillings, Nell thought. That was almost a week's wages.

"Good," Mr Crosby said.

In the café that evening Nell told Lottie about Mr Crosby, his gallery and the art student who was to help Bobby with his drawings. "He wants us to go to his studio in the morning," she said. "So I'll have to send a note to Mr Bradley. It's the second time in two weeks I'll not be at work. I hope he won't sack me." Losing her job was the thing Nell feared most. Without it she couldn't pay the rent. The hat and flower money came in useful, but it wasn't as reliable as a wage.

"He'll not sack you," Lottie said. "Josh'll have a few things to say to him if he does."

"Josh? Why? What do you mean?" She remembered it was Josh suggested the job, but she got it on her own merits surely.

"He sent a note asking his old man to take you on. Didn't you know that? Old Mr Bradley'll keep you as long as Josh says. Wouldn't want to upset his eldest son."

Nell could hardly believe what Lottie was telling her. "You mean Josh arranged the job for me? Why?"

Lottie huffed. "Well if you can't work that out you're a lot dumber than I thought," she said.

Nell's stomach knotted. If what Lottie was saying was true she owed Josh a lot more than she realised. All her resolve not to get close to him would count for nothing. She was in his debt. She wasn't sure how she felt about that.

Lottie was watching her more closely than was comfortable. "He said you were acting cool towards him at the zoo. He thought you were playing hard to get, but he likes that. What are you really up to? We'll not remain friends if you're playing fast and loose with Josh. He's a decent man and deserves better."

Nell looked Lottie in the eye. "Josh is a good man, one of the best, but I'm not in the market for anything more than friendship. I wanted him to know that."

Lottie looked suspicious. "Another man is it?"

"No," Nell said, aghast. "It's just... just..." She couldn't explain so she grabbed her things and stormed out of the café. "Come along, Bobby," she said. "It's time you were in bed."

Indoors she went back in her mind over her meeting with Mr Bradley. How he'd first thought her to be recently bereaved, looking to arrange a funeral for a loved one. How his face had cleared when she mentioned Josh and how easily he'd taken her on. He hadn't even asked for references or checked if she was up to the job and he'd even found a menial task for Robert, seemingly because of rather than despite his disability. It all made sense. Lottie was right; she owed her living to Josh.

She spent a restless night wondering whether she should tell Lottie and Josh the truth about Robert and why she'd run away with him. Would they understand or would she be putting them in danger too? Aiding and abetting a crime, even covering it up was as bad as the crime itself. If she was found out she'd be hanged, but they'd all be punished too. No, she'd have to think of something else. Another lie to keep her secret safe. The problem was where would it end?

One thing was certain. Keeping Josh at a distance would be even harder now. She couldn't afford to get involved with anyone, but keeping her heart whole when she owed him so much wouldn't be easy. She'd come to appreciate his easy-going nature and the way he managed to make even the greatest difficulty disappear. She'd enjoyed his company at the zoo and he'd brought laughter back into her life when she thought it gone forever. She wasn't one to turn her back on her friends either.

She tossed and turned but could find no solution. She vowed to put the thought to one side and see what tomorrow would bring.

Chapter Twenty Four

The next morning, after breakfast, Nell took Robert along to the address Mr Crosby had given her. It was in a part of town she thought she knew quite well, having had to walk through it every morning on her way to work, but she'd never noticed the cobbled alley that led off the main street. A long wall ran along each side of the alley broken only by shabby doors and dirty windows. The roofs of the houses almost touched. She wondered if she was in the right place. A dark alley where sunshine and light rarely ventured wouldn't be her choice of location for an art studio.

She found the door marked, *'Studio Entrance'*, in peeling paint. Another wave of doubt engulfed her. She pushed the door open. Inside a notice had an arrow pointing up a narrow flight of stairs. The hallway was dark and dingy and Nell shuddered.

Surely this wasn't the place Mr Crosby had spoken of so highly.

Upstairs another door was simply marked with a sign that proclaimed it to be, '*The Studio*'. She opened the door and went in. Inside couldn't have been more different. Sunlight streamed in through the windows. A variety of frames and canvases were propped against white painted walls around the room. The overall effect was one of airy lightness. Several artists' easels stood grouped around a long table. A young man in paint-spattered overalls stood at an easel, his back to the window. Spring-like curls of ginger hair poked out beneath his red beret. A goatee beard and ginger moustache gave his face the appearance of intense concentration. He held a paintbrush in his hand. Nell guessed him to be about her age. No more than twenty at most.

He looked up when Nell entered and put down his brush. He smiled as he walked towards her, hand outstretched. "Good morning. You must be the young artist and his aunt Mr Crosby told me about. I'm Max Pemberton and I'm very pleased to meet you."

Reassured, Nell smiled and shook his hand. "We're very pleased to meet you too," she said. "I'm Lily Drummond and this is my nephew, Bobby Robinson."

Robert glared at her, his lips pressed into a grimace.

Max crouched down. "Hello, Bobby," he said. "I hear you're a great artist and you've come to learn how to be even better."

Nell bridled. "He doesn't speak," she said. "I thought Mr Crosby might have mentioned that."

Max looked momentarily discomforted. "No, he didn't tell me that, but it doesn't make any difference. It's his drawing I'm interested in. Anything else is of no concern to me."

"I'm sorry," Nell said. "I didn't mean to snap."

Max smiled. "You're forgiven. I don't suppose you find many people as non-judgemental as me."

"No, indeed," she said. "Well, you'd better have a look at Bobby's drawings and tell us what you think." She took them out of her bag and Max spread them out on the table in the centre of the room.

He pored over them for several moments. Nell held her breath.

"These are good," he said. "How old is your nephew?"

"He's seven"

"Really? He has an eye and a good hand. Milton mentioned the drawings might be improved with a little colour. Pastels I think he said. I can see what he means." He picked up the picture of the ice skating. "This could do with a little perspective," he said. "Background colour perhaps." He took up the one of the boats on the river. "This too."

He took the portraits to the window and held them up in the light. He smiled and came back to where Robert stood.

"Now, young man," he said. "Are you willing to work hard, do as you're told and let me show you how to make these drawings even better than they are?"

Robert nodded, his blue as a summer sky eyes serious but shining with hope.

"Good. Then we'd better get started." He pulled another easel over to the light from the window, frowned and found a box for Robert to stand on so he could reach the paper pinned there. He placed some coloured chalks within reach and said, "Show me what you can do with these."

He turned to Nell. "He needs to get used to handling different materials before we do anything else. There's no need for you to stay. You can collect him at noon if that suits."

Nell glanced at Robert happily scribbling on the paper on the easel. He looked happier than she'd seen him in ages. Max must have sensed her hesitation. "It's all right. I won't eat him," he said.

Nell laughed. "Good. As you say, not everyone is as kind and non-judgemental as you. Are you sure there's nothing else I can do?"

Max shook his head.

"I'll leave him with you and come back at noon then," she said.

Her heart lifted a little as she left the alley. Walking back into town the sun beamed from an azure sky.

Nell spent the rest of the morning cleaning and tidying their room. She washed the sheets in the wash house and put them out to dry. All the while thoughts of Robert left with a stranger filled her mind. She wanted to encourage him to be independent, but she wasn't sure leaving him so soon was the right thing to do.

At twelve o'clock she was at the studio door. She hurried up the stairs, anxious now in case Robert had caused any trouble, you never could tell with him. She needn't have worried. When she went into the studio she saw Robert standing staring out of the window and Max poring over some pictures on the table. He looked up when she entered.

"Has he been all right?" she asked. "How has he got on?"

Max walked over to her, the pictures in his hand. "I must say your nephew is the most intriguing student I've ever had," he said. "He's done these. They're very good, but not what I asked him to do."

Nell glanced at the pictures, one in red pastel, one in blue and one in yellow. All drawings of Max.

"I don't need to look in the mirror to see what I look like," Max said. "Bobby has captured my likeness perfectly. The problem is that I asked him to draw a landscape, or some trees."

Nell smiled. "He draws what he sees," she said. "If you want landscape or trees you have to take him to where they are. He can't invent them in his mind. He has to see them."

"Oh, I see," Max said. "But that doesn't explain why he wouldn't draw any more when I asked him. He folded his arms and refused to draw anything further. Then he went and stood staring out of the window where he's been ever since."

Nell walked over to where Robert was standing. She turned him around. He ran and picked up his picture of Lottie, pointing to her cheeks, eyes and hair. Nell nodded.

"He was told you would show him how to add colour to his pictures. That's what he wants to do. He's not interested in anything else. I'm sorry. I think I've made a mistake bringing him here. I'm afraid I've wasted your time."

Max looked stricken. "Not at all," he said. "I didn't realise. I thought I'd get him used to the materials first."

"Well, you should have told him that," Nell said.

"I'm sorry. I didn't understand."

"Very few people do," Nell said, sadness overwhelming her. She went to pick up Robert's pictures but Max stopped her.

"Please leave them," he said. "If you bring him next week I'll start showing him the colouring." He held up the pictures Robert had drawn of him. "And I think we can do something with these too."

"What do you think, Bobby?" she said.

Robert glared, but nodded.

"That's decided then. I'll bring him again next week."

Max showed them out.

Over the next few weeks Nell and Robert fell into the routine of going to the funeral parlour in the mornings and either the park or Mrs Crosby's in the afternoons. Every Saturday Robert would go to the studio for his lessons. Nell would walk half-way with him, then leave him at the entrance to the alley to make his own way there.

Spring turned to summer and the days became longer. Nell still searched the newspapers, her stomach in turmoil, in case she found any mention of Lord Eversham's missing son. She didn't, but she worried all the same. Kidnap was a hanging offence.

One day at the funeral parlour, while searching for a new nib for her broken pen she found something else that set her mind in a whirl of worry. She couldn't find a new nib in her desk in the shop so she went to ask Mr Bradley. He wasn't in his office, so she opened a drawer in his desk to see if he had any nibs in there.

As she was searching through the papers she saw a note. It read:

'Dear Pa, If a young lady with a small mute boy comes looking for work I'd be obliged if you'd take her on. She needs to find work to pay her rent. With great affection, your loving son, J.'

A knot formed in her stomach. Lottie was right, Josh did arrange the job for her. Was that an act of kindness to someone he saw in need? Or was there more to it? She recalled the evening out at Christmas in the pub where he'd been very popular, especially with the ladies. If he was after a girlfriend he could take his pick. He seemed to know everyone and everyone wanted to know him. She also remembered how attentive he'd been and the feeling he gave her of being admired and appreciated, something she'd not felt since Ethan left the Manor. She enjoyed Josh's company and couldn't imagine a life without him now, but she couldn't afford to get involved in anything other than friendship. Would that be enough for someone who'd done so much for her?

By the beginning of June the weather turned balmy. Nell spent her afternoons teaching Robert his letters and numbers. She often took him to the park or to sit by the river with his books, sketch pad and pencils. She tried to teach him to write his name, writing 'Bobby' and spelling it out for him to learn, but he steadfastly refused. She knew it was pointless trying to reason with him. He was stubborn, determined and wilful, but so charming and charismatic with it she could only sigh and forgive him.

Mr Crosby bought three of Robert's pictures and Robert was almost finished the fourth. Nell put Robert's money in a wooden box which she put in the drawer with Robert's other belongings. It was money she could use if they ever needed it to pay doctors and lawyers to keep him out of the asylum if it ever came to that.

Chapter Twenty Five

Over the weeks the atmosphere in the funeral parlour went from bad to worse. Every day Linus had some complaint about her, or Robert or

Goose. The coach wasn't clean enough, he couldn't find the wood or tools she was supposed to have ordered. The yard hadn't been swept. Every day she thought about packing the job in, then she thought of Josh and how kind he'd been and Mr Bradley who'd come to depend on her while Mrs Bradley was still laid up. She even thought of Goose who needed the job as much as she did. At least if she was there she could keep an eye on Goose and Linus would have to kerb his temper. There had been several outbursts, which Nell reported to Mr Bradley and which earned Linus a caution.

She realised there was no love lost.

One day near the end of the month she was sorting out the accounts and found yet another query for Linus. Items that had to be paid for, but had never appeared in the workshop. She sighed. He'd never admit to falsifying the accounts, but at least she could let him know she was on to him and maybe he'd think twice about doing it.

He wasn't in the workshop but she heard an angry voice shouting outside in the yard. Fear clutched her heart. Linus was in a rage and she wouldn't put anything past him. She feared for Robert and Goose who were out there.

She rushed to the door. When she got there she saw Linus with his back to her, his arm raised in anger, fist clenched. She couldn't see who he was shouting at. It could have been Robert or Goose. It looked as though he was about to hit someone. Hot blood flushed her face and pounded through her veins. Anger like molten lava rose up inside her.

He had his back to her, his arm raised, fist clenched, shouting. Seeing him reminded Nell of the workhouse Master. A wave of sickness engulfed her. A sudden spark of fury lit a raging inferno inside her. Memories of the horror of the workhouse filled her brain. She'd often watched the Master out of the infirmary window. She'd seen him standing in the yard beating a boy around the head or bending him over a stool to take a thrashing. Boys were beaten for fainting through lack of food, or for falling asleep when they should have been picking oakum. Sometimes there didn't even need to be a reason. They were beaten for the hell of it. Boys like Robert, too small, naïve and scared to speak up for themselves or fight back.

The fire inside her turned into a swirling cauldron, like a volcano ready to erupt. A kind of madness fell over her. In her mind Linus became the workhouse Master. How she hated him. She wanted to stop him once and for all. She wanted to strike a blow for all those innocent boys thrashed to within an inch of their lives for no reason other than to give the Master his perverted pleasure. She wanted to smash his head in.

She glanced around the workshop looking for something she could hit him with. An iron pole lay on the bench. She grabbed it and rushed to the door. At the door she paused for brief moment, wondering if she should fetch Mr Bradley. Only Mr Bradley could deal with Linus when he was in a rage.

As she stood at the door, she realised the shouting had died down. An eerie silence hung in the air. Holding the iron pole she edged out of the door. Perhaps it was just a lull while he got his breath back. Or perhaps the person he was shouting at had run to escape his wrath. She wouldn't have blamed him.

She saw a man lying on the floor. Blood oozed from a wound on his head. There was no sign of Linus or any of the other lads. The yard was empty save for the man lying on the floor. Nell rushed to his side, dropping the iron pole as she did so. She caught her breath as she leaned over him. Seeing the blood seeping from the wound she tore a strip off her petticoat and tied it around his head to try to stop the bleeding.

"Help, help!" she shouted. "Someone please come and help. There's been an accident."

She tried to raise the man up to check if he was breathing.

Her own breath came in short gasps. Everything had happened so fast she didn't have time to think. She glanced around. Where was Robert? He should have been in the yard. Where was he? A huge swell of fear rose up in her. It felt like everything was closing in on her. How long had Linus been in the yard? She'd heard shouting, had he done something to Robert? Why?

A wave of relief washed over her when the yard gates opened and Charlie came in with two police constables. "Oh thank goodness," she said. "We need an ambulance. This man is badly hurt."

Then Mr Bradley appeared. "What's happened?" he said. "What are you doing here in the yard, Miss Drummond. Where's Linus?"

Chaos and confusion followed.

Charlie and the other lads milled around, shuffling their feet and shaking their heads. Nell's mind whirled. Where was Robert?

One of the police constables examined the man on the ground. He shook his head. "He's a gonner," he said. "She's done for 'im all right."

Nell was aghast. "Me? I didn't do this."

The other constable picked up the iron bar Nell had dropped. "This looks handy," he said. He took Nell's arm. "You've got some explaining to do."

Linus came into the yard. "What's the silly cow done now," he said. "I knew she was trouble first time I saw her. Old boyfriend was it, wouldn't take no for an answer. Have you been egging 'im on?"

It took a moment to realise what was going on. Who'd called the police? Why was Charlie with them? What had he told them? Why was Linus looking so smug and most important of all, where was Robert and was he all right?

Questions raced through her mind. Then the penny dropped. She was being accused by the police of murdering an unknown individual.

"It wasn't me. It was him," she cried, pointing at Linus. "He did it. I saw him."

Linus laughed. "Saw me? I bin down the stable all morning. Charlie'll tell you. I ain't even bin 'ere."

Nell's eyes widened in shock.

"That's right isn't it, Charlie?" Linus said, a broad grin on his face. "Both of us down the stable all morning."

Nell appealed to Mr Bradley. "You know I wouldn't do anything like this," she said. "Tell them. Tell them about Linus and his temper. Tell them how he can't be trusted…"

The first police constable looked at Mr Bradley. "Was you 'ere, sir? Did you see what 'appened?"

"No, no, I didn't see… but Miss Drummond wouldn't… she works in the shop, she'd have no reason…"

"We'll have to take her down the station. It seems she was the only one in the yard when this poor feller was attacked."

"No," Nell said. "There are two other people. Goose and Bobby. They're here somewhere. They must have seen what happened," she said. Tears stung her eyes threatening to overflow.

"And where might we find this Goose and Bobby?"

Nell glanced round. They were nowhere to be seen. Her heart pounded. Terror sent bitter bile up from her stomach to lodge in her throat. Where were they and what had happened to them?

"I think you'd better go with the constables," Mr Bradley said. "Sort this out at the station. Meanwhile I'll have this poor unfortunate man's body transported to the morgue. I expect that's what you will require, eh, constable?"

"Indeed, sir. Most grateful."

"But Bobby?"

"If he turns up I'll take care of him, don't worry, Miss Drummond. Mrs Bradley will be happy to look after him until you return."

Nell had no option but to go with the police to the station where she was put in cell to await a chance to make a statement.

She shivered as she glanced around. The back wall had a small window overlooking an alley. Bars lined the other sides. Bunks were placed alongside the bars either side of the cell. There was no other furniture. A man in the next cell lay on his bunk, mumbling and cursing. Nell pulled her shawl around her and shuddered. Despair washed over her. What on earth was she doing here? How had it come to this? And, more importantly, what had happened to Robert? Where was he and what was she going to do now?

The events of the last hour ran through her mind. She recalled wanting to challenge Linus about the accounts he'd put in for payment. Furious at what she saw as his attempts to defraud Mr Bradley she was determined to have it out with him. She remembered that. The rest was a bit of a blur. She recalled seeing him in the yard, fist raised, shouting. Remembered grabbing the iron bar. Remembered wanting to hit him with it – she'd have done it too. She'd have done anything.

She'd had murder in her heart that morning. But the man on the floor wasn't Linus, she knew that. It was the man in the brown suit who'd argued with Linus before. Nell hadn't hit him, but she'd been ready to commit murder. Didn't that make her just as guilty?

Some instinct had stopped her. What was it that had made her stop and think of calling Mr Bradley? It wasn't fear, she knew that. She'd been shaking, not with fear, but with anger. Her hand had gripped the bar so tightly it had left an impression on her palm. What had been in her mind in those brief few seconds? What had made her see sense through the fog of insanity?

A thousand thought had run through her mind in the few seconds she stood there. She wasn't a murderer. She wanted to protect Robert, but there must have been another way. Visions of Josh filled her mind. What would Josh do? He wouldn't rush in brandishing an iron bar that's for sure. Josh was the voice of reason in her ear. It was as though he'd come into her mind as a warning, telling her to think. Think about what she was about to do. It was thinking of Josh made her want to call Mr Bradley. She sank down onto the bunk. Her only desire had been to protect Robert, but now it looked as though she'd placed him in even greater danger.

Dusk was falling. Grey clouds covered the sky outside when a constable came to her cell.

"You've got a visitor," he said.

Behind him Lottie stood grim faced. She had a smartly dressed man with her Nell didn't recognise. The constable unlocked the door allowing them to enter, then locked it again and sat in a chair across the corridor where he could see what was going on.

Nell fell into Lottie's arms. A huge wave of relief brought a sob to her throat, but Robert's disappearance was still on her mind. "I'm so glad to see you," she said. "Have you seen Bobby? I'm so worried about him. He wasn't in the yard..."

"It's Bobby brought me here," Lottie said. "If it wasn't for him..."

"How is he? Is he all right? Has anything happened to him?" Tears filled Nell's eyes as a feeling of deep dread crept up inside her.

"Gawd love us, he's good as gold that one. Ran into the café, grabbed my arm and pulled me up to your room, he did. Showed me the picture of Josh on the wall. Course then I knew somat was wrong. He was telling me you was in trouble and I had to fetch Josh." She patted Nell's hand. "I sent a lad for 'im and went to the funeral parlour meself. When I heard what had happened I went and got Ben. Bobby's in the café with Ernie. Safest place."

Nell heaved a sigh of relief. So Robert was all right, for now anyway. "I'm so grateful to you," she said. "I don't care what happens to me as long as Bobby is all right."

"It's you we've come to see to," Lottie said. "This is Ben Crowe. He's a solicitor. He'll speak to the officer in charge and sort things out. Don't you worry, pet."

Nell looked at Ben. She managed a weak smile. "I don't know how Lottie managed to find you or how I can thank you. Only to say I am most grateful."

"You need to tell Ben all about what happened," Lottie said.

"I don't know what happened, only that I did nothing. I tried to help the man on the ground. You have to believe me, Lottie. It wasn't my fault."

Lottie nodded. "Everyone knows you wouldn't hurt a fly," she said. "We'll soon get you out of here, won't we, Ben?"

"I'm not sure what I can do until you tell me what happened this morning," he said. "Perhaps we can start from there."

Chapter Twenty Six

Under the watchful eye of the constable Nell told Ben all she could remember. She told him about Linus and his temper and how he was always finding fault, an excuse to beat one of the lads at the yard. How she feared for Robert's safety, remembering to call him Bobby in front of Lottie. How it was only Mr Bradley stopped him picking on Robert and Goose, thanks to Josh.

All the while Lottie sat beside her on the bunk, tutting and shaking her head. "Ought to be put away that Linus," she said at one point. "Always was a bad 'un. And Charlie, his brother's just as bad."

So, Charlie was Linus's brother. Nell hadn't known that.

When Nell had finished Ben said, "I'll have a word with the officer in charge, then go and speak to the other lads at the yard, see what I can find out. I'm afraid you'll have to stay here tonight, but I'll try to sort something out for tomorrow."

The constable unlocked the door to let them out. Lottie gave her a hug. "Don't worry, pet," she said. "We'll soon get you out of here."

Nell smiled but here heart wasn't in it. She still couldn't understand what had brought her to this place. Why would they think she'd kill a man she didn't even know? At least Robert was safe, for now anyway.

She lay down and tried to rest but a frenzy of thoughts crammed her mind. As she dozed her head filled with visions of being hanged, the crowd baying for her blood. Terror ballooned in her heart.

She began to see how reckless she'd been taking Robert. She was his compass. Without her he'd be lost in a world of confusion, unable to understand what was happening to him.

Even if acquitted of her current problem, it would not be the end of it. Any trial would mean public scrutiny. Her exposure would identify Robert, then all would have been for nothing. His family would have him put away just the same and kidnap was a hanging offence.

Her past life flashed before her eyes. As though in a dream she saw her life at the Manor; Robert playing in the magnificent garden, the sunshine and laughter of happier times. That was his birthright; that was what he deserved, not to be sweeping yards and polishing coaches like a labourer.

Sickness welled up inside her. That was what she had brought him to. It was all her fault. She'd taken it upon herself to pass judgement on his family and their plans for him. If she were hanged he'd be left alone, deserted with no one even being aware of who he was or the legacy that was owed to him.

If she'd obeyed their instructions he'd be locked up in a hospital or asylum, but as least he'd be safe. There'd be people to look out for him. He wouldn't be left alone in the world to fend for himself. She'd vowed to look after him and she'd let him down. Her eyes burned with tears. A web of despair wrapped itself around her, sucking her down into a pit of gloom. She'd betrayed that sweet boy's trust in not making sure there'd be someone to speak for him. Her actions had made him even more vulnerable than before. She'd have to do something about that.

She called for the constable to bring her some paper, pen and ink. "I want to make a statement," she said. "And some envelopes, I need to settle my estate."

The constable returned with paper, envelopes, a pen and an inkwell.

She sat down to write. She'd have to confide in someone, let someone know who the boy they called Bobby Robinson really was. She thought of Lottie and Josh. They were her dearest friends, but no one would believe that a child in their care could be the son of an Earl. Even the things she'd kept to prove his identity could be disputed as being stolen or forged.

She thought of Ben, the man she'd just met. Anything she told him would be kept confidential, but he was an officer of the law and obliged to reveal any known criminal act to the authorities. He'd think he was acting in the child's best interest reuniting him with his family, albeit a family who wanted him locked away. She hadn't known him long enough to trust him with Robert's secret.

Then she thought of Milton Crosby. He had wealth and position. His mother knew everyone who was anyone, knew their secrets and held no brief for people who used their influence to abuse their position, treat people badly or cover for their family's failings.

She wrote:

Dear Mrs Crosby,

I am saddened to be writing to you but I have no one else I can turn to. What I am about to reveal will rock society and burst its bubble of hypocrisy, which I am sure you will agree is long overdue.

I am in dire need of your help. Not for me, for it is too late for intervention on my behalf, but for the boy I introduced to you as Bobby Robinson, the orphaned son of my sister. He is in fact Robert Eversham, the missing eldest son of Lord Eversham and his first wife Lady Caroline.

She then went on to describe her life at the Manor, her treatment there and the second Lady Eversham's plans for Robert. She wrote about the locket, engraved photo frame with a picture of Robert's mother, the letter addressed to the doctor at the hospital, sealed with Lord Eversham's seal. Should she be charged with murder she didn't want to implicate Lottie in the crime so she wrote: *In the event of my death or incarceration these things will be among my possessions.*

At the end of what turned out to be a long missive, she wrote:

Please ensure that Robert is recognised for the amazing, talented child you know he is and enable him to claim his rightful place in society.

Tell him I loved him beyond reason and please, please, please, take care of him. Don't let him be locked away and forgotten.

She pondered a while whether to sign it Lily Drummond or Nell Draper. She decided Lily Drummond would be best as that was how Mrs Crosby would know her and she didn't want to confuse her or have the letter put in the bin as being from someone unknown, probably asking for some hand-out or other.

Satisfied that, if the worse happened and she was charged with murder, she could give the letter to Ben to post. That way at least Robert would be protected. In any event she thought it a good idea to put the letter with Robert's other things, so that someone would know who he was and could look out for him if she couldn't.

Then she remembered that the next day was Friday and Mrs Crosby would be expecting her in the afternoon. She wrote a short note saying: '*Due to unforeseen circumstances I regret I'll be unable to visit you as planned, but hope to be able to call again next week.'* That was suitably non-committal. If she was still in custody on Monday then Mrs Crosby would be able to read all about it in the newspapers. She signed it Lily Drummond as well, wrote the address on the envelope and put the letters together on the bed. She'd have to ask the constable to see the note was taken that night or early next morning. Letting Mrs Crosby know she wouldn't be there was the least she could do. The letter telling her who Robert was she'd keep until she knew her fate.

At about ten o'clock the constable came on his rounds. He huffed when she handed him the envelope. "Please ensure that this is delivered as soon as possible," she said.

That settled she tried to sleep, but sleep wouldn't come so she spent the night reliving her past and wondering if that would be all the life she had.

The next day dawned a little brighter. She gazed out of the barred window looking for the patch of blue that always made her think of her mother and wondered if she'd soon be joining her. That thought was hastily put aside. She prayed that Ben would find the truth.

At lunchtime the constable informed her she had another visitor. This time she was taken to a small room where lawyers could interview their clients in private. Ben was waiting for her, but so were Josh and Robert.

Robert ran into her arms and she held him close. She breathed in the smell of him, and the sensation of his cheek soft against hers. She stroked his hair and felt his little heart beating against hers. Closing her eyes she savoured the moment, never wanting to let him go.

Josh coughed. "He insisted on coming with me," he said. "I didn't want to bring him, but he clung on like a limpet. He wouldn't let me go."

Nell smiled and kissed Robert's forehead. "I'm so glad to see you safe," she said.

An oak table took up most of the centre of the room with chairs placed around it. Nell sat at the end of the table and pulled Robert onto her lap, her arm tight around his waist. She wanted to hang on to him for as long as she could before he'd be wrenched out of her arms. Ben sat in the chair on one side of her and Josh took the chair on the other side.

Josh took a sheet of paper from the bag he was carrying. "Bobby gave me this," he said, passing it to Ben. "It's one of his drawings."

Ben gazed at it. He looked at Nell and placed the picture on the table in front of her. It showed Linus, fist raised, face twisted in spite, about to land a punch on the face of the man standing opposite him. The man in the brown suit.

Nell gasped. "I saw Linus in the yard. Robert must have seen it too. Is this what you saw?" she asked Robert.

He nodded.

"Robert must have seen what happened," she said. "He's drawn it. He can't tell you, but he's able to show you."

Ben frowned. "Where were you when you drew this?" he asked Robert.

Robert put his hands over his face.

"Hiding," Nell said. "That's the sign for hiding."

"Where?" Ben asked.

Robert drew a circle in the air.

"That's a wheel. In the coach? Were you hiding in the coach?" she said.

Robert nodded again.

"Was anyone else with you?" Ben said.

Robert pulled his sketch pad from his bag and showed Ben a picture of Goose.

"Goose," Nell said. "Was Goose with you?"

Robert nodded.

"Where was Goose?" Ben asked.

Robert put his hands over his face again.

"Hiding," Nell said.

"Where is Goose now?" Ben asked.

Robert put his hands over his face again.

"Hiding?" Nell said.

Robert nodded.

"Surely that'll help our case," Josh said. "If there were witnesses."

Ben stroked his chin. "This could have been drawn anytime. The boy might have drawn it today, just to help his aunt. I'm not sure it'll stand up in court."

"No," Nell said. "Bobby only draws what he sees. He can't carry pictures in his head. He can't make things up. He has no imagination. He can only draw what's in front of him at the time."

Ben grimaced. "Well, it's not much to go on, but I'll have a word with the inspector. See what he says." He turned to Josh. "Is there any chance of finding this Goose chap? Would he be able to testify?"

"Me and the other traders'll find him. He'll testify," Josh said. From the look on his face Nell knew he'd stop at nothing until he found him.

"All right. I'll go and have a word," Ben said.

Josh said he'd take Bobby home and see he was fed. "I'll be back as soon as we find Goose, then we'll get you out of here," he said to Nell.

Chapter Twenty Seven

Nell was taken back to her cell to await developments. At least Robert was safe with Josh and Lottie, but she still worried what might happen to him. She hadn't committed the crime she was accused of, but she wasn't wholly innocent either. Anyone making enquiries into her background or where she came from might uncover her secret. Then she'd be hanged and Robert... She dreaded again what might happen to him. She spent the rest of the day in a sweat of anxiety.

It was late in the evening before Ben returned. Dusk had fallen and pale moonlight shone through the small window high up in the wall. A constable she hadn't seen before came to take her from her cell to the room where Ben was waiting. He smiled as she walked into the room. That surely was a good sign?

Nell sat at the table opposite Ben. "I hope you have good news for me," she said.

"Not bad news at any rate," Ben said. "I've been over the evidence against you, it's very thin. They only have a witness statement from the constable who arrested you and he wasn't there at the time. Linus and his brother have yet to appear to make their statements in writing. We have Goose and Bobby's drawing, your denial and I can produce several character witnesses to speak on your behalf." He leaned back in his chair. "You have made some good friends in the short time you have been here. That says a lot for your character."

"Not to mention the fact that I am innocent. I didn't do it, Linus did."

"Yes, that too will go in our favour." He stood to leave. "The Hearing in the morning is just a formality. With no evidence to offer the case will be quickly dismissed. Please don't worry."

Easier said than done, Nell thought.

The constable took her back to her cell, where she spent another restless night worrying about Robert and whether Lottie was looking after him. Ben's words had reassured her. She only wished she could be as confident of the outcome as he appeared to be.

The next morning she was taken in a police van with several other offenders to the Magistrates' Court. They were put in the cells beneath the court to wait their turn. Nell was called up first. Her heart pounded as she climbed the steps to the dock in the centre of the panelled room. In front of her the three Magistrates sat behind a high bench ready to pass judgement upon her. She glanced around and saw to her utter dismay the public benches filled with reporters, scribbling in their notebooks. A band tightened around her chest. If her picture appeared in the newspaper she would be recognised and all her efforts to protect Robert would be for nothing.

She swallowed as the Clerk of the Court read out the charge. Ben stood. "Ben Crowe for the defence, your worship" he said and sat down.

A slight man in a dark suit stood. "Harold Goodman, for the Crown," he said.

The Magistrate nodded. "Let us begin," he said.

Harold Goodman stood. "If it please, your worship. The Crown wishes to withdraw the charge of murder against the defendant Miss Lily Drummond."

"Withdraw the charge? On what grounds?"

"Evidence has come into our possession that proves Miss Drummond to be innocent of the crime of which she is accused."

The Magistrate looked perplexed. "Very well then, case dismissed. You're free to go, Miss Drummond." He banged his gavel on the bench. "Next case."

The court filed out. Ben greeted Nell as she stepped down from the dock. A wide smile lit his face. "I told you they'd have no evidence. Without Linus and his brother's statements they had nothing." He's as thrilled as I am, Nell thought, warmed by the realisation that he really cared.

They walked together to the courthouse lobby. Harold Goodman was waiting for them with a man Nell didn't recognise.

"Miss Drummond, isn't it?" he said, stepping forward to shake her hand. "I'm Harold Goodman, the chief prosecutor."

Nell offered her hand. She glanced at Ben. He shrugged.

"I'm sorry you've been held so long, but we have to make enquiries and check everything out."

"Of course," Nell said. "But I'd never hurt anyone, let alone a man I've never met."

"No. I realise that now," he said. "But you must admit – a man on the ground, a sturdy iron bar and witnesses who said you'd done it…"

"Yes," Nell said. "I suppose…"

"The good news is that, thanks to the drawing Ben showed us and your friend finding another witness…"

"Josh found Goose?"

"Yes and he's been in and made a statement."

"Is that the evidence you mentioned had come into your possession?" Ben asked.

"Yes, that and information given to us by Inspector Munro here."

Inspector Munro stepped forward. "Delighted to meet you both," he said, shaking hands with Ben and Nell.

"The drawing and witness statement will be used in evidence against Linus Frumly when they find him," Harold Goodman said.

"You mean he's disappeared?"

"Done a runner," the inspector said. "Once we identified the victim it became obvious it couldn't be you, but it put Linus Frumley in the frame."

"Who was he, the victim? One of Linus's friends? I saw him at the yard a couple of weeks ago," Nell said.

"It was Harry Grubstick, an opulent receiver. Well known in the manor for fencing stolen jewellery and other valuable items," the inspector said. He shook his head. "It seems the constables here were never informed, but my men at the Marylebone Station have been investigating a string of burglaries in our area. All have taken place when the houses have been empty while the occupants were attending the funerals of their loved ones. We made the connection and we've been watching funeral parlours for a few months. The drawing of Harry with Linus Frumley puts him right in the picture, if you know what I mean." He grinned. "Begging your pardon, ma'am."

"We'll need you to make a statement, Miss Drummond. For the prosecution this time." Harold grinned.

Nell smiled. "I'll be happy to make a statement if I can help you put Linus Frumley behind bars."

"Thank you, ma'am," Inspector Munro said.

Ben sat with Nell while she wrote out her statement. She included details of Harry Grubstick's previous visit when she saw Linus arguing with him and how he'd said he'd be back. It was a relief to get it all down. Ben walked her home.

On the way the warmth of the summer's day felt extra special and Nell thought she'd never appreciated walking down a grubby street as much as she did then. When they reached Lottie's, Ben told her she'd probably be required to testify against Linus when he was caught.

"I'll be in touch when that happens," he said. "And Bobby. They'll want him in court too."

"Bobby? In court?" Suddenly the realisation of what that meant hit Nell. She'd been so relieved at being set free she'd willingly agreed to make a statement and testify against Linus. She hadn't thought it through. The idea that she'd have to swear an oath that she was Lily Drummond and that Bobby was her nephew had never entered her head. Their names and probably faces might appear in newspapers. If she was recognised...

"I can't have Bobby appear in court," she said. "It would be too much for him. You must realise how vulnerable he is. No. I won't permit it."

Ben frowned. "They may insist, after all his drawing and testimony about Goose being there were key factors in the enquiry. I'll do all I can, but I can't see how it can be avoided."

Nell wanted to tell him she couldn't, simply couldn't, appear in court and nor could Bobby. But all she said was, "Linus hasn't been caught yet. He may never be, isn't that right?"

Ben smiled. "Don't worry the police will catch him. Have no fear of that."

Nell's heart quickened. She couldn't afford to appear in court, but she'd have to cross that bridge when she came to it.

Saturday morning Nell took Robert to the studio where she knew he'd be happy working on his drawings with Max. She couldn't face going to the yard, so went to the market instead to spend time with Lydia and watch the women buying the hats she decorated with silk roses.

Monday morning she decided to tell Mr Bradley they'd no longer be able to work for him. She wasn't prepared to have Robert working in the yard. She'd have a word with Mrs Crosby to see if she could recommend her services to a friend. She had nursing skills and didn't mind hard work. She'd even be prepared to take on domestic duties if it meant she could have Robert with her, although not many employers took kindly to a woman alone with a young lad in tow, no matter how good she was at her job.

If worse came to worst she could help Lydia out on her stall in the market. It wouldn't pay much but at least she'd be able to keep them housed and fed.

She packed her bag with books for Robert and his sketch pad before leaving to see Mr Bradley. Then they could go straight to Mrs Crosby's after leaving the funeral parlour. She walked briskly along. When she arrived at the shop she saw a '*Closed*' notice on the door. She knocked several times and eventually Mrs Bradley opened the door.

"I'm sorry we're closed," she began to say, then realised who it was. "Oh, it's you, Miss Drummond, with little Bobby. Please come in. Mr Bradley's not here I'm afraid. It's been quite a to-do the last couple of days, what with one thing and another, but I don't have to tell you that do I?" She wrung her hands together as she spoke.

Inside, Nell noticed how quiet it was. There was no one about. The workshop was closed up and the yard empty.

"Come upstairs and I'll make us some tea. Then we'll see what we can sort out." Nell followed an obviously upset Mrs Bradley up the stairs. "Amos is helping the police with their enquiries," she said. "Out all day he is. Looking for that Linus Frumley. I can't think what got into 'im. Killing someone like that. Not right it ain't, not right at all. It's put Mr Bradley in a right state it 'as."

Mrs Bradley showed Nell into the small front parlour. "Make yourself comfortable," she said. "I'll get some tea on. Oh what a to-do it's been." She paused and said again, "But I don't need to tell you that do I?"

Nell felt sorry for this poor woman who appeared to have the weight of the world on her shoulders.

The front parlour was a cosy room with a faded carpet and worn chairs, but the dresser standing against one wall was the most magnificent Nell had ever seen.

"Amos made that when we got married," Mrs Bradley said, seeing Nell admiring it. "I'll treasure it 'til the day I die. We didn't have much back then, but we had each other. He's a good man, Amos."

"I know," Nell said. She recalled what Lottie had said about him having a good heart and how he always believed the best in people. That was how thugs like Linus managed to take advantage of him, she thought.

While Mrs Bradley made tea in the kitchen next to the parlour, Nell set Robert at the table and spread out his books. She'd written a list of words he had to find on the page and underline them. She felt sure he could read, but without speech it was difficult to be sure. One thing she did know was that when she read to him at night he'd point to the words as she read them. Sometimes she'd test him by saying the wrong word, but he wouldn't move his finger on until she said the right one. Either he could read or he'd memorised the page. She wasn't sure which.

Over tea Mrs Bradley told Nell that Amos was thinking of selling up and going back to cabinet making. "He's devastated," she said. "He wouldn't have stood for it if he'd known. He wanted to be able to help people in their hour of need, not rob them blind." The horror of their predicament obviously weighed heavy on her mind. "He won't rest until he finds that Linus Frumley and takes 'im to police."

She put her cup down and leaned forward, whispering in a conspiratorial way, "Do you know what they found at Linus's place? Dreadful it was. Amos told me they found people's personal effects. Things relatives had left to be buried with their loved ones. Jewellery, rings, little mementoes and that." A look of disgust filled her face. "That's not all," she continued. "They found suits and boots too. Linus had taken the shirts off the backs of the dead to sell on. Fair broke Amos's heart it did. All those people who'd trusted him..."

Nell swallowed trying to imagine how Mr Bradley must have felt at the horrific discovery. She didn't know what to say.

Mrs Bradley's eyes brimmed with tears. "Amos opened the funeral parlour after our youngest boy, Ezra, died. We spent every penny we had to give him a decent funeral. Somehow it still wasn't enough, but Amos wanted to be able to help people like us when they lost loved ones." Her face hardened. She shook her head. "That Linus has got a lot to answer for," she said. She sipped tea. "Amos'll never get over it. All he ever wanted was to make sure that at least people could bury their loved ones decent, with a service and a grave to visit. We got a headstone for Ezra. Not straight away of course, but in time. That's what Amos wanted for other people. People like us."

Mrs Bradley took out a handkerchief and wiped her eyes. Her wretchedness and distress made Nell's heart crunch. "What will you do if he closes the business?" she said.

Mrs Bradley shrugged her shoulders. "I don't know. Sell up I suppose. I'd have liked to keep the mourning wear going. You know, reasonably priced outfits for the widows. But at the moment, I just don't know."

They sat in silence for a while with just the scratching of Robert's pencil to disturb the air. Mrs Bradley put her cup down. "It must be hard for you bringing up a lad on your own. I know when mine were young they ran me ragged." She laughed and the lines on her face lifted. "Right bunch of scallywags they were," she said.

Nell had visions of Josh and his younger brother, Adam, at about Robert's age and her heart warmed. "They've grown up to be fine men," she said, thinking particularly of Josh, the one she knew best.

"I tried to teach them right from wrong," Mrs Bradley said. "Luckily they had Amos to look up to. It's his guiding hand that formed them. Boys need a firm hand and a father to look up to." She gasped. "Oh I'm sorry I didn't mean…"

Nell's mind whirled back to the Manor, Lord Eversham and the way Robert's father had treated him. Better no father than a bad one, she thought. "It's all right," she said, dropping her voice to a whisper. "Bobby was very young when he was orphaned. He doesn't know any different."

"It's a shame he has to grow up without a father though," Mrs Bradley said.

Nell thought again about Lord Eversham and his treatment of Robert. "Indeed it is," she said with an edge of hardness in her voice. That wasn't true but Nell wasn't going to go into it so she tried to change the subject. "Tell me about your boys. Josh's the oldest isn't he?"

Mrs Bradley's face cleared. It was as though the sun had come out. "Yes, oldest of the three. Fearless he was, Josh. Always getting into scrapes. Liked a fight better than his dinner. It was as though he had something inside him and couldn't let it rest. Came home nine days out of ten with cuts and bruises."

Nell could imagine that.

Mrs Bradley's face clouded over. "The youngest, Ezra, was a sickly child, often ill. He had a club foot and walked with a limp. The other kids mocked him and called him names. Josh stuck up for him. That's what caused most of the fights." She paused as though lost in memory. "Josh was devastated when he died. We all were. Adam seemed to get over it, but Josh took it hard." Her brow creased into a frown. "They were close. I haven't seen Josh get close to anyone since, not like he was with Ezra." She stood up, went to the mantelshelf and took down a picture in a silver frame. "This was Ezra," she said.

Nell looked at the boy in the picture. He was about Robert's age, a sweet looking child with an engaging smile, standing next to a tricycle similar to the one Robert had ridden at the Manor. Was that the reason Josh had taken so quickly to Robert and been so keen to help her?

She glanced again at the picture of Ezra. The sadness in his eyes stayed with Nell for the rest of the day.

Chapter Twenty Eight

That afternoon Mrs Crosby appeared more fidgety than usual. Her leg had healed and Nell no longer had to dress it. She asked Nell questions about the children at the workhouse. Who were they? Where did they come from? Nell was perplexed at her sudden interest. She tried to answer as truthfully as she could.

"What happens to them when they leave the workhouse?" Mrs Crosby asked. "Is there any hope for a better life?"

Nell explained how they were expected to find work as soon as they were old enough. "That's usually about fourteen," she said. "Although some are put into service from the age of ten."

Mrs Crosby shook her head. "No hopes of finding families for them?"

Nell remembered Kitty, the girl who'd followed her around the first Christmas she visited with toys for them. "Every child dreams of finding a family to take them in and care for them," she said. "There was one girl…" she went on to talk about Kitty and her hopes of eventually being adopted by a loving family.

Mrs Crosby seemed unusually interested. "I suppose they entertain all sort of fantasies, about their lost loved ones. Perhaps imagining they have been abandoned by the most wealthy in society who are only waiting time before coming to reclaim them?"

Nell bit her lip. It was a fantasy that was all too familiar. "In a place like that we all need our dreams," she said, remembering how often she'd dreamed of her mother not really being dead, or her lost-at-sea father coming to take her away to a better life. "What else is there? The everyday drudge of hard work, poverty and being made to feel less than human. It's people's dreams that keep them going."

She was beginning to feel uncomfortable talking to Mrs Crosby. It was as though she was trying to worm some sort of confession out of her, but she couldn't think of anything she'd done to deserve such treatment.

Eventually, over tea, Mrs Crosby said, "I know a family who have been unsuccessful in having children of their own and are looking to adopt. They have asked Doctor Barnardo to find a girl and a boy they can foster. He's the leading light in placing children with caring families. Thinks that the best way to bring them up." She put her tea cup down and glared at Nell. "If you give me the name and address of the workhouse I'll contact them and ask about that child, Kitty wasn't it?"

Nell's stomach knotted. There was nothing on earth she could think of so wonderful as finding a home for Kitty, but if she gave Mrs Crosby the address of the workhouse it wouldn't take much to work out that Nell was the workhouse girl who'd been given the job of nursemaid to Lord Eversham's son and had since kidnapped him.

Mrs Crosby's steely gaze bored into her. "Come, girl, you must know the address of the workhouse where you were brought up."

Nell swallowed. "It's not something I like to remember," she said. "It was a several years ago. The name of the place escapes me."

Mrs Crosby sat back, a satisfied smirk on her face. "I trust you'll remember by Wednesday," she said. "Please bring it then. My friends could do a lot for that young girl, give her a good start in life. I'm sure that's something we all want for her."

"Yes, indeed," Nell said, blinking away the terror that threatened to assail her. She longed to help Kitty, but doing so would put her and Robert in danger. That's if Mrs Crosby's offer was genuine. Could she afford to doubt it? A vision of Kitty, her summer blue eyes shining, blonde curls bouncing around her head and her angelic smile filled Nell's mind. If anyone deserved to be saved she did

"I'll see if I can find it," Nell said. "Will Wednesday be soon enough?"

Mrs Crosby nodded. "Wednesday it is then."

The following morning, just as Nell thought she'd take Robert over the park, the storm clouds gathered. Ben came into the café to find her.

"Won't you join us for a cup of coffee," Lottie said. "On the house."

"How can I refuse? Thank you," he said, swivelling into a seat next to Nell. He glanced at Robert, put his hand into his pocket and brought out a shilling. "I bet if you took this to the sweet shop you'd find something you might like," he said.

Robert glanced at Nell. "It's all right," she said. "I expect Ben wants to have a word about something quite boring. Go to the shop but don't be too long."

Robert took the shilling, made the sign Nell had taught him for 'thank you' and went out.

"Now I don't suppose this is good news," Nell said.

"It depends how you look at it," Ben said. "Linus Frumley is in custody. He's to appear in court at the beginning of next month. The Chief Prosecutor will want to interview all the witnesses, including you and Bobby. He'll want to go over your statements and be sure the evidence they're presenting will stand up in court. It's a very serious matter. We need to get it right."

Nell's heart hammered. She could hardly breathe. She felt as though she'd been caught in a trap and someone was nailing down the lid. She could never stand up in court and swear an oath as to the truth of her name let alone that her testimony was a true and accurate record of events. Then there was Robert. He couldn't tell them who he was, but someone might recognise him from the reports in the papers. Her hands were shaking. She curled them into fists. "What happens if I refuse?" she asked.

Ben scowled. "Linus would go free and in all probability they'd arrest you in his place. At the very least you'd be imprisoned for aiding and abetting a criminal." He stretched his hand across the table to touch hers. "You'll be all right," he said. "I'll be with you. All you need to do is tell the truth. You can do that can't you?"

"When?" Nell said.

Ben shrugged. "Soon. The case is listed for next month, so perhaps a week or two."

A sigh of relief escaped Nell's lips. She managed a smile. At least she had a week to plan her next move.

Things didn't get any easier when Josh appeared, bursting with the news of Linus's capture. He looked put out when he saw Ben already there but his mood soon lightened. "They caught him down by the docks. Him and his brother," he said. "They were looking for a ship out. A sharp eyed constable recognised him from one of Bobby's drawings. You should be proud of the lad. If it weren't for 'im..." He glanced around. "Where is he by the way?"

"Sweet shop," Nell said. "Ben gave him a shilling. I don't expect we we'll see him until lunchtime."

Josh laughed.

Ben said he had to be going. He fixed Nell with a stare. "I'll be around next week to go through your statement with you," he said. "And I'll be at your side whenever you need me. Just let me know."

Nell nodded. "Thank you."

Josh's face clouded. "What was that about?" he said.

"Our testimony for court. I don't want Bobby dragged into court. He did nothing wrong. He won't understand what's going on."

"But without him they won't believe he didn't make up what happened and draw it after the event. You have to explain how he couldn't have. How he's not capable of it."

"I know. But it doesn't make it any easier."

Josh grimaced. "You know they've taken Pa into custody. They think he was party to the robberies."

"No!"

"Yes. They won't believe he knew nothing about them. It's only your word and Goose backing you up that's likely to persuade them any different."

"My word?"

"Yes. As a character witness. You know he knew nothing about Linus's game. You have to tell the court that. Ma's depending on it."

"But why me? Surely there are others will speak up for him."

"Yes, they knew him. But you were the only one, other than the lads in the yard who were all in it, who worked with him. Who knew what Linus was like and how he bullied the other lads and pulled the wool over Pa's eyes. You have to speak up for 'im. Tell them how Linus ran the yard. Pa just paid the bills." Anger and spite filled his voice.

Nell tried to control the thoughts racing through her mind. Speaking up for Amos would mean appearing in court and she wasn't prepared to do that.

Robert appeared with his bag of sweets. Her heart swelled with love as she looked at him. He'd grown up so quickly since they left the sheltered life at the Manor. She'd come to depend on him as much as he depended on her.

She stood up. "I'm sorry for your pa," she said. "He's a good man. I'll do what I can for him." She took Robert's hand. "Come on, let's go over the park and see if the ducks like those sweets."

Robert giggled and went with her.

Before she went to Mrs Crosby's on Wednesday afternoon Nell wrote down the name and address of Salvation Hall House for Mrs Crosby. She also wrote a note to Mrs Bradley, sympathising with her over her troubles and saying she'd call on her Thursday morning to collect her wages and any other money owing to her. She felt a bit callous doing it, but still hadn't been paid for the last three mourning outfits she'd made and she needed the money.

That afternoon she handed Mrs Crosby the note. "The girl's name was Kitty, but she was known in the workhouse as 'Girl No 126'," she said. "I'm sure your friends won't be disappointed when they see her. She's bright as a button and will bring them much joy."

Mrs Crosby looked bemused. "Thank you," she said. "I'll get Milton to write today. From what you tell me the child deserves better than spending the next five years picking oakum."

"Thank you," she said. "Now, what am I to read today? Is there a book you fancy, or should I read from the newspaper?"

Mrs Crosby handed her *The London Illustrated News*. "This should give me some pleasure," she said. "I believe the daughter of one my friends is to be engaged to a dreadful bore. Read all the details please."

So Nell turned to the society pages and began to read. She was half-way down the page when she spotted the small advertisement outlined in black. Her voice faltered, but luckily Polly came in carrying the tray of tea. While Mrs Crosby busied herself with the tea Nell read the advertisement.

'In Memoriam'.
Lady Caroline Eversham, wife of Lord Eversham,
mother of Ellen, Martha and Robert.
Died 29th July, 1885 – Always Remembered
Lady Mary, Dowager Duchess of Hertsbury's
thoughts are with her daughter's children, on the
eighth anniversary of her death.
Robert Eversham, Lord Eversham's eldest son, is
missing. Lady Mary would appreciate any
information leading to his whereabouts. A small
reward will be offered.

There was an address in Somerset. Nell's hands shook as she closed the paper. Saturday was Robert's birthday. He'd be eight years old. She tried to calm her thundering heart, but a swirl of memories threatened to engulf her. Memories of Robert's birthdays at Inglebrook Manor, the memorial services for his mother he was barred from attending and the way his birth was remembered only for the for the loss it had caused. She'd planned to celebrate by taking him to the National Gallery. Now those plans would have to change.

"Thank you," she said with a smile as Mrs Crosby handed her the tea, but inside her stomach churned.

Chapter Twenty Nine

Thursday morning Nell went through the chest of drawers to see what she could take with her and what would be best left behind. She put Robert's clothes, a spare blouse, petticoat and skirt for herself into her carpet bag. She'd wear her suit and shawl. She sorted out some books and toys for Robert, then sat on the bed holding the silver christening cup engraved with his name. Vivid recollections of his birthday the first year she'd been at Inglebrook Manor filled her mind. They'd been so happy then, the giggly boy and his naïve nursemaid. She recalled the laughter and fun they'd shared. He was a different boy now, more solemn and wary. She longed to put that sunbeam smile back on his face. Perhaps, once they got away, it would return. .

She wished she could go now, without delay, but she couldn't afford to lose her pay from the funeral parlour and what Mr Crosby owed her.

She packed her silks, ribbons, cottons and the silk flowers she already made into a bag to take to Lydia in the market on her way to the funeral parlour to collect her pay. She'd take whatever Lydia gave her for them. She wouldn't have room to take them with her.

She took out her writing pad and pen and wrote to Milton Crosby to let him know she could no longer visit to sit with his mother, explaining she'd suddenly been called away. She said she'd call at the gallery on Friday morning, if it was convenient, to collect her pay and outstanding money from his latest purchase of one of Robert's drawings.

Robert ran ahead of her as she walked to the market planning their escape. She'd seen pictures of seaside resorts on the South coast, with sea air and wide open spaces a world away from the grimy smog filled streets of London. She'd find a better life for Robert at the coast. The change would be good for him. No more polishing coaches or sweeping up other people's rubbish. She'd find a small shop to lease and open a millinery store where she could keep Robert by her side.

She sighed. It's all very well having dreams, she thought, it's making them come true that's hard.

She left Robert at the entrance to the market and went to see Lydia. The market was quiet at that time of day and Nell strolled around the stalls humming to herself. Planning her escape had lifted a heavy burden from her heart. She'd collect whatever she was owed by Friday night, leave a note and two weeks' rent for Lottie, take Robert to the National Gallery on Saturday for his birthday and catch a train to Brighton at noon.

A worm of guilt wriggled inside her at the thought of leaving Josh and Lottie without a word. They'd been good to her and she'd miss them as she missed Jenny, Alice and the people at the Manor, but she owed it to Robert to keep him safe.

Her cheerful mood of the day was snuffed out like a candle flame when she saw a face she recognised among the shoppers. Her hands flew to her mouth. She gasped and dodged into the shadow between two stalls. A chill ran through her veins. Thomas O'Leary was talking to stallholders, showing them a slip of paper and asking questions. They could only be about her. Had he come to London to find her and claim the reward? She wouldn't put it past him.

She watched him moving around the stalls, thankful to see the traders shaking their heads. Robert had never been with her when she came to the market; she'd always left him at the entrance, knowing how the crowds would unsettle him. She was glad of that now.

Then she remembered she'd left him at the market entrance that morning. Was he still there? Would Thomas see him and recognise him? Another frenzy of dread and panic swirled inside her. She took a shuddering breath. He couldn't have seen him on the way in or he wouldn't be asking round the market, so was Robert even there still? He often wandered away to find something more interesting to look at. As long as they were apart there would be no connection between her and the woman with a child he was looking for.

She waited until he'd moved on then asked Lydia. "What did he want? Is he looking to buy a hat?"

Lydia laughed. "No. He's looking for a woman run off with a young boy." She chuckled. "Not that he'll get any joy from the market traders. They'll reckon that anyone running away with their child would have good reason to. They'll not help an abusive husband find a runaway wife."

"What was on the paper? Was it a picture?" As far as she knew Robert's sketch pad would have the only pictures of her and she'd brought that with her.

"No. Just a name, Nell somebody. Not sure. Didn't take much notice to be honest. Yes, dear." Lydia turned away to serve a customer.

Nell breathed again. They didn't have her picture. Still, her resolve to get away from London as soon as she could hardened. When she was sure he'd gone she hurried as fast as she could to the market entrance to find Robert. Then she remembered the crossing sweepers. They'd seen them together. She'd given them her real name. Would they remember if Thomas approached them?

None of them could read, so the notice in the paper would mean nothing, but being approached by a man with the possible offer of a reward? That was a different matter. A fresh torrent of terror ran though her.

When she got there, there was no sign of Robert. Visions of Thomas finding Robert and hauling him away, a smirk on his face filled her mind. Sickness filled her stomach.

As usual a group of crossing sweepers were standing around waiting to sweep the crossing for any ladies walking that way so Nell asked them if they'd seen where he went.

"Lost 'im again?" the oldest boy said. Nell nodded, recalling the first time he'd wandered off, shortly after they'd arrived in London. She'd been blinded by panic and asked them to look for him. That time he'd found his own way home.

"Have you seen him?" she asked.

They all shook their heads.

"Have you seen a strange man around here asking questions?" She felt sure that if they'd seen a man dragging him away they'd tell her.

Again they all shook their heads. A smile flitted across her lips. Thomas O'Leary was a snob. It was most likely that he'd think talking to raggle-taggle street boys beneath him. That was her only hope. She crossed her fingers.

"If you see him…"

"I know. Tell him Nell's looking for him and take 'im 'ome to Lottie's Place."

"That's right."

"Half-a-crown, you said."

Nell smiled. She'd said sixpence, but in the circumstances…"Yes, half-a-crown."

The boy nodded. "I never forget a face when money's on offer. If we see 'im we'll bring 'im 'ome."

All the way to the funeral parlour anxiety churned in Nell's stomach. Seeing Thomas O'Leary had unsettled her more than she cared to admit. It brought the possibility of capture too close for comfort. She was more certain than ever that if she wanted to save Robert from the asylum they had to get away as soon as possible.

When she arrived at the funeral parlour the 'Closed' notice was still on the door. She knocked and Mrs Bradley let her in. She was surprised to see Josh there with Adam and Mr Bradley, all looking grim. They greeted her with subdued tones.

Inside she saw the workshop and yard had been cleared out. Although the hearse, carriage and cart remained, most of the wood and tools had gone. The place was eerily silent. An atmosphere of dull foreboding hung in the air.

"Pa's out on bail," Josh said. "He'll be appearing with Linus and Charlie at the Old Bailey next week. Ben's trying to get us a barrister to defend him. Lord knows what that'll cost. We might have to sell up.

"Josh says as how you're going to speak up in Amos's defence," Mrs Bradley said. "I knew we could rely on you. We're everso grateful, aren't we, Josh?"

"More than I can say," Josh said.

Nell glanced at Mr Bradley and saw a silent, broken man. Her stomach dropped into her boots. She was going to let them down but she had to think of Robert and his future. If she didn't escape before the trial he might not have one.

"Come upstairs and I'll put kettle on," Mrs Bradley said. She managed a wan smile.

"No, I can't stop," Nell said. "I have to get back. I've left Bobby on his own. I told him I wouldn't be long."

"Oh. Very well then, come up and I'll sort out what we owe you."

All the way home Nell fretted about the Bradleys. They'd been kind to her and she was going to let them down. A rock of despair formed in her stomach. There was nothing she could do to make things better. Robert was her only concern now.

When she arrived home she'd expected to find him on the doorstep, or in the café drinking Lottie's excellent coffee which he'd grown a taste for. But he wasn't there.

"Haven't seen him since breakfast," Lottie said.

She tried their room upstairs. He wasn't there either. She walked to the end of the street, glancing in each of the shops as she passed in case he'd popped in, not that he had any money to spend. She thought of retracing her steps to the market, but knew that Robert would know his way home from there. He had a better sense of direction than she had.

She was torn between going out looking for him and staying home in case he turned up. He knew she was going to the funeral parlour today to get her pay, would he have gone there? If he had she'd have seen him. If he'd gone there and missed her Josh would have told him and sent him home. She thought about going back, or sending Josh a note, but in the circumstances...

Anxiety swirled in her stomach as it always did when Robert was out of her sight. She struggled to convince herself that he'd be home soon and all her worrying would have been for nothing. Had

Thomas O'Leary seen him and snatched him away from her? She forced the thought out of her mind. Robert had no love for Thomas. She recalled that he'd bitten him when he assaulted her. Robert was canny enough to keep out of his way if he saw him and quick-witted enough to outsmart him.

In the end she decided to wait for him and sort out what she could take on her journey to the coast and what she'd have to leave behind. It proved to be a painful process. Every item brought a pang of memory, either something she'd acquired since arriving in London, or the memory of something she'd left behind.

By late afternoon Nell's panic was rising. Robert still hadn't come home. He'd never stay out past teatime. Meal times for Robert were set in stone: rituals that had formed part of his routine since the days at the Manor. It was almost teatime now so where was he?

A commotion outside drew her to the window. On the pavement below the gang of crossing boys were carrying a small boy she immediately recognised as Robert.

Shock hit her like a punch. A huge swell of fear surged through her. Panic she'd been suppressing exploded sending burning blood humming through her veins. Her whole body trembled as she flew down the stairs.

"This the lad you was looking for?" the oldest boy said. "We found 'im being beaten like an old rug in a doorway."

Robert was barefoot, his feet and legs scratched and dirty. His clothes were torn. Clods of mud stuck in his hair. Blood oozed from cuts on his face and a black, yellowing bruise spread beneath his half-closed, swollen eye. His lips quivered and silent tears rolled down his cheeks.

Nell's heart shattered. A swell of love for this small helpless child washed over her. She could hardly breathe as a maelstrom of fury, hate and rage engulfed her. She struggled to control the emotions swirling inside her. She wanted to kill whoever did this. Still shaking she took Robert in her arms and held him close.

"I'm so sorry," she said, pressing her face against his cheek where her tears mingled with his. Sorry was too small a word for the way she felt. It was all her fault. She was to blame. It was her fault for bringing him here and for taking him to the funeral parlour where Linus Frumley worked. She'd done it to protect him, but she'd brought pain and suffering instead. She shouldn't have abandoned him that morning. She should have kept him close.

"My poor darling," she said. "Who did this to you?"

"It was a big lad done it," the crossing boy said. "Kicking and punching 'im. Would 'ave bin worse if I hadn't shouted. He ran away when he saw us." He motioned the other lads standing around staring at Nell.

"Have you ever seen the lad before? Do you know who he is?"

The crossing boy shook his head. "Nah. He stole 'is shoes. Would've killed 'im I reckon."

One of the other boys piped up. "I seen him afore. He's in a gang wot goes thieving. I seen 'im."

Nell perked up. "Whose gang? Do you know the leader?"

"Nah. Big bloke, pudgy face, dark hair."

Nell felt sure it was Linus Frumley. "Thank you," she said, hugging Robert even closer. "I can't thank you enough. Wait here."

She carried Robert upstairs, laid him on the bed and came down again carrying her purse. She gave them each half-a-crown. They deserved much more, but they seemed happy enough with what she gave them. It was probably more than they earned in a month between them.

She put her hand to her mouth to swallow back the sickness rising up to her throat at the horror of what had happened to Robert. It was Linus's doing, she was sure of that. Linus and his gang trying to stop Robert from testifying. Molten fury swirled inside her. She wanted Linus to hang more than anything she'd ever wanted in her life before. Him and his gang of thugs who'd done this to her poor defenceless child. Maybe she should go to court and tell them she'd seen him commit murder.

She went to Robert and checked his body for broken bones. Thankfully there were none, only mud, dirt, cuts and bruises. "I'll fetch the bath," she told him. "Will you be all right here for a moment?"

Robert lay staring at the ceiling; his eyes vacant and empty, his face white as a mortuary corpse. Nell brushed his forehead and held her hand to his cheek. "I'm sorry," she said. "Sorry I ever brought you here. Sorry for the life I've made you lead. If there was anything I could do to turn the clock back I'd do it." Even as she said it she knew that, given the circumstances, she do the same thing again.

She'd heard what life was like in asylums for the mentally ill. He be put in with the chronically disturbed, vagrants, the old and infirm, people addicted to drugs and alcohol, pregnant single women who had been cast out by their relatives, in fact anyone who by hook – and not infrequently by crook – could be squeezed into whatever the law required to be 'certified'. It would be worse than the workhouse where at least his stay would be time limited.

She kissed his forehead, squeezed his hand and said, "I'm going to take you away from here as soon as I possibly can. That's a promise."

She ran down and fetched the bath from the washhouse, then carried up sufficient jugs of hot water to fill it. She tried to remove his torn and muddied shirt. As she did so he grabbed her hand.

"What is it, my love?" she said. "I need to undress you for the bath."

Slowly he released her hand and allowed her to open his shirt. To her amazement she saw his mother's gold locket around his neck. "Oh no," she gasped, thinking how easily it might have been stolen. She didn't know what to say. How could she make him understand how dangerous it was to wear such a thing? She glanced into his eyes and saw the deepest sorrow. Her heart buckled. It was all she could do to hold back the sobs that threatened to assail her.

"I'll just take if off for now," she said. "While you have a bath."

He allowed her to remove the locket. Was he trying to remember his mother? She prised it open and saw that in place of his mother's picture he'd drawn her likeness and placed it there. It seemed as though he wanted to keep her close to his heart.

She gave him a bath and washed the mud out of his hair. When she'd dried him she dabbed arnica on the bruises on his face and body and dressed the cut under his eye. He picked the locket up from the bed and put it around his neck. She gently removed it. "I don't think that's such a good idea," she said. "It might get stolen."

Robert stared. He took it from her and put it on again. She bit her lip. She didn't want to upset him further, so, she tore a strip of the petticoat she'd already torn when she tried to help the man in the yard, wrapped it around his neck, crossing it over his chest and tied it behind his back. It covered the locket completely. It would be difficult to steal it, especially if you didn't know it was there. She helped him into his nightshirt.

She made soup which she served with bread. He ate slowly as though even that caused pain. Inside, Nell seethed with anger and bitter hatred for the people who'd done this, but most of her anger was for herself, for her helplessness in not being able to prevent it.

Watching Robert silently nibbling at his tea she saw a different boy from the five-year-old she'd met on the day she left the workhouse. What had happened to that lively, fun-loving boy, full of mischief and laughter who should be playing in the sunshine in the orchard or riding his tricycle in the garden? The boy whose infectious chuckle and giggling brought her so much joy?

Wherever he'd gone she was determined to find him and bring back the happiness in his life and his magical smile. The sooner she left this place the better.

Chapter Thirty

Friday morning Robert was still unwell. Nell decided to keep him in bed at least until noon. She worried about him. In the infirmary she'd seen boys in a far worse state, but they were boys who regularly took a beating and became hardened to it. Robert's little face was ashen and his eyes almost closed. She mixed some willow herb in case he was in pain and put ointment on his bruises.

She made him beef broth with bread which she gave him on a tray and sat with him, stroking his head as he ate. Inside her heart ached.

"I need to go out for a while," she said, "but I'll be back soon." She plumped up the pillows so he could sit up comfortably and gave him some books, his sketch pad and pencils. "I'll ask Ernie to pop in and keep an eye on you." She put her shawl around his shoulders but nothing she could do for him would erase the guilt she felt for what he was suffering. She tried to tell herself the treatment at the so-called 'hospital' would be worse, which made her feel a little better, but not much.

Downstairs, Lottie had already heard from the crossing boys what had happened.

"It could have been some lad after 'is shoes and 'is coat," she said, "but if you asks me I reckon that Linus Frumley's behind it. Someone from 'is gang of thieves no doubt."

"No doubt," Nell said. Lottie was only confirming what she already suspected. "I have to run an errand. Bobby's in bed, still recovering. I was hoping Ernie could pop in..."

"Of course he will," Lottie said without hesitation. She turned to Ernie. "Little Bobby's in bed and needs company," she said.

Ernie grinned and pulled off his apron. Relief flowed over Nell. He had a way with him and Robert had taken to him. If anyone could bring the smile back to Robert's face it was Ernie.

Outside, the July sun blazed from an azure sky. Cotton wool clouds drifted lazily in the breeze. Plenty of blue now, Mother, Nell thought. She hoped with all her heart that the brightness of the day meant things would soon be getting better.

She walked briskly to the gallery. She didn't want to be out longer than necessary. She just wanted to collect the money she was owed, then she'd be on her way home again. When she got there she glanced in through the large windows. The room looked empty so she made to go in. A bell tinkled as she pushed the door open.

She'd hardly stepped inside when she saw Milton Crosby talking to a tall man, with unruly dark curls. They both turned at the sound of the bell. A jolt like a thunder-bolt hit her, stopping her in her tracks. She couldn't believe her eyes. Energy drained out of her. Her legs turned to jelly. She couldn't breathe. The only thought in her head was to run, to get away as quickly as she could.

Questions flew like swarming bees through her head, but her feet didn't wait to find the answers. She turned and ran out of the door. She paused for a few seconds on the pavement, then seeing a passing hansom, managed to wave it to a halt and jump in. She called out an address in Regent Street in case she should be overheard. The only thought in her head was to get as far away from the gallery as she could.

To her absolute horror she'd recognised the man with Milton Crosby. It was Ethan – Ethan Baines, one time gardener at Inglebrook Manor. Ethan? Here? How?

As the hansom drew away she saw him, standing on the pavement, a look of amazement on his face. Confusion filled her head. Why was he here and what did it mean for her and Robert? She'd seen Thomas O'Leary in the market. Were they working together, Ethan and Thomas? No, she'd never believe that!

Thoughts whirled through her mind going round and round in circles, like a child's windmill caught by the storm. Ethan and Thomas! No, never. Her heart turned to ice as as everything she'd believed about Ethan and all the happy memories turned to rancid ashes.

The same impulse that had driven her from that train to take Robert into her own care drove her now. Throughout the short journey all she could think about was how Robert had been treated at Inglebrook Manor, how he'd been put away out of sight, left out of every event or gathering, ostracised by a father who'd shown him no love or affection, who thought more about his standing in society than the welfare of his son. She'd be damned if she'd let them take him back, back to that life when she could take him to live with real people, people who'd care about him and love him for the amazing child he was.

A bitter taste filled her mouth as she thought of Ethan. Ethan, who'd been so kind when he was at the Manor. What had happened to him to make him turn against them? And how was Milton

Crosby involved? Had Mrs Crosby written to one of society friends mentioning her new companion and the mute boy with a talent for drawing she called her nephew? She'd have said how she didn't believe a word. It was the sort of gossipy innuendo Mrs Crosby would be delighted to share.

Lord Eversham's wife was at the back of it, she was sure of that. Lady Eversham and her brother. She recalled how she'd overheard them talking about her plans. She hadn't realised that those plans involved Ethan.

Nell glanced out of the window to make sure the hansom wasn't being followed. As they neared Regent Street the heavy traffic brought them to a halt, so she called to the driver to let her off, paid him and walked towards home, deep in thought.

The address she'd given Milton Crosby was the funeral parlour which was now closed. If Ethan went there he'd hopefully get no response. If he did manage to speak to Mrs Bradley or Josh, would they realise he was looking for her? Would they give her address to a stranger? She hoped not.

She'd planned to take Robert to the National Gallery in the morning for his birthday treat, then catch the train from Kings Cross and be long gone before her absence was discovered. Now she knew she needed to go today, but Robert wasn't well enough to travel. He needed rest. She had no choice but to leave their escape until morning and hope above hope that Ethan didn't find out where they were living.

All afternoon and evening, Nell was on tenterhooks. She kept looking out of the window, dreading what she might see. She paced the room while Robert slept, her mind in turmoil. How could Ethan think of betraying her? Was he in the pay of Robert's father? He'd left his job at Inglebrook to work for Lord Eversham's friends. Were they involved in trying to find Lord Eversham's son? Why Ethan of all people? He was the one person in the world she thought would understand her motives. Surely he knew she'd never do anything to hurt Robert or put him in danger?

Bitterness rose up inside her remembering what had happened to Robert – the beating – but that was a small matter compared to what would lay ahead of him in an asylum. She felt sick at the thought of Ethan's betrayal.

Her mind flew back to the garden at the Manor, the chats they'd had. In her mind she saw a vision of his face, always smiling, always happy to see Robert and to play with him. She recalled how her heart had lifted at the sight of him, working in the flower beds and the way the day always seemed brighter when he was around.

She remembered the way he'd mended the tricycle for Robert, the book of trees he'd drawn for him the carved wooden horse. What had happened to make him turn on them? Had he himself been threatened?

Suddenly the seriousness of her situation hit her. Lord Eversham was a Peer of the Realm. His son had been kidnapped, albeit to protect him for being locked away in an asylum, but he wasn't likely to have mentioned that. No, he'd have told the police his son had been kidnapped for a ransom. The fact he hadn't received a ransom note was a minor difficulty. It was only a matter of time, he'd say. Of course he'd never admit to planning to have his son 'certified'. A rock-like swell of anxiety filled Nell's stomach, churning like boulders in a mixer.

She sat and pondered for long while. As darkness fell the street lights outside the window were lit, the sounds of the traffic muffled and died down. The stifling heat of the summer day lingered. Nell packed as many of their belongings as she could into her carpet bag. She wrote a note for Lottie and put it on the table with two weeks' rent. She glanced around the room that been her home for almost a year. The events of the last ten months played in her mind, the people she'd met, their kindness. She wanted to write to Josh but the words never came. She'd be letting him and his family down but she had to think of herself and Robert.

Once she was packed she lay down in the bed next to Robert. He turned towards her in his sleep and she put her arm around him to hold him close, his head rested on her shoulders, his breath warmed her neck.

Through the long night the arguments in her head went this way and that. She was guilty of the horrendous crime of kidnap. At the time she'd acted on impulse. She hadn't thought it through. She'd looked at that small, innocent boy staring out of the train window and her heart had wept for him. She'd wanted to protect him at any cost. She'd grown up in an institution and knew the horrors that awaited him. The freedom he'd enjoyed at the Manor would be taken away. Any sort of freedom would be denied him, and why? Because his behaviour was at times odd and he'd never learned to speak? Because he often appeared to be lost in a world of his own? Because he'd never grow up to be the son his father wanted, never be able to take his place in society, never be the son his father could be proud of?

He'd be an embarrassment. Everyone would know he had a mental illness, a brain that didn't quite function properly. Something never spoken about in polite society.

Or was it because his stepmother had plans for her own son that required Robert to be 'put away'?

It hadn't been a deliberate act meant to deprive Lord Eversham of the company of his eldest son. That decision had been made by his second wife, but who would believe Nell's word against Lady Eversham?

Chapter Thirty One

Nell got up the next morning before dawn. She planned to sneak out before the café got busy. She couldn't face seeing Lottie this morning or the questions she might ask.

Downstairs she washed and took enough hot water back upstairs for Robert. She dressed in her best suit for travelling, then got him up, dabbed arnica on his bruises and helped him dress in a clean shirt. She'd bought him a suit, coat and shoes from the second-hand clothes stall in the market on her way home after the gallery incident the day before. She chatted to him as she helped him put them on, explaining that they were going on a journey but nothing registered in his eyes.

Fear churned in her stomach as she brushed his hair gently and put his cap on. He looked smart enough but his little face was solemn. Not for the first time Nell wondered what was going on inside his head. His body may be mending after the beating, but Nell wasn't sure about his mind.

She struggled to keep her voice calm. "It's your birthday," she said. "You're eight years old today." She held up eight fingers. He touched each one as though he was counting. "That's right, eight," she said, clapping her hands. A smile, brief as a butterfly, flickered across his lips. She had to work hard to win a smile from him these days, but when she did it was still magical.

Before they went downstairs she told Robert of her plans. "We'll be going on a train," she said. "You'll enjoy that. Remember when we came here on a train?" The memory was etched vividly in her mind. "This time we'll be going to the seaside." She smiled as she stroked his cheek, then realised Robert would have no idea what she was talking about. She grimaced. "It'll be fun, you'll see."

His brow creased. He raised his hands to put fingers to his mouth in the sign she'd taught him for 'game' or 'fun'.

Her heart crunched. "Yes, we're going to play a game," she said. Her mind spun back to the games of hide and seek they'd played in the orchard, only this would be a game of hide and seek for grown-ups.

She'd bought him a box of pastel chalks like the ones he used at the studio but she'd keep them to give to him on the train so he'd have something to do for the journey, although she knew he'd spend most of it staring out of the window.

She picked up her bag and glanced around the room once more. Everything looked in place. She took Robert's hand and led him down the stairs. Outside she saw the lights on in the café. Ernie and Lottie would be starting the breakfast. In a short while the traders and street sellers would be out and the city would come to vibrant life. Robert went to go in the direction of the café but she pulled him away. She walked briskly, tugging Robert along beside her. The morning air felt fresh and cool as the early light crept over the roof tops. Nell pulled her shawl closer around her.

Despite the early hour the streets were gradually filling with costers and traders on their way to market. Nell hurried Robert along, she wanted to get as far away from the café as possible to avoid any chance of being recognised. If they were seen it was quite likely that their meeting would be mentioned to Lottie. The traders were well known for their friendliness, camaraderie and gossip.

A horse-drawn omnibus was making its way up the street so she hailed it and got on. It was crowded with people on their way to work but she managed to squeeze in between a woman with a huge basket of potatoes on her lap and a man who smelled of manure. She pulled Robert onto her lap.

The journey to Trafalgar Square was short, but she was relieved to get off. It was good to breathe fresh air again.

She took Robert to a café near the National Gallery for breakfast. It was larger than Lottie's Place but just as busy. She found a table away from the window and ordered two breakfasts from a cheerful looking woman in a stained apron. The breakfasts soon arrived and Nell was pleased to see Robert, with a bit of encouragement, start to eat his.

It would be a while before the gallery opened, but as soon as it did she'd take him in and they could spend an hour or so looking at the paintings. It was one of his favourite places, he seemed to derive a lot of pleasure just staring at the pictures on the wall and she'd feel safe in the gallery. She wasn't likely to run into anyone she knew. She'd brought him to the gallery because she'd made a promise for his birthday, not that he'd understand what that meant, but she'd feel a lot happier once they were on the train.

Walking into the gallery the breath-taking magnificence of the place fell over her. Every visit brought renewed pleasure, not only the paintings on show, but the awe inspiring atmosphere of the place. She caught her breath as she walked in and she thought perhaps Robert did too. The quiet reverence of the people shuffling round from one painting to another had a calming effect on Robert. He seemed to slow down, whereas in other places he'd rush frantically from place to place. She breathed easily as she held his hand. She felt safe.

They were admiring the paintings in a side gallery when she felt the presence of someone close behind her. She felt his breath on her neck. She turned her head and the bottom fell out of her world.

Ethan was standing by her shoulder. She grabbed Robert's arm and tried to move away, but Ethan caught hold of her elbow. "Please," he said. "Don't run. I've come a long way to find you. We need to talk."

His hand squeezed her elbow. She tried to pull her arm away but it was too late. Robert had turned at the sound of Ethan's voice. A huge smile spread across his face and he put out his arms. Ethan bent down and picked him up. "Hello, Robert," he said. "I'm so glad to see you."

In this crowded space, with families milling about Nell was powerless to stop Ethan walking away with Robert's arms around his neck. To the onlookers they probably looked like a family enjoying an outing together. Nell ground her teeth. She had no option but to follow Ethan to the tea room. She kept close behind him fearful of losing him and Robert in the crowd. If he walked away with Robert there was nothing she could do. She wanted to scream out that he'd abducted her child, accuse him of the very thing she'd been guilty of, but the terror of losing Robert kept her silent.

Ethan found a vacant table in the tea room and ordered tea. How could he be so calmly sitting there when he'd betrayed her? She had no doubt in her mind that he was working for Lord Eversham's second wife. What other explanation could there be?

She sunk into a chair beside him. Robert sat happily on his knee. It felt as though even Robert, in his innocence, was betraying her.

She couldn't bear to look at Ethan lest the despair in her eyes gave her away. She bowed her head as she said, "How did you find us? Who are you working for now? Are you working with Thomas O'Leary?"

Ethan's face creased into a frown. "Thomas O'Leary? What on earth gave you that idea?"

"I saw him in the market. Is it just for the reward you've betrayed us?" Her voice filled with spite as she asked the questions that burned in her mind.

"Betrayed you? I came looking for Robert with his best interests in mind. And as for Thomas O'leary —" A look of absolue horror crossed his face. "I can't believe you thought that of me."

Nell blanched, she'd got that wrong, but nothing would stem the deep dread churning in her stomach.

"You're not the only one concerned about Robert's future. There are others who can do much more for him than you, even with your best intentions."

"You mean lock him up in an asylum for the rest of his life." Bitterness rose up like bile in her throat. "That's what they had planned for him. Is that what you want?" Memories of Ethan in the garden, his kindness and gentle nature swirled in her mind. She couldn't believe this was the same man. Something had happened to change him. What could it have been?

"Of course not," he said. "I wouldn't be here to help if I believed that. Trust me. Please give me a chance to explain."

The tea arrived and Nell had no option but to take a breath and let him speak. He had Robert on his lap and it would be the greatest difficulty to dislodge him. It might even lead to Robert having one of his famous tantrums and she couldn't afford that. They'd both be carted away.

Ethan put Robert on the chair next to him, furthest away from Nell. He put a buttered scone on a plate and placed it in front of him. "Scones, Robert. Your favourite. I'm afraid it's probably not up to Mrs Hewitt's standard, but good enough," he said.

Robert chuckled and started to eat the scone.

"What happened to his face?" Ethan asked, indicating the fading bruises and cut not yet healed.

Nell swallowed. Her inability to protect him still rankled. Then she saw the concern in Ethan's eyes. Surely he didn't think... "He got in a fight," she said. "You know how boys are."

His eyebrows shot up. "A fight?"

She realised how unlikely it was that gentle, placid, in-a-world-of-his-own Robert would get involved in brawling, but telling him the truth was out of the question. She nodded and said, "Yes, a fight."

He shrugged. It was clear he didn't believe her but wasn't going to probe any further. "I remembered it's his birthday," he said. "Milton Crosby said you might bring him here. So I came along in case. It seems he was right."

Nell was impressed that he'd remembered the birthday and Robert's love of Mrs Hewitt's scones, but that didn't excuse his betrayal.

"Milton Crosby?" She recalled seeing him with Milton the previous day. "So how did you find Milton Crosby and what's he got to do with it?"

Ethan grinned. "It was Milton Crosby found us," he said.

Nell looked puzzled.

"The letter you sent his mother," Ethan said. "You told her the boy you called Bobby was Robert Eversham, Lord Eversham's missing son."

Nell gasped. Her hand flew to her mouth, her heart faltered. She opened her bag of belongings and scrabbled inside to find the letter for Mrs Crosby which she'd put with the letter to the hospital. She ripped it open and found the note telling her she'd be unable to visit on Friday. A wave of desolation washed over her. How stupid!

She replayed the day in the cell in her mind. She'd written the letters, put them on the bed and went to call the constable. The letters had fallen to the floor. She'd picked them up and handed one to the constable and put the other one in her pocket. The one in her hand was clearly the wrong one.

"Mrs Crosby thought it may have been a joke, but she didn't see you as a joker. She showed it to Milton. Mrs Crosby knew Lady Caroline's mother, Lady Mary, Dowager Duchess of Hertsbury well, so Milton telegraphed her. They still weren't sure. Since offering the reward in the paper Lady Mary has had a stream of waifs and strays brought before her claiming to be her long lost grandson." Ethan poured Nell a cup of tea and said, "She thought you might be one of those."

Nell recalled Mrs Crosby asking about the workhouse children and what happened to them. Surely she didn't think Nell's letter was an attempt to gain access to a wealthy family through deceit. "So what made her realise that I wasn't?"

"As soon as Milton mentioned to Lady Mary that the boy was mute, she became interested. That information hadn't been in the papers. She made short shrift of the imposters who brought young boys to pose as her lost grandson. As soon as they opened their mouths and spoke she knew they weren't Robert."

Nell had thought the omission of Robert's disability was to save the family embarrassment. They'd never admit to the disgrace of mental illness in the family. So she was wrong on that count.

Ethan put a glass of milk next to Robert's plate. He went on, "Lady Mary hasn't seen Robert since he was two. The girls visited once or twice after their mother died, but never Robert. They told her about his lack of speech and what the doctor had said, but that was no excuse in her eyes. She still wanted to see him."

"But she never did?"

"No, Lord Eversham wouldn't allow it. She was afraid she wouldn't recognise him. She knew me from when I worked at Inglebrook Manor and knew I would. She also knew I was working for friends of hers in Kent, so she asked if I could be spared to come to London and see the boy. Tell her if it was Robert or not."

"And if it was she could have him returned to the hospital to be locked away for the rest of his life."

"No." Ethan shook his head. "You've got her all wrong. Lady Caroline was her only daughter, Robert her only grandson. She holds no brief for Lord Eversham and his wife. She hasn't seen the girls since Lord Eversham remarried. She wants to protect her daughter's children. Especially Robert."

"And you believe her?"

"Yes."

"Robert's father thinks his best interest lies in having him locked away in an asylum. I have a letter to the doctor at the Bethlehem Hospital for the Insane. How do you know she is not of the same mind? In the elevated circles they move in mental incapacity is a stigma to be hidden away and forgotten to spare them the shame of it." Nell's anger was mounting. "I know I can't give him the lifestyle he deserves, but I can give him love and acceptance of the way he is. Don't let her fool you, Ethan. You remember how they treated him at the Manor."

"Lady Mary's not like that, I promise." His voice faltered. "Her daughter died giving birth to him…"

"All the more reason to blame him and want him put away, just like his father."

Nell saw desperation in Ethan's eyes. "What have they promised you if you find him?" she asked.

Ethan's face fell. "That's unworthy of you, Nell," he said. "The Nell I knew would never have thought that."

Nell immediately regretted her words. The Ethan she knew at Inglebrook would never have done anything he didn't agree with for money.

"Please, give me a chance to prove you wrong. Come and meet Lady Mary. She's staying with the Crosbys. Then you can make up your own mind."

"And risk being arrested for kidnap and hanged?"

"Do you honestly believe that's what I plan to do?"

Nell's cheeks burned as she remembered Ethan's kindness and affection for Robert. Did she really think he'd turn her into the police? If so their early friendship was a lie and she didn't believe that.

She thought about the railway tickets in her bag. She was running away because she'd feared an appearance in court would expose their real identities and Robert would be taken from her and given back to his family. Now it seemed Ethan was intent on doing that anyway. All she had to do was give Ethan the slip and her and Robert could be on the way to Brighton.

Chapter Thirty Two

She sipped her tea and watched Ethan with Robert. She tried to work out how he'd changed over the months since she'd last seen him. He'd put on weight. Working in the garden his face had lightly tanned, he'd matured, she thought. A tidal wave of memories threatened to overwhelm her. Emotions she'd long ago tried to suppress stirred inside her. She struggled for breath as she watched Ethan encourage Robert to eat, the way he ruffled his hair and brushed crumbs from his lap. This was the Ethan she remembered and his affection for the boy was clear.

"Supposing I do come with you? What happens next?"

"Lady Mary gets to see her grandson. She'll make sure he's properly cared for and gets all the help he needs. You can't deny she's in a better position to do that than you."

Nell didn't deny it. "And you believe her?"

"I do."

"So what about me? What happens to me?"

Ethan sat back and gazed at her. "Lady Mary will be most grateful to you for what you've done. You'll have returned the boy to her she thought was lost."

"She won't have me charged with kidnapping and hanged then?"

Ethan frowned. "Lady Mary knew all about you and how you'd taken Robert. If she wanted you hanged she'd have had a warrant put out for your arrest complete with your real name and picture. She didn't do that. She wanted to protect Robert. She didn't want you harmed either."

Nell gulped. "How do you know all this?"

"I spoke to her in the coach coming here. She worried about Robert and the girls as she hadn't seen them for so long. She wrote to Lord Eversham, but every time she asked about Robert he said he was ill, something was wrong with him, there was always some excuse why she couldn't visit. She became suspicious so she asked Chadwick, her butler, to find out what was going on."

"Her butler?"

"Yes, Chadwick worked at Inglebrook Manor when Lady Caroline was alive. Apparently he's kept up a correspondence with Mrs Hewitt so he wrote and asked about Robert. When Mrs Hewitt told him about you taking him to hospital, which she called the asylum, Lady Mary was furious. She went to Inglebrook to confront her son-in-law."

Nell's mouth gaped.

Ethan smiled. "He denied all knowledge of course, but Lady Mary contacted the hospital. She wanted to get him out. They told her you hadn't arrived. That's when Lord Eversham reported Robert missing. He hadn't bothered before."

Nell recalled the article in the paper she'd read to Mrs Crosby. "It was an impulse, my taking him. I hadn't planned it. I just couldn't bear the thought of…" Tears sprang to her eyes.

"I know," Ethan said. "Your disappearing act certainly put the cat among the pigeons. There's no way they can have him put away now."

"Really?"

"If there's one thing more calculated to ruin one's reputations in society than having a child like Robert, it's the scandal that'll be caused when it comes out that you've bribed someone to have him put away."

"Bribed?"

"Yes. Lady Mary discovered that the hospital had been paid a great deal of money to exaggerate Robert's symptoms and class him as dangerous rather than merely a bit simple-minded."

"He's not simple-minded," Nell almost shouted. "He's the brightest, quickest child I've ever known. If that's what you think..."

"I don't, but that's what the family have been saying. Anyway, no chance of him being put away now."

"So I have achieved something."

"You've achieved a lot, Nell. More than you know. If it hadn't been for you writing to Mrs Crosby, Lady Mary would never have seen her grandson again and he'd have been deprived of all she can do for him."

"So, what happens now?"

"Now, we go and see Lady Mary."

Ethan stood and picked Robert up. It was clear that, having found him he wasn't going to let him go. Nell picked up her bag and followed him out into the July sunshine.

They walked in silence for a while, Robert holding Ethan's hand, a look of pure delight on his face. After a few minutes Ethan said, "I missed you, Nell. Lady Mary wasn't the only one keen to find you. I hoped I would too."

Nell's heart fluttered like it always used to when she saw Ethan in the garden. "I missed you too," she said. "And Jenny and Alice," she added, not wanting him to get the wrong idea, well, perhaps it was the right idea, but she found it hard to admit it.

"I thought about you every day," he said. "I even wrote to Jenny asking about you. I was devastated when she said you'd gone away."

"Did she say why I'd gone or where?"

"No. I think the staff were sworn to secrecy."

"All except Mrs Hewitt no doubt."

Ethan chuckled. "Mrs Hewitt speaks her mind and is not easily intimidated. She was very fond of Robert."

"I remember," Nell said, recalling the indomitable woman who'd ruled the kitchen at the Manor.

She took a deep breath and glanced around. Her desire to escape was quickly diminishing. Seeing Ethan again brought a cascade of memories and made her long for a different future, a future which included him.

"I'd never do anything to hurt you, Nell. You know I'd fight the world for you if I had to, but this isn't about us is it? It's about Robert. It's about making sure he's accepted and valued for the way he is and given every chance to fulfil his potential, whatever that might be. It's also to see that he takes his rightful place in society and is not deprived of his inheritance."

"That's what I always wanted for him," she said. "That's why I took him. To keep him safe and free from the future his family had planned."

"Lady Mary can do that."

"And have the police arrest me and cart me off to Newgate?"

"She wouldn't do that."

"And you know that because…?"

"I told her about you. She gave me her word. She promised."

Nell sighed. Perhaps Ethan was right. This wasn't about her, it was about Robert and his future. That was the most important thing, making sure he was recognised for the bright child he was and regaining his rightful place in the world. Wasn't that what she'd always wanted? Lady Mary was in a better position to do that than she'd ever be.

When they reached the end of Mr Crosby's road Ethan stopped. He still held Robert's hand. "If you think this is a trap this is your chance to run. I won't come after you or try to find you again. You'll be free to go, live your life in any way you wish."

Nell stopped. She glanced around. She had even more reason to run away now. Even if Ethan was right and Robert's grandmother didn't want him put away, she was guilty of kidnapping him and kidnap was a hanging offence.

Where would she run to? Wherever she went it wouldn't be the same without Robert. And supposing Ethan was wrong and they did plan to have him put away? She needed to see for herself that Robert was safe.

She looked into Ethan's soft brown eyes and saw the question there. Did she trust him enough to believe what he said, or was she more concerned with her own fate?

Her mind was in turmoil. All desire to escape had vanished. She wanted to be with him, stay with him, spend the rest of her life with him if she could. This was the man who'd stolen her heart the first time she saw him. Then there was Robert.

"I won't go without Robert," she said.

"He belongs with his family," Ethan said. "You can't change that."

So, this was it. They'd won. Robert would be taken away from her to join his family whether they wanted him or not. She was just the workhouse girl employed to look after him and of no importance at all.

He started to walk towards the house where Robert's grandmother waited.

Nell fell into step beside him. For better or worse her future lay in the hands of Robert's family and the man walking beside her. She only hoped it would be for the better.

When they arrived at the house Nell brushed Robert's hair with her hand and tidied his shirt collar. "You member Mrs Crosby?" she said.

Robert nodded. "Well, now you are going to meet your grandmamma. She wants to look after you. You'll be able to live in a grand house again, like Inglebrook Manor. Do you remember?"

Robert made the sign for 'home'.

"Yes, it'll be your new home," Nell said and her heart lurched again. It would be his new home, but what would happen to her?

Their arrival at the house was greeted with a great deal of excitement. Lady Mary and Mrs Crosby were sitting in a large back room with French windows open to the garden. Milton Crosby stood up as the butler showed them in. Lady Mary gasped.

"Good morning, Lady Mary," Ethan said a huge grin on his face. "I'm delighted to tell you that this is your grandson, Robert Eversham. The lady with him is Nell Draper, his nursemaid, who has looked after him for the past ten months. And a very good job she's made of it. As you can see, he's healthy, happy and well cared for with nothing worse than a few scrapes and scratches, as you would expect with a boy of his age."

Nell gulped. Would he say that if he knew about Robert working in the yard or about his being beaten?

Lady Mary held out her arms to Robert who glanced at Nell. Nell nodded and pushed him forward. "This is your grandmamma," she said. "Do you remember her?" Nell was sure he did. He had a phenomenal memory.

Robert walked towards Lady Mary. He smiled and climbed onto her lap. She hugged him and held him close. She looked lovingly at his face. "I remember you," she said. "You've hardly changed." Her brow creased into a frown. She turned to Nell. "What happened to his face? It's bruised."

Nell swallowed. "He got in a fight," she said. "But he's on the mend. Boys will be boys."

Lady Mary touched his cheek. "He's a fine looking boy," she said. "I understand we have a lot to thank you for."

"I was paid to look after him. That's what I have done." A vision of Robert's humiliation as he swept the yard that first day flashed through her mind, but she quickly dismissed it.

Robert was slipping away from her as he rejoined his family. She thought of all the other people in her life who'd slipped away, her mother, Flossie and now Robert. He was the one she'd miss the most.

As she hugged him Lady Mary touched his chest. "What's this? There's something under his shirt." She unbuttoned it and pulled out Lady Caroline's locket. "Oh my dear," she said. "It's the locket my son-in-law gave to my daughter. You've kept it."

"I kept it for Robert, along with a few other things of his that Lord Eversham didn't want. I have them here, at least the things I didn't have to sell to keep us fed."

Nell opened her bag to retrieve Robert's things. Giving them back would be another wrench. It felt as though every trace of him would be finally gone from her life. Deep sorrow squeezed her heart.

Lady Mary opened the locket. In place of Robert's mother's picture she saw the picture Robert had drawn of Nell. "He must be very fond of you," she said, showing Milton the picture.

"And I of him," Nell said, her voice cracking with emotion.

"And an excellent artist," Milton said. "I have some of his pictures in my gallery. He signed them with an 'R'. The boy has talent, Lady Mary, and there's a lot more to him than people give him credit for. He should be encouraged."

Lady Mary smiled.

"What are your plans for him?" Nell asked, fearful of what she might hear, but determined to hear it. "I trust they don't include having him put away."

Lady Mary's eyes blazed. "Definitely not," she said. "I know what Lady Eversham planned and I can assure you she's been severely rebuked and disavowed of any such idea." She glanced at the open locket in her hand. "Robert will be coming to live with me. He'll need a nurse to look after him. I trust you will be available to fill the post?"

Nell's heart leapt. She'd be able to stay with Robert after all. "I'd be delighted," she said. Happiness flowed over her.

"Won't you need Lord Eversham's approval if he's to stay with you?" Milton asked. "He is the boy's father after all. He could have him returned to him at any time."

Nell's heart sank. Of course Lord Eversham was the boy's father. Whatever his grandmother wanted would be of no account. She had no illusions about what Lord Eversham would do to her either. She put her hand to her throat. She could almost feel the hangman's noose there.

Chapter Thirty Three

Lady Mary grimaced. "Over my dead body," she said. "I'll send a note to Sir Oswald Rockingham immediately."

Mrs Crosby chuckled. "Sir Oswald Rockingham is Lady Mary's lawyer," she confided to Nell. "He's so powerful and influential there's nothing he can't achieve."

Lady Mary was formidable enough, Nell thought. She could only guess what her powerful and influential lawyer might be like.

That done Mrs Crosby suggested they all go in for lunch. They adjourned to the dining room. Nell sat next to Robert, helping him to sandwiches and fruit.

"Please tell us a little more about the boy?" Lady Mary said, helping herself to some lunch. "From what I've seen of him he's not the imbecile Lord Eversham describes. All we have heard is his excuse for wanting him sent away. You seem to have found a way of managing him which has eluded others. Perhaps you could enlighten us."

Nell smiled. "He's the brightest, most amazing child I've ever worked with," she said. She put her arm around his shoulders. "As long as he's kept to his routine, avoids anything too unfamiliar and isn't overwhelmed, he's a joy. A cheerful, giggly boy with a sunny smile and the sweetest nature."

"In other words he's a treasure," Ethan, who was sitting next to her, said. "Nothing at all like the picture painted at the Manor."

"Exactly," Nell said. "As long as he's with someone he knows he's fine. I think you'll find most children prefer the comfort of the familiar."

"So what would be familiar to Robert, now?" Lady Mary asked.

"To be with people he knows and trusts. To be surrounded with kindness," she said.

Over lunch she told them about Robert's life at Inglebrook and how he'd been treated. Then she told them about making hats and mourning wear for a living and Robert's drawing. Mrs Crosby got her to repeat some of the more entertaining tales she'd told her about life in the workhouse. She didn't mention Lottie, Ernie or Josh. An omission that burned with guilt in her mind, but if she was charged with kidnap they could be charged with helping her. She didn't mention Robert's working in the yard, the murder or his being beaten up either. If she did perhaps Lady Mary might change her mind about Nell being the best person to look after him. Looking after Robert and securing his future was all that mattered now and to do that she needed to stay with him.

When everyone had finished eating, Mrs Crosby said she couldn't remember when she'd enjoyed a more interesting and entertaining lunch.

After lunch, Sir Oswald Rockingham arrived and was taken immediately to Lady Mary in the study. When Nell joined them, Milton Crosby was standing by the fireplace, his mother sitting in a chair to one side and Lady Mary deep in conversation with an elderly, smartly dressed gentleman with piercing, granite chip grey eyes. Not especially tall, but portly, his demeanour suggested a sense of power. He had a broad boned face, heavily jowled. He wore a black frock coat over a maroon brocade waistcoat, topped with an extravagant waterfall of white linen forming a cravat at his neck. The sort of man who had little need to care for the opinions of others, Nell thought.

Lady Mary looked up. "Ah, Miss Draper. Sir Oswald, this is Nell Draper, the nursemaid I've been telling you about."

Sir Oswald touched Nell's hand to his lips. "So, this is the young lady who abducted your grandson?"

Blood drained from Nell's face.

"She prevented him being sent to an asylum," Lady Mary said. "She should be commended, not condemned.

"I'm not sure the court will see it that way," he said.

Nell's heart turned over. She'd run away to avoid one problem, now it seemed she'd run straight into a worse one.

"I know what I did was wrong," she said. "But I did it for Robert."

Sir Oswald nodded. "That may be the case but you cannot take a son from his father without good reason. You will have to prove in court that Lord Eversham is an unfit father, a difficult thing to do, although leaving his son in the care of a nursemaid who later abducts him may help to prove the case."

"And planning to have him committed to an asylum wouldn't?" Nell's eyes blazed.

"Do you have evidence of that?"

"I have a letter with his seal addressed to the Bethlehem Hospital for the Insane."

Sir Oswald smiled. "In that case we will go to court."

"I've just been telling Sir Oswald about my plans for Robert," Lady Mary said. "And asking his advice about the appointment of a guardian and what can be done should Lord Eversham raise any objections."

"The Court may appoint a Guardian where there are conflicting views concerning the welfare of a person who is unable to make reasonable judgements about their own affairs, or where there are concerns about the decisions others are making for them. It is most usually deemed necessary when there are no living relatives. In this case Robert Eversham has a father. He is alive, wealthy and respectable. We will have to show good reason for his authority over Robert to be removed. If Miss Draper can provide evidence of Lord Eversham's plans to have him committed that may suffice. However, that will be for the Court to decide."

"Miss Draper told us she was the boy's guardian when she first came to see us," Milton said.

"Guardian angel more like," Mrs Crosby said.

Nell blushed. She wasn't sure she was that.

"You'll need to name someone with standing and a good reputation. Someone Lord Eversham can't object to," Sir Oswald said.

"Like my son, Milton?" Mrs Crosby suggested, a sly grin on her face.

"If he'll agree," Lady Mary said.

"It would be an honour and a privilege," Milton said. "The boy has talent and I'd take every opportunity to see he reaches his full potential."

"Excellent," Lady Mary said "And safeguarding his inheritance? He is Lord Eversham's heir. Surely nothing can change that."

"A guardian cannot make decisions about the finances of a person with a decision-making disability. But Lord Eversham cannot disinherit his son without good reason. Of course had he been able to have him 'certified insane' then there would be no question of his taking up his inheritance and it would pass to his next born male child."

Sir Oswald coughed. "I have explained to Lady Mary that, in the current circumstances, there exists the possibility that Lord Eversham or his wife, who I understand is a most vindictive creature, could in effect bring charges against you, Miss Draper. You were employed as a nursemaid and tasked by them to accompany Master Robert to hospital, a duty you failed to carry out. Despite the positive outcome of your actions, the course you took, clearly a dereliction of duty, could still be called into question."

"Surely Lord Eversham would not court the scandal it would create by pursuing her?" Lady Mary said.

"I fear you underestimate your son-in-law's arrogance, Lady Mary. He may wish to make an example of her to prevent anyone else thinking they could do the same."

Nell's heart sank to her boots. Her worst nightmare was coming true. Suddenly there wasn't enough air in the room. The world swayed slightly. If she was imprisoned, or worse hanged, it would mean she'd never see Robert again. Never hear his giggles or see his dazzling smile. Never experience the jump in her heart his laughter brought. Never hold him close in her arms and feel his heart beating against hers. Tears welled up in her eyes. A stone of grief hardened inside her.

She swallowed, now was not the time to be faint-hearted. She thought back to Flossie and the other inmates of the workhouse who'd never had owt, and never feared losing it. At least, for a short while, she'd had Robert and he'd always be in her heart. If jail was the price she had to pay for his freedom, so be it. "It was a risk I was prepared to take," she said. "If there are consequences I must suffer them, but at least I will have peace of mind knowing that Robert is safe and I did my best for him."

"Good, then I will arrange for a Guardianship Hearing Monday morning."

After he left it was time for everyone to change for dinner. Mrs Crosby looked at Nell. "My dear, you simply can't appear at dinner dressed like that," she said, eyeing Nell's faded blue suit.

"And Robert will require a whole new wardrobe," Lady Mary declared looking him up and down with disapproval. She sent for a tailor who assured her he could produce a suit for Robert by dinner time. Mrs Crosby insisted her lady's maid find something suitable for Nell to wear.

Marie, Mrs Crosby's dresser was about Nell's size and happy to lend her a dress to wear. She chose a lavender afternoon dress with lilies embroidered on the bodice and sleeves. Gazing in the mirror Nell thought back to the rough workhouse uniforms she'd worn when she was growing up. Even the uniform she'd had to wear at the Manor was nothing like the dress she had on now. She wore the silver lily brooch Ethan had given her for Christmas. Still Sir Oswald's words rang in her head. She'd come a long way since those days of poverty, sickness and deprivation in the workhouse. The work at the Manor, keeping Robert shut away from his family was nothing like the feeling she had now. She'd enjoyed the freedom of being able to take him to the park, to the river, to the museums and galleries. She'd enjoyed sharing the experiences with him and being able to show him a better life than he'd had at Inglebrook. Was she about to lose all that?

She'd given him back to his family which was only right. Lady Mary could give him the life he deserved, a far better life than she could ever have dreamed for him, but still she felt a pang in her heart. She had to console herself with the thought that she'd done what she set out to do that day she left the train. She'd ensured that his future would be secure and he'd never be ignored, locked up or ill-treated again.

After she'd changed, Nell went downstairs to join Ethan, Mrs Crosby and Lady Mary in the sitting room. She didn't miss the look in Ethan's eye as she appeared in the lavender afternoon dress.

"Wow," he said. "I'd forgotten how beautiful you are. You put the real lilies to shame."

"Indeed, that colour suits you perfectly," Mrs Crosby said a beaming smile on her face.

Polly came in with Robert. "He's finished his tea, ma'am. Ate every bit. He's been everso good," she said.

"And I trust the tailor has finished with him?" Lady Mary said.

"Yes, M'lady. He said he'd bring the suits this evening."

"Excellent," Lady Mary said. "Come and sit with me, Robert. I'd like to spend some time getting to know my grandson."

"He likes books, drawing and things that move," Nell said. "He's good at skittles…" Her voice faded as she realised how little Lady Mary would know about Robert, his likes and dislikes, things that had become second nature to her but would appear strange to Lady Mary.

"I'm sure we'll get along very well," Lady Mary said. "Why don't you young people take a walk around the garden. It's really magnificent this time of year. Mrs Crosby's especially proud of the roses."

"A delightful idea," Ethan said, holding out his arm to Nell who forced a smile and linked her arm through his. Her stomach knotted. Please let Robert behave and not throw one of his tantrums, she thought.

Ethan took her to see the lilies in the garden and Nell's heart went out to him. She didn't tell him what Sir Oswald had said about the possibility of her being charged with Robert's abduction. The conversation played in her mind but she didn't want to spoil the pleasant mood.

At seven o'clock Nell was shown the bedroom where she was to sleep with Robert. She would have the bed by the door and he would have the one by the window. He'd no longer share her bed. Another degree of separation she thought, but knew it to be for the best. Robert was growing up. He was eight now and perhaps it was time for her to think about her own future, if she had one.

She read him a story from one of the books she'd brought with her and put him to bed. As she tucked him in she said, "I hope you like your grandmamma. She obviously loves you."

Robert smiled and made the sign for 'home'.

"Yes. She's going to give you a new home." She brushed his forehead and hoped with all her heart that she'd be going with him.

She kissed him goodnight. "Sleep well," she said. After tonight his future would lie in his grandmother's hands. She sat by his bed, as she always did, until he was asleep, then went down to join the others for dinner.

The Guardianship Hearing took place on Monday morning in a small room with light oak panelled walls and large windows. Bright sunlight shone in, casting reflections on the oak table and chair in the centre of the room. Sir Oswald explained that it would be an informal affair focussing on what was considered best for the child named in the Guardianship Petition. The Judge was a large man with a florid face and wisps of white hair curling around his ears. He sat next to a thin wiry man assiduously taking notes. Nell guessed him to be the Clerk of the Court.

Lady Mary attended as the Petitioner, Milton Crosby as the proposed guardian, Sir Oswald to present the petition and Nell to give her evidence. Lord Eversham was represented by Sir Richard Catchpole.

Sir Oswald began by setting out the facts of the matter: Lord Eversham's employment of an untrained nursemaid to care for his son, his failure to provide any sort of education or training for him and his instructions to Miss Draper to transport him to the Bethlehem Hospital. Nell produced the letter addressed to the hospital as proof of his intentions.

"He also failed to ascertain whether his son had arrived at the hospital. His attitude to his son's whereabouts has proved casual in the extreme. It was only enquires made by his grandmother, Lady Mary, Dowager Duchess of Hertsbury, that revealed his non-arrival and persuaded him to report the boy as missing. He has made no attempt to locate him."

Lady Mary spoke of her willingness to support her grandson financially and take over responsibility for his care and welfare. Milton expressed his agreement to act as Guardian in Robert's best interest.

Sir Oswald concluded, "I believe that the circumstances outlined are sufficient to warrant the appointment of Milton Crosby as Guardian for Robert Eversham."

Sir Richard Catchpole, a slight man with fine boned features, cleared his throat before speaking. He wrinkled his nose as though in distaste for what he was about to say. "I have spoken to Lord Eversham on the telephone this morning. He informed me that he was aware of Lady Mary's close bond with her late daughter and her wish to be involved in the upbringing of her only grandson. In the circumstances he has no objection to his son, Robert Edward Henry Eversham, residing with Lady Mary or with the appointment of Mr Milton Crosby as Guardian to take over his affairs. He wishes only that his son enjoy the best that life can offer, given his disability."

Lord Eversham having no objection the Judge granted the order. Milton Crosby was appointed as Robert's Guardian.

Nell breathed a sigh of relief as they left the courtroom. Lady Mary and Milton Crosby went ahead to call her carriage.

Sir Oswald was by Nell's side walking towards the courthouse door when Sir Richard Catchpole approached them, accompanied by a police constable.

"Nell Draper, I am arresting you for the Kidnap and Abduction of Master Robert Edward Henry Eversham, son of Lord Eversham of Inglebrook," the constable said. "Please come with me."

All the joy of the last few days with Lady Mary, secure in the knowledge that Robert was in safe hands, drained out of her body. A ball of ice formed in her chest, a chill slithered into her bones. Her mind whirled back to when she'd been arrested before for something she didn't do and found innocent, this time she was guilty.

Sir Oswald accompanied her to the police station where she was charged and put in a cell. She shuddered as the door clanged shut behind her. The moment she'd dreaded since that impulse drove her to defy Lord Eversham and keep hold of his son had arrived. Her worst fears had been realised. Outside the small window the sky darkened as storm clouds gathered. There was no sign of her mother's little patch of blue.

"I'll see what I can find out," Sir Oswald said. "Things may not be as bad as they appear."

Chapter Thirty Four

Sir Oswald returned an hour later. "Just as I thought," he said to Nell. "Lady Eversham's spite knows no bounds. You have deprived her son of the inheritance she had hoped to secure for him and you must be punished."

A stone of dread hardened in Nell's stomach. "What will they do to me?" she asked, although she already knew the answer.

"Nothing if I have anything to do with it," Sir Oswald said. "The law cannot be used to settle personal vendettas. She may believe she can have everything she desires, but that is not the case." He took a sheaf of papers and a notepad from his briefcase. "There will be a preliminary hearing in the morning. You will plead not guilty and the case will be committed to the Crown Court to be heard at trial before a jury." He smiled. "In view of the prominence of the people involved and the great amount of public interest I feel sure this can be accomplished fairly swiftly. We don't want you in jail any longer than necessary."

Nell breathed a sigh of relief. If Sir Oswald was as powerful and influential as Mrs Crosby had said she had nothing to fear.

"Now, you must tell me about your responsibilities at Inglebrook Manor and how you came to be on that train with Master Robert on the way to London."

For the next hour Nell explained all that had happened at the Manor and the manner of her departure. Memories swirled through her brain as she spoke. Most of them were happy, joyful episodes of her time with Robert. She was able to speak with passion about his achievements and the steps she'd taken to encourage his love of drawing.

"And since you've been in London?"

Nell sighed. The memories now running through her mind were murky and grey as the London streets where sunshine seldom called. Once again the memories of Linus Frumley ran through her mind. She may not be in a position to testify against him now, or speak for Amos Bradley, but she didn't want to put her friends in jeopardy for helping her. She told Sir Oswald about seeing Thomas O'Leary in the market and her plans to run away to Brighton and start a new life with Robert.

"Now that would have been foolhardy in the extreme," he said. "There'd be no defence for such action had you taken it."

"Well, I didn't and now I may hang."

Nell spent that night in the cell contemplating how life can change in a moment. She hardly slept. When she did, Robert's face appeared at the edge of her dreams, smiling and chuckling with unrestrained joy. She dreamt of happy hours playing in the sunshine, Robert giggling his cheeky face and eyes sparkling with glee. Pictures appeared before her eyes; memories of Jenny's smile, Alice's laughter, Ethan's hands, his slender fingers handing Robert the horse he had carved; moments of happiness she tried valiantly to hang on to before they disappeared like morning mist at sunrise.

Tuesday morning Nell was again taken to the courthouse. Memories of her appearance charged with murder haunted her. She'd been innocent then and Ben had spoken for her. Now she was guilty. Would Sir Oswald's eloquence save her?

Sir Oswald greeted her and explained that the preliminary hearing would be held only to take her plea. "The actual trial will take place this afternoon in the Old Bailey."

Nell shuddered. "Will Lord Eversham be there?" she asked, her pulses racing.

Sir Oswald laughed. "Not this morning. However, he will have to appear this afternoon to state his case against you. It's something I look forward to with great anticipation."

Nell's spirits rose at his confidence. She wished she could be as sure.

It was as Sir Oswald had said. She made a brief appearance in the Magistrates' Court where the charges of Kidnap and Abduction were read out. She pleaded 'Not guilty'.

At two o'clock in the afternoon Nell was led to the dock of the Number One Court at the Old Bailey. She glanced around the lofty wood-panelled room and her heart fluttered. Rays of sunlight shone through the high windows, dust mites dancing in their beams. A musty smell and an eerie silence hung in the air.

She saw Sir Oswald, suitably attired in his white, horsehair wig and flowing black gown sitting next to Sir Richard Catchpole in the well of the court to her right. The jury box was to her left. Behind the barristers Nell saw Lady Mary and Milton Crosby sitting on benches filled with journalists and reporters, eagerly awaiting the trial of the nursemaid who had had the audacity to kidnap the son of an Earl.

The trial began with all the ceremony the Central Criminal Court demanded. Lord Chief Justice Bowden-Brown presided. He was in his late fifties with a sombre face. A tall man, impressive in stature, he carried the weight of his office on broad shoulders. He wore a full-bottomed wig and scarlet gown. He took his place on the high bench beneath the embossed carving of the Royal Crest showing the authority of the Court. The usher swore the jury in and proceedings commenced.

Sir Richard rose. "Sir Richard Catchpole, QC speaking for Her Majesty's prosecution," he said.

Judge Bowden-Brown leaned forward. "It's not often I see you in my court, Sir Richard," he said.

"No, Your Lordship. I try to avoid criminal law," Sir Richard said.

Judge Bowden-Brown frowned.

Sir Oswald rose. "Sir Oswald Rockingham, QC for the defence, Your Lordship."

Justice Bowden-Brown nodded. "It's always a pleasure to see you, Sir Oswald."

"Thank you, My Lord."

Nell felt heartened by the exchange.

The judge leaned back and said, "Let us begin."

Sir Richard Catchpole opened by outlining the case against Nell. "The defendant, Miss Nell Draper, is charged that on 15th day of October 1891 she did Kidnap and Abduct Robert Edward

Henry Eversham, son of Lord Eversham of Inglebrook. The taking of a man's son is a serious offence," he said. "I will prove beyond reasonable doubt that the defendant, with malice aforethought, did illegally take Robert Eversham into her custody without the permission, knowledge or consent of his father Lord Eversham of Inglebrook. By her actions she has subjected Lord Eversham's son, Robert Edward Henry Eversham, to physical and moral degradation detrimental to his health and wellbeing. A complete reversal of the role she was hired to fulfil." A satisfied grin filled his face as he returned to seat.

Nell was shocked. That wasn't what she had intended at all.

Sir Oswald's eyes sparkled with glee. He lifted a heavy leather-bound book and slammed it down on the table in front of him. The sound reverberated around the room causing everyone in the benches to jump. Nell's heart skittered.

He laid his hand on the book. As he spoke his voice resonated around the room. "Kidnap – the taking away of a person or child by force, threat or deceit, with intent to cause him or her to be detained against his or her will for ransom or for political or other purposes. Abduction – the criminal taking away of a person or child by persuasion, fraud, open force or violence. That, Gentlemen of the Jury, is the legal definition of the offences for which my client stands before you." A wry smile lit his face. The people in the front of the public gallery leaned forward as a ripple went round the courtroom. Nell could see he was enjoying himself.

"I intend to prove beyond all doubt that these charges are without foundation and are in fact a ploy, dreamed up by a vicious and uncaring parent as a vendetta against a young girl whose trust has been badly abused and that the defendant has no case to answer."

He sat down.

Sir Richard rose. "I have only one witness to call, m'lord," he said. "Call Lord Eversham of Inglebrook."

A buzz of muted conversation filtered down from the gallery as Lord Eversham strode up to the witness stand, his head held high, his shoulders squared. Tall and in his fifties, he had the look of a military man. Flecks of autumn coloured his hair and tinged his moustache and beard which were neatly trimmed. His grey eyes stared straight ahead. He'd travelled to London by train that morning; his brown tweed coat was creased and his hair a little dishevelled because of it, but his shield of arrogance remained securely in place.

Apart from the Boxing Day Ball this was the first time Nell had been in the same room as her former employer. Now she saw before her a man whose demeanour had been honed by years of sustained discipline, a man of rigid mentality, intolerant of others' perceived imperfections. A shiver ran down her spine.

He was sworn in and Sir Richard walked to the centre of the court. He moved with the ease of someone who knows of his own importance and has no need to impress. His eyes burned with frightening intensity. His zeal for the task ahead was clear.

Lord Eversham confirmed his identity and his position as Nell's employer and father of Robert Edward Henry Eversham.

Sir Richard began, "On 15th October 1891 did you instruct your son's nursemaid, Miss Nell Draper, to accompany him to an appointment at a hospital in London?"

Lord Eversham confirmed that to be the case.

"The hospital was considered to be a place of safety for your son, was it not?"

"It was."

"Your son has mental deficiencies, does he not?"

Lord Eversham bowed his head. To Nell's surprise she saw tears glistening in his eyes. "Regrettably, yes. That is the case."

A hush fell over the court. The only sound the scratching of the reporters' pencils on their notepads. Nell shuddered. By morning Robert's disability would be headline news. Was that what Lady Eversham planned? To have him declared mentally unfit to inherit?

"I am sorry," Sir Richard said.

Lord Eversham nodded.

"And did Miss Nell Draper deliver your son Robert Edward Henry Eversham to the hospital?"

"No she did not."

"Do you know what happened to your son?"

Lord Eversham drew himself up to his full height. "I have since learned from my mother-in-law that for the past nine months he has been living with Miss Draper at an unknown address in London.

Nell breathed a sigh of relief. At least they didn't know about Lottie's Place and Robert working at the funeral parlour.

"To your knowledge has Miss Draper ever made any effort to follow your instructions and take your son to the hospital appointment you made for him?"

"No, never."

"Has she made any attempt to return him to you at Inglebrook Manor, the home where he grew up?

"No."

"Did she have your permission or consent to take him to live with her in London?"

"She did not."

"Do you believe that the abduction of your son has been injurious to his health, wellbeing and mental state?"

"Without doubt."

"Thank you, Lord Eversham. Your witness." He returned to his seat.

Sir Oswald Rockingham stood. "My condolences for the difficulties your son has faced. It cannot have been easy bringing him up with the stigma attached to any sort of mental incapacity."

Lord Evesham bridled. "Thank you," he said.

Sir Oswald continued, "My client, Miss Draper, was employed by you as a nursemaid and given the responsibility of caring for your son, Robert Edward Henry Eversham. Is that correct?"

"Yes."

"To your knowledge was Miss Draper a qualified nurse having experience of working with the mentally disabled?"

Lord Eversham's face flushed. He coughed before answering. "I believe she had previously worked in the infirmary at Salvation Hill House, the local workhouse. She came highly recommended."

"I see. So not your regular nursemaid?"

"No."

"Did you engage a workhouse girl to look after your other children?"

Lord Eversham's jaw clenched. Anger shone in his eyes. "My wife was alive then. She engaged the nursemaids."

"A responsibility that has passed to your second wife?"

"Yes, naturally."

"I see. So a girl from the workhouse wasn't employed because your son was mentally deficient then?"

A gasp went round the court. Sir Richard jumped up. "My Lord!"

"Yes, yes." Judge Bowden-Brown said, waving him to sit. "Sir Oswald, I find that question offensive."

"I apologise, m'lord. I withdraw it."

"Members of the jury, you are to ignore Sir Oswald's last remark."

The members of the jury nodded but Nell didn't miss the look of disgust on their faces when they stared and nodded at each other. Sir Oswald had made his point about Lady Eversham's possible hostility to her husband's eldest son.

Sir Oswald continued, "Lord Eversham, can you please give us an idea of the duties and responsibilities involved in the care of your son? Was Miss Draper, for example, able to make decisions regarding his education, health, everyday routine and activities?"

"Yes, within reason that was her role."

"And these responsibilities were given with your full permission, knowledge and consent?"

"At the time, yes."

"Responsibilities she took seriously and duties she diligently performed during her employment at Inglebrook Manor?"

"While in my employ, yes."

"When did you last see you son, Lord Eversham?"

Lord Eversham looked shocked. "I am a busy man," he said. "It may have been some time ago. I'm afraid I can't recall."

"Within the last year? Or maybe two?"

"I can't recall."

"You have not seen your son or spent any time with him in the last five years, Lord Eversham. Is that not so?"

A ripple of disgust went around the room. Sir Richard jumped up. "M'lord, Lord Eversham is not on trial here. It's Miss Draper's behaviour that is in question."

"Sir Oswald?"

"I apologise, m'lord. I was merely trying to establish the fact that, during Lord Eversham's extensive absence, Miss Draper was '*in loco parentis*'."

"Oh. I see where you're going, Sir Oswald," Judge Bowden-Brown said. He grinned. "For the benefit of the jury, Sir Oswald contends that Miss Draper's responsibility for the day-to-day running of Robert Eversham's life gave her the authority to make decisions on his behalf 'in his parent's place'. Is that correct, Sir Oswald?"

"Precisely so, m'lord. Thank you. Would you agree that that was the case, Lord Eversham?"

Lord Eversham's face reddened. "In my absence and during the term of her employment I suppose that could be seen to be the case," he said.

"When Miss Draper left Inglebrook Manor she was in sole charge of your son. Is that correct?"

"Yes. She was to accompany him to the hospital."

"Were you not concerned when she failed to return to Inglebrook? After all she was in your employ. Was there no expectation that she would report back to you upon Master Robert's safe arrival at the hospital? Did you make any enquiries as to her whereabouts?"

Lord Eversham sniffed. "Since her services were no longer required once she had delivered my son to a place of safety, we presumed she had found alternative employment and decided to remain in London."

"Was her employment terminated at that time, either by you or by Miss Draper? Was she paid off and given a reference?"

Lord Eversham looked uncomfortable. "There was no official termination, no."

"So to all intents and purposes she was, and still is, in your employ and as such still responsible for Robert *in loco parentis*?"

"I suppose one could argue…" He glared at Sir Oswald.

"On 15th October 1891 you instructed Miss Draper to travel with Master Robert Eversham to London with the intention of taking him to the Bethlehem Hospital for the Insane. A place you have today described as 'a place of safety'. Is that correct?"

Lord Eversham lowered his head. He looked as though he wished he could be anywhere but where he was. He couldn't deny it. "Yes," he said.

"At the time did you stipulate any given time for Miss Draper to arrive at the hospital?"

"Er. No I don't believe we did."

"So her failure to arrive may be a delay, not a disregard of instructions?"

"There was an expectation that the boy would be taken immediately to the hospital."

"Ah. But an expectation is not an instruction is it?"

"I suppose not."

"Where is your son now?"

"He is with his grandmother, the Dowager Duchess of Hertsbury."

"Would you say the home of the Dowager Duchess is a 'place of safety'?"

"Of course it is."

"So, whilst in your employ Miss Draper has delivered your son to a place of safety. In doing so she has followed the spirit, if not the letter, of your instructions, albeit with some delay. Wouldn't you agree?"

Lord Eversham took a breath and pulled himself up to his full height. "I might agree had she informed us of her plan to do so."

"So, it is her lack of communication that is the problem. Not her actions? There is no need to answer."

Sir Oswald paused to consult a paper he picked up from the table. He lifted his head to stare at Lord Eversham. "Is it the case that your son, Robert Edward Henry Eversham, is to reside permanently with his grandmother, the Dowager Duchess of Hertsbury, and that a Mr Milton Crosby has been appointed his Guardian by the Court?"

Lord Eversham looked stricken. He swallowed. "A decision I fully endorsed knowing of Lady Mary's fondness for the boy," he said.

Sir Richard jumped up. He too looked decidedly uncomfortable. "My Lord," he said. "The appointment of a guardian for a mentally unstable boy is not unusual or relevant to this case. I ask that this evidence be struck from the record."

Judge Bowden Brown raised his eyebrows. "Sir Oswald?"

Sir Oswald tossed the paper onto the table. "I believe the Court may draw its own conclusions," he said.

"Very well, continue."

Sir Oswsald hooked his thumbs into the lapels of his robe and raised his head. His voice resonated around the courtroom. "Lord Eversham, I put it to you that Miss Draper, employed by you and given responsibility for your son, Robert Eversham's welfare, had no intention of depriving you permanently of his presence. She merely, while *in loco parentis*, saved him from incarceration in a place wholly unsuited and likely to be detrimental to his wellbeing."

Blood coloured Lord Eversham's face, a vein in his neck pulsed. He gripped the rail in front of him. His eyes blazed. "She disobeyed my orders. She took him without consent. That is a crime and one for which she should be punished."

Sir Oswald's eyebrows shot up to his horsehair wig. "That, Lord Eversham, is for the jury to decide," he said.

Sir Oswald referred to the book now open on the table in front of him. "To the best of your knowledge, when Miss Draper took your son was any force, threat or deceit used against your son?"

"Not as far as I am aware," Lord Eversham said. "But who knows what force, threat or deceit may have been used against him while he was in Miss Draper's custody."

"Has a ransom been demanded?"

"No."

Sir Oswald referred to the book again. "A fraud committed?"

"Not that I am aware of."

Sir Oswald raised his head. "Thank you, Lord Eversham. That will be all."

When Lord Eversham stepped down from the witness box he appeared deflated. Nell almost felt sorry for him. Then she recalled how Robert had been treated at the Manor and all sympathy disappeared.

"Now we come to the allegation that Miss Draper subjected Robert Edward Henry Eversham, to physical and moral degradation detrimental to his health and wellbeing. If it please the Court I would like to call Dr Peter Jameson, an eminent psychiatric physician to the stand.

Dr Jameson was duly called and sworn in.

"Dr Jameson, you are a practising psychiatric physician of some note and considered by the profession to be an expert on the subject of mental health in children. Is that correct?"

"Indeed. It is true to say that within my profession I am considered an expert," Dr Jameson said.

"And you have had the opportunity of examining Robert Edward Henry Eversham within the last twenty-four hours?"

"Yes. I spent an hour with him last evening. You have my report."

Sir Oswald picked up a file of papers. "A highly detailed and comprehensive report," he said. "You have a copy, m'lord. As does Sir Richard."

Judge Bowden-Brown nodded and picked up a file of papers.

"Can you give the Court a brief outline of your findings?"

Dr Jameson nodded and addressed the Court: "Robert Eversham is eight years old. He is mute.

Whether that condition is temporary or will remain permanently I am unable to say. He is able to follow simple instructions. His cognitive and reasoning abilities are as I would expect for a boy of his age with his disability. He has a low level of concentration with periods of in-attentiveness. He is easily distracted, however if the subject is of interest to him his interest can border on obsession. He demonstrated his ability to recognise simple written words. His talent for drawing is extraordinary, far in excess of what I would have expected in so young a child. Although unable to speak he can communicate effectively using signs, facial expressions and physical action."

"Thank you, Dr Jameson. Is it your professional opinion that the time Robert Eversham spent in Miss Draper's custody has been detrimental to his health and wellbeing?"

"On the contrary. I would say it has been highly beneficial. Robert has made friends, is able to integrate socially and communicate using signs she has taught him. Apart from some traces of the type of physical injury most young boys experience at some time in their lives, he is extremely healthy."

Nell swallowed at the memory of the still fading bruises on Robert's face and body. At least the swelling around his eye had gone down.

"Thank you, Dr Jameson. You have heard of the Bethlehem Hospital for the Insane?"

"Of course. It is an institution for those with serious mental disorders who are dangerously deranged and likely to be injurious to the community were they at large."

"Would you consider the Bethlehem Hospital a suitable place for Robert Eversham?"

Dr Jameson looked aghast. "Good heavens no! The child I met is a happy, healthy, quick-witted boy who, with the right encouragement, will no doubt reach his full potential by the time he is fully grown. You would be mad to send him there. He'd not survive five minutes."

"Thank you, Dr Jameson. That is all." Sir Oswald returned to his seat.

Sir Richard stood and walked to the centre of the room. "Dr Jameson, thank you for your well constructed report on the mental state of Lord Eversham's son. I'm sure your findings will be welcomed. However, is it fair to say that your professional assessment of Robert Eversham's mental state is a result of a recent, time-limited consultation?"

"Yes. I spent an hour with him last evening."

"You were not aware of his mental condition prior to his visit to London?"

"No, I was not."

"So you are in no position to pass judgement on the improvement or otherwise of his mental condition during the time spent in the defendant's custody. Is that not so?"

"I can only use my professional judgement. I was unable to identify a decline in his mental capacity from that which I would expect of a boy of his age with his disability – unless of course he was previously a genius."

A ripple of mirth went round the courtroom.

"Thank you, Dr Jameson. No further questions."

Sir Oswald rose. "That concludes the case for the defence, m'lord."

Nell glanced around. Her heart hammered. Had Sir Oswald done enough?

Judge Bowden-Brown glanced at the clock on the wall above the dock. "I see the hour is late. We will adjourn for summing up tomorrow. Thank you, gentlemen." He banged his gavel and Court was adjourned.

Chapter Thirty Five

Nell travelled, shackled to two police officers, in a closed carriage to Newgate Prison. Two wardresses accompanied her to her cell. A cot with a rough grey blanket stood along one wall. A bench with a hole in it and a bucket beneath stood across one corner next to a small table holding a metal wash basin, a jug and a tin cup were chained to the wall. The only light came through a barred window high up on the wall. The floor and whitewashed walls were solid stone.

Nell shuddered. She hugged her arms across her chest and sank onto the cot. The day's events ran through her mind. Had Sir Oswald done enough? Would the jury believe she thought she was still employed by Lord Eversham and had only taken Robert to delay taking him to the hospital? Even she doubted it. The men on the jury were Lord Eversham's contemporaries, landowners themselves who may have had trouble with staff. Would that go against her? If she was found guilty of the charges she would undoubtedly hang.

She didn't fear death, in the workhouse it visited daily. For most of the inmates, like poor Flossie, it came as a blessed relief. She recalled what Flossie had said about going to a better place and hoped she was right.

She prayed to God for the strength and courage to face whatever lay ahead. She prayed for Robert. The thought of never seeing his face, lit up with a magical smile, not watching him grow up, never knowing the man he would become, these things brought on a torrent of despair so strong it took all the willpower she possessed not to give in to a fit of weeping. She fought it back.

Now was not the time to be faint-hearted. Robert was safe in the arms of his adoring grandmother. Milton, Max and even Ethan would be there to make sure he had the loving care he deserved. His happiness and safety meant more to her than her own miserable life. She'd done what she set out to do that day when, on a sudden impulse, she took him with her rather than deliver him to a place of living hell where he'd be incarcerated for the rest of his life. Now she was ready to face whatever lay ahead.

That night was the longest of her life. She lay in her bed shivering, her feet numb with cold waiting for the dawn to come. Whatever was going to happen to her, she was powerless to prevent it.

The next morning the Court reassembled. Judge Bowden-Brown presiding. The Clerk of the Court read out the details of the matter before them and Judge Bowden-Brown called on Sir Richard to sum up the case for the prosecution.

Sir Richard Catchpole stood to address the jury. Despite Sir Oswald's eloquent performance the previous day he appeared supremely confident. Nell shuddered.

"Gentlemen," he began. "Let us look at the indisputable facts of this case. On 15th October, 1891 Miss Nell Draper did take Robert Edward Henry Eversham from a train at Kings Cross without the permission, knowledge or consent of his parent and then guardian, Lord Eversham of Inglebrook in blatant contravention of his instructions to her that day. She then forced, yes forced, him to live with her at an address we have yet to identify. During the time Robert Eversham was living with her she has made no attempt to inform his parents of his whereabouts. If that's not Kidnap and Abduction I don't know what is."

He took a step closer to the jury box. "You are all landowners and employers and will share Lord Eversham's expectation of unquestioning loyalty and obedience from your staff. Whether Lord Eversham's instructions were fair or reasonable is not for you to decide. He is not on trial today, Miss Draper is. The unlawful removal of a son from his father's jurisdiction is a serious offence and one of which I have no hesitation in recommending you find Miss Draper guilty." He grinned at Nell as he made his way back to his seat. A huge stone of despair fell into her stomach. She felt the hangman's rope getting closer.

Sir Oswald rose. He smiled at Nell but it didn't make her feel any better. He approached the jury box. "In order to find the defendant guilty of the charges against her you must believe, beyond reasonable doubt, that she did, with malice aforethought, use force, threat, fraud, violence or deceit, with intent to cause him or her to be detained against his or her will for ransom or for other purposes. That is the legal definition of the charges against Miss Draper. You have heard directly from Lord Eversham's lips that this was not the case.

"You have also heard Lord Eversham's instruction to Miss Draper to take his son to a 'place of safety' and that, in Lord Eversham's exceedingly long absence from his son's life, Miss Draper was *in loco parentis* which means she had the authority to act as a parent and make decisions about Robert Eversham's welfare based on her own judgement and at her own discretion. Miss Draper's overriding duty was that of a duty of care to Robert Eversham. It was her judgement that the Bethlehem Hospital for the Insane was not an appropriate place of safety for a child like Robert. A judgement with which Dr Jameson, an expert in the field of child psychiatry, concurs. She has followed Lord Eversham's instructions and ensured that Robert Edward Henry Eversham was taken to 'a place of safety'. No time frame was stipulated for Miss Draper to follow these instructions, so she used her discretion. That is not Kidnap.

"Cases of Kidnap and Abduction must of necessity focus on the needs and effects upon the victim, or the Abductee, in this case Robert Eversham. Dr Jameson, a consultant psychiatric physician, an expert in his field, has testified that no detriment or damage has come to Robert Eversham as a result of Miss Draper's action. In fact, his opinion is that her custody has been highly beneficial. You have heard the evidence. Based on what you have heard you have no alternative but to find my client Not Guilty." He returned to his seat. Nell was taken back to the cells below the court to spend an agonising half-hour awaiting the verdict.

When she returned Judge Bowden-Brown called upon the foreman of the jury. "Have you reached a verdict?"

"Yes, My Lord."

"Is it the verdict of you all?"

"It is, My Lord."

"Very well. What is your verdict?"

"We find the defendant, Miss Nell Draper, Not Guilty of all charges."

The Court erupted. Reporters rushed out to file their copy. Nell felt the breath squeeze out of her lungs. A huge weight lifted from her shoulders.

Mrs Crosby was right. Sir Oswald Rockingham could do anything.

She didn't miss Sir Oswald's wry smile as they left the court.

When they arrived back at the Crosbys' house, Lady Mary insisted they open the champagne. She poured them each a glass.

"Sir Oswald, I hope you can stay for dinner," she said. "We have much to celebrate."

"Thank you," he said. "It will be my pleasure."

Lady Mary nodded at Ethan, glanced at Nell and said, "This young man has told me a lot about you. It seems he's rather fond of you. I suggest the two of you spend some time together before we depart to Somerset next week."

Ethan blushed.

The mention of the following week brought the memory of Linus Frumley and the court case crashing into her mind. "Next week? But I can't. I..."

She glanced around as though looking for an escape, but there was none. In her worry about her own future she'd pushed the case against Linus Frumley to the back of her mind. How could she explain to Robert's grandmother about her and Robert witnessing Harry Grubstick's murder? Her knees turned to water. She sank onto a chair and put her head in her hands.

"What on earth is it, my dear?" Lady Mary said. "Whatever it is I'm sure it can be sorted out."

Nell didn't know what to say. Robert was with his family, his inheritance would be assured. Milton would see that his talents were recognised, all fear of the asylum had been removed. There was no reason their true identities couldn't be revealed. She wanted justice for Linus Frumley. She wanted him to pay for what he'd done to Robert. The Bradley's were relying on her. Now she had no need to let everybody down.

"Robert and I have to appear in court next week. We were witness to a murder. We have to testify to the facts and make sure the truth comes out."

Everyone stared. Even Mrs Crosby was lost for words. Nell told them all about her job at the funeral parlour, Mr Bradley, Goose, Linus, witnessing the murder and being arrested. She noticed Sir Oswald listening intently.

"That's when I wrote the letter," she said. "I wanted to be sure Robert would be protected if anything happened to me."

"We are all grateful that you did," Lady Mary said.

Then Nell went on to tell them about Robert's drawing saving her from prison and being used in evidence.

"Good heavens," Milton said. "When that gets out the value of his pictures will rocket." He looked suitably impressed.

"I think that's what prompted the beating," she said.

"The beating!"

"Yes, a young thug beat Robert up. I didn't want to say anything before, but that's where he got the bruises."

Everyone was horrified. "Well, my dear," Lady Mary said. "I'm sure Sir Oswald will be able to sort it all out."

"I'll certainly try," he said. Nell's hands shook as she told him about the murder she'd witnessed and the part Robert played in getting her freed from prison and Linus Frumley arrested.

"Hmm. This sounds like a serious matter," he said. "I'll make some enquiries."

Then she told him about the beating. "The crossing sweeper who chased the assailant away said he was an older lad, part of a gang. I feel sure he was put up to it by Linus Frumley."

Sir Oswald looked perturbed. "Rest assured you'll have my full backing to protect the boy and ensure that the perpetrator is caught. Can't have the son of an Earl beaten up and get away with it."

Nell stuttered, "B-but of course he didn't know who Robert really was."

Sir Oswald smiled. "He soon will," he said.

After dinner Nell went for a walk around the garden with Ethan.

"Tell me more about where you've been living with Robert," he said. "It sounds fascinating. You made friends too, what are they like?"

At the mention of her friends Nell recalled the note she left for Lottie with the rent money. She'd said she wouldn't need the room any longer. Lottie would think she'd done a runner, which was exactly what she'd planned. Lottie'd be sure to tell Josh and they'd all know she was about to let them down by failing to appear in court. She caught her breath. If she wasn't there to testify against Linus and speak up for Mr Bradley…

She'd been so tied up thinking about her own future and the threat of imprisonment for abducting Robert, she'd forgotten about the note to Lottie. Now they'd all know what a traitor she was.

"I have to go back," she said. "I have to go back and tell them I'm going to speak up in court."

"You mean they don't know?"

Nell swallowed. "I left a note. I wasn't going back. It wasn't just a visit to the gallery for Robert's birthday, I was running away. I had tickets to Brighton. I was taking Robert. I…I was going to let them all down." A swell of misery engulfed her. At the time she'd seen no way out other than going away. Now she'd have to explain that to Lottie, Josh and his family.

"Oh, I see," Ethan said. "You saw me in the gallery and that prompted you to run away, letting your friends down and leaving everything you valued behind." Confusion filled his eyes.

"No, you don't see," Nell said. "Yes, it was seeing you made me want to run that day, but I'd been planning it ever since I heard that I'd have to appear in court. I was afraid my identity would be discovered and Robert would be taken back to the Evershams and then on to the hospital. That was what I was running away from."

"Not me then?"

"No, not you, only the people I thought you represented, the Evershams."

He nodded, reassured. "If you want to go back in the morning I'll come with you," he said. "I assume there's no reason now why you can't appear in court? Now your identity has been uncovered and Robert is safely with his grandmother."

"As long as Lady Mary's lawyer is able to protect Robert I don't care what happens to me."

"I care," Ethan said. "I care a lot, Nell."

Chapter Thirty Six

The following morning Nell rose early. Robert was up before her, staring out of the window into the garden. She washed and dressed quickly and dressed Robert in one of the new suits the tailor had delivered the previous evening. He seemed to have grown several inches since they left Lottie's, but perhaps that was just because he stood taller, his sunny disposition had returned and Nell realised that he understood the improvement in their fortunes.

"Are you looking forward to going to live with your grandmamma?" she asked. His broad smile and the sign for 'home' spoke more eloquently than words ever could.

Breakfast was served in the dining room and when Nell arrived Ethan was already there.

He rose as they arrived. "Good morning," he said.

"Good morning," Nell said. She had hoped to be able to get out early before Ethan as she'd have preferred to go to see Lottie alone, but it soon became clear that wherever she went, Ethan was sure to go with her.

Robert ran to a seat at the table and Nell put some eggs and ham on a plate for him. Then she served out some for herself. After the usual pleasantries, the 'Did you sleep well?' and 'How are we today?' Ethan sat beside Robert. Nell's heart warmed seeing them together.

"I've spoken to Lady Mary," Ethan said. "I told her we had urgent business to attend to. She suggested we leave Robert with Milton. He has a surprise for him."

"A surprise? Whatever is he planning?"

Nell's voice betrayed her concern. She'd trusted Milton and Mrs Crosby with Robert's secret, but handing him over completely, that was a different matter.

"You'll see," Ethan said, but wouldn't be drawn further.

After breakfast Robert was allowed out to play in the garden. "He'll be quite safe," Ethan assured her.

"I'll keep an eye on 'im," Polly said. "He's so bonny, who could ever think of harming him, that's what I'd like to know."

Satisfied that Robert was in good hands Nell set off with Ethan to visit Lottie.

It was warm in the sunshine and early enough that the cabs and carriages rushing along the road were not so many as to make their journey unpleasant. The rattle of wheels on cobbles and the clatter of horses' hooves prevented any meaningful conversation. As they walked towards

Lottie's Place the streets became narrower and darker. In her mind Nell compared it to the wide open spaces where Ethan would be working in the garden in the estate in Kent, a far cry from the crowded city.

She watched him glancing around, unable to make sense of his expression. He was keeping his thoughts close and hardly spoke until they were almost at the café.

"Were you happy here, Nell?" he asked, glancing around the tall buildings and crowded streets.

Nell thought for a moment before replying. "Yes," she said. "I was happy here."

"Tell me about it."

Nell drew a breath. "I loved the freedom," she said. "The knowledge that every decision was mine to make. I managed to provide a home for Robert and keep him fed by my own labours. I won't say it wasn't hard, it was, but also very satisfying."

"You did a good job," Ethan said. "The boy is happy, everyone can see that. Despite his difficulties you gave him hope and showed him he was valued. You gave him confidence too. I noticed how different he was from the small uncertain boy I saw last."

"He gave me something too," she said. "He gave me the courage to fight for the things I believe in. He brought me great joy and showed me a different way of life. I owe him a lot."

"Will you be happy working for Lady Mary in Somerset? You'll lose your newly gained freedom."

"I know. I'll be a domestic servant again, but as long as it's for Robert's sake I'll manage." She bit her lip. "I'll never leave him, you know, unless it's what he wants. I'll always do what's best for him."

"I know," Ethan said.

When they arrived at Lottie's Place Nell went up to the room she'd shared with Robert to retrieve the note she'd left for Lottie. All the time her heart pounded. She'd left on Saturday morning, today was Thursday. She hadn't been in for breakfast with Robert. Lottie would have missed her. Would she have come upstairs to check in the room and found it empty? Would she have realised that Nell intended to leave Mr Bradley to his fate? Would she have told Josh?

She breathed a sigh of relief when she saw the note still there. The vase of flowers she'd left on the table by the window, the chairs pulled out when they stood up from breakfast, two of Robert's wooden toys left on the floor, all still undisturbed. It felt strange being here after all that had happened. Was it really only six days? It felt a lot longer.

Ethan followed her. "So, this is where you lived." He gazed around. "It looks clean and cosy. I can see why you liked it."

She picked up the note and money. "I'll take the rest of Robert's toys today," she said. "There wasn't room in the bag when I left." She started picking up the toys.

Ethan walked over and drew back the curtain that hid the bed. She stood behind him, glancing around in case she'd left anything there. Then she saw it; the picture of Josh, still on the wall.

"Who's that?" Ethan asked.

"A friend," Nell said reaching over to take it down. "I'd forgotten it was there."

"Oh."

Nell rolled the picture up and put it in her bag. She took a last look round. Everything looked neat and tidy. Lottie would have no trouble re-letting the room. Downstairs they went into the café. Sunday was the busiest day in the market, but the traders would be out early so the café was quiet.

"Lottie greeted them with a smile. "I've missed you this week," she said. Then she glanced at Ethan and back at Nell. Her eyebrows rose.

"This is Ethan, an old friend," Nell said. "Please join us for coffee. I have something to tell you."

Lottie made the coffee. "I 'opes as how it's good news," she said. "We've 'ad our share of the other sort."

Nell immediately thought of Josh, Mr Bradley and the court case. "I hope you'll think it good news," Nell said taking the coffee. "But you may find some of it surprising."

"I'm all ears," Lottie said.

Nell went on to tell her about the boy she knew as Bobby and who he really was.

Lottie's eyes sparkled with incredulity as she spoke. Her jaw dropped at one point and she stared at Nell. "No," Lottie said. "You're joshing me. That little lad? Well, fancy that."

"We'll be living with his grandmother, Lady Mary, Dowager Duchess of Hertsbury. She's going to take care of him," Nell said. "So, you see, I won't need the room any longer." Nell took out two weeks' rent and laid it on the table.

"Well, I'll be..." Lottie was stuck for words. Then her face clouded over. "What about Josh, the court case, Goose and Mr Bradley?" she said.

Nell swallowed. "I'll still be giving evidence," she said. "We won't be leaving for at least a week. I want Linus Frumley to hang for what he did." Bitterness echoed in her voice. "And for what he did to Robert."

Lottie nodded. Her gaze flitted to Ethan. "And Josh?"

Nell smiled and turned to Ethan. "Josh was a good friend. He got me the job at the funeral parlour. I don't know what Robert and I would have done without his help." She looked at Lottie. "I'll talk to Josh. I'm sure he'll understand."

Lottie's eyebrows shot up. "Well, I guess you could always leave him a note," she said.

Then a customer came in and Lottie got up to serve him. Nell's heart dropped. Had Lottie been up to the room and seen the note? If she had she was certainly keeping quiet about it.

When they'd finished their drinks Nell went out to the kitchen to say goodbye to Lottie and Ernie. "I want to thank you for all you've done for me and Robert," she said. "I'll never forget you."

Ernie gave her a kiss on the cheek, Lottie gave her a hug. "I wish you all the best, girl," she said, wiping a tear from her cheek with the corner of her apron. "I'll miss you and the young 'un but you 'ave to grab at any good fortune that comes your way, whatever shape it comes in."

"Thank you," Nell said. "I'll see you at the trial. I won't let Mr Bradley down."

Lottie nodded. "I know you won't," she said.

Ethan and Nell walked for a while in silence. Then Ethan asked, "This Josh? Is he important?"

Nell let out a long breath. Visions of Josh raced through her mind. The evenings they'd gone out together, the fun, the way he smiled and brought laughter back into her life. He was like the red ribbon on a plain straw hat that lifted it from the ordinary to the desirable. He'd been important in her life, but now her life had changed. She couldn't decide if he still was.

"I'm not sure," she said. "He was a good friend at a time I needed a friend." She turned to him. "Just as you were."

"Were?" Ethan's brows drew together in a frown. "I hope I still am." He stopped. "In fact I was hoping there might be more between us than friendship," he said. "I missed you, Nell. When Jenny said you'd gone away and I learnt about you and Robert disappearing, it wrung my heart. I so wanted to be the one who found you, I wanted to be the one to save you. Now it seems someone else has taken that place."

Nell's mind spun back to the time she spent with Ethan in the garden at the Manor and the way her heart had lifted at the sight of him. She'd never stopped thinking about him. It was a long time ago but the memory of those days had never dulled. Could she feel the lift in her heart again and the way it used to sing when she saw him. Could she get those feelings back?

If Josh was a red ribbon, Ethan was a golden field of corn waving in the breeze. Josh was dashing and exciting, Ethan steadfast and reliable. She recalled how Josh had charmed the ladies in the pub at Christmas and how at ease he was amidst the fairer sex. Ethan, on the other hand had always been reserved, tongue-tied sometimes. But when he spoke as he was speaking to her now she knew it came from his heart.

"I never thought I'd see you again, Ethan. I thought you'd moved on. I had to move on too. Things change, people change."

"Feelings don't change, Nell. Nothing will change the way I feel about you."

They arrived at Mr Crosby's gate. Nell looked into Ethan's deep brown eyes and her heart jumped, just the way it used it.

He touched her face. "Just say there's a chance for me, Nell. I know things are difficult now, but if there's a chance I'll wait."

Suddenly her heart flooded with love for this man standing in front of her. "There's a chance," she said. "A very good chance."

Inside they went through to the sitting room where Lady Mary was watching a young man she recognised as Max Pemberton reading to Robert.

Milton was standing by the fireplace a satisfied grin on his face. He stepped forward when they entered the room. "No doubt you remember Max Pemberton," he said to Nell.

"Yes. He was Robert's art teacher," she explained to a perplexed Ethan. "But I'm not sure why he's here now."

"Milton asked him to come," Lady Mary said. "Robert is eight. He'll need a tutor and Milton has recommended Mr Pemberton. You said Robert needed to be surrounded by people he knew and who would be familiar to him. Milton assures me that Mr Pemberton is eminently suitable."

"He's travelled extensively, is well qualified and can provide Robert with expert tuition in all subjects," Milton said. "We're lucky to have him."

Max stood up. "It's my privilege to be able to teach such an avid student," he said. "In the short while I've known him this young man has made a considerable impression upon me. I feel sure we will do very well together."

"I've asked him to come to Somerset to be Robert's permanent tutor," Lady Mary said. "And I'm pleased to say he has agreed."

Nell smiled. "I suppose I shouldn't be surprised," she said. "I know Robert will be thrilled to be able to continue his studies with Mr Pemberton." She put out her hand. "Welcome," she said.

Max shook her hand. Ethan held his out and he shook that.

"Excellent," Milton said. "As Robert's Guardian, I am delighted."

Chapter Thirty Seven

Monday morning Milton arranged for Robert to spend two hours each day after breakfast in his study with Max Pemberton. "It will give Max a chance to get to know the boy and assess his understanding of scholarly subjects," he said. "He can help with his art work in the afternoons, perhaps twice a week?"

"The routine will be welcome," Nell said. "It's what he needs after all the changes he's been through." She felt confident that Robert could read and understand the words in the books she read to him and he had no problem understanding how many pennies made a shilling.

Max set out a rigorous schedule of lessons, including reading, writing and arithmetic, for Milton's approval. Robert couldn't read out loud, nor call out the answers to sums, but Max produced answer sheets so he could point to the answers of questions or sums to demonstrate his understanding. As his nurse, Nell would be responsible for his meals, his laundry, care of his clothes and his general health and wellbeing.

In the afternoons when he wasn't with Max working on his drawings, she would be able to take him out.

On Wednesday Nell received a note from Sir Oswald Rockingham asking her to attend his office that morning. Her stomach churned. "He'll want to go over my statement," she said to Ethan over breakfast. "I'll be glad when the trial is over." She'd been trying to put it to the back of her mind. Living in the Crosby's house with Robert had seemed a world away from the funeral parlour, the yard, Linus Frumley and all the anxiety they brought.

"I'll come with you," Ethan said. "Moral support. Unless you'd rather go alone."

Nell thought about it. Did she want Ethan to be present when she went over all the gory details of the fight in the yard, the atmosphere, the thefts that had been uncovered? Looking back now it all seemed sordid and unreal. Doubts about the wisdom of taking Robert there resurfaced. The experience wasn't one she cared to share.

"I'm sure you can find more pleasant ways to spend a morning," she said. "It'll be dull, boring legal stuff. Perhaps we can meet for lunch afterwards."

"If you're sure."

"I'm sure. I'll be fine. I expect it's just a formality."

She donned her straw bonnet, pulled on cotton gloves and wrapped a shawl over her shoulders. Marie had remodelled a pale blue day dress with a fitted bodice and long sleeves for her to wear. The morning sun was beginning to light the sky but Nell still felt a chill as she walked along.

Sir Oswald's chambers were in Temple which was a short walk from Lottie's Place. Walking along the familiar streets her mind filled with memories of Josh: the day she met him in the café, Christmas evening in the Crown and Anchor, the theatre trip. She recalled his smiling face, the fun they'd had and the way he always made her laugh. She hadn't seen him since she moved out of the room above the café. How would he feel when he found out the truth about her? Everything she'd told him was a lie. She'd deceived him. He'd befriended her when he thought she had nothing and needed a hand. The truth would be a revelation, one she wasn't sure he'd understand. Add to that the fact that she was going live in Somerset with Robert's wealthy grandmother and it felt like the ultimate betrayal.

She still felt guilty about her intention to leave them in the lurch when she planned her escape with Robert. Had Lottie told him of her new situation? Had she seen the note left for her and told Josh of her plan to run? In any event she owed him an explanation. She needed to tell him face to face. She owed him that much.

If all went well she could call in to Lottie's and see if he was there, alternatively she could go to the funeral parlour. It wasn't a confrontation she relished. She felt ashamed of her deceit. Guilt about intending to let them down gnawed at her stomach, but telling him the truth had been out of the question. Her life depended on remaining undiscovered. Would he appreciate that?

Nell found Sir Oswald's chambers behind the Royal Court of Justice. Her knees trembled as she walked up to the daunting 17th century building carrying Sir Oswald's note in her shaking hand. A plaque on the wall identified the address. Inside it felt like walking into church, the silence oppressive. A clerk greeted her. She showed him the note and was immediately taken into Sir Oswald's office.

She caught her breath as she entered the room. Her heart raced, but it wasn't the heavy furniture, the sombre atmosphere or the opulent surroundings that took her breath away. Sir Oswald rose from behind his solid mahogany desk. Ben and Josh, who were sitting in carved-back chairs in front of the desk, also stood to greet her.

Her footsteps faltered. Ben was the first to stride forward and shake her hand. A smile lit up his face as he said, "I understand it's Miss Draper now. So good to see you again."

Sir Oswald guided her to a chair between the two men. "I've explained the recent change in your circumstances to Mr Crowe and Mr Bradley," he said. "It seems they were unaware of your true identity."

Nell bowed her head as the blood rushed up her neck. Josh was sitting next to her. He hadn't spoken and she daren't look at him for fear of what she might see. Her heart hammered at his closeness. His presence exerted a powerful influence over her. The unresolved issues lay between them like shards of broken glass along a carriageway.

Sir Oswald resumed his seat behind the desk and consulted the pile of papers in front of him. "Now, let's get down to business," he said. "As I understand it Miss Draper, known to the police as Lily Drummond, is a witness for the prosecution in the matter of the murder of Harry Grubstick by Linus Frumley." He glanced up.

"Yes, I am a witness," Nell said. "I was accused of involvement in the murder but cleared by a drawing produced by the boy known to the police as Bobby."

"I'm acting in defence of Amos Bradley, Josh's father," Ben said. "He's accused of being Linus's accomplice and involved in the theft of valuables from clients of the funeral parlour he owns. Miss Draper, who worked at the funeral parlour and is well acquainted with Mr Bradley, has agreed to speak on his behalf. Miss Drummond, or Miss Draper as we now know her to be, is a witness in his defence."

Nell glanced at Josh. His head was bowed, he turned his hat in his hands, a look of pure misery filled his face. She'd never seen him so subdued.

Sir Oswald nodded. He leaned back in his chair and folded his hands in front of him. "I have spoken to the Chief Constable and I am happy to be able to tell you that the charges against Amos Bradley have been dropped."

Josh's head jerked up. "Dropped?"

"Yes. They were purely circumstantial and would never have stood up to any cross-examination."

A look of relief passed across Josh's face. "I can't thank you enough," he said, his eyes sparkling with life. "Whatever it cost we'll be happy to pay. My mother will be so relieved."

Sir Oswald waved his hand. "Consider it settled," he said. "Now, the case against Linus Frumley." He looked again at his papers. "The police have caught the boy who assaulted young Master Robert Eversham, although of course at the time he was masquerading as Bobby Robinson, the orphan child of Miss Drummond's sister." He sighed. "My client was most anxious that this boy be brought to justice, but, in view of the testimony he agreed to give against Linus Frumley, he is to serve a short sentence in a Reformatory School. We would have wished for a something harsher, but his testimony has been crucial." He paused to consult his notes again. "Mr Frumley's brother, Charles Frumley, has also been," he glanced up, "shall we say convinced – to tell the truth and testify against him. With the additional evidence held by Inspector Munro the case against Linus Frumley is so strong that he has been persuaded to enter a guilty plea in hope of avoiding the rope."

"You mean he won't hang?" Nell's eyes sprang wide.

"Sentencing is in the hands of the Judge, my dear," Sir Oswald said. "It may be that the guilty plea will allow more leniency, but it's not certain. It may merely ease his conscience when he goes to meet his maker."

"Conscience? I doubt he has one," Josh said.

"Well, whatever the reason, my client's wish that Miss Draper and Master Robert Eversham should be spared the ordeal of the court case has been fulfilled. That is the outcome I have been charged to obtain."

"Well I'm glad," Nell said. "I think I've seen enough of the inside of a courtroom to last a lifetime."

Sir Oswald grinned. "Did you not find it a thrilling experience, my dear? The cut and thrust of argument, the energy of debate, the rise and fall of fortunes on the turn of a word or a phrase?"

Nell saw the passion is his eyes as he spoke. "No," she said. "I fear my experience was quite different."

Sir Oswald chuckled. He glanced again at his papers. "There was another witness statement from a Mr George Duckworth." He looked up. "Unfortunately I have been unable to contact Mr Duckworth."

Josh chuckled. "Goose. You mean Goose."

"Do I? Well, whatever he chooses to call himself I need to let him know that his presence in court is no longer required."

Josh grinned. "I can let Goose know. He'll be glad not to have to appear in court. If you're sure."

"Yes, I'm sure. Thank you, that will suit very well," Sir Oswald said.

"How is Goose? Is he all right?" Nell said as she realised she hadn't given him a thought when she decided to run away. "When Robert was attacked I worried the same thing might happen to Goose."

"He's fine. He's working with a coach-builder in the Strand. It's a good job with prospects. He misses Bobby of course. He took to the lad, same as we all did."

Nell sighed with relief. "I'm sure Bobby, I mean Robert, misses him too. He enjoyed working with him and learned a lot." Nell remembered Robert greeting Goose in the café. The warmth of the greeting assured her that Robert had taken to Goose. Whether he missed him was another matter. The workings of Robert's mind where relationships were concerned were a mystery she had yet to solve.

"I'm sure we are all very grateful," Ben said.

"Yes, a satisfactory result all round," Sir Oswald said.

Josh stood and extended his hand across the desk to Sir Oswald. "You have the gratitude of the Bradley family," he said. "We'll never forget and if there's ever anything we can do in return please be sure to let us know."

Sir Oswald smiled as he shook Josh's hand. "Thank you. I hope I won't be in need of the services of a funeral parlour for some time to come, but your offer is well received." He stood up. "Thank you all for your attendance today."

Ben stood to leave. Nell stood too. Sir Oswald shook their hands, wished them "Good day," and showed them out.

Outside in the fresh air Nell breathed again. It felt as though the sun had come out, the sky was now azure blue. She turned her face to feel the sun.

"That's a turn up," Ben said. "Last thing I expected when I came here. Good news though. I'll let Lottie know. She'll be as surprised as me when I tell her." He turned to Nell. "If I can ever be of any assistance, please don't hesitate to call me."

"Thank you," she said.

He nodded to Josh and walked away leaving Nell standing on the pavement with Josh.

"So, it's Miss Nell Draper, nursemaid to the Honourable Master Robert Eversham. And I thought it was Lily, the beautiful aunt of an orphaned boy."

"I'm sorry," Nell said, embarrassment turning her face red. "Sorry I couldn't tell you the truth, but I couldn't risk anyone finding out, no matter how dear they were to me."

"Sir Oswald explained," he said. "Fair knocked me sideways when he said he was taking Pa's case. Course that was nothing to the shock of finding out why."

"I know, and I regret having to lie to you, but I can't regret anything else." A spark of determination lit her eyes.

"I should've known you were too good to be true. A classy lady like you being interested in a chancer like me."

Nell laughed. "You're not a chancer and I wouldn't describe myself as classy. I'm a girl from the workhouse who had the good fortune to meet a gentleman who offered help at a time of need. Something I'll always be grateful for."

"It's Pa should be grateful to you," he said. "If it weren't for you being who you are Sir Oswald would never have taken the case, nor spoken to the police to get the case dropped. I reckon it's us as should be thanking you."

"I'm glad it worked out for your father. He didn't deserve to be charged with something he knew nothing about. How is he? And your mother?"

"They'll be much better when I tell 'em they don't have the threat of the court hanging over 'em." His eyes twinkled as he said, "Come and see for yourself. They'd both be happy as bees in summer to see you. Any excuse for Ma to put the kettle on."

Nell smiled. "Give them my best wishes, and Goose when you see him. Does your father have any plans? Your mother said he was thinking of giving up the funeral business."

Josh pouted. "I can't see 'im doing owt else. He's a natural at it. Puts people at their ease and he's good to them as can't afford a proper do. Keeps 'em out of Potter's field, that's the main thing."

Nell smiled. Potter's field was what they called the place where paupers and unclaimed bodies were buried. Mr Bradley made sure even the poorest families were able to give their loved ones a decent funeral.

"No. I think he'll carry on. I might even give 'im a hand. At least it's secure and I suppose it's time I settled to something."

"I'm glad to hear it," Nell said. "While I was there I learned how comforting it can be to know your loved ones are given a good ending. It's something we should all be able to rely on."

"There'll always be a place there for you, if you want it," Josh said. Nell saw a glint of hope in his eyes.

"Thank you, but I have to go with Robert," she said. "It's where I belong. He has my heart in his hands. I could no more part from him than fly to the moon." She bowed her head. This was harder than she'd imagined, but she owed it to Josh to tell the truth at last.

"I'd be lying if I said I wasn't sorry to lose you," Josh said. "But I get it. You have to do what's best for you and the boy. I reckon you mean everything to him an' all."

"I do hope so," she said, thankful for Josh's understanding. "I'm glad we can part on good terms. Your approval means a lot to me."

"Hardly approval," he said. "But I do wish you well." He lifted her hand to his lips. "I'll always remember you as the Lily, the girl who brought sunshine into my life."

"You'll always be part of my life," Nell said. "A big part."

"But regrettably not the most important part." Nell shrugged.

He let her hand go and leaned over. His lips brushed her cheek. "Goodbye, Lily," he said. "I'll never forget you."

"Nor me you," she said.

Chapter Thirty Eight

Friday morning Sir Oswald arrived with news of the case against Linus Frumley. Polly showed him to the sitting room where the ladies were having coffee. Milton was called in from his study and

Ethan and Robert came in from the garden to hear his news.

Lady Mary offered him coffee which he accepted. "I expect you're waiting to hear the outcome of the case against Linus Frumley," he said to Nell. "I came as soon as the court adjourned. He has been sentenced to life imprisonment, with hard labour." He frowned. "Not the outcome we might have wished for, but you can rest assured he will not be troubling you or your friends again."

Nell sighed. She touched Robert's shoulder. "Did you hear that, Robert? Linus Frumley will spend the rest of his life in prison. We don't need to worry about him ever again."

Robert's eyes filled with tears which quickly overflowed to run down his cheeks. Nell made the sign for 'sad'. She guessed it was the memory of seeing the murder and the beating he associated with the mention of his name. She hugged him and brushed the tears away. "It's all right," she said. "He's gone away. We won't mention him again."

"Thank you for telling us," Milton said. "It's put our minds at rest."

Max arrived to give Robert his lessons for the day.

Sir Oswald had other business with Lady Mary so they went into Milton's study. Max took Robert into the garden for his lesson. Outside, the early August sun was warm and pleasant. Nell went with them. She was delighted to see Robert's progress and how well he got on with Max. Max was a kind but persistent tutor, just the kind Robert needed.

At twelve o'clock Nell was called into the study where Sir Oswald was ensconced with Lady Mary and Milton Crosby.

Lady Mary greeted her. "I have told Sir Oswald that I wish to make provision for your future," she said.

"She wishes to offer you her protection and make you her ward," Sir Oswald said.

Nell gasped. "Can she do that?"

"It would be unusual, but not impossible," Sir Oswald said. "Given that you have no living family."

"That's with your agreement of course," Lady Mary said. "You would be treated as one of the family. I may even say you would take the place of my daughter, Robert's mother, as I know you already have in his heart. The picture in Caroline's locket makes that very clear."

"Milton would be Robert's Guardian as far as making decisions about his future," Sir Oswald explained. "But Lady Mary has suggested you be responsible for the day to day care of the boy. What do you say?"

"I don't know what to say." Lady Mary had taken Nell's breath away and with it the power of speech.

"I take it you have no objections?" Sir Oswald's eyebrows rose as his piercing grey eyes twinkled.

"None whatsoever," Nell said. "I'm overwhelmed by her Ladyship's kindness and generosity."

"I have asked Sir Oswald to set up a Trust to ensure that, whatever happens to me, you will be well cared for. I also wish to remember you in my Will," Lady Mary said smiling at Nell. "Robert will be the main beneficiary, but you will not be forgotten. I want to ensure that both you and Robert will always have a home. It will allow me to die with a peaceful heart knowing you are safe."

Nell was stunned. "Just letting me look after Robert would be enough. You have been more than generous," she said.

"Nonsense. It is I who should be grateful to you and my action today will go some way to show my appreciation of your care and compassion when dealing with my grandson." She grinned. "I am also aware that his continued wellbeing rests on securing your presence as a constant in his life. I fear that without you to rely on he would sink into a decline from which he'd never recover."

Nell laughed. "I think you'll find he's more robust than that, but I am grateful all the same."

"I'll have the papers prepared and bring them along tomorrow," Sir Oswald said.

Nell thought Mrs Crosby was right. There was nothing Sir Oswald Rockingham couldn't arrange. Lady Mary was lucky to have him as her lawyer.

Milton, who'd been standing by the fireplace watching proceedings, stepped forward. "I know how much Robert means to you and you to him. I commend Lady Mary for her good sense in ensuring your continued participation in his life." He glanced at his pocket watch. "It seems it's almost time for luncheon. Sir Oswald, will you join us? I understand the cook has prepared a veritable feast."

"I'd be delighted," Sir Oswald said.

Milton offered Nell his arm, Sir Oswald helped Lady Mary and together they went into lunch.

They met Mrs Crosby in the hall. Max was invited to stay for lunch but said he had to go home to help his mother with the packing for their move to Somerset.

"She has found a delightful cottage we can rent," he said. "It's near to Lady Mary's estate and has a conservatory which she tells me will make a wonderful studio. There's also a small barn she intends to turn into a gallery. The thought of moving out of London has given her a new lease of life. There's a lightness in her step too."

"That's excellent news," Milton said. "I may still look forward to receiving your paintings to hang in the gallery then?"

"Indeed you may."

Max left them and they went in to lunch. Mrs Crosby produced a letter she'd received that morning. "It's from the friend I was telling you about," she said to Nell. "The sister of my dressmaker. She's married to a vicar. He has a parish in Shropshire. You remember, they were keen to foster a child with a view to adoption."

Nell gasped. "You mean you wrote to the workhouse?"

"Well, you gave me the address. What else did you think I was going to do with it?" Mrs Crosby's brows puckered. Nell bit her lip. She'd thought the request for the address was a ruse to look further into her background. That was when she'd feared discovery. How silly it all seemed now.

"They've been to Salvation Hill House and taken the girl you mentioned, Kitty I think you said?"

Nell nodded. Her voice was still stuck somewhere in her throat.

"Yes, her and a small boy, name of Archie. About six they think." She looked up from the letter. "They are good people and your little friend will have a good home."

Emotion threatened to overwhelm Nell. So much had happened in the space of a few hours. It seemed dreams did come true: hers and Kitty's and the little boy Archie's. "That's wonderful news," Nell said.

Mrs Crosby slid a photograph out from the envelope and passed it to Nell. Nell thought her heart might burst when she saw the look of unrestrained joy in the eyes of the two children pictured. Memories of Kitty following her around that Christmas flashed through her mind, with visions of all the children in the workhouse. She saw the boys sitting in rows in their ill-fitting workhouse uniforms, their eyes reflecting the misery of their lives and the girls picking oakum until their fingers bled. If there was hope for these two, there must be hope for the others, she thought.

"Thank you. That's marvellous," she said, but words couldn't express the happiness in her heart.

After lunch Lady Mary decided she'd like to take Robert for a ride through Hyde Park. "If one comes to London, one must be seen," she said. Lady Mary's coachman brought the carriage around with its top down. The excitement on Robert's face as he climbed into the open carriage was obvious. He beamed with delight. Nell and Ethan accompanied them for the drive through the park. Robert was fascinated with the wheels, the movement of the carriage and the scenery passing by. He bobbed up and down making signs for the wheels, trees and horses. His lively animation entranced Lady Mary. "I can't believe this is the same boy Lord Eversham said was sullen and unresponsive. He's really quite spirited and vivacious."

"I don't believe he's ever ridden in a carriage before," Nell said.

"Well, shame on his father for the omission," Lady Mary said and settled back to enjoy the ride watching her grandson's glee at the new experience.

It was a splendid afternoon, one Nell vowed she'd never forget. She couldn't have been happier. She was riding through the park on a glorious summer day, with the people she cared most about in the world. All her dreams were coming true. Robert would have a good home where he'd be loved and appreciated. She'd be to spend the rest of her life with him.

She glanced at Ethan. He wasn't the most exuberant of people but this afternoon he appeared particularly subdued. She wondered what was worrying him. Was it the fact that their stay in London was soon to come to an end? He'd have to return to his job in Kent while she went to live in Somerset with Robert. Was that what was on his mind?

Her heart flipped at the thought of losing him again, but she wasn't going to let that stop her enjoying the best day she'd ever had in her whole life.

Chapter Thirty Nine

The next morning Sir Oswald brought the papers for Lady Mary to sign. Once that was done she said she saw no reason for them to continue to encroach upon Milton's hospitality. Arrangements were made for them to journey to Somerset on Monday morning. In the meantime she arranged for her dressmaker to call. She ordered two gowns for herself and several for Nell.

"I can't have my ward dress in hand-me-downs," she said, so Nell spent Saturday morning with the dressmaker, being measured and choosing several outfits. She marvelled at the dressmaker's suggestions. It was clear that her future life as the ward of Lady Mary would be significantly different from that of a nursemaid, or even a milliner come clerk at a funeral parlour.

The dressmaker assured her that her travelling outfit would be ready by Monday and the rest of the outfits would be sent on to Lady Mary's home in Somerset.

As they were leaving London, Nell wanted to take Robert to say goodbye to Mrs and Mrs Bradley, Lottie and Ernie. She'd already said goodbye to Josh. "They've been so kind to us. I don't know what I would have done without their help."

"Of course you may. Please give them my thanks," Lady Mary said. She ordered hampers from Fortnum & Mason for Nell to take with her. Nell smiled when she imagined the look on Lottie's face when she walked in with the hamper. "It's most generous of you," Nell said.

"Nonsense. I only wish I could do more," Lady Mary said.

Ethan insisted on going with her. Nell wondered why, as he'd never met the Bradleys. As they climbed into the carriage Nell had the feeling he had something on his mind. Surely he understood why she had to go with Robert? She wished he could come too but that would be too much to hope for. She told herself that she'd been blessed in being able to stay with the boy who'd become so much part of her life. That was the only thing that mattered.

In the coach Robert was distracted looking out of the window and pointing at the passing buildings. Nell named as many as she could until Robert settled to just looking out.

Ethan was particularly quiet. "You seem troubled, Ethan," she said. "The events of the last few days have surprised us all, but I would hope you of all people would be happy for me and wish me well."

"I do, Nell. It's just…" He gazed at his boots. "You will no longer be a servant. You'll be part of the family, well above my station. Lady Mary can offer you a lifestyle beyond anything I could offer." He bowed his head. "Battling hardship brought out qualities in you I came to admire. I fear an easy life in the country may…"

"What? Change me? Turn me into a simpering mess of gratitude?" She shook her head. "I thought you knew me better than that. Anyway, I'll be Lady Mary's ward in name only. I'll still be looking after Robert. A new life won't make me forget my old friends. I'm still the girl you met in the garden, the girl you bought this brooch for." She touched the lily brooch she wore every day.

He glanced at her. "I fear for the girl I knew. The one who fought like a tiger for the boy in her care. The one who wouldn't allow him to be locked away. The girl I knew was all heart and fire and wanting to do the best she could, no matter what the personal cost."

"The girl who missed you every minute we were apart."

"Did you, Nell? Really?"

"Yes. And I'll miss you again when I go to Somerset, but you must see I have to be with Robert." She ruffled the boy's hair. "He needs me."

"I'm glad," he said. "I have something to say but was afraid of broaching the subject for fear of your disapproval."

"Well, you'll never know unless you tell me."

He took a breath, as though unsure how to continue. "Lady Mary has offered me the position of Manager of her Estate in Somerset. It'll be a promotion..."

He didn't get any further. Much to Robert's amusement and Ethan's astonishment, Nell threw her arms around him. "That's wonderful," she said.

"I was hoping you'd approve," he said. As the coach drew up outside the funeral parlour Ethan took her in his arms and kissed her. Nell responded with all the fire and passion she'd just learned that he admired in her.

Later, in the splendid grounds of Lady Mary's Somerset mansion Ethan proposed to her. Nell said she'd have to get Robert's approval. She took him into the garden and explained to him what would happen if she married Ethan. How she'd have to move out of the big house into a cottage in the grounds, but she'd always be near and she'd be there for him any time he needed her. "So, what do you think? Will you be happy for me?"

Robert's beaming smile and hug was all the answer she needed. As soon as she let him go he ran indoors to see Max. She realised he was growing up, growing away from her. That was the way it should be. He was becoming independent. Her heart swelled with pride at the person he had become.

A June Wedding – 1892

Ethan and Nell were married the first week in June of the following year, in the church on Lady Mary's estate. The week before the wedding Nell travelled to London to have her trousseau made. She visited Lottie, Ernie and the Bradleys, inviting them all to the wedding. Then she went to see Goose, remembering his special friendship with Robert to make sure he was included.

"You can travel down by train and back the next morning," Nell told them. "Lady Mary has provided the tickets."

The smile on Goose's face told her how pleased he was. "Will I be able to see Bobby... er... I mean Robert?" he asked.

"Of course," Nell said. "I'm sure he'll be delighted to see you."

Lady Mary invited Milton and Mrs Crosby to stay for the month. She wrote personally to Lord Eversham requesting that Ethan's father, Harvey, his sister, Jenny and her friend Alice attend, letting it be known that any difficulties she experienced would become the talk of society. He graciously accepted the invitation on their behalf, informing Lady Mary that he and his wife and daughters would be abroad so the staff in question could be spared from household duties.

Ethan's mother accompanied them, saying how pleased she was that the baby she'd delivered on that fateful day had grown into such a charming, sweet-natured young man.

Mrs Hewitt declared she wouldn't miss it for the world and insisted on coming along as well. Miss Bannister didn't attend.

The day dawned with an early mist that lay over the fields, followed by brilliant sunshine. Nell had the help of Lady Mary's dresser to get her ready. She glanced up at the pale summer sky. She pinned her 'little piece of blue' to the bodice of her dress so everyone could see it. The silk was tattered and faded, her mother's brooch tarnished, but to Nell it was the most important piece of her outfit. "It will remind me where I come from," she said. "And I want my mother to be proud of me."

"I'm sure she is," the dresser said.

Nell walked down the aisle on Milton's arm to stand next to a beaming Ethan, the man she'd fallen in love with when she first saw him in the garden. Robert was her page and looked bemused throughout the ceremony. Ethan and Nell would be honeymooning in Devon, so Jenny was staying on to look after Robert. "He knows me and I'll see he has everything just right," she said.

Max and his mother came and again Nell saw how fond Robert was of his new tutor. She knew then that he'd be in safe hands.

The reception was held in Lady Mary's grand ballroom. Windows opened onto a terrace where tables and chairs were set out for the guests. Mrs Hewitt declared it was even grander than the summer balls at Inglebrook Manor. The wine flowed, a quartet played in the ballroom and Nell ~ught she'd never been so happy in her life.

When Lady Mary heard of Goose's part in protecting Robert from Linus Frumley at the yard she offered him the position of Assistant Coachman in her extensive stables.

"I'm sure Jenkins will be glad of the help," she said, "and Robert will be delighted to have found a familiar friend." She also made sure Goose had a significant pay-rise and the offer of a cottage in the grounds for his family.

Later that afternoon, amid the festivities, Milton approached Nell. "I've been reading about a school in New York where a teacher has been working with a blind, deaf mute. Apparently she's had a great deal of success. They call her the Miracle Worker. I wondered whether it worth sending Robert there?"

Nell frowned. She watched Robert playing with Goose. He was teasing him and Robert giggled and chuckled just like his old self.

"There's no guarantees, of course," Milton said.

Nell sighed. "Robert's lack of speech has never stopped him enjoying life to the full, making friends and learning to read and add up. In fact he's very bright. I'm not sure any benefit could be gained from taking him from a familiar environment into a strange and difficult one."

"No you're probably right," Milton said. "It was just a thought."

"Well, it would have to be Robert's decision. One he's perfectly capable of making. Personally I think he's just perfect as he is. We should accept him for the smart, happy, intelligent boy we know him to be. Whatever happens I couldn't love him more than I do now."

She saw Ethan laughing with Robert and Goose. She and Ethan would have children of their own one day, and of course they'd love them, but Robert, her amazing silent boy, would always have a special place in her heart and she'd always be his Guardian Angel.

About the Author

Kay Seeley lives in London with her husband Michael. She has two children, both married and three grandchildren, all adorable. She is a novelist, short story writer and poet. *The Guardian Angel* is her third Victorian novel. Both her previous novels have been listed as finalists for The Wishing Shelf Book Award. She also writes short stories and has had over fifty published in *The People's Friend, Woman's Weekly, Take a Break* or *The Weekly News.* She has published twenty of these in *The Cappuccino Collection.* Kay's stories have been short-listed in several major competitions. Kay is a member of The Alliance of Independent Authors.

Contact: www.kayseeleyauthor.com

Acknowledgements

Firstly my thanks go to my family for their unending patience and support especially to my lovely daughters for reading the manuscript multiple times. Special hugs must go to my littlest grandson, who's autistic and non-verbal, for being the inspiration behind the book. Extra hugs too for my other grandchildren who are also truly inspiring. Also thanks to my husband, Mick for making it possible for me to spend my time doing something I love.

Thanks to the members of my writing groups, you know who you are, for their helpful suggestions and to the brilliant Helen Baggott whose eagle eyes and sound advice helped in the production of this book.

A huge 'thank you' to my writing friends, ALLi members and supporters for their continued encouragement and, once again, to Jane Dixon-Smith for another wonderful cover.

Lastly I want to thank the readers whose enjoyment of my previous novels prompted me to keep writing and made it such a pleasure.

If you have read and enjoyed this novel I would love to hear from you via my website:
www.kayseeleyauthor.com

I would also appreciate a review on the appropriate Amazon page
Many thanks.

If you've enjoyed this book you may also enjoy Kays other books. Here novels are available in Large Print.

A Girl Called Hope

A heart-wrenching saga of love, loss, courage and resilience from the author of *The Guardian Angel*.

In Victorian London's East End, life for Hope Daniels in the public house run by her parents is not as it seems. Pa drinks and gambles, brother John longs for a place of his own, sister Violet dreams of a life on stage and little Alfie is being bullied at school.

Silas Quirk, the charismatic owner of a local gentlemen's club and disreputable gambling den her father frequents, has his own plans for Hope.

When disaster strikes the family lose everything and the future they planned is snatched away from them. Secrets are revealed that make Hope question all she's ever believed in.

Can Hope keep them together when fate is pulling them apart?

What will she sacrifice to save her family?

A captivating story of tragedy and triumph you won't want to put down.

A Girl Called Violet

A gripping saga of courage and human relationships from the bestselling author of *The Guardian Angel*

When the feckless and often violent father of Violet Daniel's five-year-old twins turns up out of the blue, asking to see them she recalls the abuse she suffered at his hands. He never wanted them before, why would he want them now?

Terrified that he might snatch them from her she takes them to a place of safety. There she meets the handsome and charming Gabriel Stone who shows her a better way of life.

But is he all he appears to be?

When Violet decides to stop running and finds the courage to return to London, vowing to confront the children's father, she finds a far greater evil than she ever thought possible.

How far will Violet go to protect her children?

Set against the background of two very different worlds in Edwardian London's East End this is the second book in the Hope Series.

Perfect for fans of Catherine Cookson and Dilly Court.

The Water Gypsy

When Tilly Thompson, a girl from the canal, is caught
stealing a pie from the terrace of The Imperial Hotel,
Athelstone, the intervention of Captain Charles Thackery
saves her from prison.

The Captain's favour stirs up jealously and hatred
among the hotel staff, especially Freddie, the stable boy
who harbours desires of his own.

Freddie's pursuit leads Tilly into far greater danger
than she could ever have imagined. Can she escape the
prejudice, persecution and hypocrisy of Victorian
Society, leave her past behind and find true happiness?

This is a story of love and loss, lust and passion, injustice
and ultimate redemption.

The Watercress Girls

Annie knows the secrets men whisper in her ears to impress her. When she disappears who will care? Who will look for her?

Two girls sell cress on the streets of Victorian London. When they grow up they each take a different path. Annie's reckless ambition takes her to Paris to dance at the Folie Bergere. When she comes home she takes up a far more dangerous occupation.

When she disappears, leaving her illegitimate son behind, her friend Hettie Bundy sets out to find her. Hettie's search leads her from the East End, where opium dens and street gangs rule, to uncover the corruption and depravity in Victorian society.

Secrets are revealed that put both girls' lives in danger.

Can Hettie find Annie in time?

What does the future hold for the watercress girls?

A Victorian Mystery

You may also enjoy Kay's Short Story Collections@

The Cappuccino Collection 20 Sstories to warm your heart

The Summer Stories 12 Romantic stories to make you smile

The Christmas Stories 6 stories about the magic of Christmas.